THE "PAYDAY" CONSPIRACY

A Berlin Noir

Mike Blumenthal

Solanum Press
Princeton

Also by Mike Blumenthal (W. Michael Blumenthal)

Nonfiction:
The Invisible Wall: Germans and Jews, A personal exploration
From Exile to Washington: A Memoir of Leadership in the Twentieth Century

In memory of my sister,
Stefanie Dreyfuss

ISBN: 9798330365128

Cover design by: Duncan Blachford
Book design by: Diana Wade

Published by Solanum Press, Princeton, New Jersey

Prologue

*T*he Honorable J. deWitt Emerson, deputy chief of mission at the American Embassy in Berlin, vanished on a gray and dreary November afternoon, never to be seen again.

Alive, that is. An early morning jogger found him two days later elegantly attired in a Savile Row suit resting against a Grunewald birch, dead from a bullet through the back of the head. On the evening news, a police spokeswoman said the shot came from a handgun fired at close range. No further news was available. Ambassador Benninger was out of the country, and the embassy didn't respond to requests for comment.

Emerson—"Witty" to his friends, "Dimwit" to his detractors—had cut a wide swath through Berlin almost from the moment he arrived in town four years earlier. With his excellent German—not all that common for American diplomats—he had quickly become a familiar face on the capital's countless TV talk shows and on the dinner party circuit a popular guest appreciated by hostesses for his chivalrous old-world manners. Not exactly an intellectual heavyweight, but a good conversationalist and storyteller fluent in six languages not counting English.

Murders are pretty rare in Berlin, and mostly gang-related or honor killings within immigrant communities. A senior diplomat shot dead in the Grunewald Forest was sensational news.

As soon as the story broke, the capital's rumor mills started grinding. Commentators on ZDF and ARD, the two major TV channels, agreed that it was unlikely the American diplomat was a suicide or victim of a robbery gone wrong. They pointed out that he typically moved around town in a protected embassy limo, especially while his ambassador was away and Emerson was acting as chargé.

Conspiracy theorists claiming to be in the know suggested that Emerson's official job had been a front and that he was really CIA. Some whispered they had it on good authority that the BND, Germany's spy service, suspected that some foreign counterpart outfit had taken out a contract on him and that the chancellor's office had been so informed. Another school of thought was pushing a more salacious, if less political, explanation. At fifty-nine, the American diplomat was a bachelor, rarely seen in public in the company of a woman. The police, they claimed, were already looking into the sex angle, scouring their sources in Berlin's well-established gay community. One or two male lovers were said to be in their crosshairs.

The reality was that as the weekend passed, nobody really knew a thing. The embassy remained silent, and the police weren't talking either. The only new news was that the chancellor had been on the phone with the American president to express her shock and to offer condolences. A full investigation has been promised. Both heads of government agreed that US-German relations weren't at risk in this tragic event.

World stock markets opened slightly higher on Monday and appeared to be unaffected.

Chapter 1

Berlin

Friday afternoon, November 3

*S*hortly after 4:00 p.m. on what would be the last day of his life, Witty Emerson has mustered himself in the full-length mirror of the ambassador's top-floor embassy dressing room, and likes what he sees.

A self-satisfied half smile emerges below his permanently rosy cheeks, a bulbous, somewhat asymmetrical nose, hooded baggy eyes, and thinning gray hair carefully parted down the middle. With his pudgy 230 pounds on a five-foot-eight frame, he isn't much to look at, but is a fastidious dresser, and this afternoon he has chosen his outfit with care.

With a gold chain across his vest, the charcoal double-breasted suit—English worsted wool and discreet stripes—is one of his favorites for conveying the understated Savile Row look of affluent elegance he likes to project. The Turnbull & Asser pink shirt with white cuffs and collar and the patterned blue silk tie with matching kerchief set off the whole thing rather nicely, he notes.

Keeping up appearances is what Witty Emerson is all about,

and the right kind of attire is a big part of it. Looking "right" is so ingrained that he has long ago lost his grip on what is real and what merely pretense, not only in his clothing, but in much of what he says and does. That his wardrobe isn't actually the genuine article no longer crosses his mind.

Who, on a Foreign Service salary, could afford real Savile Row these days? Or Turnbull made-to-order shirts at $600 apiece? No one would know, and even he hardly remembers that what he is wearing is actually mere Savile Row-ersatz from the workshop of Durukan, the Turkish tailor he uncovered in Kreuzberg, one of Berlin's low-rent districts and home to the city's Turkish minority. In Witty's book, Durukan is a genius, better than any London bespoke master tailor, and at half the price.

This afternoon, Witty savors his free run of the embassy's impressive ambassadorial suite. As acting mission chief, he is taking full advantage by lounging around here and soaking up the aura of prestige and importance.

The rightful occupant of these quarters, Ambassador Nick Benninger, likes to spend as much time as possible back in Oklahoma, where he is the owner of a string of car dealerships. The President had offered him the Berlin Embassy as payoff for his prodigious bundling of massive campaign contributions from right-wing friends, and Benninger happily accepted the job and the title that went with it. Once installed, however, he never shook the feeling of a being a fish out of water. The Chancellor and her senior ministers he sees only rarely, and the diplomatic protocol and chitchat with his counterpart ambassadors baffle and bore him. He likes neither the weather nor the food, and apart from an occasional *Auf Wiedersehen* or *Wie geht's?* delivered in an Oklahoma twang, he remains a stranger to the language. The day-to-day affairs of the embassy he has been content to leave to professionals on staff and to his deputy, who doesn't complain at all.

For Witty, nearing retirement after a so-so career, the prospect of an embassy of his own faded some time ago. Number two in Berlin is a plum assignment for a younger officer on the way up, but as an end-of-career posting, it is no more than a consolation prize.

Not that he hadn't tried to press his case, tirelessly cultivating the fruited plains of Washington's Foggy Bottom by seizing every opportunity to lobby the State Department's Executive Personnel Office where the Secretary of State's recommendations for top appointments originate. His Ivy alma mater had rarely gone unmentioned, nor had gentle allusions to the Emersons, not excluding Ralph Waldo, his alleged New England forebears. Even Johan deWitt, a seventeenth-century Dutch political leader, had occasionally been thrown in. Pedigree mattered when representing America abroad, and his mastery of six languages was always duly noted and stressed.

None of it, alas, had worked. Just recently, over drinks at the Old Ebbitt's Grill, a popular watering hole in the shadow of the White House, a Foreign Service personnel officer named Oscar Ramirez, a man years Witty's junior, had once more brushed his best arguments aside. Substance trumped pedigree, Ramirez had observed gently, and mastery of foreign languages counted for less than how effectively one did business in them.

That it might not be smart strategy to tout his New England Ivy roots to Ramirez, a state college graduate and son of immigrants, hadn't occurred to Witty. Rather, he was infuriated that the forces arrayed against him were trade school types from colleges for the masses rather than an establishment institution with the tradition to educate the nation's socio-cultural elite.

He'd joined the Foreign Service straight out of Dartmouth in the late seventies, when substantive expertise was actually frowned on and reaching the top of the Service was reserved for the generalist possessing a certain "habitude du monde."

Sadly, no more. Now you had to have a graduate degree or two in some boring specialized field, and promotions went to those who had served tours of duty in miserable South Asian or African hardship posts or—God forbid—Afghanistan or Iraq. Witty had skillfully avoided such unpleasantness, and now it was being held against him while the Ramirezes, women, and other minorities were getting the nod.

For a long time, he has been in a slow burn at all these changes depriving him of the end-of-career prize he thought his due. The way he sees it, all this "wokeness" is misguided and grossly unfair and that what really motivates Ramirez and his ilk to block him is nothing less than envy of those with the class they don't possess.

For a long time, the injustice of it gnawed at his insides, but now that is in the past. Retirement is in sight, and Witty has a plan for glory, success, and, possibly, a good deal of money.

"Let's see who has the last laugh," he says to the image in the ambassador's mirror, and the thought buoys his spirits. "Time to move," he mutters. "Carpe diem!"

Witty briskly exits into Benninger's adjoining office with its large picture window fronting Pariser Platz, Berlin's most photographed square. A deputy nesting in the ambassador's office during his absences is highly unusual and distinctly outside Foreign Service traditions. But to do business there, even temporarily, gives Emerson an irresistible kick, a feeling of power and privilege. He especially likes to receive visitors in this oversized domain and to impress them with the aura of the surroundings.

He stops briefly by the window and takes in the scene below. It is raining, and the resident street artists and performers have taken cover, but hordes of tourists under a sea of umbrellas are snapping selfies by the Brandenburg Gate. Across the square, others are crowding the currywurst and souvenir kiosks, cruising pedicabs hustle for riders, and the usual touts and hucksters are working the crowds looking for suckers.

After this moment of silent contemplation, Witty turns, reaches for the umbrella and mackintosh resting on one of Benninger's chocolate-brown chairs, and continues to the next-door reception area where Betty Kowalski, the ambassador's secretary, and her German assistant, Greta, are busy clicking on their keyboards and shuffling papers.

In Washington, a popular adage reputedly coined by the legendary George Ball, deputy secretary of state under Kennedy and Johnson, and a man wise as few others to the ways of inside-the-beltway power players, noted that "nothing 'propinqs' like propinquity." If you work near the boss and have his ear every day, you have more power than your seniors situated farther away from where the decisions are made.

Betty is living proof of Ball's observation. She knows all the tricks to navigate and outwit bureaucratic arcana, her bosses rely on her discretion, and Berlin's FSOs treat her as a dependable counselor and interlocutor on their behalf. Next to her nameplate, a second one reading "Too Blessed to be Stressed" encapsulates her operational style. Witty fears and resents her propinquity in about equal measure, but chooses to cloak his feelings with a mix of flattery and superior airs when in her presence.

"Betty, dear," he chirps, stopping at her desk, and then, trying to sound cordial and decisive at the same time, "any action stuff I need to see?"

"Only this one, marked priority," Betty replies, handing him a one-pager from atop an inbox pile. "State wants our take ASAP on the new German budget numbers. You may want to handle this personally."

Betty is pulling his string, but the subtle dig is wasted on him. She figured out Witty long ago, his aversion to hard work and his pretensions, posturing, and little tricks. His dislike for budget numbers, trade statistics, and any kind of detailed work—matters he prefers to fob off on what he calls the "green eyeshade boys"—is no secret to her.

Witty glances briefly at the paper and does not disappoint her. "Send it to Joe in Econ and tell him to get busy on this," he says airily. Then, more sternly, "And tell him I want the draft on my desk by noon Monday."

"Already did it," Betty replies. "But Monday may not work. He's got that outside conference to attend all day."

"Well, he's got the weekend and nights," Witty replies, this time in a no-nonsense tone of command. "Isn't that what FSOs are supposed to do? Burn a little midnight oil?"

"Some do it, some don't," she replies sweetly, proffering him another impressive stack of folders resting on the edge of her desk. "With the ambassador's return still iffy," she explains, sticking the needle in a little deeper, "you may wish to handle these personally. Most of it is German PR, invitations and stuff. He always insists on attending to that himself. Just so you know."

Witty waves her away, bends over her desk, and in a low voice meant to stay out of Greta's hearing from across the room, intones conspiratorially, "This will have to wait, Betty. I have to leave for an important meeting right away. Can't talk about it. Very important. That's all I can say, even to you. Trust me."

A short silence follows. Betty looks at him and thinks, *Important meeting? Not likely. At least it explains the fancy dress at this time of the afternoon.*

"Don't forget, you have a dinner tonight at Graf von Trachtenberg's residence out in Dahlem," Betty says. "Business suit, seven thirty for eight."

Gräfin Bettina von Trachtenberg, a descendent of ancient German nobility but with little to say in Germany today, is the kind of hostess Witty adored. Her dinners and soirees invariably feature an assembly of society types most embassy officers avoid as a waste of time. But for Witty, who would descend from his limo chauffeured by Walter, his driver, and with security conspicuously hovering nearby, it is what makes diplomatic life worth living.

Greta, Betty's German assistant, crosses from her desk to hand him a single sheet of paper. "Tonight's guest list. I told them you asked for it and they emailed it over."

Greta handles the non-classified traffic, social correspondence, invitations, appointment requests, and serves as a liaison with the German world outside. Her flawless, if slightly British-accented English, had been honed to near perfection during an earlier two-year stint in London, interning in a firm of solicitors with a smattering of German clients.

Witty pockets Greta's list and reaches for his coat and umbrella.

"I'll call security and tell Walter to bring the car around," Greta says.

Witty waves her away. "Not necessary," he tells her. "Just going over to the Adlon next door. Tell Walter and security to meet me there at 7:15."

"No security now?" Betty asks, genuinely surprised.

"Yep."

With a parting wave of his neatly rolled umbrella, Witty turns his back and heads out the door.

Emerging from the ambassador's elevator, Emerson makes straight for the staff exit, guarded that afternoon by Lance Corporal Terrance Hopper, a young African American generally known as "Skip." Behind his glass screen, the young marine rises smartly and works the security gate, as Emerson hurries past him and out the door.

Hopper will later testify that, at the time, he thought Witty's behavior unusual.

The Adlon, Berlin's historic temple of luxury for over a hundred years, sits just east of Pariser Platz, a few hundred feet from the embassy's back door. Samuel, the six-foot-seven Nigerian doorman at the front portal, wearing a black cylinder hat and gold-braided topcoat, is a Berlin fixture, integral to the Adlon brand.

Normally, Witty took special pleasure hearing Samuel's booming, "Welcome, Excellency," publicly announcing his arrival as he ascended the red-carpeted steps leading into the elegant Great Hall. That afternoon, though, his hope was to slip in unnoticed, and he notes with relief that Samuel is busy at the curb helping some VIP out of a shiny white limousine. Collar turned up and face low into his raincoat, Witty briskly traverses the hall, past the afternoon tea crowd in the center and the early drinkers crowding the bar to his right.

Checking his watch, he hurries out of the hotel's unattended Behrenstrasse rear entrance, gets into the lead cab in the taxi line, and asks to be taken to the Zoo Bahnhof in West Berlin. His heart is pounding. Being on a secret mission exhilarates and frightens him at the same time. Leaning back, he closes his eyes and tries to relax.

Fifteen minutes later, he joins the crowds of homeward-bound commuters flooding into the Zoo rail station. A few minutes after that, he emerges from a different door and hails another cab. He looks out the window, left, then right. Nobody following. So far, so good.

One more cab change continuing west, and at 5:20 by his watch, Witty still warily monitoring his surroundings, steps to the door of a well-kept, prosperous-looking prewar apartment building on Wielandstrasse, a quiet side street just off the Kudamm. A polished brass nameplate with individual bells lists the tenants. He's been there before, but to make sure, he extracts his glasses from an inside coat pocket, glances over the names, and presses the bell next to a single name, Holzapfel. The wait seems much longer than it is. The buzzer sounds, and Witty pushes past the unlocked door.

An old-fashioned elevator slowly works its way to the top floor, then deposits Witty, slightly nauseated with anticipation.

There is no name to mark the single apartment. Witty knocks, then waits nervously, listening to the sound of locks being worked. At last the door opens to reveal a tall, middle-aged woman gazing at him wordlessly in a stern head-to-toe inspection. Her eyes are heavily mascaraed, lips painted dark magenta, and her long red hair, neatly arranged in a single braided *Zopf*, dangles over her left shoulder. The black bustier bodysuit hugging her Amazonic frame ends just above her hips and keeps the midriff bare, except for a G-string over her crotch. Thigh-high black lace-topped net stockings cover her unusually long legs. In her stiletto boots, she towers at least a foot over her trembling visitor.

When she breaks her silence, her voice is cold, matter-of-fact. "Late again, you worthless *Stück Scheisse*."

"Forgive me, Mistress!"

"Down," she orders as the door closes behind him.

An hour later, Emerson reemerges from the Wielandstrasse house, turns left, and walks to the Kudamm corner. The rain has stopped, night has descended, and the boulevard is brightly lit. Prada, across the street, and the other boutiques in the vicinity are closing. At the Gucci store behind him, the lights are just being turned off. A large clock at the corner shows the time as 6:43 p.m.

Witty checks his watch, steps to the curb, and observes the traffic. Almost immediately, the black Audi A8 he was looking for turns the corner and comes to a stop where he stands. The rear door opens and Witty slips into the back seat.

He is in an excellent mood, relaxed and refreshed after his visit with Madame Holzapfel, and full of eager anticipation for what lay ahead.

That it is a bullet through the head never crosses his mind.

Chapter 2

Berlin

Friday morning, November 3

2:00 a.m.

*M*idlife crises are supposed to come in your fifties. I'm only thirty-eight, but I may be ahead of schedule.

It's two o'clock in the morning. I'm still dressed, the bedroom's a mess, and I can't sleep. I'm sprawled across the unmade bed, my mind doing laps trying to figure out what's going on, and getting nowhere. I get up and walk to the window. Outside it's raining, a dismal drizzle on empty Wittelsbacherstrasse in the dead of night. Not the kind of weather to lift one's spirits. I stare out morosely for a minute, light my third Montecristo for the night, then get back on the bed and start chewing my cud all over again.

Twelve years ago, when I joined the Foreign Service, I took it for granted that I was in for the long haul. I loved every part of the life, in Washington and overseas. Working on policy in the department and serving abroad, understanding foreign cultures, negotiating and representing the US, being respected and feeling important.

My career has been on track, and the little frustrations that come with the job—the mountains of paper, bureaucracy, idiot bosses—never bothered me. Not even the low pay. Yet these days I'm sick of what I'm doing, and my quandary about staying or quitting surprises and depresses me.

The embassy here is a dysfunctional mess, and I'm stuck in it. That's part of my funk. Amateur ambassadors appointed as political payoff are a long time American tradition, and all presidents do it, I keep reminding myself. Backstopping them is what we professionals are supposed to do and, God knows, I've been through it before. So, what's different now?

Maybe it's because this one, Nick Benninger, is a far-right know-nothing and an embarrassing caricature of the Ugly American abroad. He's AWOL half the time and without a clue of what's going on when he's here. His deputy—my boss, that dimwit Witty, posted here to wait for retirement—is an incompetent ass full of pretentious bullshit and petty demands.

The two of them together, Benninger and Witty, are the worst possible combination. The Germans know we have no credibility and politely ignore us, raising their eyebrows as they ask about our policies, barely able to conceal their schadenfreude at the mess the mighty Americans are in, with an irrelevant embassy and a crazy man in the White House.

No wonder I feel like calling it quits. But where's the red line, I keep asking myself, the point at which I can no longer explain and defend the president's snubs of the German chancellor, his trashing of NATO, the crazy fixation on tariffs, and his weak spot for authoritarian bullies?

But what to do if I quit? Try to patch up my miserable marriage, go to work in real estate for Fiona's father back in New Jersey, which is what she wants, or run away and start all over again? Become an

Uber driver or a bartender?

I look at the clock. Quarter to three. I go to the bathroom, wash up, and talk to the guy in the mirror. "Adam, you're a mess. Get a life. Do something," I tell him.

I go back to the bed, close my eyes, and turn off the light.

8:00 a.m.

The alarm jars me awake from a benumbed sleep. I feel stiff, and there's a sour tobacco taste in my mouth. Even the best Havanas don't taste so good the morning after. I drag myself out of bed and head for the shower, letting the cold water pound me awake. My remedy for hangovers, and it usually works.

In the kitchen, I down a glass of OJ from the fridge, start the coffee, and sit down to my usual breakfast: cornflakes with lots of sugar. Sipping my coffee, I scroll through my cell for my appointments for the day.

Shit. It's Thursday, which means Witty's weekly staff meeting, at which I have to serve as note taker. These meetings of his are usually deadly and mostly useless. The department heads don't say much because they don't trust him, and he loves to ask for useless reports that he may never read. They also cut into my main job as political officer, trying to gather info from my German contacts.

A dismal prospect for another lousy day. Some minutes later, when the full absurdity of my situation hits home, I come up with the obvious solution, lifted from my high school playbook. Brilliant. I'll call in sick, but with a technological update to avoid arguments or questions. I tap out a message to Charlotte, my secretary. *Feeling lousy, running a fever,* I lie happily, *tell Emerson I can't make it. Hope to be okay by Monday. I'll try to get some sleep now.*

The last bit to make sure nobody tries to call back.

By the time I'm heading out of town, my duffel bag stuffed with clothes and books beside me, it's the middle of the afternoon, and the end-of-day commuter traffic is building. Berliners call it *Berufsverkehr* and gripe endlessly about normally free-flowing roads clogging their trek home. They don't know how good they have it. Compared to the permanently constipated roadways of most big cities, Berlin during the worst times of day is still a snap.

I'm in my well-aged Opel, dodging double-decker buses on the Kudamm, heading to the A-11 and the Baltic coast, two hundred miles to the north. I'm off to Heringsdorf, a seaside resort on Usedom Island, where I know the perfect place to hide. I'm wearing jeans, a knitted black sweater, and white tennis shoes. My padded seaweed-green winter jacket is slung over the seat next to me and a duffel bag stuffed with clothes and books is on the floor.

On Indira Gandhistrasse, I pass Weissensee, home to Europe's largest Jewish cemetery, and one of the biggest in Berlin. I've wandered around there many times. I have a thing for cemeteries, especially the great ones, like Père Lachaise in Paris, and Weissensee, which is much larger, with its hundred thousand gravesites spread over a hundred acres. It was built in the nineteenth century, when Berlin's Jewish population was large and prosperous. Along the inside fence are dozens of elaborate mausolea, some larger than an average Berliner's apartment.

The Nazis tried to rid Berlin of all traces of Jewish life, so the survival of the cemetery is a miracle. Maybe focusing all their energies on hunting living Jews didn't leave them with enough time or interest for the dead ones. A handful of underground Jews actually stayed alive during the war, hiding inside the cemetery at night because their pursuers found it spooky in the dark and avoided it.

There's a small plot in the cemetery with a marker in memory of my grandparents, Hermann and Rosa Jakobsohn. A year before the war, they managed to get their teenage son, my father, into the US to save him from the Nazis. Their own visas never came through, and in 1942, they disappeared in the east and were never heard from again. So, it's not really a gravesite, just an empty plot with their names.

Not surprisingly, my father hates Germany and all things German, and to this day he can't understand why I agreed to be posted here. Long ago, he vowed never to set foot in Germany again, and he never has. Once on a family vacation in Europe, we had to pass through a small corner of Germany driving from Switzerland to France. I remember that he refused to stop and that none of us were allowed to get out. At the French border, he noisily spat out the window with only a single word: "Bastards!"

Growing up in New Jersey, where my folks owned a boutique store selling antiques, I didn't know much about family history. One day, someone mentioned the grandparents I'd never known, which raised my curiosity.

"Hey, Dad," I asked him, "if your father was Jakobsohn, how come our name is Jackson?"

He looked at me and said nothing for a moment and then answered. "Well, Adam, you know how I feel about Germans. So, from the moment I came to this country I wanted nothing more to do with them, not even the German name. To be a real American, I had to get rid of all traces of the past. Jackson sounded about as American as you can get. So, I took it."

"When did this happen?" I wanted to know. "And why not Smith or Jones? Sounds American too."

"Simple," he explained with a sheepish grin. "It was sort of an accident. When I got my citizenship after the war, I had to fill in a lot of forms and put down a name. That's when I made the decision. I looked in a phone book—we still had phone books in those days—and near the Jakobsohns was a whole page of Jacksons. That's how you got your name."

Heringsdorf

9:00 p.m.

It's dark now, and I'm out of Berlin heading toward Usedom Island. Traffic is light and I'm listening to Radiohead and Oasis. I'm getting close to Heringsdorf and singing along with, "*You gotta roll with it, you gotta take your time.*" *My plan; good advice*, I'm thinking.

Shortly after nine, I roll up to a well-weathered two-story house and pull the Opel into a narrow lane to the right. There's a low picket fence in front and a tiny *Vorgarten* sprouting patchy grass and a few nondescript bushes in need of trimming. The house is dark, except for a single light downstairs, a glimmer behind drawn curtains. Anna Rotbein is waiting up for me.

Her place, the Villa Ostwind, sits on a short and narrow street a few hundred yards in back of the Seeweg, Heringsdorf's main beach thoroughfare where the pricier new hotels, *Pensions*, and rooming houses have sprouted in recent years. In prewar days, Heringsdorf was the seaside resort of choice for Berliners with money to spend their summers enjoying the sugar-white beaches. These days, only a few villas remain as reminders of that era. Under the Communists, the town decayed, and after the Wall came down, Heringsdorf devolved into what some now call "Berlin's bathtub," the destination for masses of budget tourists crowding the rooming houses and bed-and-breakfasts. Some new hotels went up in hopes of restoring Heringsdorf's past glory, but with indifferent success. Berlin's upper crust long ago decided that the resort is too close to Berlin and prefers to congregate on the North Sea islands of Sylt and Norderney.

Like most everyone in Heringsdorf, Anna rents rooms in the summer, breakfast included, but she's picky about the guests. Her rates are modest, but apparently enough to keep her going during the off season when no one's around.

A villa, her place is not, not even close. The fading yellow walls outside are badly in need of paint, but Anna hasn't seen fit to do much about it in years. "What's outside is for show," she once told me. "What's inside's what counts, and my guests know the difference."

I climb the red brick steps to the door, it opens, and there she is in a pair of corduroy pants and a loose-knit red sweater.

She says, "Adam Jackson, my American diplomat, you look like hell."

"Really?"

"Baggy eyes. You need sleep. *Komm rein.*"

"Thanks for the warm welcome," I tell her. "How about a hug?"

I walk in, drop my duffel, and she obliges. Then we sit down on the well-worn sofa in her front room and look at each other for a moment, not saying much.

Anna is special, a unicorn. At five feet or thereabouts, she's almost as broad as she is tall. She is eighty if she's a day, but you wouldn't know it from her remarkably clear-skinned face, cheeks the color of crabapple, and the sparkly and expressive bright blue eyes of a woman half her age. Her gray hair is arranged in a bun and she wears it like a crown.

Anna likes crazy jewelry and tonight's no exception. She's hung a twisted lava bead necklace around her neck, and four vaguely Ethiopian-looking Wollo rings decorate the fingers of her left hand. Only two rings are on the other, I note, which is unusual. An exotic-looking wood and resin blue one graces her pinkie and a bulky turquoise creation of unknown pedigree fascinates me, but defies further description. She has put it on her middle finger. Inexplicably, the ring finger has been spared.

Two years ago, on a starless night in the middle of a fearsome rainstorm, Fiona and I were coming back from a trip to the north when I ran the car into a construction ditch just outside Heringsdorf. That's when we stumbled into the Villa Ostwind and I first met Anna.

Fiona hated our life in Berlin and was nagging me to quit my job and go home, which I had no intention of doing. For months there had been no honest talk between us, just recurring arguments between bouts of icy silence followed by tears, protestations of love, and wild love-making—sometimes angry, always passionate. I guess it's the great sex that's kept me from facing the reality of our situation. Just as it had first bewitched me twelve years ago when I met Fiona at Rutgers. I thought it was a wondrous, perfect love at the time. Now I think it may just have been perfect lust.

Sex has always been Fiona's way to get what she wants, and she is superb at leveraging her looks and lovemaking to maximum effect. From the beginning, she was quick to sense what I wanted in bed and to cater to it. When to be coy, seductive, submissive, and when to take charge, relentlessly aggressive and inventive.

For me, the challenges and rewards of representing the US abroad more than offset the little annoyances that came with it. For Fiona, it was a different story. It's the spouses who bear the brunt of the downsides of diplomatic life without the rewards, and Fiona was never the type to bear her burdens in silence.

"Marry me, take me with you," she had breathed into my ear while laboriously tonguing it as we lay, limbs entwined. No other woman had ever made me feel like that. Her nakedness enfolded me, and overcome by the odor of spent love, I was blissful, paralyzed, and speechless.

She wanted an over-the-top wedding. I never asked her father what it cost him.

Things started off pretty much according to plan. My first eighteen months in Basra, a hot, dirty, and dangerous shithole of a post infested by untold numbers of flies, Shiite bomb throwers, and 110-degree heat, I served alone. Fiona joined me for short leaves spent with wild abandon in Rome, Athens, and once, in Paris. That was the good life of Fiona's reveries. Next came our first joint posting to pleasant and problem-free Geneva, with lots of good Fendant du Valais to drink, and great skiing in Verbier and Gstaad. Thereafter Washington, Rabat, and, finally, Berlin.

It took four moves in ten years before Fiona's dreamy expectations of diplomatic life gave way to the reality of what she began to bemoan as our "gypsy existence." Then, she became relentless and infinitely inventive in her maneuvers to impel me to quit and go home.

In our short time together in Berlin, her campaign reached its peak. She refused to learn German or get to know the city; she was put off by the weather, the food, and the people. She complained bitterly about her boredom and our poverty and rootlessness. Sometimes she would plead pitiful homesickness, at other times angrily demand that it was my turn to respect her needs and agree to find other work.

There were days when she refused to leave the apartment, meet friends, or accompany me to embassy events. When she did agree to show up, she would deliberately embarrass me with too much liquor and inappropriate talk, or try to provoke me by flirting her way across the room. And for Fiona, of course, there always was the sex, her preferred strategy for getting her way. No doubt it infuriated her that this time, none of it had worked.

I avoided my wife when I could, made excuses, stayed away overnight pleading real or pretend business out of town. I guess she must have felt the same way, so one day she simply packed her bags and left. Her mother needed her, she told me. She'd be back soon, she promised, which I knew was a lie. To tell the truth, I was relieved.

In the last year I've seen her once, briefly in DC. We email or talk on the telephone, usually at night. She says she misses me, and I tell her the same thing. For me, it's a way to avoid the hard stuff, probably for her too. So, we just chitchat and go on pretending, sharing the rut we're stuck in.

Sunday, November 5

10:00 a.m.

Anna likes to serve her guests plentiful breakfasts. Sunday mornings, plentiful becomes humongous, and though I'm the only one in the house, today is no exception.

I've slept in late, and when I come down from my room, she is standing at the kitchen stove dressed in a wine-red, loose-fitting tracksuit, with a large, multicolored wooden bead necklace dangling down to her ample belly.

She's laid out a stunning spread for us. There's a large platter of various Baltic fish specialties, little *Sprotten*, smoked eel, pickled *Brathering*, and a flat aquatic delicacy I suspect is flounder. Another plate is loaded with several kinds of wursts and ham and a tray with a selection of cheeses. In a well-stocked breadbasket, I spot a couple of giant pretzels. There's also an impressively large *Apfelkuchen* on the table, and the freshly baked aroma greets me as I descend the stairs.

"*Gott*, Anna," I groan in mock horror, "you think there's a famine in Berlin? Who's supposed to eat all this?"

"Sit down," she orders. Then she asks, "You want eggs, or maybe a little *Schinken* omelet?"

"Stop it," I tell her sternly. "Get away from that stove and sit down."

She pours us coffee, sits opposite me, and we go to work on her idea of an ordinary Sunday breakfast.

Anna won't allow cigarette smoking in her place, but doesn't mind pipes and cigars, which she considers a more civilized alternative. She likes to smoke herself, so, after we've eaten, she opens the fresh box of Montecristos I brought her, and we light up.

Outside, it's a blustery, cloudy day. The sky has the same dark, slate color as the ocean, and gusts of Atlantic wind are blowing the last leaves off the old beech tree outside the kitchen window. Anna is an oral miser. She talks only when she's got something worth saying. She doesn't ask many questions and answers even fewer.

I'd spent most of Saturday up in my room reading or climbing around on the dunes, trying not to think about anything important. I wasn't in the mood for talking, and Anna kept out of the way and silent, as I knew she would.

Now, as the clouds of cigar smoke drift through the air and gradually overwhelm the smell of her *Apfelkuchen*, I watch the tree outside bend and billow in the wind. Anna, half chewing, half sucking on her cigar, follows the tiny smoke rings she is blowing toward the ceiling.

It crosses my mind that I owe her an explanation for showing up out of nowhere. "It's a fucked-up world out there," I tell her.

"Uh-huh."

She sends a silent appraising look my way, but now her sphinx-like silence doesn't fit my mood. Actually, it irritates me.

"I'm thinking about quitting my job, my marriage—the whole shitshow." I wait a beat, then I turn to her and ask, "Surprised?"

She fixes me with her steely blue eyes. "Yes to the first, no to the second."

"What do you mean?"

"You seem to really like the diplomatic bullshit, so I'm surprised you want to give it up." I nod, then she continues. "As for your Fiona, I met her only once, that first time you were here. She's beautiful, your wife. These walls aren't exactly paper-thin, but I still heard the two of you in your room. . . ."

"*Du Missststück*! I wish I'd known—"

"Forget it, *mein Freund*, it wasn't the ruckus of your screwing that stuck with me. It was more the way the two of you came across down here. You didn't exactly seem like soulmates. So, no, I'm not surprised."

"There was a time . . ." I started, but then I let it drop.

"No," she announces. "Time for a beer." She walks to the fridge and comes back with two bottles of *Erdinger Weissbier*.

We clink silently, Anna smiling faintly in almost a motherly fashion. "*Prost*," she says.

"*Weisst Du.*" I tell her after swigging beer for a while, "Oscar Wilde once observed that all women become like their mothers. That's what I think happened to Fiona. I never did like her parents, and the feeling was mutual. Her nagging mother didn't approve of her marrying a civil servant. But Fiona swore she didn't care about that and only wanted to be my wife and in my life. My mistake was that I believed her. With her head full of romantic dreams of glamour and glory, she probably believed it herself."

"What changed?" Anna asks.

"It just took her a while to discover what life with me was really like and for me to see that she was just as spoiled and selfish as her parents. Spoiled in the breeding, I'd say."

"Looks like the two of you have wound up separated by more than distance." Anna shrugs. "You'll figure it out."

She fingers the wooden necklace dangling from her neck with the idle distraction of an Arab working his beads.

I stare into the distance and eventually, I laugh. "There may be some real irony in working it out."

"How so?"

"If working it out means I resign and go home, it's exactly what Fiona seems to want. Except I might not be coming home to her."

"But why would you resign?"

"It's a tough call. Quitting may make things worse. If I stay, I might have some small amount of influence."

"The Weizsäcker dilemma," she says.

"I don't follow."

"Freiherr Ernst von Weizsächer," she explains. "Our ex-president's father, one of the old-school diplomats with titles and striped pants. Joined the service in the 1920s and stayed on well into the war. Even joined the Nazi Party working for Ribbentrop, thinking he'd use his influence on the inside to prevent the worst.

"Didn't work," she continues. "They made him put his signature on all kinds of shit, including the order to deport French Jews to the death camps in Poland. In '47, he found himself on trial as a war criminal. Wound up in Landsberg prison."

She leans back, exhales, and gives me a challenging look. She seems drained.

Maybe I should lighten things up a little, I'm thinking, so I wave her away with a smile.

"Interesting bit of history. We have a lunatic in the White House, but he's no Hitler. And the US isn't Germany."

Anna gives me a skeptical look. "Are you sure? I lived through Hitler as a kid and forty years under the Communists. There are only so many moves in the dictator's playbook, and your guy seems to be checking all the boxes: keep the pot boiling; stoke anger and fear; blame the minorities; attack judges who rule against you; and attack the media when they write stuff you don't like. The Nazis called it *Lügenpresse*, the lying press. He calls it Fake News.

"And the rallies! All the banners and slogans and screaming for blood. A real déjà vu for me, Adam. Only the Nazis and the commies were better at it. Your guy's an amateur."

Then she laughs. "So, maybe there's hope for America after all."

I smile, but there's really nothing funny in what she says. History has made Germans super-sensitive to dictators and demagogues, so they're pessimists. But there's also a bit of "you're not so special, it can happen to you too" triumphalism.

I'm trying to think of something pithy to say when my phone rings. Reflexively, I look at my watch and realize that it's early morning in DC. *Sorry, Fiona*, I'm thinking, *not now*, and decide to ignore the ringing.

Anna moves toward the living room, and I'm about to follow her, when the ding of a text message followed by renewed ringing gets my attention. I look at the screen and realize that it's my secretary, Charlotte, not Fiona, who's after me.

The text says, *We have an emergency. You are needed ASAP. Call immediately.*

I push the pictograph of a telephone receiver and say, "What's up, Charlotte? Where's the fire?"

Her breathing is labored, her voice heavy. "Someone shot Mr. Emerson," she says quietly. "He's dead. You're wanted back here at once. Please hurry."

"I'm on my way," I tell her and end the call.

Ten minutes later, I'm throwing my gear into the Opel with Anna coming down the steps to see me off. We hug and she kisses me on one cheek, then the other. She doesn't ask what's happened, and I don't explain.

"Watch yourself, Adam," she tells me, "and keep in touch." I smile and give her a thumbs-up as I get in the car and pull away.

Chapter 3

Berlin

Sunday, November 5

S unday mornings, Emmett Cunningham and his neighbor Wolfgang Trieber have a standing tennis date. Two sets of singles, which Emmett always loses, followed by a beer and some Berlin gossip.

It's a tennis friendship of opposites. Trieber, a German banker, is passionate about the game, takes weekly instructions from the pro at the nearby Rot-Weiss tennis club, and likes to win. Cunningham is an Irish-American diplomat who hasn't had a lesson in his life. His playing style is unorthodox, to say the least, with a contorted service motion that defies gravity and has to be seen to be believed. He plays for fun and exercise and hustles exuberantly around the court, chasing Trieber's lobs and slices. A happy loser as long as he takes at least three games per set.

1:00 p.m.

Another Sunday, another tennis trouncing. Emmett, bushed and sweaty, is returning home. Over six feet tall, broad-shouldered and barrel-chested, Emmett is fifty, but looks younger. Trim except for the hint of a spare tire around his midriff, he looks more like one of his cherished New England Patriots than a seasoned diplomat. With a head full of tousled, ginger-red hair, bushy eyebrows, and an impressive handlebar mustache, he's not easily overlooked.

"I'm back, honey," he bellows, drops his tennis gear in the hallway, and crosses the downstairs reception area to join his wife, Liz, on the veranda fronting a spacious flower garden. Emmett is Minister-Counselor for Political Affairs, the number three spot at the American Embassy, and the rather grand Dahlem residence at 14 Rosengasse that the Cunninghams presently call home is meant for the inevitable receptions and dinners that come with the job. Its checkered history, Emmett likes to tell his American visitors, is a paradigm of twentieth-century Berlin drama.

The original owner was a prosperous Jewish brewer who had the villa built in the 1920s. The next occupant was one of Heinrich Himmler's SS deputies who appropriated the place for himself after the rightful proprietor had been conveniently shipped off to the gas chambers. Himmler's deputy shot himself when the Russians appeared at the door in 1945. Thereafter, Dahlem became ground zero in Berlin's American sector, and so it fell to a succession of US generals to enjoy these elegant quarters over the next forty years. When the Wall came down and the military pulled out, the State Department appropriated the prized property for the residence of Berlin's Minister-Counselor.

As Emmett collapses on a cushioned wicker lounger next to his wife, she puts down her *New York Times* crossword and sends him a fondly appraising look.

"Why so happy, Em?" she asks. "Don't tell me you won."

"Six-four in the first set," he announces triumphantly.

"You won?"

"Of course not. But I took four games, which scared the bejeezus out of Wolfgang. But thanks for the question, darling. A man needs a wife who believes. And how's the puzzle coming? Got it all done?"

"Ha! What's the meaning of *mephitic*, smart ass?"

"Google it." Emmett laughs and leans forward to plant a kiss on top of his wife's head.

Liz Cunningham is an attractive, slender woman a good two heads shorter than her husband, with a delicate round face and once dark hair now mottled with middle-age gray.

They are Foreign Service lifers and proud of what they do. In their twenty-five years together, they have raised their two kids in four countries on three continents. As Emmett successfully negotiated the Department's obstacle course into the senior ranks, she organized their living quarters and settled the kids in each new post, has been a gracious hostess for his guests, and is a discreet and smiling companion at his side.

On a typical day, Emmett is at his desk before eight, and most evenings there are meetings, conferences, receptions, and dinners, which they sometimes do together, but more often she may not see him again till late at night. Sundays they keep for themselves.

Liz has laid out the Sunday brunch: Greek salad, a plate with bread and cheese, and a pitcher of Bloody Marys. "I'm starving," Emmett announces. He moves to the table, fills their glasses, and starts picking tomatoes out of his salad.

"Where's the feta?" he asks. "There's no feta. I like feta."

"Sorry, we're out of it."

"Greek salad without feta is like screwing in the dark. No zip, no passion."

"That's my husband—everything boils down to sex."

"Hell yes, do you mind?"

"Not really," she smiles slyly. "Try the Limburger; it's the stinky kind you like. It'll take your mind off the feta."

Emmett drains half his Bloody Mary and leans back contentedly on his lounger.

"What's the rest of the day look like?" Liz asks. "Any plans?"

Emmett looks up at the sky where some patches of blue have appeared between the gray cloud cover.

"How about we bike to Grunewald Lake and back?" he tells her. "And tonight, I'll take you to the Taverna and tell Luigi we want candles on the table and a bottle of that Barolo you like."

"Sounds good. When's Benninger coming back?"

"God knows. Which reminds me . . . Looks like our man in charge left the reservation. Tony Alcaro from security called me yesterday. Seems Witty missed a dinner at the von Trachtenbergs', and yesterday morning he didn't answer his phone. But Tony didn't call back, so I guess he came home. Not like Dimwit, though. He loves those dinners with the snob brigade."

"Maybe he had a hot date," Liz says with a grin.

"Are you kidding?" Then, as an afterthought, "Anything's possible, I suppose."

Emmett emerges from the shower and is toweling off when he hears Liz calling from downstairs.

"Em, the phone. It's Tony. He says it's urgent."

Emmett picks up in the bedroom. "Hey, Antonio. What gives?"

"It's Emerson. The cops just found him. He's dead. Somebody shot him."

Emmett drops the towel, clasps the phone tight, and stands buck naked by the bed. For a moment he's paralyzed, unable to think.

"What? How? What do you mean?"

"This police *Kommissar* said they found a guy this morning shot in the head. Off a place called Im Jagen, in the Grunewald. They just confirmed the ID."

Emmett struggles to get his emotions under control, his mind to function. Then the feeling rises from his stomach and into his throat. *It's the biggest mess at this embassy in fifty years, and I'm in charge.*

"Who knows?"

"I've sent a 'No Dis, Immediate' to the Department, that's all."

Emmett does his best to sound authoritative. "Okay, Tony. Here's what I want you to do. First, tell Public Affairs until I get there it's 'no comment' with the media. Second, tell Gunny I want his marines to lock down the building till we figure out what's what. Third, you get on the phone and call the senior team. I don't care where they are. It's an emergency and I want them assembled in the embassy ASAP. Got that?"

"Yes, sir," Tony answers, "I'm on it." He sounds relieved.

"And send a car, Tony. I'm coming in."

"Done," Tony replies.

Chapter 4

Berlin

Sunday, November 5

5:00 p.m.

*D*aylight is fading fast by the time I reach the embassy. The police have barricaded the entire Behrenstrasse block around the entrance to the Chancery, which is brightly lit. Two green armored vans and a couple of police cruisers are parked in front, and several cops in protective gear wielding automatic rifles patrol the area. Aside from a handful of tourists still wandering around the Holocaust Memorial to the south, the only civilians are in an ARD television truck parked nearby.

Since leaving Anna, I have been in a barely controlled state of agitation, and seeing the floodlit, barricaded embassy does nothing to ease my anxiety. What if Witty's murder wasn't a fluke or private misfortune, but the beginning of something truly sinister coming our way?

The cop at the police barrier eyes the Opel's diplomatic tag, and as I flash him my ID, he pushes the wooden stopper aside and lets me pass. Inside, the marine on duty is all business.

"Hey, Mr. Jackson," he says. "You're expected downstairs in the Tank."

"The Tank" is a super-secure space in the basement for sensitive meetings when top-secret material is being discussed. It's an odd-looking contraption, a cross between a barracks and a tent, with an outer skin supposedly immune to electronic penetration and regularly swept for listening devices.

Oh boy, I'm thinking, as I ride the elevator down.

The marine at the door to the Tank has seen me a hundred times, but tonight he carefully checks the badge around my neck before he steps aside to let me pass.

Emmett Cunningham is seated at the head of the long metal conference table that's bolted to the floor and fills most of the room. Within easy reach to his left is a small stand with three phones, each a different color. The red one is in the middle. An oversize television screen for secure communication with Washington is mounted along one wall. A bunch of chairs around the table complete the room's sparse furnishings, except for a niche near the door with an industrial-size urn for coffee and some bottles of water. The air feels heavy and fetid. Ventilation in the Tank has always been a problem, and tonight's no exception.

"Sit down, Adam," Emmett calls out and motions to one of the empty chairs. Next to me, on his right, are Tony Alcaro, our security officer, and Erica Baumholzer, head of Public Affairs. Jack Castelyou, our legal attaché, and Austin Trotter, the CIA station chief, sit across from them.

Castelyou is actually an FBI agent. Tall and athletic looking, about forty, he wears rimless glasses, a salt-and-pepper crewcut, and a black tracksuit and sneakers. He spends a lot of time in the gym, where he must have been when they called him in. Usually, he's one of the few officers around the embassy wearing the white shirt, suit, and tie that's the FBI uniform.

Trotter is the exact opposite—stout, balding, and perennially gloomy-looking, with thick glasses and circles under his eyes. Normally we don't see much of him or his team, who keep to themselves in their secured quarters on the top floor. There are plenty of rumors but no hard facts about what they do up there, and I doubt that even the ambassador has a clue.

Castelyou and Trotter sitting side by side is a first. Castelyou hates Trotter, and vice versa. They hardly talk to each other, let alone sit together, and spend much of their time fighting over turf and hatching petty intrigues. *It took Witty getting himself killed to have these two in the same room*, I'm thinking.

Emmett leans forward and rests his large hands on the edge of the table, dominating the room. His bushy handlebar moves up and down with little twitches showing some inner tension, but his voice is calm.

"Okay," he says, "let's take stock of what we know, which is pretty sketchy. Tony, bring us up to date."

Tony is visibly nervous. In his midfifties, short and skeleton-thin with sparse gray hair, he looks more like a bookkeeper than a diplomat. But he's a career FSO, conscientious to a fault, a stickler for rules and procedures, and easily upset by the slightest infraction of even the most chicken-shit regulation.

He shuffles some notes in front of him and launches into his report. "According to Betty Kowalski," he starts off, "the DCM left the embassy a little after four on Friday afternoon. She says he was acting strange. He'd been working out of the ambassador's office—"

"Working?" interrupts Trotter, and rolls his eyes.

"Spare us, Austin," Emmett cuts him off. "Go on, Tony."

"Betty says he told her he had a meeting at the Adlon but wouldn't say more. Insisted on walking there without security, which is unusual for him."

Tony pauses to consult his notes, and Trotter shifts in his chair and makes a face. I feel embarrassed by the school-boy antics at dead Witty's expense, and apparently I'm not alone.

"Mr. Emerson had a dinner in Zehlendorf that night, at the Trachtenbergs," Tony continues, "and his driver Walter was supposed to meet him at the Adlon at 7:15, but called Betty at 7:51 to report that he never showed. She wasn't overly surprised, she says, because she thought it had to do with that meeting thing of his. So, it wasn't until 6:10 yesterday evening that the alarm bells went off. That's when Gräfin von Trachtenberg's social secretary, Katharina Willmans is her name, phoned Greta to ask whether Emerson was ill, because he'd missed the dinner. When I couldn't reach him on the phone, I immediately called Jack, who alerted the German authorities, and that's when they started looking for him."

Tony looks up from his notes and mutters, "That's the story. At twelve past two today, we got the call that they'd found him. Jack can tell you the rest."

Castelyou takes a moment to glance around the room, then says, "I got a phone call from Hans Schnittker, Berlin Interior Senator's State Secretary, my main contact point here for law enforcement. He reported that a Caucasian male had been found in the Grunewald, dead from a bullet through the back of the head. Small caliber, very close range. Berlin homicide took him to their morgue on Kaiser Friedrichstrasse and identified him as Emerson."

"That's it?" Emmett asks.

"Well," Castelyou says, "we sent an 'Immediate' to the Department. I also contacted the Staatssicherheit, the federal office of state security, who no doubt briefed the chancellor's office and the BND. I have a call in to them now."

"Goddammit, stay the hell away," Trotter thunders. The BND is the German spy organization he considers his territory. "You don't know what the fuck you're doing. You'll screw up everything. I'm handling this."

"Just doing my job," Castelyou tells him quietly.

"The hell you are, motherfucker," Trotter bellows, "this ain't amateur hour."

"Relax, Austin," Castelyou smiles, which really enrages the CIA chief.

"Fuck you," he says and bangs the table.

Emmett leans forward and stares wordlessly at the red-faced Trotter.

"Right," he says after a long silence, "let's wind this up. Adam, any idea what Witty's meeting could have been about?"

"None," I say, and shake my head. "I wasn't even here on Friday."

"So, I'll sum up," Emmett says. "First, Witty's murder is a tragedy. We don't know how or why this happened, and until we do, we'll treat the assault on our colleague as an assault on all of us. Let's remember that Witty was an FSO representing the president and our country. So, it's an attack on the US as well. I expect us to pull together as professionals and act as a team. That goes for everyone in this room and this post," he adds pointedly, but does not look at Trotter.

"Second. This afternoon, I ordered the building locked down and secured. Pending new developments, I plan to reverse that in the morning. Flags will fly at half-mast, but otherwise let's get the embassy back to normal. The ambassador, I expect, will be back very shortly.

"Third, we can expect holy hell to break loose once this hits the news—"

"It's already on the wires, and my phones are going apeshit," Erica Baumholzer breaks in. "What's our public posture, Emmett? What can I say? We need to meet with the media ASAP. I recommend we call in the usual suspects—German and US—the key networks certainly, and you personally brief them later tonight—"

Cunningham cuts her off. "Not yet, Erica. It's 'no comment' until we know more. German Homicide will do the talking and they won't say much either. We'll stay mum, at least until God knows who all is going to descend on us from Washington in the morning."

"I disagree," Erica insists, waving her arms like a traffic cop at rush hour. "We have to keep the initiative on this. The pressure will be huge and—"

"I know, Erica, I know," Emmett says. "You can handle it. You're the expert. But 'no comment' till you hear otherwise, okay?"

Emmett stands up. "Okay, folks. Stay cool, and get some rest. You'll be glad you did come tomorrow morning."

"Adam," Cunningham calls, motioning me back to a chair. I reverse course and we sit down together as the Tank's door closes behind the others.

Emmett is a great guy. He's my idea of an FS professional, a sharp analyst who knows how to keep his cool under pressure. I tell him I admire the way he handled the meeting.

He gives me a thin smile. "What a fucking mess."

"Yeah," I answer. "Good old Dimwit, of all people. The poor bastard was six months from retirement."

Emmett strokes his handlebar, stares into space, and then leans toward me. He tells me he's been thinking about what might have happened and wants to kick some ideas around and think it through together.

He says he can think of three reasons for what happened: a robbery by some random stranger, a beef over money or sex, or something to do with Witty's mysterious meeting.

He says, "The *Polizei* told Jack they don't think it was robbery because neither his wallet, cell, nor other valuables were missing.

I asked specifically about that stupid diamond signet ring of his, and they told me it was still on his pinkie where it always was. So, I'd have to agree that a botched holdup is an unlikely explanation.

"Frankly, knowing our late DCM, I just can't picture the guy entangled with someone over money or sex. Just doesn't fit. Which leaves us with the meeting. Make sense to you?"

I nod slowly, still pondering. "Witty never mentioned money or complained about it. You never know, but I also agree about the sex angle. Some people thought he was gay, but if so, he would have been way deep in the closet. Personally, I just think he wasn't interested in getting laid."

Emmett's bushy eyebrows travel north and he looks at me skeptically.

"Yep, Emmett," I grin, "such people do exist. Even though a horny bastard like you can't imagine it. But if you ask me, Witty got off on society, not sex. He was an old-womanish type, the kind who sits down to pee."

We look at each other and laugh. Then Emmett gets serious again, and there's a note of urgency in his voice. "That leaves the alleged secret meeting," he says, "which really bugs me. Perhaps it's nothing, but there's a chance it was real, and a chance it involved important US interests. I'm worried the Germans could stumble on it before we do."

Emmett studies my face, assessing my reaction.

"Could be," I say, "but I can't see what we can do about it now. Our security types should dive into that when they get here in the morning."

"Might be too late," says Emmett, shaking his head. "Officially it's the German Kripo's case, and they're out there poking around right now, and due in here in the morning, incidentally. We have to get a jump on them tonight.

"Tony and I already went through Witty's office this afternoon.

Checked his desk, his computers, and all his files, including the classified ones. Didn't find a thing. Nada."

He pauses to take a breath. "Which leaves his apartment," he says.

Then he leans forward and looks me directly in the eye. "Adam, I need you to go over there tonight and see what you can find. Obviously, on the QT."

I hadn't seen this coming, and for a moment I try to think of what to say. Then I ask, "You want me to break into Witty's apartment?"

"Yep," he nods, "if necessary."

"Like a burglar."

"You might put it that way."

"You're joking."

"No, I'm dead serious. I've thought about this long and hard. I wouldn't ask you to do it if I didn't think it could be really important."

I don't know whether I'm being drawn down some sinister rabbit hole or suddenly dropped into a Monty Python routine, but I'm shaking my head and laugh. "No way."

"Why not?"

"Because it's nuts. Ever hear of Watergate? And what makes you think the Kripo isn't parked outside with their binoculars, just waiting to see who shows up?"

"Relax, Adam. Let's think this through together, okay?"

"I've already thought it through," I say, "and I think we should let our security people handle it. I grant you it'd be nice to get there first, but if the Germans beat us to it, we'll survive. Going rogue and burgling Witty's place can't work and is way too dangerous. I sure as hell am not up for it. I'd make a lousy burglar and wouldn't have a clue about getting in and out again without being nabbed *in flagrante delicto*. I'm an FSO, remember? And so are you. We're not supposed to do illegal stuff on foreign postings. Hell, Admin busts a gut when I so much as get a traffic ticket."

Emmett shakes his head. "That's where you're wrong. Who knows what's at stake? It could be nothing, or it could be a major threat to national security. Protecting the national interest is what we do, right? There are plenty of people out there who want to cause serious trouble for us."

"And they'd begin by killing Wit Emerson?"

"We just don't know. You may think he's a fool, but at the time of his death, he was the man in charge of the US Embassy in Berlin. Sure there's risk, but it's our duty to try, not just as citizens, but as FSOs. And I can't think of anyone better suited than you."

"You think?"

"Sure. You have the smarts, and you have the guts."

"Yeah," I nod. "Smart enough to say no. Besides, I don't have guts. I'm a coward."

So, we go back and forth a while longer. But Emmett is good, really good. He appeals to my values, my pride, and my ego. He pushes all the right buttons. I know what he's doing, but—damn him—he's succeeding.

After half an hour of working me over, he pauses, gives me a warm smile, and says, "Enough talk. It's your call. The decision is entirely yours."

I stare at him for a long moment. Then I say, "Okay, I'll do it."

Emmett gets up and gives me a hug.

"Bless you," he says. "I've got your back."

Chapter 5

Berlin

Sunday night, November 5

8:00 p.m.

*B*ack at my apartment, I have a panic attack. I'd just promised to burglarize Witty's place, and I have no idea where to begin.

I visited there several times and knew the basic layout. I also remember Witty's self-important insistence on beefed-up security, meaning that his doors had electronic in addition to standard key locks. How was I supposed to get past those? And even if I could, I still didn't know what I was looking for.

I also saw it as more than a fifty-fifty chance that the German cops would be sitting on the doorstep, watching and waiting. If I got caught, what would I tell them? The whole thing could backfire because they'd naturally suspect we were after something worth retrieving or covering up. Not to mention the fact that I'd be on the hook for attempted burglary and suddenly the prime suspect in a murder.

The sane thing was to phone Emmett and call it off. More than once I reached for my cell phone, but each time I pulled back. It was crazy, but as much as I dreaded getting involved, I was also drawn to it. My entire life I'd beat myself up for being too timid, too nerdy, too much the straight arrow. When other guys were joining the Marines or covering wars from the front lines or putting bad guys in jail, I was learning how to file reports and make chitchat at embassy cocktail parties. At long last, here was my chance to be a badass, maybe for a good cause—and with diplomatic immunity!

I sit back and take a deep breath. To hell with it, I'll do it.

An hour later, I emerge from the U-Bahn a block away from Witty's apartment. Im Dol is a quiet, tree-lined street of mostly private villas behind fenced-in gardens.

Walking through all this peace and prosperity, I realize I'm decked out in full burglar regalia, as if I'd bought it in a kit labeled "Breaking and Entering." Jeans, wool shirt, sweater, and raincoat, all in black, plus sneakers and a baseball cap—also black. None too subtle. Like Santa Claus on a Heringsdorf beach in July.

I'd picked up two pairs of surgical gloves at a drugstore, then on my way out I saw a small first aid kit and bought that too. Just in case. The larger issue was that I still had no idea what I was doing. My only hope of getting past the electronic lock on Witty's door was to guess the code, which seemed an impossible long shot. As for the key lock, I brought along a few safety pins and some metal kebab skewers from my kitchen drawer. This kind of shit worked in the movies, and that's all I had to go on. For whatever reason, I also packed a small hand towel, three different size screwdrivers, and a pair of pliers from my home tool kit. I stowed it all in a small backpack strapped beneath that outer layer. For Witty's computer, assuming I got that far, I'd stuck a couple of thumb drives into the pocket of my raincoat. The only flashlight I owned was too big and bulky, so I'd left it behind, relying instead on the light from my cell phone.

Im Dol looks deserted. No one seems to be around, and unless they're lurking in the bushes, I detect no visible signs of *Polizei*, which is a relief.

The sparse street lighting isn't doing much to dispel the misty gloom, which is fine by me. I try to stay in the shadows and walk purposefully, as if I belong here. I tense up when I hear someone coming up behind me, but it's just a woman on a bike, pedaling fast as she passes on my left and vanishes into the murk. Minutes later, a couple walks toward me on the other side of the street. Another momentary case of nerves, but they're talking to each other without a glance in my direction, so I relax again.

Witty's building is postwar vintage, one of the few apartment houses on this street. I remember Witty's penthouse as being over-sized for a single occupant, and furnished to reflect his idea of what would elicit the proper respect due a senior diplomat. Wildly over the top, and not my idea of comfort or good taste, but Witty loved it.

There's a curved driveway in front and a lone streetlamp shining at the entrance. No one is in sight, so I approach and look into the lobby. Mirrored walls, a couple of chairs on either side of a table, and a huge vase of blue and white lilies. I can make out red-carpeted stairs next to the elevator in back.

A brass plate left of the entrance displays the tenants' names, two for each floor, except for the top, with just the initials W.D.E. Below the names are numbers where you're supposed to punch in your access code and what looks like a visitor's intercom.

I'd read somewhere that more than half of people use some variation of their birthday, so before leaving home, I'd checked Witty's DOB. Now I pull out the piece of paper on which I've written April 7, 1956, and then the digits in various combinations. After a quick look around, I punch in 4-7-5-6—nothing. No click, no door unlocked. Next, I invert the 4 and 7, which is how Germans do calendar dates. Nothing again. Next, in quick succession, I try the four numbers in all their combinations—7456, 4765, 6547 and so forth, eight in total. All duds.

I'm beginning to feel conspicuous, standing in the lighted doorway, punching in numbers. Especially in my cat burglar attire. I need a less exposed spot to think through my next move.

Across the street, I make out what looks like a sizeable villa set back from the street. There's a garden with some tall trees and a massive hedge of leylandii bushes in front. I hurry across and get behind the hedge and breathe deeply. No one will see me here, not on a night like this, but hiding in the dark isn't going to get me into Witty's building.

I stand there and stare across the street, hoping in vain for inspiration. It's a clammy night, and I'm getting chilly. On either side of the building, I see some greenery, flower beds laid out neatly with German precision, and behind them a shrubby hedge of boxwoods about waist-high. Further back, I can make out more bushes and some tallish trees. Then I realize that there's a narrow walkway on the left, leading into the dark toward the back.

I take a quick look around, sprint across the street, and move up the alley. Sure enough, it leads to a back door, not glass, but solid wood and—dammit!—the same code lock as out front. Opposite the door sit a bunch of garbage cans, behind which I hide.

There's no light over the back door, and it's mercifully dark. Minutes go by. Nothing happens, and I'm beginning to think that no one may be in the mood for housekeeping late Sunday night, but it's getting even colder and I pull the raincoat tight around me to keep out the chill. I'm also assaulted by the smell of garbage, which makes my new hiding place distinctly inferior to the one behind the hedge.

I'm out of bright ideas about new scenarios when I hear someone approaching from inside the door, which makes me crouch as low as

I can behind the garbage. A moment later, an elderly man in a wind-breaker, slippers, and pajama pants appears at the door and swings it wide open till it catches and stays that way. He's toting a big plastic bag of household detritus and shuffles directly toward the containers behind which I'm down semi-prostrate. He's close enough to touch me when he opens the lid and drops in the bag, then turns around and hurries back inside. In this weather, I don't blame him.

What catches my attention is that it's an automatically con-trolled door, which closes after him in slow motion. My heart skips a beat, but it's unfortunately not slow enough for me to sprint out from my hideout and catch it in time. The grim thought crosses my mind that I've just missed my best chance. Who else is likely to do outside KP on a wet and chilly Sunday night in a fancy building like this?

Which is when my eyes catch the lettering on one of the contain-ers—*Müllabfuhr, Montag/Donnerstag, 8:00–12*. Monday morning early is when the garbage man comes, it says. My spirits soar—maybe there's hope—so I settle back behind the bins and wait. With luck, garbage could actually be the answer to my prayers, and the thought makes the smell of it easier to bear.

A few minutes go by before there's more action behind the door, but it's been long enough for me to have figured out my next best line of attack. The moment I hear someone approaching, I rush into the dark and lie down flat among some grassy bushes in a spot I've picked out, about ten yards off to one side of the door. This time it's a teenage girl who appears. She's got two bags, one in each hand, and she uses her foot to secure the open door while she gets rid of her load. When she turns back, I'm ready. As the door slowly closes, I rush forward and manage to stick my foot inside, just in time to keep it from snapping shut all the way. Then I wait till she's gone and the inside light goes off. I push the door open gently, step inside, and noiselessly let it shut behind me.

I take the stairs, and a few moments later, I'm standing in front of Witty's door. All is quiet, except for the muted sound of classical music from somewhere below me, maybe Beethoven. It occurs to me that it's useless to pick one lock if I don't know the combo for the other. Which is when I notice that there's another door to the right, which, to my astonishment, leads to an outside terrace, seemingly wrapped around the entire back of the apartment.

The door has an ordinary bolt lock, and on the other side I can see a key stuck in it. I fish out my kebab skewers and screwdrivers, slip on plastic gloves, and start trying to jimmy the thing open. We used to pick locks for fun when I was a kid, but I only vaguely remember how we did it. Even so, it takes only about five minutes of poking and twisting with the skewer and a bent safety pin before I've got the key straight so I can shove it back and hear it land on the terrace floor with a ping. I freeze, hold my breath and wait, but nothing stirs below, so I cautiously start in on the lock itself.

Now I'm actually beginning to enjoy this. I explore to the right, then the left, poke around to locate tumbler and spindle, apply some pressure, and keep fiddling. The minutes fly by until I finally succeed in maneuvering the lock's lever so I can shove the bolt aside. I push once with my screwdriver, twice, and—presto—the lock snaps open.

I step quietly through the door, relock it, and cautiously make my way around to the front of the terrace where some outdoor furniture has been stacked under a tarp, and a large umbrella, folded and lashed for the winter, stands beside it. A solid oak door leads into the apartment with locked and shuttered windows on either side. For a guy who never traveled around Berlin without a guard in his protected limo, what Witty was thinking with this setup on his terrace baffles me.

No matter. I go to work again, and three minutes later, I'm standing on the other side of his fancy oak door.

It used to be a tradition for junior FSOs to make formal social calls on their seniors when arriving at a new post. Marginally helpful for the wives to get acquainted, but mostly just a stilted ritual of being "looked over," less a pleasure than an embarrassing time-wasting pain. Nowadays it's rarely done, but Witty still insisted on it, and Fiona and I had dutifully called on him for afternoon tea shortly after we arrived. This was before Fiona started getting pissy about Berlin, and the visit sticks in my mind mainly because Witty was totally taken in by her shamelessly flirtatious bullshit to impress him.

After she went back to the States, I tried to avoid his dreadful dinners with every lame excuse I could think of, though once or twice I hadn't been able to duck them. I have a vague recollection of the layout.

I close the terrace door behind me and stand still to listen while my eyes slowly adjust to the dark. Then I take off my sneakers, lay the raincoat next to them, and tap around to check the windows. Next, I switch on the light on my cell and orient myself.

I see that I'm in the reception area and tiptoe around, using the tiny light to look for anything of interest. I'm pretty proud of myself, but I'd feel a whole lot better if I knew what exactly I'm looking for. All I see is a large room furnished in Witty's aspirational idea of elegance. I check out the liquor cabinet, look behind the paintings on the walls, and then move to the dining room. Nothing of interest.

There's a powder room on one side and the kitchen on the other, both of which I decide to ignore. Two doors open to a couple of guest bedrooms, but I'm looking for Witty's private quarters and remember them at the end of the hallway. Bedroom and study, side by side. I'm listening for sounds and get edgy again.

I decide to tackle the study first, shine the light around, and see that it's surprisingly small. What looks like a Bokhara rug covers the floor, heavy floor-to-ceiling wine-colored drapes hide the window, and a largish antique desk takes up most of the space in front of it. No bookshelves anywhere, which, given Witty's less than towering intellect, doesn't surprise me. But there is a laptop computer sitting on one side of the desk.

This has possibilities, so I sit down, power it up, plug in my flash drive, and wait. Then the screen comes up asking for a password, and I feel like an idiot. If whatever I'm hoping to find is in digital form, we're never going to get it.

Next, I go through the desk drawers but come up empty yet again. One has stationery, pens, and visiting cards in it, the second is full of assorted junk. In the third drawer are a few files, which I inspect with some care. One contains a bunch of bills from Witty's tailor and a flower shop, plus a list of restaurants. Another file holds what appear to be routine bank statements from a savings account at a Washington branch, the last one for September, with a balance of just over $17,000. Another file has stuff from a broker-age account with assets worth about $500,000, mostly stocks and a few bonds. I guess that's his retirement nest egg. *Not bad*, I think. With his FS savings and pension, he wouldn't have been rich, but in good enough shape to get by in his golden years.

There's a connecting door to the bedroom, my last stop, and by now, I am definitely losing hope of finding anything of interest. A burglary to nowhere. Emmett will be disappointed, which, at this point, is the least of my worries. I've done my bit. Now I just want to wrap it up and get out of here.

I shine the light on a king-size bed, covers neatly folded back, and a pair of slippers on the floor beside it. Maybe his *Putzfrau* has been around. There are two easy chairs in one corner and a small table with some German magazines on it, two *Spiegel* and one *Die Bunte*, a glossy weekly specializing in gossipy society puff pieces. No doubt one of Witty's favorites.

My one remaining possibility is a walk-in closet on the far side of the room. I walk over, open the door, and find myself staring down an astonishing phalanx of suits and jackets crammed onto two long racks. On either side are shelves stacked with dozens of dress shirts and scarves, row upon row of ties, and below it as many pairs of shoes lined up in neat German rows. Witty's temple of sartorial bliss.

His enormous array of haberdashery leaves me breathless. The sight of it borders on the grotesque, and I struggle not to laugh out loud when thinking about how to describe this craziness to Emmett. We all knew Witty had a thing about how he looked. Obviously, our DCM was even more of a weirdo than we thought.

I push some of the suits aside and—what's this? There's a good-sized wall safe behind them. My heart skips a beat, and I move in for a closer look. Locked, of course. For want of a better idea, I randomly work the combination lock's wheel back and forth, then try the birthday numbers, but nothing's moving. Just like with his computer, without password or code, I'm stumped. Again.

My impulse is to get out of there fast and report back to Emmett about that safe. I'll have to confess that I had no way to get into it and turn the problem over to him. Perhaps we'll have to pull in one of Trotter's guys from upstairs. Cracking safes might be routine for them, but not for me.

One moment I'm telling myself to cut and run, and the next my ego kicks in and I stay put. I'd hate to admit failure to Emmett, and, even more so, to myself. Besides, I'm curious to know what Witty's squirreled away in there. He's got a big safe at the embassy, why does he need this private one at home? I've got to give it one more try. One final Hail Mary pass.

I hesitate and pause, then take a few deep breaths. I knew Witty pretty well, so what other numbers, if not his birthday, might have stuck in his mind?

I think for a while, and it occurs to me that being a diplomat was key to his self-image. He always said that joining the Foreign Service in '78, straight out of college and the youngest in his class, was the proudest day of his life. Each new class of Foreign Service recruits is called up in April, so, what the hell, I'll try 4-78, but I need four digits. I don't know the precise day, so I'll go from 1 through 9 and see what happens. I tap in 4-1-7-8, left, right, and left again. Nothing budges. I try 4-2-7-8, nothing again. It feels hopeless, but I keep going and am about done at 4-8-7-8 when I hear a whirring and clicking noise from inside the safe, followed by a beep. My heart stops and there's a lump in my throat as I pull on the door and it swings open.

"Jesus Christ!" I exclaim. "That was it. It's a fucking miracle. I'm in."

I'm shaking as I step in close, thinking I've found my next career—bank robbery. I shine my light inside the safe, and to my astonishment see the entire back wall stacked with money. Bundles of fifty-euro bank notes. Lots of them.

I stand and stare, spellbound and speechless.

When I recover, I rifle through one of the packs and count a hundred bills, which is five thousand euros. I force myself to stay calm and quickly add up the bundles: ten rows against the back, stacked six high and six rows deep. Then I do the arithmetic—once, twice, three times. Math was never my strong suit, but Witty's safe appears to be loaded with 1.8 million euros. That's $2 million US.

I've never seen such a pile of cash in my life. My mind's racing as I try to decide what to do next. Emmett was right. This guy was involved in something large, and I don't think it was official State Department business. If this blows up into some kind of crisis, it could be a big one for the service. Right now, seeing to it that it doesn't blow up is on me.

I quickly look through the rest of the safe. The money fills up most of the space, except for a manila folder and a big yellow envelope in one corner. Inside the folder, there's Witty's birth certificate, Dartmouth diploma, Foreign Service Commission, and a hard-to-decipher family tree. The envelope is tightly sealed with layers of scotch tape, which makes me think it may be where the action is. I can feel some papers inside it, so I go to work trying to get past the tape, which is something of a challenge while wearing surgical gloves. It takes a while, until I find two smaller plain white envelopes inside, also double-taped shut.

I'm more and more anxious by the minute to get out of Witty's apartment, so I just stuff the envelope and the letters into my backpack. No one will miss them, and I can check out the contents when I'm someplace safe. I grab a bundle of euros to take back for evidence, but then reconsider, carefully put them back, and snap a few photos of the cash stash instead. Burglary is one thing, robbery is another.

I'm starting to lock down the safe when I notice a small piece of paper with some numbers on it taped to the inside of the door. I recognize Witty's handwriting, but what he's posted there doesn't register at first.

The top line reads XG455111BDID, which means nothing to me. But right below that I'm reading WINST78@gmail/8642.

That's when a bolt of lightning hits me. My God, has Witty just left me his computer password and entry code?

I quickly stuff the paper into my pocket, lock up, and hurry back to the study. My hand is shaking as I type in the codes, then watch the computer come alive. Any sufficiently advanced technology is tantamount to magic, right?

I go to "Documents," plug in my thumb drive, then drag and drop.

Five minutes later, I'm done. I can't wait to get away now, shut the computer down, gather up my stuff, and silently tiptoe back to the terrace. My plan is to disappear in the same incognito way I made it in, but I'm in a state of barely repressed euphoria and struggle to stay focused and alert. It's cold out there, but I can feel the sweat on my face and running down my back.

I've stumbled onto something big, but what is it? What was Witty up to? Political or criminal? There was a lot more to the guy than we knew, and his pretentious bullshit may well have been just a façade.

Or maybe not, and what now?

Chapter 6

Berlin

Sunday, November 5

10:00 p.m.

O n the street, it's still misty, and the wind has picked up. It's turned colder, and I can feel its sharp sting on my face. I dive deeper into my raincoat, put my hands in the pockets to draw it tighter around me, and start walking.

Im Dol is quiet and dark, except for some streetlights by the U-Bahn stop in the distance, where I can make out a few people waiting around the entrance and a few cars parked at the curb. The urge to put distance between me and Witty's apartment propels me toward the lights, but I force myself to keep a normal pace. I've covered half the distance to the corner when a figure emerges out of the shadows, falls in behind me, grabs the back of my coat collar and shoves something sharp into my lower back. He's big, and he's pushing me forward, his face close to my left ear.

"*Maul halten, weitergehen*," he orders. "Keep your hands in your pockets and keep walking." Then he increases the pressure against my back and says, "Feel this? Do as I say; no blood."

"Let me go," I croak and try to pull myself free, but the guy is strong and has me at a disadvantage.

"Try that again, and this knife goes right through you, asshole," he threatens.

His German is not the best, as he adds, "You and I are going for ride."

He's steering me toward a black automobile with two other men in it, just ahead. My mind races as I try to think of some way out of this. Whatever he's got jabbed into my back feels big and sharp, but if I get into that car, I'm done for.

Across the street, a train has just pulled in and passengers are filing out of the station. What I do next is hardly a James Bond move, but it's all I can think of. I take a big breath and start screaming as loud as I can. At the same time, I lurch forward with a shrug and pull my arms out of the sleeves. While he clings to an empty raincoat, I swing around and drive my knee into his crotch.

I try to get a look at him, but he's doubled over now, also wearing a hood. All I can see is a pair of eyes glaring at me from above a scarf covering the rest of his face.

The knee to his testicles has not made him any more personable, and he still has the knife. I'm still yelling and screaming as we both try to control the arm that has the weapon. I manage to throw myself forward, hitting the ground and pulling him down with me. We roll around, limbs flailing and feet kicking, but he's clearly getting the better of me, and I'm picturing that knife slicing my throat when I hear the sound of rapid footsteps and excited voices hollering in German.

Next thing I know, two men and a young woman are on top of us, screaming at my assailant and dragging him off me and back on his feet. I'm still on the ground, but above me it's bedlam. The guy with the knife twists and turns, knocks one of my rescuers to the ground, and races off into the fog of Im Dol, the others in hot pursuit.

A group of bystanders with lots of German *Zivilcourage* had rescued me from disaster and saved my mission. Minutes later, however, their ingrained civic discipline will almost do me in.

I've rarely seen Germans cross the street against the light. Even at night when nothing's in sight, they'll patiently stand at the curb and wait. That's what they've been taught, and that's what they do. Rules are rules. *Ordnung muss sein.*

It's a commendable civic virtue, but when the crowd that gathered refused to let me go and insisted I sit tight while they called the cops, I would have preferred a looser interpretation of civic virtue. They thought they'd witnessed a robbery, which suits me fine, and they say nothing about kidnapping. Even so, they insist that protocol has to be followed, details recorded, IDs registered, the crime properly dealt with.

Never mind, I assure them, I'm okay, everything is fine. Here's my wallet and watch, see? The bum didn't get a thing. No need to bother the police, who surely have more important things to do at this time of night. I'm tired and will report it tomorrow from home, I tell them.

I argue, smile, feign exhaustion, and do my best to convince them to let me go, but nothing works. Witnesses do not leave the scene of a crime. That's how it's done.

While waiting for the law, they put me on a bench outside the station. Someone brings me a bottle of water, and there are lots of questions and lively speculation about the evildoer. Foreigner, immigrant, asylum-seeker, welfare cheat? Opinions differ, but on two things they agree: unlikely that it was a "real" German, and the police would never catch him. Those foreigners have tricks up their sleeves and live in a world of their own.

Eventually, all but a few of the bystanders fade away, and the formidable female who'd helped tackle my assailant had returned and taken charge. She said her name is Ute, and the guy was lucky to have escaped her. She is truly Amazonian, well over six feet tall. Ice hockey, she explains, semi-professional, on her way home from a playoff in Reinickendorf, way on the far side of Berlin.

She is also a determined upholder of the law, and she assures me that the police will likely show up any minute. This means I was running out of time. My two male guardians just disappeared into the station to answer the call of nature, leaving Ute alone with me, creating my last chance to make a break. So, I suddenly wince and pant, grab my stomach, and tell her I feel faint, and could she please refill my water bottle? I'll just sit here—promise.

Taking pity on me, Ute dutifully runs off into the station, and I just as quickly take off the other way toward the taxi stand at the corner.

"Where to?" asks the driver as I slide in behind him.

"Reinickendorf," I say, smiling happily and leaning back in my seat.

The prospect of a fat fare to Reinickendorf had apparently thrilled my cabdriver, because he mutters something unpleasant when I divert him to midtown west, two blocks from my apartment.

It's close to midnight, and I am dead-tired, but the nippy odor of currywurst from the kiosk at the corner reminds me that I haven't eaten all day. I stop and down two quick ones with some sauerkraut on the side and a slightly stale roll, a Berliner *Schrippe* I dunk into the pungent sauce. Then I hurry home.

I call Emmett, who must have been waiting up, because he answers on the first ring.

"You okay?"

"Yeah. Tired, but still in one piece. And you were right. You won't believe what I found—"

"Get some sleep," he interrupts. "We'll talk in the morning."

"But, Em, listen to this—"

He stops me again, and this time it sounds like a command.

"No. Not now. Tomorrow. The usual, 9:15." And he ends the call.

For a moment, I'm puzzled and stare at the phone. What gives? Only a few hours back, Em had sent me on a mission he said was so urgent that it couldn't wait till the morning, yet now he refuses to talk about it and tersely cuts me off.

I was annoyed, but then I realize he may have been sending me a message that using our cell phones is a bad idea. That also would have explained his mentioning "the usual," a veiled way of telling me where to meet him in the morning.

The lump on my head is the size of a goose egg and aches, so I go to the kitchen, kick off my shoes, and get some ice to try to reduce the swelling. Then I pick up a beer, lie down on the bed, and put a bag of ice on my head.

I was coming off a high, feeling both tense and drained. The mission had been a success, but I'd escaped a kidnapping, and/or the cops by the skin of my teeth. Which left me with more questions—and worries—than when I'd started out.

Having talked to my friendly rescuers at the U-Bahn, the cops might figure out who I was and catch up with me still. The guy with the knife and the sore scrotum probably had no doubt who I was, and might show up any minute as well. Then there were those stacks of euros in Witty's safe. Was he a crook, a traitor, or what? And what was that going to mean for the rest of us? Was I now on the radar of Russian agents, or drug runners, or God only knows who?

That's the last thing I remember thinking before falling into a dazed sleep.

Chapter 7

Berlin

Monday, November 6

8:20 a.m.

Dawn has given way to a blustery morning with a cold wind blowing in from the northeast.

Oberkomissar Bodo Kranmüller is a cheerful man who loves his job, but today he's in an irritable mood. "BK," as he's known around the Charlottenburg Landeskriminalamt (LKA) building on Keithstrasse, is the chief inspector in charge of the homicide division, one of eight such teams in Berlin. After just five hours of fitful sleep interrupted by several phone calls, he's resigned to a rough day ahead. He's also twenty minutes late to work. Twelve minutes of brisk walking in lousy weather to cover the distance from his car to the LKA office, and that's not counting the extra time driving around before finally nabbing the first free parking spot on a side street eight blocks away.

For Kranmüller, punctuality is a personal responsibility that brooks no excuses. But that it's a bad day for him when he's late for work is missing the point. Being precisely on time has deeper meaning for him. It's what gives him the comforting sense of being in control of his world and of himself.

That one of Berlin's top homicide detectives does not rate a reserved parking place near his office has been a sore point for years. Yet the way he sees it, the city's shabby niggardliness doesn't absolve him from failing to arrive at work precisely at eight a.m. each morning.

The ugly, fortress-like LKA building on Keithstrasse is more than a hundred years old. With a somber façade of dirty gray rocks, only a few narrow windows, and a heavy, twelve-foot-high iron portal facing the street, it has the forbidding look of a prison.

Kranmüller hurries up the stone steps and pushes past the big door into the reception area, where Elfriede Kaçmarek, a large, solidly built *Polizeibeamtin* well north of fifty, intercepts visitors from behind a thick glass enclosure with a stern and slightly intimidating air that matches the building's exterior. He nods at her and Frau Kaçmarek nods back, an unsmiling, silent ritual repeated each morning. She buzzes him past the barrier, and he heads for the elevator to the third floor, where he is greeted by a mini-chorus of "*Morgen, Herr Oberkomissar*," from his office staff. He returns a friendly "*Hallo, die Damen*," enters his office, and closes the door.

Bodo Kranmüller has a quarter century of service under his belt, the last seven as chief of the Charlottenburg homicide team. Under six feet in height, he is devoid of middle-aged flab with an unblemished face, soft voice, ready smile, and understated demeanor. He comes across more like a social worker than a relentless chaser of bad guys, but he is one of the best homicide detectives in Berlin, methodical and relentless, and a stickler for detail. His father was a cop before him, an uncle works on murder cases downtown, and Felix, his eldest son, is just out of law school and a recent recruit in the prosecutor's office.

Kranmüller is tired because he's been up most of the night. Each of Berlin's eight homicide teams, the *Mannschaften*, do ten-day turns of standby duty for any suspected murder in the city. Sometimes it's quiet, and sometimes not, so it's the luck of the draw that BK's *Mannschaft* has landed the capital's highest profile case in memory. Top diplomats in Berlin don't usually wind up with a bullet through the head, so this one's likely to be an international cause célèbre, and a feeding frenzy for the media. Kranmüller's got no illusion about the pressure, politics, and second-guessing that awaits.

He takes off his jacket, settles behind his desk, and considers what's ahead. How are we going to do this one methodically and without being rushed? he wonders. Not going to happen. We'll be in the glare of publicity all the way and everyone from the chancellor's office down will be on my ass wanting action and quick results. Not to speak of the horde of Ami investigators sure to get in the way.

He leans back, stifles a yawn, and closes his eyes. A moment of quiet before the storm.

Half an hour later, five men and three women gather around his desk, slouched in their chairs, some clutching paper coffee cups. The air is tired, and so are they.

Kranmüller leans back and smiles, hoping to project a calm he doesn't even remotely feel. It's occurred to him that none of the team, especially the younger ones, has ever been up against a case like this one, with the Federal Security Services, Berlin's Interior Affairs Senator, and US investigators—not to mention CNN and the German media—all pushing to get into the act.

"*Guten Morgen, liebe Kolleginnen und Kollegen,*" he begins. "Aren't you the lucky ones? Seems like you got yourselves an interesting case. Everyone had a restful night, I take it?"

"Sure, *Chef*," deadpans Karl Holzer, the team's senior investigator. "Great night for you too, I'm sure. By the way, how's the parking this morning?"

There's a moment of silence, and then Kranmüller wags a finger at him, laughs noisily, and everyone joins in. Holzer is his deputy, a veteran with a massive head and bald shiny pate, bulbous nose, and red cheeks. He's the expert interrogator on the team, and he and Kranmüller are longtime friends. His black turtleneck is straining to cover his bulging belly, and a heavy brass bracelet dangles from his wrist. It's his good luck talisman, he claims.

Kranmüller leans forward, lets his eyes roam across the room, and says, "Okay, *Kinder*, quick inventory to see what we've come up with overnight. Keep it short. Es, what've you got?"

Each team has its mix of specialists, and Eslem Osman is Kranmüller's *Spurensachbearbeiter*, the expert evidence tracker. A university-trained science nerd not much past thirty, she's the newest member on the team. Given her olive skin and long black hair, most Germans still think of her as a Turk. She's the daughter of former guest workers, but in fact a born and bred Berliner with the local vernacular to prove it.

She studies her notebook, carefully cleans her glasses, puts them back, and starts her report. "The lab downtown pulled an all-nighter and here's what they've got as of oh-eight-hundred this morning. Still provisional, of course.

"Number one, autopsy shows estimated time of death between nineteen and twenty-two-hundred hours Friday. Powder marks at entry point on back of head indicate two shots from twenty-to-thirty-centimeter range, at junction of parietal and occipital bones."

She pauses, then looks up and adds, "In plain language, roughly the midpoint of the back of the skull. I've got photographs." She waves them in the air.

"Number two, shell casings retrieved at site confirm shooter's weapon a Makarov 93.5 millimeter, probably Bulgarian."

"Makarov 93.5?" Holzer interrupts.

"That's what I said."

Holzer stands and stares at the wall behind Kranmüller's desk, which is plastered with a dozen mug shots of tough foreign-looking men, with lines and arrows connecting them up, down, and sideways. It's a rogues' gallery with names, dates, color codes, and question marks.

"I suppose no one's got a monopoly on Makarov 93.5s," Holzer says, "but I don't know anyone else in Berlin other than our friends here who use them. Coincidence, or what?"

"Why would the Hassanis want to kill an American diplomat and not even rob him?" one of the team challenges. "Not their style. Doesn't make sense."

"I didn't say they did," Holzer answers, then sits down. "Interesting, though."

Kranmüller purses his lips and nods. "Well, it's a thought. We'll look into it. Go on, Es."

Osman maneuvers her glasses back on the bridge of her nose and continues. "They worked his cell phone, which, oddly enough, didn't get taken. I've got a list of calls the last few days before Friday. Needs more work, but appears to be a dry hole. Checking the cell towers, they picked up a line on Emerson's movements Friday afternoon. At least part of the time. Looks like he was in the Adlon around 16:30, then we got a cell signal near the Zoo Banhof a half hour later, and on the Kudamm near Wielandstrasse at 18:27. They think they may have another hit at Halensee around 18:35, but they're still working that. Sorry, BK. That's all."

"Thanks, Es. Good job. Keep working it."

Then, turning to Holzer, Kranmüller asks, "What about the victim, Karl. Anything new?"

"Not much. Full name is John deWitt Emerson, age fifty-nine, deputy chief at the Ami Embassy and chargé last Friday in the ambassador's absence. Bachelor, well known around town. No known partner, male or female. We've picked up some rumors about his sex life, but nothing definite at this point.

"The embassy hasn't been talking, but an inside source told me he left there alone after 16:00 Friday. Normally he travels around town with protection, so that's unusual, but no one knows why, or at least isn't saying.

"He has an apartment on Im Dol in Dahlem. We need to get in there pronto, BK."

"One moment—Im Dol?" Angela Franke bursts out; she's a young detective trainee. She leafs through a file balanced on her knee, then looks up triumphantly.

"It's in the overnight incidents report. Says here there was an attempted hold-up at Im Dol last night. Attacker was a foreigner who got away. Victim, an unidentified male, midthirties, may have been hurt but took off before the *Polizei Streife* got there. According to witnesses, probably a foreigner as well, with an English or American accent. Dahlem precinct is looking for him."

"What's the connection, Angie?" a detective named Stummer asks and sends a look her way that signals part pity and part superior wisdom.

"It's a short street," she says.

Kranmüller closes his eyes, and the room watches and waits. He gets up, walks to the narrow window fronting the street and silently squints at a fleck of gray sky, returns to his desk, and looks at his watch.

"Nine thirty-five a.m.," he announces to no one in particular. Then says, "Here's the situation. We dig into the victim's bio, trace his movements Friday, and search his home and workplace for possible leads. Basic stuff.

"*Staatsschutz* and BKA, the Bund Criminal Division's international liaison, have contacted the Americans who promised their full cooperation. I'm on my way to the embassy this morning to settle the details of our working relationship. Shouldn't be a problem," Kranmüller adds confidently, while thinking *God knows how that's going to go down.* By the dubious looks in the room, the team seem to feel the same way, which he chooses to ignore.

"Es," he says, "continue to push the labs. I want the cell phone wrung dry, all calls in and out recorded and analyzed. All the way back. Get me a printout.

"Karl, you take charge. Talk to your canaries on the street. Check out the Hassanis' hangout around Moabit for rumors. See what you can pick up. And have someone trace back the victim's movements on Friday, in depth. Check the taxis. What was he doing for a couple of hours around Wielandstrasse? Look for witnesses. The normal drill.

"After I've talked to the Americans, we'll go to Emerson's place. I may come along on that one."

He reaches for his coat, then adds, "And by all means, have someone follow up with the Dahlem precinct about that hold-up. May not be any connection, but Angela is right. You never know."

Chapter 8

Berlin

Monday, November 6

6:00 a.m.

With just five hours of sleep, I'm up again and heading for the bathroom. I realize I'm still wearing last night's cat-burglar outfit, minus raincoat and sneakers. The backpack with my tools and Witty's envelopes is on the floor next to the bed.

More sleep is out of the question because my mind is racing. The first order of business is to put some distance between myself and last night, so I empty the backpack, bury the rubber gloves at the bottom of the kitchen trash can, and put the screwdrivers and kebab skewers back where they belong. If uninvited visitors show up at the door, at least the evidence of my nocturnal escapade won't be in plain sight.

That done, I hurry into the shower, then make myself an extra strong double espresso and head back to my desk. I rip open the yellow envelope from Witty's safe and find two smaller double-taped white ones inside it. I pry the tape off the first one and extract a single sheet of paper with five long lines of bunched-together numbers and letters in Witty's unmistakable handwriting.

CH93 0076 2744 6785 3111 8

011 738 476 3485

011 426 113 2785

MFG 685 213 22 X

SSL 237 8567206

Some kind of code, but what is it? I take my time to study the numbers from all angles for some clue or pattern, but nothing specific comes to mind, and a half hour later I give up trying.

The contents of the second envelope reveal the last thing I would have expected—a handsome post-Foreign Service employment contract from an outfit I've never heard of. There's no letterhead, the signature is an illegible scrawl, and for anyone who knew Witty's level of competence, the deal it describes sounds far too good to be true.

15 October 2017

Dear Mr. Emerson,

This is to advise you that the partners have agreed to all the particulars concerning your joining MFG as Executive Vice President. The base salary is €300.000 p.a., plus a sliding-scale bonus based on volume, as discussed.

The partners suggest that we announce your appointment at a time closer to your retirement from the Foreign Service on 1 April 2018. Until that time, your arrangement with MFG continues as in the past.

Welcome aboard!

Sincerely,

I read the letter several times, and it doesn't smell right. As an employment letter, it leaves a lot to the imagination. What is MFG, where's it based, what's its business, and what exactly is Witty's job?

One thing is clear: there was obviously a lot more to our DCM than anyone knew.

8:00 a.m.

First, I notice the blinds on my window letting in daylight. It's past eight o'clock. Then the mobile phone goes off.

Fiona!

Damn.

Ignore or pick up?

Hesitation—then guilt, so I try the light touch.

"Hi there, is this by any chance my wife?"

"Adam, for God's sake. Why don't you answer the phone? I've been trying for days."

"Days?"

"Days!"

"Really?"

"Really."

"Sorry. It's been a shitshow here."

"Too busy to give me some consideration?" she asks. "I've worried about you, Adam."

"Sorry," I repeat. "On duty at the embassy until late at night." And I leave it at that.

"Maybe I shouldn't even have called."

"No, no. I'm glad you did."

"I heard about Witty. It's because of Witty, right?"

"Yeah."

"What happened?"

"We don't know yet."

"Who did it?"

"We don't know."

"How could this have happened?"

"That's what we don't know."

"How is everybody at the embassy?"

"Tense. Nervous. But we hope this week it's back to normal. Life goes on."

"Mmm."

Sometimes on our transatlantic calls, we compare notes about the weather. The safe stuff. Witty's murder is a sensational new way of not talking about our situation. We both know what's next, and the prospect of it hangs in the air: the point where we're like two Olympic duelers, epee blades at the ready, warily awaiting the first thrust, which is usually Fiona's.

"You haven't asked me how I am," she jabs.

"I was just about to. How are you?"

"Lonely."

"I know."

"Do you?"

"Yeah, sure."

"How about you? Are you lonely too?"

"Yeah. I guess. Sure. But my head's been full of the crisis here."

"You guess!"

Admittedly, my phrasing left something to be desired.

"So, Adam," she goes on, "since you're lonely too, why don't you come home? We'd be together again and"—she lowers her voice suggestively—"neither of us would be lonely and we'd have fun getting reacquainted. Remember?"

"Of course, I remember," and I mean it. "The sooner the better. Unfortunately, home leave isn't until next June."

"How about Christmas?"

"Depends."

"On what?"

"On what happens here."

"Always your fucking job," she bellows. "What about us? There are good jobs here too. Dad's offer still stands."

Here we go again.

"Look, Fiona, even if I came home, I wouldn't go to work for your father. No way, and you know why. I've told you this a hundred times. I'm a career Foreign Service Officer, and right now my job is in Berlin. I'm sorry you don't want to be here. But you're the one who left. There are consequences for both of us, and I don't like it any better than you do. The sooner we face that reality and talk about it, the better."

It's as close as we come to mentioning the elephant in the room.

I hear a sound at her end that's a cross between a snort and a sigh.

There's a brief silence, and then she tries a different tack.

"My friend Susannah—remember her?"

My wife's pretty predictable, and I know what's coming. I decide to play dumb. "Susannah—do I know her?"

"Of course you do. The redhead. You used to leer at her tits, remember?"

"Yeah, now I do," I laugh. "Wiggles. Not only an imposing front, but an impressive ass too. Three times divorced—"

"Twice."

"Sorry, twice."

"She wants me to fly down to St. Croix with her for some R and R."

I'd seen it coming. Fiona has dealt a new hand that's all too familiar, but I'm not picking it up.

"Great," I tell her. "Have fun with Susannah. Enjoy the sunshine."

"You'll have some fun, too, won't you?" she says, and I know what she means.

"Will do," I say brightly.

Then I add, "I'm late, Fiona. Got to be at the embassy in twenty minutes. Call me from the beach."

Morning Jo's is a hole-in-the-wall coffee bar on Rudi Dutschkestrasse, a ten-minute walk from the embassy.

Dutschke (a.k.a. "Red Rudi") was a radical student leader in the 1968 movement who survived getting shot by an anti-Marxist, only to drown in his bathtub eleven years later during an epileptic seizure said to have been the result of the shooting. He's a kind of folk hero for his generation, and Berlin named this street after him because it's close to the Springer media chain's giant headquarters, where Dutschke liked to lead mass protests.

These days it's a busy commercial street where students rub shoulders with office workers, and tourists visiting nearby museums crowd into the area's shops and restaurants.

Morning Jo's sits next to Suppen Theater, which offers a choice of eight different daily soup creations. On the other side is a beer *Kneipe* with two giant screens for soccer enthusiasts. On warm summer days when there are tables outside, the aroma of goulash soup mingles with that of beer and freshly baked pretzels.

Emmett and I like Morning Jo's because the coffee is great, the clientele is interesting, and it's far enough from the embassy that we don't to have to make nice with people we deal with all day. Mostly though, we like to stop in there because of April May, the woman who runs the place. She's half African-American and half German, the daughter of an ex-GI from deep-south Georgia and a German mother. She speaks Georgian-accented English as well as her native Berlin German.

Her father, ex-US Army Sergeant Asa May, stayed behind when the US Army left Berlin and now is the head concierge at the Hyatt on Potsdamer Platz. April says he's the one who convinced her mother to name their identical twin daughters April and June.

We call them Plus and Minus. They think it's hilarious.

It's twenty past nine when I walk in, but Emmett is nowhere in sight. April gives me a big smile from behind the counter where she and her helpers are managing the organized chaos of morning rush hour.

The dozen or so bare-bones wooden tables and cushioned benches along the wall are occupied by the usual mixture of locals, tourists, and regulars. One of them is Vito Heckelgruber, a dapper elderly man with flowing white hair and goatee to match, who is at his usual table by the window. He looks up and gives me a brief welcoming nod, then buries his nose again in the *Tagesspiegel*. Vito is a retired tenor from the nearby Komische Oper who arrives precisely at eight o'clock each morning, orders his caramel cappuccino and croissant, and doesn't leave until he's carefully read each of the four daily papers April lays out for her customers.

Nearby I see another familiar face, a flamboyantly tattooed young woman in her midtwenties with pierced nostril and lower lip and long, stringy hair dyed fire engine red hanging down to below her eyes. Unlike Vito who likes to gossip and has been known to break into bits from Lehar and Strauss operettas on special occasions, she's a mystery woman who, to the chagrin of the other regulars, doesn't socialize at all. No one knows her name or what she does at Jo's every morning for several hours, pounding her tablet while consuming a fresh cappuccino—with lots of milk—every thirty minutes. April is happy to oblige and doesn't ask questions. With up to a half dozen cappuccinos at one morning's sitting, mystery woman is one of her better customers.

The place is filled to capacity, but April points me toward a table being vacated by two Asian women, likely from the nearby Eisler

Music Academy. As I elbow my way past the giant cello case one of them is dragging behind her, I hear April's voice calling out, "the usual?" in my direction, which is more a statement than a question. A few minutes later, one of her helpers sets a double espresso and a spoon with two little fake sugar pills in front of me, announces triumphantly "the usual," and departs.

By now it's past 9:30, and there's still no sign of Emmett, which is unlike him. It occurs to me that there may have been a change of plans, so I pull out my cell phone and start scrolling for messages. They have accumulated overnight, but none are from Emmett, and most of what's come in are call back requests from all kinds of people fishing for information about the murder. Most I'll ignore, and the few I'll answer can wait, including a new text from Fiona who wants to talk again tonight.

10:00 a.m.

Vito's head is still in his paper, mystery woman hasn't budged from her tablet, and an American tourist couple at the next table are trying out their broken German on April, who thinks it's funny and winks at me with a grin. Emmett is almost an hour late, and when I try his phone, there's no answer. *Something's come up*, I'm thinking, but just as I'm about to check with Charlotte for messages, I finally catch sight of his favorite long black-and-white knit scarf dangling around his neck as he's pushing his way hurriedly toward my table. That scarf is hard to miss; it's a Christmas gift from Liz in the colors of Holy Cross, his alma mater, and Emmett's rarely without it these days.

"Hi." He sits down, carefully scans the room, finally turns toward me, and says, "Glad to see you. Everything okay?"

"I should ask you the same thing. What kept you?"

"Something came up. Let's get out of here and I'll explain." It's clear that he's in a hurry.

"Fill me in. What's going on?" I ask him, but he ignores my question and asks how I got to Jo's this morning.

"Walked. Left the Opel at the embassy."

"See anyone who might have followed you?"

"Not that I know of."

"Anything else happen to you this morning on the way here?"

"Nothing, if I don't count you being an hour late."

That earns me the morning's first reassuring smile from Emmett. "Sorry, buddy," he says. "This ain't the biggest surprise in store for you today."

"Let's go," he calls out over his shoulder. He's already five paces ahead, with me trailing behind and wondering what's next.

Chapter 9

Berlin

Monday, November 6

10:15 a.m.

*E*mmett listens silently while I brief him on the break-in. When I finish, he gives me a high five. "You did it. I'm impressed."

"Thanks a lot," I say. "But don't expect a repeat. That line of work is definitely not part of my job description. You took me way out of my comfort zone."

We're sitting on the top steps of the Konzerthaus, a Berlin architectural jewel of the early nineteenth century. Perched up there all alone, looking down on the largely empty Gendarmenmarkt piazza. The concert hall and the beautiful square, and the two domed cathedrals on the north and south sides draw thousands of visitors, but not on a gray and dreary November morning like this.

Emmett seemed edgy, frequently looking over his shoulder.

"So, what do we do now?" I ask.

He takes a deep breath and starts to fill me in.

As expected, he says, a small army of investigators had arrived from Washington, and he'd been at the airport at seven a.m. to meet their government plane. FBI, CIA, and State's security were all in on the act. They'd headed straight to the embassy where Alcaro, Trotter, and Castelyou were to brief them.

He sighs and raises his bushy eyebrows. "They'll turn the place upside down, but God knows what good that'll do, all those guys tripping over each other." He pauses for a moment, then shifts his weight on the hard stone. "The senior guy from the Agency pulled me aside. Apparently, Witty had his hand in the wrong cookie jar. Washington had been watching him for weeks."

"Who exactly?"

"I don't know. FBI, the Agency."

"Were Trotter and Castelyou in on the surveillance?"

"He didn't say."

"So, what had Witty been up to?"

"That's why he wants to talk to you."

"Me?"

"That's right," Emmett says, looking at his watch. "We have a date with him just about now. When you tell him what you found, maybe he'll clue us in."

"Or not," I say, which prompts Em to raise those eyebrows one more time.

Most FSOs are not too fond of CIA types, and I'm no exception. They never tell you what they're doing, and you couldn't trust them if they did. They're not fully accountable to the ambassador, and there's always the suspicion that their secret games will blow up and undermine everything we're trying to do. Witness the Bay of Pigs, Abu Ghraib, and a hundred other fuckups.

"But why me?" I ask. "Did you tell this guy about Witty's apartment?"

"As a matter of fact, I did," Emmett nods, "which is why he wants to hear what you found. He also knows you worked for Witty and knew him better than any of us."

"You told him we did something illegal? Not smart, Emmett. Now he's got us both by the shorthairs."

"C'mon, Adam." He laughs. "Break-ins are what these guys do every day. If anything, he'll respect you for having pulled it off."

"Look," I say, "you know as well as I do what our station chief here is like. Trotter is a devious creep and can't order breakfast without hedging the truth. And he's got the judgment of a horny nineteen-year-old. All Agency people are like that. Are you telling me this one's different?"

"I trust him," Emmett nods. "Up to a point."

"What point?"

"Fair question," Emmett says. "But meeting with this top spook isn't a question of trust, but of utility. Each agency has its own turf to protect, its own interests, same as we do. You and I care about the impact on US-German relations and protecting the good name of the Service. That's why it's up to us to make sure the cops and spooks don't cross us on this. We'll learn what they have on Witty, and we'll tell them about the safe and the euros—but not about the letters you took. Those we'll keep back as our ace in the hole. You with me on that, Adam?"

I nod politely, but the fact is I'm not thrilled about getting involved with the CIA, especially not one of the pooh-bahs from Langley. We have no idea what they'll do with whatever we tell them. I mention this, along with their long history of screwups.

Emmett shakes his head dismissively. "Every nation has an intelligence service," he says, "and ours isn't any worse than the others . . . probably better than most."

"Saddam's weapons of mass destruction?" I say.

"That was a long time ago," he says.

"The Murphy fiasco in Guatemala?"

"Look, Adam. We've got no choice. We're in it, whether we like it or not. This guy is waiting for us. We'll be careful, but we have to chance it. We need to find out what they have on Witty, so we can protect the Department."

"Okay," I mumble, reluctantly. Then I ask, "Does this guy have a name?"

"McLean, Mortimer McLean. At least, that's what he says."

"What a pile of horseshit. McLean, Virginia. Next door to Langley and CIA HQ. Now that's what I call tradecraft. Lord help us."

We cross the Gendarmenmarkt, and Emmett heads for a line of cream-colored taxis in front of the Hilton, then changes his mind, hustles down the block, and waves at an empty one just rounding the corner.

"Charité," he tells the driver.

"Who's sick?" I ask him, trying to catch my breath, but Emmett ignores me and consults his watch yet again. "We'll just make it," he announces. I expected us to go back to the embassy for our meeting, so to be heading to the hospital is a surprise, but I don't ask any more questions because Emmett obviously isn't in the mood for talking.

We cruise through a working-class section of Berlin that was on the wrong side of the Wall till '89. There's plenty of activity around the hospital, with ambulances parked near the main entrance, cars pulling in and out, people on crutches and in wheelchairs, doctors in lab coats coming and going, and staff in multicolored scrubs out for a smoke.

This has never been a particularly desirable residential area, and the years of Communist neglect did nothing to improve it. The apartment houses are from the late-nineteenth century, but lately the low rents have attracted some bohemian types and art galleries. There are a couple of coffee bars across from the hospital, next to a small Thai restaurant, and down the block I can make out a flower shop, which is where Emmett is now steering us.

"Where're we going?"

"We're about to find out," he tells me.

Standing in front of the flower shop, Emmett extracts his phone from a coat pocket, punches in a number, puts it to his ear, and listens. A moment later, he's nodding into the phone, and I hear him saying, "Hello, yeah. Rob couldn't make it, but his friend is here." Then he listens again, nods once more, and snaps the phone shut.

"This way," he says, and motions for us to turn into a side street to the left of the flower shop. "Look for 22b," he says.

"Who's Rob?"

"Damned if I know."

The building we're looking for turns out to be a typical nondescript prewar Berlin apartment house. The faded yellow brick façade fronting the street is showing its age, and 22b is the *Gartenhaus* in back reached by traversing an indifferently maintained inner courtyard, a *Hof* which, its name notwithstanding, isn't much of a *Garten*. It's devoid of greenery, except for an ancient linden tree in the center and some patchy bushes against the back wall. Several garbage cans are lined up on one side of the door, and a half dozen bikes and a child's stroller are chained to a stand on the other.

It's a four-story building, and inside it smells of fried potatoes and onions. There's no elevator. "Top floor," Emmett announces, and we start climbing.

Chapter 10

Berlin

Monday, November 6

Noon

"My apologies, gentlemen. These accommodations are definitely below our usual standards, but we had a little difficulty getting organized at short notice."

The man, who calls himself Mortimer McLean, wears corduroy pants and a maroon cardigan that look as if he might have slept in them on the flight to Berlin. He smiles amiably and motions us toward a couch and some upholstered chairs in a corner of a tired-looking living room.

"Phoebe has done her best under the circumstances," he adds, then nods encouragement toward a platter of sandwiches and fruit laid out on a side table. "Help yourselves. Come sit."

Phoebe, I surmise, is the middle-aged woman who greeted us at the door and ushered us in.

"Coffee and soft drinks are on the table," she announces. "And there's cold beer in the kitchen, plus a bottle of Johnny Walker Black Label for whoever's interested."

I can make out daylight through an open kitchen door, but the curtains have been drawn tight in the living room, leaving us in a spooky semi-darkness.

This whole cat-and-mouse situation is getting to me. Emmett's unexplained nervousness and all the rest left me wondering what he knows but hasn't told me. Now it crosses my mind that the apartment's creepy atmosphere might be a deliberate staging for my benefit. It adds to my unease and puts me on my guard as I sit back, cross my legs, and size up our host.

Sitting in the chair next to me, he isn't at all what I'd expected. Short and chubby, he looks past retirement age. Beneath his full head of curly gray hair, there's nothing in his rosy-cheeked open face and friendly hazel eyes that suggests a tough operative from the top of the Langley circus. Especially in his rumpled comfort clothes, he comes across more like everybody's favorite uncle.

Em has settled down next to me, and I'm eager to get going when McLean pulls a cell phone out of his pocket and announces apologetically, "I'm afraid there's one more piece of housekeeping. Let's all power down our phones."

We follow his lead, after which he says courteously, "Thank you. Rule book says the brains should come out as well, but we'll take a little shortcut."

Just then, Phoebe appears out of the darkness, carrying what looks like a small strongbox.

"Cells go in here for the duration," she states matter-of-factly. We drop our phones into the box, and she snaps the lid shut. As soon as Phoebe has faded back into the darkness, McLean begins. "It's a pleasure to meet you, Counselor, I've heard good things about you."

We smile at each other pleasantly, and he says, "I bet you like your posting. Berlin's one of my favorite cities. Brings back the memories. The *Pflaumenkuchen mit Schlagsahne* at the Kranzler Eck!" He sighs contentedly and pats his middle. Then he asks, "Tell me, is the Paris Bar still around? Lousy food but great for networking."

He's talking about landmarks in the West Berlin of Cold War days, but I'm not in the mood for small talk, or for going with him on a walk down memory lane. No doubt Emmett feels the same tension that I feel, and McLean must be aware of it, but he persists in chitchatting about Berlin in the good old days of gun turrets and Checkpoint Charlie. It crosses my mind that maddening small talk may be a psychological ploy they teach you at a CIA boot camp.

So, I lean back, trying to be patient, but then Emmett sits up and says, "Let's talk business, Mort. The murder of an acting chief of mission is not a trivial matter. It goes to the heart of our mission here and to the US-German relationship. So, fill us in. Who's running the investigation? What do you already know? As I told you, Adam volunteered to look around in the DCM's apartment and he's come up with some intriguing stuff."

McLean turns toward me expectantly, but remembering Em's idea of a tit for tat information trade, I'm not sure how much of my story to unload up front, so I decide to turn it around and say, "Before we get into that, I have a question, Mr. McLean—"

"It's Mort, Counselor," he interjects with a friendly nod.

"Sure, Mort. And I'm Adam." Then, "With all due respect, Mort, why are we talking to the CIA? It's a murder investigation. Isn't that FBI turf? And if we're doing CIA, where's Trotter, our station chief? He's your guy on the ground here, isn't he?"

McLean doesn't bat an eye. "My compliments," he says, "you've asked the right questions. By way of answering, let's just say that we have a national security situation on our hands that needs urgent action. We're under big-time pressure to resolve it very quickly, gentlemen. Plus, this thing also hits a sensitive nerve in our bullshit domestic politics, so there are people around the White House who really have their pecker up on this one.

"There's also an international dimension, which is a problem for both the Bureau and for ourselves and why our cousins and we have a common interest. To be technical, it's covered by Section 702 of the FISA Act of 2008, involving certain persons abroad. I promise you, what we're doing here is legal."

He pauses, settles back into his easy chair, and shoots Emmett and me another one of his disarming, jovial smiles. "Both of you with me, so far?" he asks.

We nod back at him, though inwardly I don't feel comfortable and have some questions about what he's said. I don't trust him. Why this great hurry? And I don't like the contrast between his sunny smiles and ingratiating joviality on the one hand, and his barracks' room mouth and cynical attitude toward Witty's murder on the other. He is putting on an act, but I can't tell what the act is.

McLean continues. "Emerson may be gone, but our interest in him and his playmates, as well as the games they're playing, didn't disappear with him. His untimely demise adds a little complexity, but it only confirms our suspicions and raises the stakes. We need to know what happened and why."

McLean lowers his voice down into a conspiratorial register. "I don't mind telling you we'll all be up shit's creek if we don't clear this one up PDQ. The FBI's credibility is on the line, the Agency still has some black eyes that haven't gone away, and we have a guy in the White House for whom the word *intelligence* is an oxymoron.

"So, we're giving this one our special TLC outside regular channels, which explains why you won't be talking to Trotter. He's not in that silo."

I'm not sure what he means and decide to say nothing.

He turns directly to me and says, "So. Tell me about your little caper."

I look over at Emmett, who nods encouragement. So, I tell McLean how I'd made it into Witty's place, about the safe and the money, and about the attempted kidnapping that followed.

McLean regards me fondly. "I'm impressed," he says. "Improvisation, ingenuity, and guts. Smart thinking and balls. You're in the wrong outfit, Counselor. You should be with us. If you want to switch careers, let me know. Might be a promotion in it."

Then he suddenly announces, "Gotta go," stands up, and unceremoniously disappears. Presumably he's gone to the toilet, but once again it occurs to me that this, too, might be part of some weird "psych ops" routine. Then again, he could be checking in with Langley.

Em and I pass the time with Phoebe's snacks. I pour us coffee, and neither of us is in the mood to talk, so we sit there eating grapes, lost in our separate thoughts.

After about ten minutes, when McLean returns, he's holding a bottle of Fachinger mineral water, from which he takes a healthy swig before sitting down. "What you found in the apartment is very helpful, Adam, and it fits."

"Fits how?" Emmett asks, but McLean brushes him off with a wave of his arm.

"Patience," he says. "First, there's the matter of security. You'll be briefed on highly sensitive intel being held very close. Strictly need-to-know. Your clearances have been checked, but what I'll tell you is for you and no one else. No one. Not even your ambassador, and no pillow talk either. Best not even to talk to each other about it. Are we clear?"

Emmett and I nod in agreement.

"Good," McLean says. "Now, let me ask you a question, Adam. Your boss made three trips back to the US in nine months. Did he give you a reason?"

"Actually, he did," I say. "One trip early this year was for consultation at the Department, and the other two were on personal time. I think he mentioned a medical checkup and family business."

"Three trips in nine months. Wasn't that unusual?"

"Maybe. But Emerson's work ethic left a little to be desired. He was due to retire next spring, and, actually, I thought he might be looking for a job."

Emmett nods and says, "That's more or less what I thought."

McLean chuckles. "Good guess, gentlemen. There's evidence that your esteemed colleague had launched his new career already. For a lot better pay, I suspect. Except what we think he was doing was a bit problematic or, to be blunt, illegal as hell."

McLean pauses, takes a few more gulps of Fachinger, then at long last gets to the point. "We all know that right-wing politics is having a moment in the US. Authoritarian, neo-fascist, even. Both domestic and foreign. Which is why the Agency is working alongside the FBI. That's what this is about. Witty showed up on our radar as a likely US liaison with a certain group of conspirators. Which is why we're pretty sure his murder was no ordinary homicide."

He exhales, shifts around in his seat, and looks at us for a reaction.

"I don't get it," Emmett says. "I'd like to see your evidence. I can't imagine Witty having the balls for something like this."

"I agree," I say. "In all the time I worked for him, I never heard him talk about politics. He was all about his wardrobe and his décor. Getting facials, probably."

McLean shakes his head. "We have him on tape. He was up to his eyebrows—plucked or not—spouting the same 'white people are an oppressed minority' as the rest of that crew. The money also could have been an incentive. Not to mention ego. Maybe revenge for being passed over. As I said, you never know. Traitors are never obvious. Betrayal is the ultimate aphrodisiac for middle-aged angst. We know a thing or two about that."

"So, who are these conspirators?" Emmett asks again. "Who was he in bed with?"

"Most of them you've never heard of," McLean says. "Some have inherited wealth or run big family businesses. A few are politicians or retired military. In some places, they've got their lines into the local National Guard and even law enforcement, believe it or not. From all over—Texas, California, the South, the Midwest—you name it.

"Quite a network. Some are real right-wing nuts all the way back to the Birchers, but they all want the same thing: a government run by rich white people for rich white people.

"They think their time has come, and they aim to speed it along with unrest. Screw up elections, stoke job fears, create an alternate reality where they're the true patriots for destroying democracy."

He pauses for a moment, then asks, "What do you know about Dwayne Hollander?"

"An American businessman," Emmett tells him. "Been here for years. I think he represents some American companies, but I'm not sure. Adam?"

I nod. "He's on the board of the US-German Chamber of Commerce. You're saying he's part of this?"

"We think he was Emerson's link to the group's European counterparts," McLean says. "He's close to Adalbert von Trachtenberg. According to the guest list, he was at the dinner party Emerson missed the night he disappeared. When your boy no-showed, they waited twenty-four hours before they called his office. Odd, don't you think?"

He looks at us, but doesn't wait for an answer. "By the way, Adam, the guys who jumped you—what do you think they were after?"

"No idea," I lie, thinking of the sheet with the numbers and realizing that we're getting into sensitive territory. "Maybe the money."

McLean gives me a long, thoughtful look, and then asks quietly, "How'd they know you'd been in there?"

I shake my head, not quite knowing what to say.

Suddenly, he stands up, stretches, and yawns. "The overnight is getting to me. I'm too old for this crap," he says, and consults his watch. "Lunchtime!" he announces. "Time for a drink."

A moment later, Phoebe emerges out of the shadows and hands him a good-sized tumbler filled to the rim. "No ice," she reports. "But the water I added was cold. Anyone else?"

McLean tosses back the scotch with impressive speed and gusto, making it plain that Johnny Walker and he are longtime friends. Without further prompting, Phoebe produces a generous refill.

McLean sips it, returns to his seat, and then launches in. "From what they described as the testimony of 'civic-minded witnesses' at the scene, the *Polizei* have identified you as the elusive almost-victim of the previous night's kidnapping, Adam. They also deduced that you'd been in the area and broke into his place. Fortunately, they haven't yet figured out why."

He pauses for another sip of scotch, then resumes. "At a meeting at the embassy earlier today, the top detective investigating the murder, a certain *Oberkommissar* Kranmüller, offered a theory about a contract killing, possibly involving a violent street gang well known to the cops. They detected the gang's operating style in the way your assailants tried to snatch you, suggesting that the two events were related. Kranmüller thought we might shed some light on a possible explanation, which, of course, we said we could not.

"This is bad and good," he adds. "If Kranmüller's right, these guys are professionals. They don't play around and they're probably still after you. Also in the 'bad' column, the *Kripo*s are well aware that you've broken German law twice: burglarizing the apartment, then leaving the scene of your own mugging."

He stops to look at me, as if expecting some reaction. I'm too stunned to say anything, still waiting for the good news.

"On the other hand," he says, "the fact that they'll be coming for you again is great. If anything, it should be encouraged. They know you were in there, and they want something they think you found."

I must have looked appalled, because he quickly adds, "Not to worry. We'll have your back the whole time. In close contact with the Germans, we'll nab them when they make their move, then squeeze them for information. The money trail, Hollander, Trachtenberg, and all the rest. Kranmüller, the top cop, is a good detective and a reasonable guy. Under those circumstances, he'd never press charges against you and honor your FSO 'get out of jail' card."

He stops and smiles broadly. "What do you think?"

"Great," I said, "a terrific plan. You want to dangle me as bait to catch some psychopaths."

He smiles again. "That's a crude way of putting it. But you're part of the team, Adam. We'll have you covered all the way."

"What if I don't want to play?"

"I've thought about that, but I don't think your options are great," McLean says quietly.

"Oh, yeah? Tell me why."

"Well, we couldn't stand in the way of the Germans pressing charges, and the Foreign Service would pull you out and send you home. Maybe it would end your career, maybe not. Mostly, you wouldn't be any safer. The group might still come after you, but you wouldn't have our protection. All kinds of messy possibilities, Adam, none of them good."

For a long while, silence.

Next to me, Emmett stares at the floor and says nothing. McLean rubs his tired eyes and nips at the last drops of his scotch.

The feeling of being trapped gives way to me feeling angry.

"Goddammit, Emmett!" I yell. "You got me into this. And you knew all along what this devious prick was up to. He wants me to hang out there, hoping the goons will come after me.

"I should have known better," I say, turning to McLean. "You're blackmailing me. No doubt 'in the national interest.' Like waterboarding, right?"

McLean takes no offense and gives me yet another friendly smile. "I understand how you feel," he said. "What I'm suggesting has some real upsides for you. Besides, you want to catch these fascist bastards as much as we do, don't you? Go home and think it over. You have my number. It's secure."

Then he adds, "I need to hear from you before midnight. I know you'll make the right decision."

Chapter 11

Berlin

Tuesday, November 7

6:30 a.m.

George Hartfield was fighting jet lag. He had never learned to
sleep on airplanes, and red-eyes hadn't become any easier with
the years. Though he now rated one of the Agency's Gulfstreams,
in-flight sleeping was still a bridge too far.

Using his working name of Mortimer McLean, he'd checked
into a small *Pension* on a side street off Bismarkstrasse, near the
opera house. He'd stayed there on previous visits to Berlin, and
he liked its ample breakfasts, as well as the fact that it was off the
beaten track. A back door exit down a narrow lane leading directly
to the nearby boulevard was another plus.

He'd swallowed two melatonins, hoping for a decent night's
sleep, but by four a.m. he was awake again, feeling washed out and
irritable. An hour later he'd thrown in the towel, and at 6:30 a.m.
arrived at the embassy and settled into the CIA's private tank—a

small secure conference room inside the station's sealed-off confines. The code clerk pulling the graveyard shift had brought him a pot of coffee, and when the door was securely locked behind him, he'd punched in the encrypted direct line to Langley.

"How can I help?" The duty officer in the communications center sounds sleepy and unenthusiastic.

"Put me through to the DDO," Hartfield orders.

The communications guy hesitated. The deputy director for operations isn't someone to trifle with.

"Sir, it's one o'clock in the morning," he protests. "We have strict instructions not to wake the DDO unless it's a true emergency."

"Cut the crap," Hartfield growls back at him. "I know it's fucking one a.m. Get me the DDO. Now."

"Goddammit, George," the DDO grouses when he comes on the line. "It's the middle of the night. What the fuck? This better be good. Where are you?"

"Where the hell do you think I am? Berlin, and I'm jet-lagged. You got me into this, so don't give me a hard time."

They were both clandestine service veterans. Hartfield, the recently retired older of the two, whom the DDO had talked into coming back in for this special assignment, had briefly been his superior.

The idealistic hubris they'd shared as recruits had long since faded into a world-weary cynicism. A half dozen directors with varying degrees of competence, along with misguided programs and PR disasters too numerous to mention, had led to the departure of some of the best of the Agency's senior professionals. Cloak and dagger had ceased to be a grand adventure, and the company had lost both respect and influence with policymakers, and especially by the current occupant of the Oval Office.

The DDO had brought Hartfield back in by appealing to his

institutional loyalties, as well as his ego. "We're under the gun here. You're the only man with the skills to pull this off," he'd said. "The Agency really has its tit in the wringer this time. We need you to pull it out." It was the flattering thought that he might be the one to score a great coup for his blemished alma mater that Hartfield had found hard to resist.

"Have you seen the Berlin traffic?" Hartfield asks. "Did you read the transcript?"

"Did he bite?"

"We'll see. He hasn't yet, but he's probably just sulking."

"Let's hope so," the DDO says. "We're up against it. We need to move."

There was a brief lull in the conversation. Hartfield pours himself some coffee, then the DDO says, "What do you think he knows about Emerson and Trotter? What makes you think it'll work?"

"We'll find out," Hartfield says. "He doesn't like us, that's obvious. And he damn sure doesn't like Austin, so I'm pretty sure he hasn't told us everything he knows. But we'll get there."

"Good. The clock is ticking, but no pressure. Nothing but the fate of the Agency in danger here. Maybe the Free World. So have some fun. *Gaudeamus igitur*, as the Germans like to say."

"Sure, Dickey boy. Up yours too," Hartfield replies.

8:00 a.m.

As Bodo Kranmüller settles into his LKA office across town, the *Oberkommissar* checks his watch as he does each morning: *8:00 a.m.*, he notes with satisfaction.

The previous day at the embassy, the strange, rotund American had introduced himself, without further identification, as Mort

McLean, one of the team of overnight arrivals from Washington. He'd said very little, then left the meeting early.

That McLean hadn't identified himself as CIA from Washington headquarters was only one aspect of the get-acquainted session that had irritated him. In typical American fashion, everyone had been relaxed, even chummy, with lots of first names bandied about. German leadership of the murder investigation had been readily acknowledged, a channel for information exchange established, and full cooperation pledged on all sides.

But behind the façade of collegial cordiality, the Americans had been less than forthcoming, which didn't bode well for a healthy working relationship. It had puzzled Kranmüller that, in spite of his gentle probing, no one acknowledged mention that Emerson had been under observation by FBI and CIA for some undisclosed reason, an important piece of information passed along to him in a BND intelligence briefing prior to his visit.

Kranmüller had spent part of the previous evening in extended discussions with Germany's security services, including staff of the chancellor's office. Clearly, the high visibility of this politics-laden case meant that it wouldn't be an ordinary homicide investigation, and the bureaucratic implications depressed him.

This was the third day since Emerson's body had been found, and he hadn't yet managed to find any order in the jumble of facts, suspicions, and open questions swirling around in his head. He was an experienced detective with an orderly mind, accustomed to a careful and methodical, step-by-step investigative routine, free from outside interference. This time, he would not have that luxury. It bothered him greatly that the intense attention of the media and likely constant questions from his judicial and political superiors would prevent him from doing his work in the usual manner.

Moreover, the reticence behind the Americans' happy talk and first names had struck him as arrogant, as if they were the ones calling the shots in Berlin, still ruling their postwar *Imperium Americanum*.

Kranmüller had dispensed with the usual nine a.m. meeting of his *Mannschaft*. The team were still busy interviewing witnesses and chasing leads, and the *Oberkommissar* wanted the quiet time to organize his thinking. For a few minutes, he sat back in his seat, kept his eyes closed, and tried to formulate the issues, but his mind had largely remained blank.

Exasperated, Kranmüller exhales, stands up, and walks to the window. For once it isn't raining, and a weak sun has become visible through breaks in the clouds. Still lost in thought, he turns, stops at the clothes rack in the corner, and carefully straightens out the sleeves of his leather jacket.

Back at his desk, he pulls a yellow pad out of the drawer. After staring at the ceiling for a moment, he sits up straight and carefully writes *Mordopfer-Motif* at the top of the page. Then he underlines the words twice.

Motive had to be the starting point. He had to come up with some plausible reasons why someone might have wanted Emerson dead, which required knowing why the Americans had been watching him and more about the man himself: Who was he? Who were his friends and enemies at the embassy? Who had he gone to meet the day he disappeared? Who he was, his friends and enemies at the embassy, and some ideas about whom he'd gone to meet the day he disappeared. Like it or not, all this would require taking another crack at the Americans.

The fact that they had kept Emerson under surveillance, and refused to say why, made politics the lead hypothesis, but sex and money—the classic incitements to homicide—were strong contenders as well. Emerson was a never-married fifty-nine-year-old, with rumors about an iffy sex life. That needed checking out.

Under his previous notation, Kranmüller writes *Sex?* and underlines it. The large amount of cash found by the authorities in his safe the previous day was unusual, to put it mildly. What diplomat has almost two million euros stashed away at home? He adds *Money?* to the list.

Kranmüller decides to pursue the political angle, which would require the help of the BND, or perhaps even the chancellor's office. He writes down *Ami-Surveillance (BND?)*.

He is making progress with ideas, but he needs to move on to action. The first step was obvious. He writes down the name *Adam Jackson*. He had to talk to this young man as soon as possible. Where was he hiding, and was his absence a deliberate ploy? Jackson had been Emerson's assistant, and probably knew more about him than anyone. Their relationship required careful exploration.

Most important, Jackson had to be questioned about his break-in into Emerson's apartment, who'd sent him, and what he'd found. Finally, he wanted to hear what he remembered about being attacked, and why he hadn't waited for the police. Under the American's name, he writes *Relationship? Break-in? Attack?*

He rises from his desk and heads for the office refrigerator in the hallway. His throat is dry, but it's too early for beer; a Cola Lite sounds appealing. He uncaps the bottle and takes a first satisfying long swig when Karl Holzer, his deputy, emerges from the elevator, looking winded.

"Been out jogging?" Kranmüller asks.

Given Holzer's impressive potbelly, this is meant as a joke, but his friend isn't smiling.

"Let's go to your office, *Chef*," he pants. "I've got news that might interest you."

Holzer closes the door behind them. "We may have cracked the case," he announces. "Or at least we're getting close. We've figured out what Emerson was doing on the Kudamm before he disappeared. And, if we're right, it probably will tell us what else we want to know."

Holzer pauses, evidently hoping for a reaction.

"Slow down, Karl," Kranmüller advises. "Take your time and tell me what you found."

"It's Es Osman, Bodo," Holzer explains. "She worked round the clock with Technology. They picked up cell signals at Bahnhof Zoo and the Kudamm. There was a one-and-a-half-hour gap, then another brief hit at Halensee, remember?"

Kranmüller nods, and Holzer takes a deep breath. "They've filled in the gap. Between 5:00 and 6:20, the phone was at 111A Wielandstrasse!"

Kranmüller waits for the other shoe to drop. "So?"

"We checked the tenants. Mostly families, except for the apartment under the roof. A commercial establishment—if you care to call it that. The studio of a certain Antonia Holzapfel, a lady well known to the colleagues at the precinct."

"A *Bordell*? So what? He went to get laid. That's not a crime in this city. What does that get us?"

"Ah," Holzer says, grinning triumphantly. "Two things about that. First, we're not talking about your usual sex shop. Madame Holzapfel is a solo operator specializing in disciplining naughty boys. And very expensive. She's also a widow. North of forty, I'm told. Her dear departed husband was Franzi Holzapfel, a thug who was doing fifteen in Moabit for attempted murder. Cancer got him three years ago."

"Interesting," Kranmüller says. "But I still don't get it."

"Before she married Franzi," Holzer goes on, "she was Antigona Duka. A not uncommon Albanian name, I'm told. Bottom line, *Chef*, remember the Makarov 93.5 that killed Emerson? And the foreign guys in the A-8 who tried to grab Jackson on the street? We've got an Albanian connection. Most likely our friends, the Hassanis. So, we might finally nail this gang if we can figure out who let the contract on the American."

"It does raise possibilities," Kranmüller says. "Maybe you should pay the lady a visit. Who knows? A little discipline might do you good."

Chapter 12

Berlin

Monday, November 6

4:00 p.m.

*B*ack from McLean's, I am in a kind of fog, unable to think. I feel trapped and abused. The sharks were in the water, and I am the bait. "Jump in and we'll spear them when they come after you. And don't worry, we've got you tethered. We'll haul you out before you get eaten."

I'm stewing about that for a while, and then I get mad.

Screw you, Mortimer McLean, I'm thinking. You're betting I have no choice, but I do. The last thing I'll do is trust you. Not you, not the FBI, or any of the Washington gang who want to use me for their own purposes. I do have a choice, because I've got what my pursuers are after, and you don't. You don't even know what it is. But I do. That's my ace in the hole. I'll help get the bastards, but I'll do it my way. I'll be the one calling the shots and making McLean jump, not the other way around.

Fear is a fine spur to action, but so is rage. I'd thought it over and concluded that yielding to either one would get me nowhere. I have to be smart, stay cool, and take charge of my own situation.

The first part of my game plan is to get a gun. Protecting myself has to be job number one. The next challenge would be to keep the envelope with the numbers hidden, both from my attackers and from McLean. Thinking of a safe hiding place doesn't take very long. Figuring out what the numbers mean will be the hard part, and I still have no idea how to go about doing that.

Next, I need to make peace with the German *Kripo*. They are sure to be on my tail, and I'll have to find a way to mollify them and keep them—and McLean—out of my hair. They are all watching me, which I assume is both good and bad. It might give me a degree of protection from my attackers, but I'll be hamstrung trying to operate on my own.

Thursday, November 9

4:00 p.m.

By Thursday afternoon I am ready for action, which means going underground. I need a safe harbor, both for security and as a base from which to operate unobserved. In an odd way, the decision to pull a disappearing act had a strange appeal. It would be an adventure, and now I was eager to get started.

I'd put a suitcase filled with clothes by the door. Next to it lay my duffel bag, stuffed with the overflow—toiletries, stationery items, diplomatic passport, and a few long-unread books from my bedside stash.

I hadn't heard from McLean since we'd parted company on Monday, even though I'd snubbed him and not called back. That surprised me, but Emmett's more than a half dozen insistent and increasingly annoying messages had not. Now I had to talk to him. I sit down at my desk and punch in his number.

"Hi, Emmett," I say brightly. I was ready for an angry tirade, but he sounded less upset than relieved.

"Adam, for Christ's sake, what the hell's happening?"

"I'm fine," I say. "Don't worry, I'm okay."

"We need to talk."

"Soon, I promise."

"But—"

"I'm taking a few days off to clear my head. You'll have to cover for me at the embassy. Won't be for long and you'll be my contact. I promise to keep in touch."

"How can I reach you?"

"You can't. I'll be calling you. It's safer that way."

I hear a groan, but ignore it.

"Tell McLean I've decided to play ball," I say. "Since it's my neck on the line, it'll be by my rules. If there's progress to report or I need his help, he'll hear from me. Through you. If he's got messages for me, he should tell you."

"I don't like it," Emmett says.

"I've thought it through every which way, and I'll be okay. What's the *Kripo* guy's name, the one who's after me?"

"Kranmüller. And he wants to see you right away."

"Yeah, I want to see him too. But first I need to know that he won't make trouble, have me declared persona non grata, or whatever. See if you can get his promise, and let me know."

"Okay. I'll talk to him."

"One more thing. Is the ambassador back?"

"Yeah, got in yesterday."

"Give him my best, tell him what you like about me, but keep me on his good side."

"I've got a million questions."

"Not now, Emmett. There's no time. Gotta go."

The Opel is parked near the front door, which doesn't happen very often. I pop the trunk, stow my gear, relock, and head for the Deutsche Bank ATM a block away. It's close to five p.m. and the last light from a weak November sun is fading fast.

With the temperature dropping, pedestrians are moving fast, and throngs of homeward-bound cyclists pass by with their heads down. I keep a sharp lookout for anything unusual, or anyone lingering nearby, but I see nothing suspicious. It's only when I'm about to climb the stairs leading into the bank and give one last look that I feel a tightening in my stomach.

A young guy in a leather jacket, jeans, and a black knitted cap pulled low has come up behind me, stops at the corner, and turns to watch me enter the bank. *Damn, where did he come from?*

Once inside, I look back through the glass door. The traffic light has changed, but leather jacket is still standing there, sipping from a paper cup. My heart pounds. *Who is this guy? A cop? One of McLean's people? A would-be kidnapper ready to go again?*

I step into the line behind a young mother with two small kids who seem determined to torment her. The younger one whines to be held, and the other ignores her and amuses himself by picking discarded rubbish off the floor. I watch in admiration as the mother operates the card machine, holding the toddler on her arm while threatening futile retribution to the floor scavenger. When my time comes, I step to the ATM and pull 3,000 euros from my account, the maximum permitted. I stuff the cash into my inside coat pocket and step back to the door, considering my options. Problem is, I can't think of any good ones.

When I come out, leather jacket is nowhere to be seen, which doesn't greatly reassure me. Since he'd come up undetected, he's probably a pro, and knows how to keep out of sight. But he's unlikely to jump me in a busy street in broad daylight. The only thing to do is to get into the Opel and find some way to shake him.

I walk fast and get into the car without turning around, pull the Opel into the street and start driving, checking the rearview mirror. I speed up and slow down, turn down side streets and double back, and as far as I can tell, nobody's on my tail. I must have been seeing ghosts, I tell myself.

The gun is my next challenge, because there aren't a lot of gun shops around, and you can't just buy one the way you can in the US. You have to show it's for a legitimate purpose, like hunting, or that you have a proven need for self-protection. Even then, the *Waffenschein*, the official permit, is hard to come by. There's plenty of red tape and the process takes time.

In my situation, the black market is the only way to go. Carrying a gun without a permit would add to my expanding rap sheet, but at least, given diplomatic immunity, I'm unlikely to wind up in jail. They might well declare me persona non grata, however, which is a surefire career-killer.

Luckily, I have a friend who knows things like where to get a weapon. He manages a joint called Die Bienen, one of the smaller clubs in East Berlin near the Hackescher Markt. I've made a date to see him around midnight, when the joint gets jumping.

The Berlin club scene is like no other. Places range from the legendary wild techno club Tresor, to the Berghain, to the Watergate, gay and straight, catering to every conceivable taste. Most of them stay open all night and will help you sober up with breakfast in the morning.

I get to Die Bienen at dusk rather than dawn, and the streets are still brightly lit and crowded. I find a parking space on a side street and, with six hours to kill before the place opens, I join the throngs. Being on the lam makes me feel liberated, even celebratory.

I'm also hungry and decide I deserve a special dinner. Chez

Max is nearby, and one of the best restaurants in Berlin. It's a small French bistro, where most patrons don't arrive until later in the evening. Only one of the dozen tables is occupied, and Max hustles over to greet me like a long-lost friend. "*Quel honneur*, Monsieur," he says, turning on his Gallic charm and lacing his accented German with French, which is part of his standard routine. Then he rattles off the day's specials. I follow his suggestion and order a leg of lamb with garlic cream, a salad of endives and greens, three kinds of sheep's cheeses and a very special prosciutto, and then *tarte aux myrtilles*. A half bottle of Chateau Smith Haut Lafitte 2009 to wash it all down.

Some two and a half hours later, I'm sipping the last of a double espresso and signal for the tab. While awaiting *l'addition*, I risk powering up my cell phone to check emails and texts. The phone is one of my unsolved problems. I don't want to be without it, yet I realize that carrying—let alone using it—exposes me to being followed and traced.

I decide to scroll through the large number of unread messages as quickly as possible, then turn it off. As usual, my inbox is filled with spam and routine stuff that can wait. There are several messages from Fiona, which I'll ignore for now. We haven't talked in days, and her missives full of hurt and reproach are no surprise. Emmett has emailed me twice, which I decide to ignore as well. The only one that requires action is from *Oberkommissar* Kranmüller, requesting a callback as soon as possible.

I'm about to shut the phone down when a new message appears on the screen. The sender is Dwayne Hollander. When the name registers, my stomach tightens.

Dear Counselor,

I was devastated by Witty's tragic death. He always spoke so highly of you, and this must be a difficult time for you.

His dear friends, Bett and Adi von Trachtenberg, have asked me to inquire what the plans are for a memorial service. Naturally, they and I would like to be a part of that.

I'd be grateful for a quick word with you or, better yet, a brief visit to discuss our own plans for a fitting tribute from his many German friends, which the Trachtenbergs are most anxious to organize. Perhaps we might briefly meet to discuss it.
Hoping to hear from you soon,
Sincerely, Dwayne H.

I hardly know this guy. Why has he written to me rather than to the ambassador or Emmett, the acting DCM? Obviously, the answer is that it's me the conspirators have in their sights, and the memorial thing is merely a pretext.

If McLean is right, they know I've been inside Witty's safe. Sending their goons after me hasn't worked, and now they're trying a direct route to size me up and find out what I know. They've lobbed a ball into my court, and I have to think carefully about how to play it back. I have something they badly want, and meeting them just might help me understand what that is.

It takes two of my one-hundred-euro notes plus change to settle Max's bill, but I wasn't complaining. He embraces me warmly, kisses both cheeks, and then we shake hands. It's half past nine when we finish this ceremony amid the *au revoirs* and *à bientots*, and I'm back out on the street with another two and a half hours to kill until midnight.

Going to the movies hadn't been on my mind, but a funky little art film theater at the corner is showing a French war film that catches my attention. What intrigued me aren't the photographs outside of soldiers with fixed bayonets and fighter planes overhead, or one of the heroes locked in a passionate embrace with a half-naked girl. It's the film's title, "Toutes les balles ne tuent pas," *not every bullet kills.*

I'm on the run from danger and some bad people are after me. The title's message hits home and lifts my spirits. *Right on,* I'm thinking. And go to the movies.

The theater is mostly empty. The seats are soft and comfortable, and I sleep peacefully through most of the film. I'd been up much of the previous two nights, and Max's Chateau Smith Lafitte has done the rest.

When the lights come on, I awake content and refreshed.

It is just after midnight when I arrive at the club.

Chapter 13

Berlin

Friday, November 10

12:30 a.m.

*T*ommy stares at me, then laughs. "You're joking."

I shake my head. "No joke. I'm in trouble, and I really need a gun. Where can I get one?"

We're in a booth off to one side of the dance floor. The club is filling up, the DJ is blasting electronica house music, and a dozen or so people are gyrating to the beat as strobes flash against the colored lights. The aroma of weed hangs heavy in the air.

Tommy's no longer laughing. I can tell he's shocked, and Tomislav Bubic doesn't shock easily.

"Without a *Waffenschein*? This isn't Texas," he says. "What's going on?"

"It's a long story, which I'm not going to tell you for your own good. Just trust me."

"Emerson's murder, I'm supposing?"

I nod. "In a way."

Tommy stares at me again, then waves toward the bar and says, "Let's first get you a drink. Then we'll talk."

A young woman behind the bar picks up his signal.

"This is Claudia," Tommy says. "She's from Moldova. Kishinev. Claudia, this is my friend, Adam."

"Hullo, Adam," Claudia says, leans forward, puts her arms around my neck, and plants wet kisses on both my cheeks. Her amber eyes match her long, black hair, shining when she smiles.

Tommy grins. "Claudia is a new colleague. She'll do well here, don't you think?"

"I have no doubt," I say.

"Claudia likes to please," Tommy explains. "And my friend is her friend, right?"

Claudia smiles demurely.

Then he says, "It's too damn noisy here. Let's go back to my office where it's more private. And bring us a bottle of Jägermeister, darling, would you? The premium stuff. And two beers for chasers."

Tomislav "Tommy" Bubic is a native Berliner whose parents came to Germany in the seventies from a small town in Croatia, and, like most guest workers, stayed to help create the German economic miracle. Tommy loves his hometown, and there isn't much going on he doesn't know about or can't find out in a hurry.

The last time I'd seen him was at his fortieth birthday party in the spring, but you'd never guess his age by his looks. His face is smooth and unlined, and his thick black hair shows no trace of gray. Tommy rarely misses his regular workouts at the gym, and at a broad-shouldered six feet, there's no sign of middle-age flab on him.

We met just after I arrived at the embassy, while he was briefly filling in as a motor pool driver. He was having "cash flow problems," he confessed to me, and had taken the first job he could get. Three months later, his fortunes took a sudden turn for the better, and he was gone.

Tommy occasionally drove me to appointments around town in one of the embassy's two slightly over-aged Chevys, and we'd talk about Berlin or anything else that came up. He's smart and knowledgeable about city life and German politics, with that special style they call *Berliner Schnauze*: brash irreverence, common sense, and a wicked tongue. A huge soccer fan, with a love-hate relationship for the two Berlin teams, Hertha and Union, he's close to several of their German-Croat players and thinks that gives him an inside edge with the bookies.

Unfortunately, he'd bet big with some private Moabit types who offered better odds, lost just as big, and didn't have the money to settle. Stiffing them wasn't an option, so I lent him the money, which cemented our friendship.

One month later, his luck changed, and he paid me back. He'd helped one of his Croat soccer friends negotiate a new contract that earned him a handsome fee. It's how he bought himself a piece of Die Bienen, and the club, he says, is a gold mine.

Tommy's office is a cubbyhole crammed with boxes filled with bills and receipts. The walls are plastered with club posters. A largish porcelain Berlin bear stared at me from a shelf behind him.

He pours us a healthy slug of schnapps, and we down it silently with a few swallows of Pilsner Urquell.

"Look," he says, "I want to help, but I need to know what's going on."

"Okay," I nod. "But some of it involves government secrets, so don't even ask. *Kapiert?*"

"I get it," he says and smiles.

So, I tell him about my break-in into Witty's place, about the kidnappers, and the *Polizei*. "The goons could be Chechians or Albanians," I say, "hired by people who want something they think I took from Witty's apartment." I leave the rest unsaid. "They're still after me. Which is why I need you to help me get a gun."

Tommy shakes his head. "A gun won't help you."

"Why?"

"Because they're a lot better with guns than you'll ever be. I grew up with some of these types in Moabit. They're the real deal."

"Then what am I supposed to do?"

"Make sure they don't find you," he says and leans toward me. "Here's what you need to think about if you want to stay alive . . ."

Friday, November 10

10:00 a.m.

Someone is banging on the door. "Time to get up, Herr Miller," I hear a voice calling and think I'm dreaming. Then I hear it again, louder, and that brings me back to life. Ten a.m., my watch says. Still semi-stupefied from a dead sleep, I stumble to the door, fighting to come awake.

The kid can't be older than eighteen. He's wearing blue jeans and a red hoodie over dirty-blond hair.

"*Ich bin der Wolfgang, Herr Miller*," he says, then hands me a shoebox-shaped package wrapped in elaborately taped newspapers. I take it and Wolfgang says, "*Tschüss*," and is gone.

Inside the box are three cell phones and a small metal-lined leather case. Just as Tommy had promised.

According to Tommy, there are three basics for staying hidden. Ditching my regular cell phone was number one. Unless I disassembled it and stored the parts in the case, he'd explained, it would reveal my location, even if I kept it turned off. The three cells he'd sent me were harder-to-trace burner phones.

Switching to public transport or taxis was number two. So, before parting company, I'd given him the key to the Opel, which he promised to move from the street to a friend's private garage.

Number three was finding an under-the-radar place to sleep. Given that reputable hotels don't register guests without a credit card and ID, the solution, he'd suggested, was to find a disreputable one. "Most of the guests are couples in a hurry, and no one's fussy about names," he explained.

"You should have a drink with Claudia later on. She'll take you over there and tuck you in."

"Some other night," I said and waved him off. "All I want to do tonight is sleep."

Which is how I'd ended up Mark Miller in the dump that was called Osthotel, where Wolfgang had just pounded me awake.

It's close to one p.m. when I get to the coffee shop down the street. Two young girls are giggling at the bar, waiting for their takeouts, and a woman has her nose in a book at a table in a corner. The rest of the place is empty, with nothing to set off my mental alarms.

I choose another corner and settle down with a buttered croissant, double espresso, and the morning paper. So far, so good. At least the Osthotel had a shower and plenty of hot water. I'm fully awake again and ready to enjoy a leisurely breakfast.

A half hour later, I pull out one of my burner cells, power it up, and make the first call.

Anna answers after maybe the sixth ring.

"It's me," I say. "Sorry I ran off last Sunday."

"*Ach*, are you coming back?"

The connection to Heringsdorf is lousy; I'm hearing swooshing noises, and Anna sounds like she is talking from under water.

"Can you hear me?" I ask, trying to keep my voice down.

"No problem."

"I'll come back soon, but meanwhile, I have a favor to ask."

"What?"

"A young man, his name's Wolfgang—blond hair and he'll probably wear a red hoodie—is going to bring you an envelope. Inside, you'll find a smaller one. Stash it somewhere where no one else can find it. Don't tell anyone where, not even me."

Anna hesitates. More swooshing noises, then I hear her say again, "No problem."

"Thanks a million, Anna. I'll explain later. And just one more thing. If I don't call back, or if you hear that something unusual has happened to me, contact Emmett Cunningham, my friend at the embassy. He'll know what to do."

There is a moment of silence, then Anna says, "No problem. Just so you know, it took time to answer this call because I was outside raking leaves near the beech tree. The one by the kitchen window. But don't worry. The thing you're sending will be safe."

For Anna, that was talking a lot.

I guess she's sending me a message, but I don't really want to know.

"Thanks, Anna," I say.

"*Ach, schon gut*," she replies, and I'm pretty sure the envelope will be in good hands.

I pick up another double espresso from the bar, then switch to the second of Tommy's throwaway cells. This call might be tricky, so I've prepared carefully.

"*Hallo, Ja, bitte?*" Dwayne Hollander answers.

"It's Adam Jackson from the embassy," I say, calm and business-like. "I want to thank you for reaching out about Witty Emerson. It was much appreciated by everyone here."

Hollander doesn't miss a beat. "I can only imagine." His tone is solicitous, sounding genuinely concerned.

"Well, it's a shock, obviously," I say. "Lots going on here, so I only have a minute."

We go back and forth a few times, offering variations on the theme of shock and grief, along with enumeration of the late Witty's virtues, while I wait for him to come to the point.

Eventually, he says, "So, about the memorial. Do let us know what's being planned, officially. The Trachtenbergs were his closest German friends, and they want to be a part of anything the embassy will do. Adi and Bett are great people. Surely you know them?"

"Not really," I say, hoping I sound regretful. "But Witty often spoke of them. Very favorably," I lie.

"Right, right. Tragically, it was their dinner for him he missed the night he, er, disappeared."

"I know."

"They're most anxious to arrange a private memorial by some of his friends and would love to meet you and get your advice. Since you knew him so well."

"Oh, yes," I say, with all the conviction I can muster. "I worked for him, but we were close. We talked a lot. About many things."

This was a carefully rehearsed lie, but Hollander doesn't pick up on it. He's meeting the Trachtenbergs for tea Sunday afternoon to discuss ideas, he explains. No doubt I don't have much time these days, but if I could drop by—just for a little while—they'd be most grateful.

"Can I let you know later today or tomorrow?"

I explain that even the weekends are loaded with work these days. I'll have to check my schedule.

"Certainly," Hollander says. "Try your best. I'll tell the Trachtenbergs to expect you, tentatively. Just call Katharina

Willmans to confirm. She's Gräfin von Trachtenberg's assistant. Do you know her?"

"Er, I think I do." Which is an understatement.

"Good," Hollander says, "I'll be there too. I'll tell her to expect your call."

The coffee shop has filled up and begins to feel overheated. I decide I need a change of venue—fresh air to clear my head—and a place for a Montecristo and quiet thinking. Fresh air followed by cigar smoke is somewhat contradictory, which makes me smile, but it's what I need.

The Old Havana Cigar Lounge is exactly the kind of place to enjoy a premium Cuban. It will take a brisk walk to get there, and so I bundle up against the damp weather outside and head over.

A half hour later, I am lounging comfortably on one of the establishment's wine-colored leather chairs, my feet resting on a matching footstool. I have just lit up and am enjoying the first drags from my cigar when the full force of my present situation hits me.

I think of myself as a pragmatist who doesn't waste time with abstractions or philosophical introspection. Things are what they are, and there's no use obsessing about the whys and wherefores. You take it as it comes and make rational decisions as best you can. Yet all I can think is that my life has been completely overturned.

Less than a week ago, I'd been doing a job with meaning and plenty of promise. I had my share of problems—having to defend a dangerous president's wrong-headed moves, dealing with a hopeless boss, a crumbling marriage—but they suddenly seemed trivial compared to what I was facing now. I was underground and on the run, hiding from killers and international conspirators in a seedy hotel where hookers noisily serviced their customers and doors slammed open and shut all night. But for all the danger and discomfort, I'd never felt more alive. It was like hang gliding or alpine climbing, where the risk was exhilarating, competence matters, and survival is up to you. After years of comfortably sleepwalking, I was now fully awake.

I have no idea what Hollander has in mind for that Sunday meeting at the Trachtenbergs, but what he doesn't know is that I have a history with the Trachtenberg assistant I'm supposed to call. It was hardly a passionate affair. Katharina and I had met only once, but that single encounter sent a shock wave through my entire body and left a lasting imprint. She's never really been out of my mind. It might be just ego—I'd prefer to see it as an accurate reading of the signals—but I think she felt at least some of the attraction that I felt. Now I might find out.

I could simply leave a message, but I keep trying to get her instead, and the third time around, she finally answers the phone. "It's Adam Jackson, from the American Embassy."

"Hi, Adam," she says. "They told me you'd call. Will we see you on Sunday?"

Her voice sounds just as I remember and gives me the kind of jolt I remember. Yes, I tell her, I'd be there.

"They'll be pleased," she says, still all business.

"Nice to hear your voice, Kati. I wasn't sure you'd remember me."

I hear a slight chuckle, then she says, "Of course I do. How's Fiona?" Which is not what I want to hear. It could be a means of deflection or a simple pleasantry.

"She's fine, back in Washington," I reply, then ask the return question. "How's Guillermo?"

"Great," she says and laughs again. "Still hoping to become the new Egon Schiele," she says, referencing the famous Austrian artist.

"The work, not the life, I hope."

"An excellent point," she says.

I have no idea how she fits into the Trachtenberg picture, and I need to find out. Could she possibly meet me before Sunday, I ask her, and explain that I don't know her employers and hope she'd fill me in. To add a little mystery, I say that I want advice on a sensitive issue best not discussed over the phone.

I'd thought this feeler might be a long shot, though I needn't have worried. "You want to see me and talk about Adi and Bettina? Sure, I'd be glad to," she says and gives me an address. "Will 18:00 tomorrow work for you?"

"I'll be there," I promise.

"Ciao," she says and wishes me a nice day.

Chapter 14

Berlin

Saturday, November 11

*I*t must have been around eighteen months ago when I first met Kati Willmans. I remember, because Fiona left town shortly after.

An art dealer named Hanno something, a friend of a friend, had invited us to a party celebrating the opening of a new exhibition. Fiona and I had been locked in trench warfare for months, and I'd suggested that the change of pace might lighten things up a bit.

The address was on Käthe Kollwitzplatz in the Prenzlauerberg area, a once dilapidated part of East Berlin now sprouting boutiques and trendy eating places among the handsomely restored nineteenth-century houses.

We got there late and found the place crammed with artsy, noisy, and well-lubricated revelers talking and laughing loudly over the pulsing soundtrack. The tightly packed dancers seemed to have found inspiration in the erotic art on the walls.

I got us some drinks and Fiona downed her margarita in a flash and asked for another. Then she started swinging her hips to the music and announced to everyone and no one in particular that she wanted to dance. My lovely wife isn't hard to read. I knew what she was up to, and she knew that I knew, which, I suppose, was the point. She was out to provoke, embarrass, and make me jealous, but we'd been through this enough times in recent months that she should have known it no longer worked.

"Have fun," I told her and tried to lose myself in the crowd.

Her antics did still manage to annoy me, and I sighed at the prospect of the inevitable eruption between us on the way home. For the moment, though, I tried to shut my emotions down, force a benign smile on my face, and circulated.

In the next room, I found a nice looking blonde to smile at, and she smiled back, which was promising. I began to edge my way toward her, which was no easy task, given the crowd. I was nearly there, trying to think of something clever to say, when a short man with a Vandyke and a ponytail blocked my way.

"Herr Jackson from the American Embassy!" he announced triumphantly. "Hanno said you'd be here."

"Actually not," I said. "I'm his twin brother," and tried to elbow past him.

Failing to get the message, he erupted in a cascade of laughter, then gripped my arm firmly and explained that he was a sculptor and that his name was Boris something. He absolutely had to ask me a question, and he said, "After I get you a drink."

It's common these days that Germans want to quiz you about the president and share their own views about him. As I'd expected, Boris was no exception. It took me ten minutes to get rid of him.

The blonde meanwhile had faded away into the crowd.

Berliners like to party into the wee hours, and Hanno's little get-to-gether was still going strong at midnight. Food was being served, and couples lounged on the furniture "making out," as if they were in high school.

I had just decided to look for Fiona in case she was ready to leave, when I heard her familiar voice loudly coaxing someone to dance. I moved in for a closer look.

She was far from ready to call it a night. Sweaty, booze-happy disheveled, and screeching laughter, she had one hand firmly on a man's wrist, and the other arm draped around his neck, struggling to pull him from his chair and onto the dance floor. A thin guy in his thirties, he clearly was not in a dancing mood, but Fiona was having none of it. Her dress had ridden up above the knees and her remarkable breasts were inches from his face, but it was a standoff. She pulled and insisted, and he sat tight and politely suggested that she best get lost.

People were watching, and Fiona was making a spectacle of herself. I was embarrassed for her, but also disgusted, because I knew how this would end. At home she'd make a scene, we'd fight, then she'd sulk, eventually she'd cry, and we'd wind up in bed, wildly fucking our hurt and frustration into temporary oblivion.

A moment later, I heard a woman's voice close to my ear. "Somebody should tell your wife that it's hopeless," she whispered.

I turned to face her, and she smiled at me.

"You underestimate her," I said, smiling back. "She's relentless when she's like this."

"She won't succeed with him. Believe me."

"You know this guy?"

"He's a painter. His name's Guillermo Francke, and he doesn't dance."

"Hmm, we'll see," I said. "My name's Adam, by the way. What's yours?"

"Kati," she said, and gave me that smile again. Then she asked, "How do you feel about Neil Diamond?"

"Why?"

"Because this is his song, and I'd like to dance to it."

"Come on," I said and reached for her hand.

She wore jeans, a black blouse, no jewelry, and stylish brown boots. I guessed she was about my age, not particularly beautiful but definitely attractive, even striking. But what really got to me was the air of someone completely comfortable in her own skin. So unlike Fiona. Was it the way she'd taken the initiative? And not in a brash way, but almost shyly, slightly detached, but curious and observant. When we danced, her slender waist and willowy frame had me hopelessly ensnared.

We danced, but mainly we talked. Over several glasses of prosecco, she told me she was an art historian, and we talked about her visits to the US and all the great museums she'd toured in New York, Chicago, and LA. She'd come from Freiburg three years ago for a job at the Berggruen Museum.

I asked her about her work, but she steered the conversation to all the places I'd served and the diplomatic life in general, but mercifully never asked about the political shitshow going on in the States. Nor about Fiona, who'd shimmied by a few times and shot me heavy looks.

At two in the morning, the party was still going, but the crowd had thinned out. Kati and I stepped out on a small balcony for some air and stood side by side, silent, not touching, but leaning out toward the street to take in the quiet of the night under a cold, clear sky. I had a wife of many years in the next room, and yet it was this woman I'd just met that I felt I'd known all my life. I felt completely at home with her. I didn't want that feeling to end. Had she felt it too?

"You better take her home now," she said.

"Yes, I better," I said, yielding to reality, but with great reluctance.

"*Es war schön*, Adam," she said. A very nice evening.

"*Schön* isn't the right word," I said, "and all because of Fiona. Why were you so sure Francke wouldn't dance?"

There were several very long seconds of silence between us, then she turned and we faced each other.

"Because I've lived with him for over a year."

She looked at me, and this time she wasn't smiling. She stepped forward, wrapped her arms around me, and kissed me. Open-mouthed, first softly, then very hard and for a long time.

When she pulled back, I drew her back to me, and she didn't resist when I kissed her again and held her very tight.

"I don't want this to end," I said. "Does it have to?"

"Perhaps . . . perhaps not. Berlin's a very big town," she answered.

Then she turned, waved, said ciao, and didn't look back.

Berlin

6:00 p.m.

Kati's apartment house, not far from Kudamm, looks like all the others along this block of Emserstrasse, a quiet residential street. I step to the door and press the bell next to the nameplate that reads Francke-Willmans.

A moment later, I hear her voice through the speaker saying, "Be right down."

After another moment, she opens the door and greets me with a big smile. "How nice, Adam," she says. She's wearing a padded brown coat, leather boots, and a furry cap against the cold. We brush cheeks and look at each other. Seeing her lights up something warm and pleasant inside me.

"You look great," I say as she steps out onto the street. "Thanks for doing this."

"I'm glad it worked out. How long has it been?"

"A year and a half."

"Really?"

"Almost exactly."

She hooks her arm through mine and maneuvers us down to a wine bar just around the corner. It's crowded, but we manage to find a table in the back, take off our coats, and sit down.

"Prosecco?" I ask.

She laughs. "You remembered. I'm impressed."

I grin triumphantly, and when the waiter comes by, I order one prosecco and one Negroni on the rocks.

As soon as he's gone, I turn to her and say, "So, tell me about your new job. Why'd you leave the Berggruen?"

"I got bored with the politics. The bureaucracy. Not to mention the low pay. The Gräfin Bettina needed an arts advisor. They give away quite a chunk of money each year; she's on two museum *Freundeskreis* boards, and these private support groups needed backstopping. She offered me the job, the pay was good, so I took it. Simple as that." There is a hint of defensiveness in her voice.

"That surprises me," I say. "They don't seem like your kind of people."

"How do you mean?"

"Aristocrats. Socialites. Snobs. I don't see you fitting in."

She shrugs and waves her hand dismissively. "I don't, but so what? They amuse me. You'll see," she says.

"Who'll be there tomorrow?"

"Just the two of them, and Hollander, plus de la Marre. Do you know him?"

"Witty mentioned him once or twice," I lie. "Wasn't he a guest at the dinner Emerson never got to?"

She nods as our drinks arrive.

We raise our glasses, and then she says, "Jean-Luc is a banker. From Geneva, and very rich. Close to the Trachtenbergs, and to

Emerson too."

"I see. Will you be there tomorrow?"

"Yes, if you don't mind."

We look at each other and smile. "It's a terrible imposition," I say, "but I'll carry on."

We laugh, then look at each other the way we had on that balcony eighteen months ago. It takes me a moment to get back to business.

"I've been wondering what's on their minds," I say. "What do they want from me with this memorial?"

Kati shakes her head. "No idea," she says. "Are you concerned?"

"I'm worried they'll ask me about things I can't talk about. Like the murder investigation. Embassy matters in general."

"Then don't tell them. But if it's a big concern, why did you accept the invitation? Or is there something you want from them? Perhaps I can help."

A strange question and a stranger offer.

All evening long, I've been on the lookout for a hint of how she fits into the picture. There's been no indication of anything other than restrained attraction, but this offer puzzles me. Is she telling me something? I watch her face closely, but see nothing to suggest any hidden meaning.

I shake my head. No, I say, I want nothing from them. The question is what they want from me.

We talk for over an hour, and I wait for the right moment to get to the heart of the matter: How had Emerson gotten in so tight with her employers?

"He was really Hollander's friend," she says. "Hollander was the one who brought Emerson into the Trachtenberg circle. I'd heard the two of them talking about going into some kind of business together, but perhaps you were aware of that."

No. Quite the contrary. I am stunned, but I try not to show it.

I take a deep breath and ask, "How about another drink?"

"I've got to leave soon," she says.

I fix my eyes on her. She's just given me a key piece of information, with the promise of more. But the fact is, I am looking for more than help with the investigation.

"I've got to come clean," I say. "Hanno's party was pure misery for me until you came along. I've thought about you ever since, and I wanted to call you many times. You've got to tell me what that kiss was all about."

She looks down into her empty glass and simply shakes her head.

"Fiona left soon afterward," I say. "She never came back."

"Do you miss her?"

"On rare occasions. In weak moments."

Kati looks at me with her wonderful brown eyes, then puts her hand on my arm. "Guillermo never mentioned his run-in with Fiona," she says quietly.

"How is Guillermo?"

"About the same. He doesn't change."

"You said he fancied himself the next Egon Schiele."

"More in life than in art, unfortunately."

"Schiele died young, right? Not a happy guy, as I recall."

She shrugs. "Narcissistic. Suicidal. Schizophrenic. Perhaps a bit of all of three."

"The perfect boyfriend," I say.

She grins slyly and says, "I have to get back."

We leave the bar and walk through the cold back to her building. At her door, we stand close to each other for a moment. I reach out to embrace her, and she leans in and holds me tight. When she lets go, she brushes her lips lightly across mine.

"Until tomorrow," she says. And then she goes inside.

I could take a taxi, but I want to walk just so I can think. Then it starts to rain, but only lightly. I turn up my collar, put my hands in my pockets, and trudge along, lost in thought. On one level, I am floating along on a cloud of infatuation. On another, I am trying to process the implications of what Kati had told me.

Who was this de la Marre, for one? And Witty's possible business venture with Hollander—that must be what the letter in the safe was all about. But how had Kati become aware of it? Her role remains a puzzle, and her explanation for taking the Trachtenberg job had not been entirely convincing. She'd offered to help me, but why was she involved in the first place?

I was beginning to wonder—was meeting her the best thing that had ever happened to me, or was it the setting of a trap that was going to get me killed?

Chapter 15

Berlin

Saturday, November 11

10:30 a.m.

*A*mong Berlin's cognoscenti, Antonia Holzapfel's standing as the city's foremost—and most expensive—practitioner of her craft is beyond dispute.

Most of her clients are repeat customers, fully aware of the strict rules and procedures for requesting an appointment, and that even minor deviations in that regard were certain to have serious and painful consequences. In other words, obedience, discipline, and fearful anticipation—the stock in trade of any dominatrix—begin with Antonia, even before a client is allowed into her presence.

Her working hours are limited to weekday afternoons, 3:00 to 8:00, so appointments are hard to come by and have to be booked well in advance. For a client seized by an irresistible urge for punishment to be received outside of her regular schedule—even with a hefty premium fee—is exceedingly rare.

On weekends, regardless of emergency or willingness to pay, it is impossible. Saturdays she does her shopping, and the evenings are for enjoying music with friends. She is passionate about Verdi's operas and Mahler or Bruckner symphonies. All day Sunday, without fail, she devotes to her wheelchair-bound mother, installed in an expensive private retirement home in Friedenau.

Of all things in the world Antonia didn't want to do, disrupting her cherished Saturday shopping routine topped the list. But on this occasion, the call to appear at the city health department, the *Gesundheitsamt* on Hohenzollerndamm, had been unequivocal.

The summons had come by phone the previous afternoon. Anke Schuster, the bearer of bad tidings, had been apologetic about the short notice, though vague about the reasons for it. As the official in charge of monitoring the district's bordellos, Anke is a motherly type who takes her job of enforcing rules and regulations while watching over the health and welfare of the area's sex workers very seriously. Antonia has known her for years, and a bond of mutual trust and friendship had developed between them. In this instance, though, Frau Schuster hadn't been able to tell her much. Orders from upstairs, but not to worry. Something about a brief interview and survey to complete was all she'd said.

Antonia is in a dismal mood as she mounts the health department's steps and asks to be directed to room 207. She's wearing comfortable low heels and a simple skirt and sweater under a plain black overcoat, and no makeup. Her long, reddish-black hair has been braided and neatly pinned around her head.

A strong institutional odor of floor wax and carbolic disinfectant greet her as she enters the ugly red-bricked building. The large clock by the entrance confirms that it is 10:30 a.m., precisely the time at which she had been summoned to appear.

The sooner I'm out of here the better, she thinks.

Room 207 was at the end of the hallway on the second floor. Antonia knocks, opens the door, then hesitates. The large, pot-bellied stranger waving her a friendly greeting was not the person she'd expected to see.

"Do come in," he calls out, smiling pleasantly.

"I'm looking for Frau Schuster," she tells him.

"*Ja, ja,* that's right!" he nods, urging her forward. "Come in and take off your coat. Anke sends her apologies. She may be around later. Meanwhile, you and I can do our business together."

"Are you the one I'm seeing?" Antonia asks, puzzled.

"I hope you don't mind," the man says and makes another welcoming gesture. "Will you join me in a cup of coffee?"

Antonia advances warily, sheds her coat, and sits down at the table opposite her host. The desk in the corner is bare. Not even empty in and outboxes on it and no phones or desktops to be seen anywhere. On the table in front of this man, she notes the absence of any kind of files or papers for the survey Anke Schuster had talked about. Only a pot of coffee, a bottle of water, plus cups and glasses.

Alarm bells go off in her head. The atmosphere doesn't smell right. The man opposite her doesn't look like a health department bureaucrat, and Antonia is afraid she knows why. When it comes to the law, she has a well-developed sense of smell, a vestige of her years with Franzi, her husband who'd died in Moabit Prison three years ago.

"Why was I called here?" she asks. "You're from the *Polizei,* aren't you?" She tries to sound relaxed and unconcerned, which decidedly she is not.

The man laughs and says, "How did you guess?" He then fishes a small leather fold out of his pocket and slides it across the table.

"*Hauptkommissar* Karl Holzer," he announces helpfully. "Coffee?"

"Thank you." She nods and pushes the ID back at him.

Her face is a blank, but she senses danger, and her mind is racing. She's never been in trouble with the authorities; she runs a legitimate business, her permits are in order, and her tax payments up to date. There is only one reason that comes to mind, and it fills her with dread.

Holzer has become absorbed with stirring liberal spoonsful of sugar into his coffee. Thereafter his gaze seems fixed on an invisible object somewhere above Antonia's head, while he absentmindedly fingers the large brass bracelet on his left wrist. She watches him out of the corner of an eye, noting the small fly that briefly settles on top of his massive bald head, then takes flight again. Holzer apparently hadn't noticed.

The quiet, along with his trance-like state, feels oppressive, and Antonia's anxiety is rising as she waits for his next move.

But her interrogator knows what he is doing. He lets Antonia sit and fret for a while, then turns to her, scans her face, and feigns benevolent concern. "You seem nervous, Frau Holzapfel."

The heat rises to Antonia's face. "I'm not nervous. Why should I be?" she answers, attempting to sound definitive and unconcerned. "But I would like to know why I'm here."

"Good," he says, smiling jovially. "So, let me fill you in. We're working on an important investigation, and we think you might have information that could help us. My apologies for the little trick to get you in here. Don't blame Anke Schuster. She was reluctant to do it until we explained the reasons, and then she realized it was in your own interest. This case is high profile with lots of publicity. Issuing a formal summons would have involved reams of bureaucratic paperwork likely to leak to the public, with people certain to draw the wrong conclusions. Bad for your business. This way we can meet quietly, out of the limelight, and nobody knows you've talked to us."

Antonia waits silently.

Holzer grins. "You probably have a pretty good idea what case I'm talking about."

She shrugs her shoulders. "How can I? I have no idea."

"Really?" he says, his eyebrows moving north.

"Yes."

"I'll give you a hint. I work for the *Mordkommission*; it's a murder case. Now you know, right?"

"What do I know about a murder?"

"The victim was one of your clients."

"A client? Who?"

Holzer sticks a hand into his pocket, pulls out a photo, and passes it to her. "You know him?"

Antonia stares at the image. "That's John Taylor, an American," she says.

"An American, yes. But not John Taylor. His name is John deWitt Emerson. And not just any American, but a diplomat. Want to see what he looked like when we found him in the Grunewald?"

No longer smiling, he hands her another photograph.

Antonia glances at it, then looks away. "My God," she whispers. "How horrible. I didn't know."

Holzer waits, his arms folded over his bulging midsection as he observes her closely. She has regained her outward calm, but inside she is fighting nausea, and her head is pounding.

"You didn't know?" he asks.

She shakes her head.

"It's been in all the papers and on TV. For days."

"I don't watch the news."

"I see."

He pauses again, then asks, "When did you see him last?"

"I don't remember."

Holzer leans forward, looks straight at her, and says, "Let me help you. It was last Friday, five p.m. Now do you remember? He was killed immediately after he left your flat."

"My God," she mutters.

"Anything unusual happen that day?"

"No. It was a normal session."

"Normal? I see. Whatever that is."

Her anxiety bursts out in anger. "You wouldn't understand," she barks. "It is what it is."

Holzer gives her a conciliatory nod. "You're right," he says. "It is what it is. But in these sessions, is there ever private conversation where you get to know your client's life beyond his predilection?"

"Never." Antonia's fear is rising steadily. *Where is this leading? What's he getting at?*

"He never mentioned his work?"

"Never."

"Did he talk about money, perhaps tell you that he was making lots of it?"

"He paid my fees. In advance. That's all I cared about."

"So, you had no idea who he was or anything else about him, is that right?"

Antonia hesitates, faces Holzer, and says, "Look, my clients appreciate discretion. He never told me any of the kinds of details you're asking about. But yes, I guessed he was with the embassy."

Holzer looks pleased, hits the table with his hands for emphasis, and nods appreciatively. "Of course you did," he tells her. An intelligent person like you. It would have been surprising if you hadn't guessed, right?"

She nods, feeling equally pleased with herself. *That was the right way to play it*, she thinks.

To her surprise, Holzer suddenly rises from his chair and heads for the door.

"Excuse me for a moment. *Dienstgespräch,* a quick business

phone call," he explains. And is gone.

———

Holzer closes the door behind him and wanders down the hall to the toilet, taking his time. The phone call had been a pretext to leave her alone with her thoughts for a while, wondering and worrying about what would come next. When he returns, he hopes she'll be ready for the next act.

Interrogation is like a three-set tennis match, Holzer would tell his young officers. A professional doesn't hit with full strength during the first few games, but studies his opponent, using different strokes to probe for chinks in his armor. Hits it to the left, then to the right, then a few down the middle. Throws in some cuts and slices and gives him a couple of softies to tempt and provoke. By the second set, he'll have figured out the guy on the other side. That's when it's time to turn up the heat, go on offense, and hit him hard where he's weakest, crack his defenses, and break his will.

Always go in with a plan, Holzer would conclude his lecture. Observe your subject, study his reactions and vulnerabilities, bide your time, and know when to pounce.

———

Ten minutes later, Holzer steps back into the room but remains standing. He leans forward, looking straight at Antonia, his bulging belly resting on the edge of the table between them, his chummy mien gone. He seems more like a very disappointed headmaster, ready to lower the boom.

"You haven't been telling me the truth," Holzer says. "Why is that?"

"What do you mean?" The fear in her voice is very real.

Holzer exhales a heavy breath of exasperation. "Because it's obvious. Number one. You claimed you didn't know about your client's murder when all of Berlin's been talking about it. Number two. You said you didn't remember his last visit when the news that he was killed that very afternoon was all over town. Are you Sleeping Beauty, in dreamland for a week? Number three. You told me he never revealed anything personal about himself. But he was a longtime client, and in your business, that means a pretty intimate relationship, right? So, not entirely believable. Number four,"—Holzer is bluffing now—"you insisted he never bragged about money he was making, when he was known to talk about it all the time.

"So, I ask myself: What's Antonia Holzapfel hiding? She must know something about this situation she's not willing to talk about. You didn't kill him yourself, so who are you shielding?"

Antonia shakes her head vigorously and pleads, "I told the truth, and I'm not shielding anyone. Herr Taylor—or Emerson—was a nice man. I'd never harm him. I'm sorry he's dead."

Holzer notes the tiny beads of sweat glistening on her forehead, even though the room is pleasantly cool. He sits down again and fiddles with his bracelet. Antonia picks at chipped nail polish on her left index finger.

Holzer breaks the silence with a tone that is softer, more understanding. "You must be careful, Frau Holzapfel," he counsels. "This is serious business. If you know anything at all, better tell me now. It's in your own best interest. I promise we'll protect you."

"Protect me—from whom? From what?"

"I'll tell you," he says. "So, listen carefully.

"We believe it was a gang killing, a contract job. And we're thinking—it's just a theory—your deceased husband Franzi had his connections in such circles, and you've got family.

"Remember, Frau Holzapfel, Germany is an orderly place. We believe that careful documentation of civic life is the hallmark of a law-abiding society. It's a German tradition that goes back to before Frederick the Great.

"So, we have all those files. We're pack rats. You change your address and there's the *Anmeldung*, you register with us. You're born, marry, divorce, or die, and we'll keep a file on that. You go to court or to jail, there's a record of that until long after you're dead. A passport application, a fender-bender, or your neighbor complains about too much noise—you name it—we'll keep a file. Nothing's ever thrown away. Not in a hundred years.

"We looked at your file and we asked ourselves: Who were Franzi's friends and who are hers—from before—when she was still Antigona Duka?"

Antonia stares at him, her blood rising. "*Lieber Himmel.*" Her voice is shaking. "Now I see what you're trying to hang on me. *Verdammt.* What is this—guilt by association? I have nothing to do with those kinds of people. Nothing."

"You're sure?"

"Of course I'm sure!" she says, near-shouting.

Holzer waits a beat, then pulls a card from his pocket, pushes it toward her, and stands up.

"Thanks for making that clear, Frau Holzapfel. And sorry to have kept you so long," he tells her. "My number is on the card. If anything comes up or you think of something, call me anytime. Day or night."

He walks around the table and offers her his hand.

Antonia, unprepared and astonished by his sudden gallantry, rises hurriedly, and takes it. "We're finished?" she asks nervously.

"Indeed. I've asked all my questions. So, I'll say *tschüss*, or per-haps,"—his eyebrows rising—"*Auf Wiedersehen?*"

In a half daze, Antonia gathers up her things and follows him to the door.

He is about to open it, his hand on the doorknob, when he turns to her once more and says, "By the way, Antigona is such a beautiful name. Too bad you changed it. Do you know its origins?"

She looks at him blankly and shakes her head. "My parents liked it, but I didn't. It's common in Albania."

"A Greek name, originally," he explains. "Antigone is the main character in *Sophocles*, a famous Greek drama. She is a tragic figure. She sticks to her belief in her family, and because of misplaced loyalty, pays for it with her life."

Hurrying out onto the street, Antonia forces herself not to break into a run. Hohenzollerndamm is filled with bundled-up shoppers out in force as a weak November sun pierces a patchy cover of gray clouds.

Shopping is now far from her mind. She is filled with confused emotions—relief mingled with fear and alarm. The police are on their tail, and she'll have to warn him. But how? What she needs is a quiet place to compose herself and think.

Walking at a fast clip, she heads toward a nearby cabstand and breathes a sigh of relief to find a single empty taxi just pulling in. She climbs in, gives a street name, leans back, and forces herself to relax, her eyes half closed. It only dimly registers with her that she has drawn a very slow driver who's got himself bottled up in traffic and takes a couple of wrong turns before reaching her destination, a Turkish restaurant on Ansbacherstrasse, close to the Kudamm.

1:25 p.m.

At the Metehan Taverna, Antonia picks at a large tomato and cucumber salad, while Holzer and *Oberkommissar* Kranmüller sit together at the Landeskriminalamt on Keithstrasse, monitoring reports from the situation. All in all, they're in good moods.

"You handled that well, Karl," the *Oberkommissar* says. "I hope you scared her enough to do something stupid."

"Like lead us to some hard evidence?"

"Exactly."

Just then, the voice of Angela, the detective trainee, intrudes via an intercom hidden in the ceiling.

"Markus makes a lousy cab driver, so we got here first. She just wrote something on a paper and then used her cell. Two-minute, thirty-five-second call," she reports in a low voice.

"Understood," a male voice acknowledges.

Kranmüller and Holzer listen closely.

"What's she doing now?" the male voice inquires.

"Eating her salad."

"Understood."

Holzer says, "Bon appétit." And grins.

Nothing much happens for a while. Then Angela reports in again. "Woman just walked in and sat down with her. Balkan-type, I think midsixties, round face, darkish, gray hair, wearing heavy coat, brown I think, matching wool cap. Subject just passed her a piece of paper."

"Understood. We got her covered," the male voice says.

The two detectives exchange looks.

"Again, good work," Kranmüller tells his deputy.

Chapter 16

Berlin

Sunday, November 12

9:20 a.m.

*T*he meeting is in progress, and I arrive twenty minutes late, just to assert a little independence.

The conversation stops when I walk in, and their eyes turn toward me. I scan their faces and note that some look surprised that I've shown up at all.

"There he is!" Emmett says, striking a cheerful note to break the silence. "Get yourself breakfast and grab a seat, Adam."

I nod politely to the other four men in the room, pour myself a glass of orange juice, and sit down next to him.

McLean slouches in an overstuffed easy chair across from us. Castelyou sits on a couch next to a big middle-aged guy in jeans and a gray sweater. Another stranger, a young man in his thirties, dressed head to toe in Brooks Brothers conservatism, has the place on Emmett's right. The only notable omission is Austin Trotter, our CIA station chief. "Not in this silo," according to McLean. Whatever that means.

Emmett makes the introductions. "Two colleagues from Washington you haven't met yet," he starts in. "Charlie Hinton from the Bureau is over there next to Jack, and Eldrige Rivas, on my right, is in from Foggy Bottom. Special assistant to the deputy secretary. They've come over with Mort to liaise with the Germans. That's the team—you included. Our colleagues have emphasized that there's a definite sense of urgency to get a handle on this situation. It's top priority in Washington. I've assured them that the embassy is 100 percent on board."

He pauses briefly.

McLean gives me a thin smile, engaging only his mouth, not his eyes. Hinton, with the Book-of-Mormon look of an FBI agent, nods with downcast eyes, and Rivas stares at me while twiddling with a yellow pencil. No one speaks. Everyone seems to be waiting for me to tell my story.

"So, Adam," Emmett continues, "this morning's agenda is to take stock of where things stand and for you to brief us."

"Glad to." I nod.

At my insistence, we're meeting at the Cunninghams' Dahlem residence. It has been four days since I disappeared from the embassy, with no desire to show my face there again. I've agreed with Emmett that it's time to explain why I vanished and what role I intend to play going forward. Keeping the lines open made sense. Sooner or later, things are liable to get dicey, and I might need their help.

What Emmett knows that our visitors don't is that I intend to make it a short meeting. I have no intention of putting myself back under their control or peeling myself open and telling them everything I know. Least of all, where I was hiding. Or that I have another relevant meeting coming up before noon.

Emmett plays his role as friend and peacemaker and turns to me with an encouraging smile.

"I've filled the team in on your contribution so far. Everyone is impressed and grateful. So, now tell us what's been happening since the night of the break-in and the attack."

I take a couple of breaths and look around the room. "Sorry about my vanishing act," I begin. "It wasn't because I don't consider myself a member of the team—"

"I'm certainly glad to hear that," Rivas interjects. He has a reedy voice and his tone is prep-school bitchy and sarcastic.

"Here are the basics, as I see 'em," I continue, ignoring the interruption. "First, our DCM was murdered. Obviously, we need to find out who did it, and why.

"Second, I understand there's evidence he was involved with some illegal group, and the government needs evidence to roll them up and expose their suspected collaborators in Germany. Specifically Dwayne Hollander, a US citizen, as well as the von Trachtenbergs, and others."

I pause and look over at McLean, whose face has remained a blank, devoid of expression. Hinton and Castelyou nod their agreement.

"You got it," Hinton says.

"Good," I reply. "I accept my responsibility to do my part. I already got myself into the middle of this thing anyway. I'm told my would-be kidnappers may be the ones who murdered Emerson and that the local conspirators around Hollander and von Trachtenberg may be the ones pulling the strings. We don't know that, but have to assume it.

"So, here's my main news, which sort of points in that direction. Two days ago, Hollander—a guy I barely know—phoned and invited me to meet him at the von Trachtenbergs. He made some bullshit excuse about wanting advice on a memorial they're planning for their dear friend Emerson.

"And?" Rivas pipes up.

"I accepted," I say. Then I stop to let that sink in.

"Excellent," McLean calls out, smiling his approval.

"Interesting," Hinton echoes, and Castelyou gives me a nod, one colleague to another.

"When?" Hinton asks.

"Next day or two, most likely. Not sure yet," I lie. I don't want these government clowns hanging around the von Trachtenbergs' villa tailing me. "My guess is they want to look me over and pick up whatever they can. But that goes both ways. Maybe I'll find out a thing or two from them. At any rate, it gets us on the inside. I'll let you know what I discover."

"Specifically, what's your plan?" Hinton asks.

"I'll look for opportunities to draw them out. Mainly, though, I'll play it by ear and see what develops at the meeting."

"Feed their suspicion, subtly. Let them follow you. We'll be right there when you leave, and—" Hinton says.

"No," I interrupt him. "Absolutely not. I'm doing this on my own. Stay away until we can consult again. Otherwise, I'm out."

"Why?" Rivas asks. "We need to be in on this, to approve your strategy and to know where to find you. You're under our orders!"

"Here's why," I say, addressing the room. "These guys are dangerous. They've already put a target on my back and getting directly involved with them ups the ante for me. They were looking for me where I live and around the chancery, which is why I went AWOL. That's how it stays until further notice. I'm willing to stick my neck out to get on the inside, but only on these terms. Emmett is my contact. I'll keep in touch with him, and he'll know when I need your help."

I am looking at a lot of distressed faces. Obviously, my defensive crouch doesn't please anyone.

It's Castelyou who speaks up first. "We hear you, Adam, but as a friend and colleague, please listen to me. As Emmett said, we're operating under a big time constraint. The conspirators—they call themselves The Group, incidentally—are far advanced in their planning. We don't know exactly when they'll strike, but it's soon. We need to move quickly, and Washington is looking to us to run the show. We can't let you wander off at your own speed, making it up as you go along. We're professionals, trained for this. You're not. We'll guide and protect you. You need us, and no one will know we're there with you."

From across the room, McLean joins the chorus, exuding benevolent concern. "And we'll help you keep the German cops off your back. They're after you too, you know."

I'd expected that. "Thanks, Mort. It's a comfort to know you'll vouch for me with the *Polizei*, if that becomes necessary. I'm hoping they'll be understanding. If and when they catch and arrest me, I'll depend on you to bail me out."

We go back and forth like this for another fifteen minutes, but we aren't getting anywhere. I'm looking for an opening to bring it to closure when Rivas rises from his chair, glares at me, and again raises his irritating voice.

"This is totally unacceptable, Counselor," he announces with authority he doesn't have. "The Department will not allow it. This investigation is being run way above your pay grade, and you take orders from us. We're running this show and I strongly advise you to fall in line. If you mess this up, it might cost you your job."

"You're suggesting I'll be fired?"

"If you disobey us, quite possibly."

"I'm shocked," I tell him. "Will that be before or after I take all the risk? If it's before, are you going to volunteer to take my place?"

Emmett laughs, and so does McLean. Rivas just stares, fuming.

"Seriously, Mr. Rivas," I say. "I have a question for you. How long have you had this job with the deputy secretary?"

"Since March," Rivas answers proudly. "I came in with the

deputy secretary when the president appointed him."

"Well, as a political appointee, you may not know this, so let me enlighten you. I'm a Foreign Service Officer and my commission was signed by President Bush thirteen years ago. Firing me isn't that easy. There are laws and regulations for that, precisely to protect me from the kind of arbitrary action you're suggesting. Maybe you can get me reassigned, but not fired. Except if you can prove criminality, moral turpitude, or gross malfeasance. Incompetent officers can be 'selected out,' as it's called. But we have a process for that in the Foreign Service, and my record's pretty solid. So, firing me isn't much of a threat. Not from you, not from your beloved president."

The room is silent as Rivas sits down and I stand up.

"I've got another appointment I can't afford to miss," I explain. "I'll be in touch." I head for the door without looking back.

It's a quiet Sunday morning, and Rosengasse is deserted. Outside the Cunningham residence, the sky is blue, speckled with puffy white clouds, and the temperature is in the midfifties, which is unusual for Berlin at this time of year. There's not much wind, and the air is dry and smells of chestnuts. My appointment is in Charlottenburg, a good five miles from Dahlem, but in deference to the weather, I intend to walk. I also need the exercise and time to process.

Everything seems normal as I turn into Clayallee, with no reason for me to take special note of the young couple walking arm-in-arm on the other side of the boulevard.

Meeting the crew from DC wasn't particularly reassuring. If anything, it confirmed my suspicion that having my back isn't my so-called teammates' top priority and that they are more interested in using rather than protecting me. Not to mention the underlying mood and body language among the attendees conveying their lack of trust, and the clear impression that each agency is playing its own game. The atmosphere of thinly veiled duplicity and deception repels and worries me.

If they don't fully trust each other, and instead of leveling with each other spend their energy maneuvering for bureaucratic advantage, how can I put myself unconditionally into their hands? Rivas was too lightweight to matter, but I couldn't help noticing how McLean and Hinton had stubbornly ignored each other, focusing all their eye contact on me, each competing to enlist me on his side.

The absence of Austin Trotter also continues to bother me. The creep is hardly my favorite, yet as the local CIA chief of station, he is the senior US intelligence officer in Berlin. If Witty had been under observation for weeks, Trotter should be working closely with the FBI. So, why is he out of the loop? What's happened to him? For whatever reason, Trotter's absence dramatically increases my sense of risk.

The reality is that I have been thrust into a perilous situation and have no choice but to go it alone in a role for which I'm ill-equipped. Dangerously exposed, I've got no one genuinely looking out for me. Tommy Bubic's my friend, but he and his bouncers are no match for the kind of criminal—maybe terrorist—gang we seem to be up against. And I still don't have a gun.

I hate to admit it, but Jack Castelyou was right: I lack the training and experience to pull off a tricky undercover operation on my own. I'd never even risk taking a Vespa into highway traffic. So why am I up for this?

Yet the fact is, exposing a conspiracy against US democracy exerts a powerful pull on me. Especially after three years in Germany, where the scars are still evident from when its own democracy was snuffed out. The totalitarians who took over in the thirties succeeded only because of the more "respectable" enablers who opened doors for them: businessmen greedy for profits, small-time politicians hungry for big-time power, and reactionaries hoping to regain lost privileges. Meanwhile, those who knew better stood by and did nothing because they didn't have the guts.

I figure this is my gut-check moment not to repeat that error. Trying to be a hero can get you killed, but being a coward and a quitter would be very hard to live with.

For more than an hour, on my way to Keithstrasse, I've been absorbed by my thoughts and looking for answers that haven't come. I've been so deep in thought that it's slow to register that I've seen the young couple coming up behind me somewhere before. I find it difficult to swallow, difficult to breathe, as I push past the *Landeskriminalamt's* heavy iron portal for my appointment with *Oberkomissar* Kranmüller.

Chapter 17

Berlin

Sunday, November 12

*K*ranmüller likes to warn young recruits in the *Mannschaft* that homicide work is mostly tedious, rarely exciting, and never glamorous. Avoid shortcuts and beware of the seemingly obvious, he tells them. There's no substitute for step-by-step, methodical detective work to get to the truth and to nail the perpetrator. Assemble all the available evidence, including motive. The whole package has to be complete to hold up in court.

More often than not, murders are committed on the spur of the moment or in the heat of passion, with little forethought or planning, he tells them. "Those we can wrap up pretty quickly," he says.

The tougher cases are the carefully prepared ones by a perpetrator who is really smart. Fortunately, that's pretty rare. But by far the worst are those that generate the kind of public excitement that gets in the way of orderly detective work. And the worst of the worst are part of some larger situation where the top brass gets involved.

The murder of deWitt Emerson, Kranmüller had been told in

confidence by the *Innensenator's* state secretary, his big boss, was that kind of affair, with political involvement all the way to the top of the government. Every step of the investigation would have to be coordinated with several other agencies. Along with being sworn to absolute secrecy, he'd been invited into a series of classified meetings with the *Bundesnachrichtendienst* (BND), the German CIA; the *Landesamt für Verfassungsschutz*, the German FBI; and *Staatssicherheit*, state security people close to the chancellor's office, where information on the case was being coordinated and the national security and international ramifications thrashed out.

Bottom line: the Emerson homicide wasn't a simple case of murder. In all likelihood, it was part of a larger anti-government conspiracy on both sides of the Atlantic with significant and immediate security implications.

Though the evidence in the murder increasingly pointed toward one of Berlin's better-known street gangs, their hands-on involvement was only part of the story. No matter who'd fired the bullets, the bigger question was who'd paid for them and how the homicide fit into the overall plot. The goal of the investigation no longer was merely to nab the shooters, but to roll up the plotters as well. The pressure was on because their timing was still unclear and the BND—fearing the worst—was working overtime to find out more. The US side didn't know either, or wouldn't tell.

That, Kranmüller realized, created a completely new situation for him. Weeks earlier, the Americans had informed German Intelligence about Emerson being a suspect in a US domestic security investigation with a German connection. The problem was that little additional information had been shared, even after Washington investigators had arrived in Berlin. To the annoyance of the Germans—assurances of full cooperation notwithstanding—the Americans were holding their cards very close to the chest.

One plausible explanation was simply intra-bureaucratic rivalries and game-playing among the various American services, which was not uncommon. Or perhaps, others thought, the secrecy was driven by domestic politics and led all the way to the White House.

If the reasons for the American reticence were unclear, the German reaction to it was not. They had answered in kind, pursued their separate investigation, instituted electronic surveillance of the suspects, shadowed them, and tried to penetrate their activities by various means. And none of what they found would be shared with the American team in Berlin.

Effective penetration of the conspirators remained a problem, and Adam Jackson could be the key to unlocking the case. What had he discovered inside Emerson's apartment? Why, after his foray into burglary, had he fled from the embassy and gone to ground?

With no help from the embassy, the young American had been devilishly hard to find. But then the Mitte precinct had reported a tip that Jackson was holed up in a sex hotel under an assumed name. Miraculously, the American himself had now phoned and offered to meet, provided that no one else knew, not even the embassy.

So, following gut instinct, Kranmüller had humored him and agreed. But he was too good a cop to leave anything to chance. People change their minds, and for the previous twenty-four hours, he'd discreetly posted his people around the Osthotel. Their mission: keep a watchful eye on an unusual resident named Mark Miller, alias Adam Jackson.

11:30 a.m.

The office isn't what I'd imagined. It feels quiet and non-threatening. Nothing about it says cops or homicide.

Kranmüller greets me at the door. We shake hands, he returns to his desk, then motions me to take one of the two chairs facing him on the other side. The second one is occupied by a rumpled-looking, bald-headed, beer-bellied man with red cheeks.

"This is my colleague, *Hauptkommissar* Holzer," Kranmüller explains. Holzer and I repeat the hand-shaking ceremony, and I sit down next to him.

I can't help noticing that, except for a computer screen on one side and a few knick-knacks, including a miniature Berlin bear, Kranmüller's desk is clean. No files, papers, or anything else. *A man with orderly work habits,* I'm thinking.

He folds his hands, rests them on his desk, and opens the conversation with a welcoming smile. "Thank you for coming, Herr Counselor," he says. "We've been looking forward to meeting you." His voice has a pleasant tone, and he speaks a cultured German with no trace of the harsher Berlin argot. In contrast to Holzer, who's in a well-worn leather jacket, flannel shirt, and jeans, Kranmüller wears a white dress shirt, gray pullover, and black sports coat. Not my idea of how a German cop would look.

"My apologies for not coming in sooner," I tell him. "Things have been a little . . . hectic."

"Yes, of course. How do you like the Osthotel?" Kranmüller deadpans.

Maybe he has a sense of humor; he's clearly enjoyed springing this opening surprise on me.

"It's not too bad," I say, feigning nonchalance at the obvious fact that they've been watching me. "I think I'm the only guest who stays longer than an hour."

"You're probably right," he nods. "We know the place. Maybe you'll tell us why you're staying there. But first, tell me about the night you were attacked. The night you broke into the Emerson apartment."

His voice is calm, but he's all business now.

It's the question I had expected and see no reason to hold back, so I tell my story in detail—except for the safe and its contents.

When I finish, Holzer is the first to speak up. "Did you get a look at the guy who grabbed you?"

"Not really. He wore a hood. All I could see were his eyes. They were dark, I think."

"Anything else you noticed? Anything at all?"

"He was taller than me. And smelled bad—garlic or some pungent spice. And he was damn strong, I must say. At one point, he cursed at me in a language I didn't understand. Oh, and he spoke German with an accent."

"Russian, perhaps?"

"I don't think so. I'd recognize Russian."

"Some other Slavic language?"

"Could be."

"Asian? South Asian?"

"I wouldn't think so. Definitely not Chinese or Japanese."

We go back and forth like this for a while until Holzer suggests that he show me some photos later on to jog my memory.

He looks over at Kranmüller, who hasn't said a word, then turns back toward me and asks, "By the way, why didn't you wait for the *Polizei*?"

"To be honest, because I didn't want anyone to know what I'd been up to in the apartment. Besides, I was in a hurry to get home."

"Hmm."

"Did I break the law? Are you going to arrest me?"

That's when Kranmüller cuts in. "Why would we do that?"

"I don't know. If I broke the law—"

"*Ach, Unsinn*; maybe you did, technically. But we're not interested in that," Kranmüller says. "That would be stupid. We want to find the murderers, and you're an important witness who can help us. That's all we care about. You should have come to us earlier, though," he adds, reproachfully.

"Again, sorry about that," I say, "but the embassy gave me contrary advice, which scared me."

That elicits a quiet stare from Kranmüller, who shakes his head in disbelief, as if rubbing it in how much of a fool I'd been to even half believe McLean's scare scenarios. Why should the Germans care about my entering a colleague's apartment, with or without a key? Or leaving before the cops arrive? The bastard was trying to frighten me, and I was fool enough to buy it.

"I can't imagine why they'd do that," he says. And throws in the afterthought, "But you know your people better than we do."

There's another moment of silence, then he asks, "Is there anything you found in the Emerson apartment that your attackers might have been after?"

"I can't imagine," I say, disingenuously, "the embassy's got it all. You'd have to ask them."

That elicits another quiet stare from Kranmüller. "I see," he says. "But what I don't understand is why you left the embassy and went underground."

We are on thin ice now, and I choose my words very carefully. "I'll be honest with you," I start in, but honesty is not exactly what I have in mind. "I was told my attackers might be the ones who killed Emerson. More to the point—that they might come for me again. So, I decided to disappear."

"All by yourself?" Holzer asks, his eyebrows traveling north.

"May not make a lot of sense to you, Herr Holzer," I tell him. "Maybe it was foolish. But that's what I decided to do."

"It's understandable, Karl," Kranmüller says, and gets out of his chair, suggesting that it's time for a break.

He heads down the hall to the washroom, Holzer and I trailing along behind. I glance at my watch. Almost two o'clock. Time has passed faster than I realized.

On the way back, he stops at a refrigerator, hands out Cokes, and we stand around in the hallway like three guys at a bus stop, sipping and chatting about nothing in particular. The two German cops seem totally relaxed and in no hurry to get back to work, but to me, the whole thing feels odd. I can't shake a gnawing sense of doubt and foreboding about what's behind their bonhomie and what's next for me.

The building is semi-deserted, but it still has the gray and airless feeling of bureaucrats at work. The only living souls I've seen are two secretarial staffers in Kranmüller's outer office and a bored-looking cop lounging in front of a TV, watching a Bundesliga soccer match.

"I'll finish up with Mr. Jackson alone, Karl," Kranmüller tells his deputy. Then he downs the last of his drink and expertly tosses the empty can into a trash stand some ten feet away.

Holzer doesn't seem particularly surprised.

"*Ach, stimmt*. It's Sunday, my day off, and I almost forgot," he says sardonically. He waves at me, and is gone.

———

Had it been an ordinary homicide, Kranmüller's next move would have been routine, and Adam Jackson would not have been so important for Kranmüller.

His people had watched Antonia Holzapfel's note travel to a Turmstasse garage. Its owner was one Jermir Duka, her cousin and no stranger to the *Polizei*. With prior convictions for robbery and fencing stolen goods, he had served with Antonia's husband in Moabit Prison and moved in the same circles as the Hassanis. That would have been enough to pull in Antonia and her cousin for intense questioning with the hope of extracting more evidence or a confession.

But now the Emerson homicide was no longer the highest priority. The German government's conspiracy investigation had moved to the top of the list, and in this, Adam Jackson was a key witness. The suspicion was that the American had taken important information from the Emerson apartment and that his entanglements with the suspects had the tantalizing potential for critical insights and intelligence about the conspiracy and its members.

Who were they and what exactly was their plan?

Kranmüller had been tasked to enlist Jackson for the German side and to persuade him that his collaboration was in their mutual interest. That he would agree wasn't a foregone conclusion, however. For whatever reasons, the American diplomat appears to have resisted cooperation with his own people; his efforts to hide, as well as his less than forthcoming answers to questions, had made that clear. It was the kind of human relations challenge to which Kranmüller was accustomed, and he had thought long and hard how best to handle it.

———

Back in Kranmüller's office, it's clear that Holzer's sudden dismissal was prearranged. I'm not sure why, but it does nothing to dispel my unease.

Someone has laid out a plate with open-faced sandwiches on Kranmüller's desk: liverwurst, prosciutto, and what looks like Edamer cheese. There's also a dish with two pairs of wieners.

"I hope you're hungry," the homicide chief says, and reaches for the wieners.

"Actually, I am," I say and follow suit.

He pours me a glass of seltzer, and we sit silently and chew for a while.

"You know," he says, breaking the silence. "I've been thinking that we have something in common. We're both *Beamte*. Civil servants. Bureaucrats. You a diplomat and me a policeman. Different countries, but public service work is much the same everywhere, right?"

"If you mean lousy pay and lots of paperwork, I agree," and take the last bite of my sausage.

"I learned that on my exchange visits to the US," he explains. "In New York with the NYPD and at the FBI Academy. Unforgettable experiences for me."

"I bet."

"Highly professional colleagues, but very friendly. What I especially liked was the American custom of using first names right away. Helps break the ice."

"Yeah, we do that."

Kranmüller has been watching my face. He hesitates for a moment, then asks, "So—should we?"

"Sure, Bodo," I shrug, with an encouraging smile, but I'm thinking, *What's with all the happy talk?*

"*Gut*, Adam," he says. "First names aren't usually a German thing. We're more formal and we like titles. I think it's a kind of German disease. But you and I have something else in common. We're both in a tricky situation and should cooperate. So, I was thinking, first names might help."

"Can't hurt, especially now that I know you're not going to lock me up." I say this cautiously, giving him one of my best smiles.

"You can forget that, Adam. Still, you're in danger from some very bad people. We think we know who they are. It's a murky situation with lots of people involved. That's why your instinct to trust no one, look out for yourself, and stay out of sight was correct. So far, it's worked. You've been smart."

"Or lucky?"

"You made your luck. Someone once said that luck is a special kind of genius."

"Ha!"

Kranmüller is looking straight at me now, and I note that he is choosing his words carefully.

"I hope someday you'll tell us why you've cut yourself off from the embassy and what your attackers are after. It would help a lot. Meanwhile, I want to tell you a few things and warn you. We've traced a connection from Emerson back to his probable killers, and you have reason to worry. They're a nasty gang, and going it alone isn't going to work against them. You need help and protection. That's why we've had you under surveillance for the last few days. To get more evidence on the gang that's after you and to protect you. Did you know that?"

"You've had people tailing me?"

"You didn't notice?"

"I saw two people following me on the way here."

"My guys," Kranmüller chuckles, not without a note of professional pride. "We've had you in our care since you checked in to the Osthotel. I told my people to be discreet. I'm glad they succeeded."

Kranmüller pauses, leans in a little closer, and looks at me intently for several seconds. For the first time, I notice the unusual blueness of his eyes, which for some reason startles me.

"Please listen carefully, Adam," he tells me, his voice calm and deliberate. "I sent Holzer away because I want to discuss some highly confidential matters with you. *Staatsgeheimnis*, state secrets coming from the top of the German government. Not something we usually share with foreigners, but I'm authorized to speak frankly with you. I need your word that you will not talk about this with anyone."

I'm suddenly aware that I'm feeling warm and a bit sweaty. Not because the room is hot, but because my inner alarm system has kicked in.

"Of course," I say and throw in a couple of reassuring nods.

He continues. "Your government informed us some time ago that Emerson was a suspect in a US security investigation with connections in the Federal Republic. When he was murdered, we saw the likely link, and when your people came from Washington, we expected a joint US-German investigation exercise. Didn't happen, unfortunately. In spite of nice words, your colleagues aren't telling us much." Kranmüller speaks dispassionately. "Any idea why that is?" he asks.

"Not really."

"It's puzzling. There's a clear common interest. Why aren't they telling us what they know? We don't get it."

"You're right," I say and crack a wry smile. "Outside the States, the CIA is in charge, and they've been known to make some bone-headed moves. Sometimes I think the word *intelligence* in *Central Intelligence* is an oxymoron. As often as not, they screw up because of bickering over who's in control and who gets the credit."

"We've thought of that," Kranmüller agrees. "Anyway, we've gone ahead with our own investigation, and we've got better resources than the Americans do. They should know that. It's our country, after all.

"We think we've identified the killers, and we've got the von Trachtenberg group under tight surveillance. But there's still a lot we don't know. Like the full cast of characters, their actual plan, the timing, and where the money's coming from. The biggest unknown is why Emerson was killed. We need more evidence before we can act on any of these fronts."

I've been listening closely, trying to figure out where Kranmüller is taking this. The uncertainty makes me nervous.

"Another thing we don't know, Adam, is how you fit in. Are you with your investigators, or are you alone?"

"Actually, both," I reply. Which happens to be true, but is also a safe nonanswer.

"Whatever it is, you can't escape being deep in the middle of it."

"Why?"

"Because these people think you have something they want and will use any means to get it. So, they'll have to make their move, and that brings them in the open and creates opportunities for us."

"I've thought of that."

"Opportunities and risks. For you. Like your visit with the von Trachtenbergs today. At 18:00, right? You shouldn't go there without a clear game plan and backup. Have you thought through all the risks?"

"Who told you about the meeting?" I blurt out, unable to hide my surprise. He even knows when it's scheduled!

Kranmüller dismisses my question with a wave of his hand. "We have our sources. One of the many resources for nailing the killers and neutralizing the conspirators. That's why your people should have been working with us. We think it's a pity there hasn't been enough trust between allies."

I say nothing, but probably he can tell that I agree.

"Perhaps you should be the one to trust us. You know us pretty well. In fact, you have an opportunity to be the missing link between our two teams. Strike a blow for the US-German alliance. Think about that."

He knows how to push my buttons, but I let him talk.

"Here's my idea," he says. "Let's agree to work together. We share information and coordinate action. All our resources will be behind you. I promise we'll never leave you in the lurch, and we'll be straight with you at all times."

I wait a moment, absorbing his proposition. Then I say, "You want me to tell you everything I know and everything I plan to do?"

"Right. We agree to brief each other fully, and we're behind you all the way. You have my word on it."

"I'll have to think about that," I tell him.

We talk for another hour before parting company. I promise to be in touch. Then I head down Keithstrasse toward Kudamm. A young man in a brown leather jacket and a wool cap pulled low over his eyes has been studying a pharmacy's window display across the street. Now he is walking in the same direction.

The fresh air feels good, and so do I. I think about Mortimer McLean. And smile.

Chapter 18

Berlin

Sunday, November 12

5:30 p.m.

Stepping out of the Osthotel, I head for the red BMW parked in a no-standing zone. Tommy is behind the wheel, rakishly attired in a gray turtleneck and baseball cap, a cigarette dangling from his lower lip.

"You're smoking," I note, wagging my finger.

"Look who's talking. Better than a lousy cigar."

"Cigars don't kill you. Besides, they smell better."

"Says who? Get in."

A red-headed giant with no visible neck and the shoulders of a Pamplona bull is in the front seat. I get in the back and we pull out into the traffic.

"Meet Börries," Tommy says. "The club's best security guy. Also good on the drums."

Without turning around, Börries acknowledges me with a spare wave of his arm. "Drums are fun," he announces in a gravelly voice. "I like to hit things."

"What did I tell you?" Tommy laughs. "The right guy for this job. All set?"

"Sure," I answer, projecting the confidence I don't feel. "Never better. Good to go."

The Trachtenbergs' villa in Zehlendorf, Berlin's poshest western suburb, sits on a small side street of villas hidden behind fenced-in gardens. You might call it a ghetto for the super-rich.

We are just about on time when Tommy pulls up outside the gate. He and his sidekick are going to be my backup, and we've worked out elaborate contingency plans in case I don't make it out of there. As a last resort, he has instructions to call Kranmüller for reinforcements. His people are probably hanging around in the area anyway.

All in all, having joined forces with Kranmüller's *Mannschaft*, and with Tommy and Börries nearby, I consider myself pretty well-protected for this venture into what likely is unfriendly, and possibly dangerous, territory.

I dressed for the occasion in suit, tie, and a dark-blue cashmere overcoat. Diplomat's attire. But no hat. I draw the line there: I never wear them.

Someone once observed that walking around with a gun in your pocket is very different from walking around without a gun in your pocket. A very astute observation. The gun inside my jacket pocket feels conspicuous and heavy, though I realize that it mostly just weighs on my mind. They don't teach firearms in Foreign Service orientation. Tommy had brought the little Ruger LCP earlier in the afternoon, put me through a quick tutorial on its finer points, and assured me—not without pride—that it was one of the most dependable small handguns in the world. Also easily concealed.

I admit there is something empowering about it, but whether I'll really be ready to use it if needed remains an open question.

I wave to my two escorts, step up to the tall, handsomely carved gate, take a deep breath, and announce myself on the intercom. A moment later the electric lock hums and clicks, the gate noiselessly swings open, and I start up a long winding path paved with small stones flanked by dense shrubbery between a row of stately trees.

Daylight is fading fast. The path lies in semi-darkness, and thin wafts of low fog have settled over the ground. Only a few widely spaced ground lights point the way, and the house isn't yet visible. Walking up the path in the eerie quiet makes me feel queasy. Not even my rubber-soled shoes make a sound.

I've stopped momentarily to fish out my cell as a lamp to guide my way when the lights of the villa finally appear through the mist and the trees ahead of me. Suddenly, I hear something crashing through the shrubbery to my right. I freeze, then duck behind the nearest tree, hold my breath, and wait. My heart is in my throat as I consider the possibilities. A falling tree? A Doberman on patrol? The kidnappers, ready to go again?

I stick my hand into my jacket pocket, wrap it around the Ruger, and wait. That feels good—the gun thing. But then a shadowy figure swaddled in black suddenly crosses in front of me, stops for a split second, looks left and right, and then quickly sprints into the bushes on the other side. He hasn't slowed down long enough for me to get a good look. But the split second he's turned his head my way is enough for me to recognize the face of Austin Trotter, our CIA station chief.

A circular driveway leads to a large turn-of-century *Jugendstil* villa. Impressive, by any standard. I half expect a footman or butler to do the honors at the door, but the man who greets me with a smile and an extended hand is the *Hausherr* himself.

Bowing slightly, Graf von Trachtenberg says, "Welcome to our home, Herr *Botschaftsrat*."

"*Freut mich*, Graf von Trachtenberg, a pleasure to meet you," I answer and give him one of my sunny smiles.

We step into the vestibule, I shed my coat, and we stand facing each other for a moment of small talk.

Adalbert von Trachtenberg is a tall, trim man in the foothills of his seventies. Standing remarkably erect, especially for his age, he cuts an impressive figure with an angular face, straight Greek nose, and blueish-gray eyes. His shock of gray hair has been neatly parted down the middle. Speaking in a quiet yet clear voice, he conveys the authority of a self-assured man used to giving orders, a man accustomed to controlling himself and his surroundings. His clothing—well-pressed dark-gray slacks, lavender shirt, and canary-yellow bowtie, topped off with an elegant wine-colored velvet lounge jacket—reinforces the impression.

He leads me from the hallway into what he calls the salon, a generously sized sitting room, filled with an eclectic assortment of expensive-looking furnishings. Biedermeyer appears to be the dominant motif, though I catch sight of several items that look like eighteenth- and nineteenth-century French and English art. The whole thing whispers *money*. Old money and lots of it.

In one of the far corners, the lady of the house, Bettina von Trachtenberg, sits in a high-wing chair pouring tea for a dapper middle-aged man in a charcoal-gray suit. He has a thick crop of salt-and-gray hair and wears wire-rimmed glasses. Bettina introduces him as Jean-Luc de la Marre. The friend and dinner guest Kati had mentioned. The Geneva banker.

Bettina's hair is in a simple bun, her makeup is subdued, and her jewelry is limited to a multi-stranded pearl bracelet with a stunning diamond clasp. A woman with an aristocratic name, she looks the part, with none of her husband's touch of natty chic.

Introductions made, she invites me to a flowery sofa on her right; her husband sits down next to her, and she busies herself once again pouring tea. After the shock of my encounter with Trotter outside, I appreciate the calming atmosphere. It's hard to imagine danger in such a genteel environment. At least if you discount most of European history.

I'm staring at a painting, which has to be a Klimt, when I hear Bettina announce, "And here is Frau Willmans, my assistant."

Kati, looking great in an A-line skirt and black cashmere sweater, appears with trays of canapés and petit fours to go with the tea and cordials being passed around.

We smile demurely at each other. Seeing her improves my mood dramatically.

But then Hollander trots in, huffing, puffing, and abjectly apologizing for his tardiness. I can't help noticing that Trachtenberg barely acknowledges him, and that Bettina offers no more than a perfunctory nod.

The party is complete, and I wonder if the fun is about to start, even as the conversation continues to meander aimlessly for a while. Where I lived in the US, street demonstrations disrupting traffic near the Brandenburg Gate, dysfunctional municipal politics, the latest on Berlin's gay mayor, that sort of thing. When the talk finally gets around to Witty, everyone agrees about his sterling qualities and that his untimely demise—not to mention its deplorable circumstances—are an unspeakable tragedy.

Not a word thus far about plans for a memorial in his honor, the ostensible purpose of my visit.

It's Dwayne Hollander who's the first to turn the conversation in a more sensitive direction. Which does not surprise me. Unlike the tightly controlled Trachtenbergs, or the politely inscrutable banker, de la Marre, Hollander's shown visible impatience with our aimless tea-party gossip from the moment he walked into the room. A balding, overweight guy in his late sixties with a doughy face and bagged eyes denoting too much liquor and too many late nights, he tends to smile a lot. Toward me, it is a smile of arrogance and self-esteem—the smile of a bully. With Trachtenberg, he smiles a lot too, but when addressing his good friend "Adi," the smile suggests subservience.

Even before we get into the meat of the matter, I have come to two conclusions. Whatever has brought this odd pair together, it's clear who is top dog. And Trachtenberg doesn't like his American partner any better than I do.

De la Marre is telling us about Verbier, his favorite ski resort in the Valais, and has paused to reach for a smoked salmon canapé.

Hollander seizes the moment to change the subject, with all the subtlety of a Sherman tank. "So, Adam, who do the police think killed Witty? And why? What are they telling the embassy?" Leaning toward me, he makes each question sound like a challenge.

The conversation stops, and all eyes turn my way.

I've been faking interest in the Swiss banker's skiing stories while thinking about my encounter with Trotter thrashing around in the bushes. His appearance inside the Trachtenberg compound adds a new level of complexity that worries me.

Hollander's questions jar me back into the present, and they fit nicely into my plan for the evening, which is to pretend to know more than I do and to raise questions intended to pry up the rotting log under which this group is operating.

I give a conspiratorial look around, then lower my voice an octave, as if about to confide some vital piece of secret information.

"I shouldn't talk about it," I say. "But you being his friends, I suppose it's okay to tell you that the police suspect that someone wanted him dead and put out a contract on his life."

"*Lieber Gott*," Bettina says, shaking her head mournfully. "Who would do such a thing? Such a fine man."

Her husband agrees. "A fine man and an American patriot," he says. "My guess is that it was indeed a political assassination. Probably with a Communist angle."

"You may well be right," I nod. "I heard the authorities are looking in that direction. Witty was a true American patriot, indeed. And an unashamed nationalist, I might add. Foreign Service Officers are officially apolitical and nonpartisan, but he and I had many frank discussions."

I glance around, mostly for effect, then clear my throat, as if readying myself for the big reveal. "Hush-hush politics is definitely getting the investigators' top attention, though they're understandably very closemouthed about it," I say. "From the questions they've been asking, it looks to me that they're also following up two of the classic leads: sex and money."

I have turned to Trachtenberg to gauge his reaction, but it is Dwayne Hollander who jumps in with a quick laugh.

"Ridiculous," he snorts. "They're barking up the wrong tree. He was a gentleman and properly discreet about his private life, but it was perfectly correct and trouble-free. Sure, there were rumors about interests in another direction—if I may put it that way—but they were completely false. That always happens when a man's a bachelor."

No one seems inclined to pursue the subject, so I decide to poke a little further.

"That may not make much of an impression with the cops," I say. "Gay or straight, sex is always one of the first motives homicide investigators want to check off the list. I certainly have no reason to disagree with you, Dwayne, but it makes sense to me. Life is full of surprises. How can you be so sure about Witty?"

"Because he was my friend," Hollander says with a huff.

I nod thoughtfully, pretending to accept the answer, while trying to size up the rest of the room. Did Trachtenberg and de la Marre know that Hollander was lying through his teeth? According to Kranmüller, he knew all about Witty's connection to Antonia Holzapfel, and that his contact with the Albanians had come through her. Assuming they were all in on it, it would have been the reason they said nothing while Dwayne fed me a line.

Sensing a minefield all around me, I move on to other matters. "So, what about money?" I ask, looking toward Trachtenberg. "What's the likelihood that money's the motive?"

Once again, Trachtenberg keeps his silence, and Hollander rushes in.

"Out of the question. Witty was a committed public servant working for government pay. He didn't care about money, and he certainly didn't have any."

"Who knows? Maybe he did and just hid it?"

"Most unlikely," Hollander insists.

"I'm not so sure."

Trachtenberg looks up, and Hollander tenses. Both scrutinize my face closely.

"You worked with him. Why do you say that?" Hollander asks.

"Well, the last few months, Witty talked quite a bit about having made some real money. He said he was on his way to bankrolling a glorious retirement. I assumed he'd been playing the stock market, but then he mentioned a lucrative new job. Come to think of it, he said you were helping him line it up. Ring a bell, Dwayne?"

"Sure," he says, a bit hurriedly. "We talked about opportunities, and I gave him some leads. I told him that with his international experience and deep knowledge of Germany, he could have a bright future in transnational business. I promised to make some calls. Nothing specific had jelled, as far as I know. Anyway, he was still on the government payroll, right?"

"So, nothing firm yet, and no real money?"

"Obviously."

Another lie. Apparently, Hollander never imagined that Witty would have kept that offer letter anywhere it could have been found. And Kati had told me their business partnership had been openly discussed by the Trachtenbergs, yet no one's mentioning it now.

Hollander seems agitated now, glancing around at his coconspirators.

"Unless you know something we don't," he says. "I assume you were part of the team that went through his things. His files at the embassy, maybe at home?"

That is as direct a challenge as I've heard yet. Buying time to think about how to respond, I pick up the snifter of brandy I'd been nursing and sip from it pensively. "All US-classified material stayed with us," I say. "Everything else of possible interest was turned over to the investigators."

I have chosen my words carefully, hoping to both obfuscate and tantalize. Trachtenberg looks at me suspiciously, and Hollander scowls.

But it's de la Marre who speaks up. "Monsieur Emerson was my good friend," he explains, "and quite naturally, he did consult me occasionally about his finances. Without divulging any confidences, I can report that, to my knowledge, he had only limited investments, all held in the United States. Except for a Deutsche Bank checking account in Berlin. He was not a rich man. He occasionally expressed an interest about another account in Europe, but that was for after his retirement."

De la Marre seems to have chosen his words with as much care as I have. Whether such a European account actually exists, he's left unsaid.

The banker then rises from his seat, consults his watch, runs his hand through his hair, and turns toward me. "It was an honor to meet you, Mr. Jackson. A most interesting afternoon," he tells me. "Unfortunately, I must hurry to Tegel, else I miss my flight to Geneva. It's the last one this evening."

Crossing to Bettina, he bends and gallantly air-kisses her hand, old-world style.

"*A bientôt, chérie,*" he tells her. "*Merci, mille fois.* Another instance of your exquisite hospitality."

Trachtenberg also stands. "It's almost seven," he says, sounding oddly relieved. "Thank you, Mr. Jackson, for giving us so much of your valuable time. What you have told us will be very helpful for planning a suitable memorial for our friend. May we be in touch if we have further questions?"

Trachtenberg is seeing his guests off in the foyer, but I excuse myself to visit the washroom at the end of the hallway. I need privacy to text Tommy and tell him that I'm coming out. I haven't forgotten that long walk in the dark to the street, and I need him to guard against any funny business as I'm exiting.

I step in and am surrounded by marble and mirrors and elegant fittings. But before I can close the door behind me, there's a sudden shove against it from the other side. I let go, take a step back, and am stunned to see Kati stepping in behind me. She locks us in, puts a finger to her mouth to signal silence, and maneuvers me into a corner, as far away from the hallway as possible.

We're standing close together, almost touching, and it's a great feeling, especially after the last hour with Trachtenberg and his cronies.

She searches my face and smiles at me faintly, but only for a moment.

"Talk quietly," she whispers.

"Is this a date?"

She shakes her head, not smiling. "A warning. You handled it well in there. But now be careful. This is a complex situation. More than you think. They want to use you, and they're not your friends."

"What else do you know?"

"Just that. To make you understand. There's no more time."

She hugs me, then turns and puts her ear to the door, eyes closed.

There are voices nearby, and my mind races.

"What's our story if they catch us coming out together?" But she's way ahead of me.

She opens the door wide, steps out, and announces in a loud voice, "Not to worry, just leave the aspirin bottle on that little shelf. No problem; you're welcome, Mr. Jackson."

Chapter 19

Berlin

Sunday, November 12

*E*ither Kati's gutsy play has worked, or no one noticed in the first place.

When I step out to take my leave, Trachtenberg is being a model of polite cordiality and insists—absolutely insists—that I stay for a light supper, *en famille.* "A quick *Imbiss*," a snack.

He'd probably planned it all along, but it occurs to me that this might actually turn out to be the most interesting part of the visit. So, Kati's warning notwithstanding, I accept. I didn't think breaking bread at the Trachtenbergs' supper table carried much risk.

8:45 p.m.

Trachtenberg leads me up a richly carpeted staircase to his second-floor library.

A fireplace to the right of the entrance has a crackling fire going in it, with two leather armchairs in front of it and a coffee table between them. Over the mantle, an oversized oil painting of a helmeted Prussian soldier brandishing a saber atop his galloping horse dominates the room. The walls and floor-to-ceiling bookcases are of an exotic, dark wood I've never seen before.

He waves me to one of the club chairs and takes the other.

"This is where I spend much of my time," he tells me. "It's my favorite room in the house. My Shangri-la."

"Who's the rider?" I ask, pointing to the Prussian warrior towering over us.

Trachtenberg, who has busied himself meticulously filtering coffee from a silver urn into two small cups, continues the ritual and answers without looking up.

"Adalbert Wilhelm Lutz von Trachtenberg, my great-great-grandfather. A soldier who led a regiment of East Prussian Cuirassiers during the Napoleonic Wars. Fought at Jena, Stralsund, and under Gneisenau at Kolberg. The Prussian king rewarded him with the first tract of land that became Gut Königsglück, our family home for generations. It's near Osterode in Ostpreussen. Not far from Allenstein, if that geography means anything to you. Poland now. We lost it in '45. I was born there."

He pauses and grimaces slightly before handing me my demitasse. I sense that the subject means more to him than he is letting on.

With the room in semi-darkness, the flames in the fireplace give off a warm glow and light up our faces. We are finishing our coffee when Trachtenberg suddenly suggests first names. Do I mind?

An unexpected proposal I hadn't seen coming. In Germany, people who have just met rarely go to first names, especially not older people, and certainly not in the circles the Trachtenbergs move in. Coming from Adi, this is a surprise. But Adi and Adam it will be, I'd agreed, though my internal defenses are on alert.

He brings his cup to the lips and drains the last of the coffee.

"So, first of all, Adam," he continues, "thank you for agreeing to stay. In the privacy of my library, we can speak frankly. That will be helpful—under the circumstances. To both of us. If you know what I mean."

My stomach tightens. "Certainly, Adi," is all I say, cordially.

I could see now that the afternoon and dinner had merely been the prelude for the main event in his library. But what is his game? Does he plan to sweet-talk me, or to squeeze and threaten me somehow? Am I perhaps even in danger of becoming his prisoner up here? All kinds of scenarios flash through my mind. Suddenly, the weight of the LCP in my jacket pocket has a comforting feel to it.

What comes next is anything but threatening, however. He reaches for a handsome crystal decanter on a small table next to him and carefully pours us generous portions of its contents into matching crystal snifters.

"Cognac?" he asks.

"*Dankeschön*, and I like your beautiful glassware," I say.

"Waterford Lismore crystal. A Christmas gift from Bettina."

He lifts his glass to the nose, closes his eyes, and slowly samples the aroma. He is taking his time. I watch him in fascination, then decide to imitate the ritual and perform the same smell test.

"I hope you like it. It's a Brisson Napoléon, *ier cruier*," he notes, and makes a show of watching me take my first sip.

I'm not much for telling one cognac from another, but it isn't the moment to say so. So, I take my time, coaxing the Napoléon around in my mouth before downing it, and then gently let my tongue caress my upper lip before nodding my approval.

"Extraordinary," I nod.

"A good brandy demands a good cigar," he replies. "I'm told you're a smoker."

"You're well informed. Who told you?"

"One hears things," he says. He lets me select a Churchill-size Cohiba from a humidor sitting on a silver tray and hands me a cigar cutter and a box of matches the size of chopsticks.

"Hmm. A Cohiba. What a treat," I rejoice.

Actually, I consider Cohibas an overpriced cult brand for cigar snobs. When word got around years ago that Fidel Castro smoked them, they quickly became the most sought-after Cuban brand in the world. And, of course, also the most expensive. I much prefer my Montecristos, but am not about to tell him that.

Adi clearly is in love with his Cohiba, and I watch him, spellbound, as he prepares his smoke. This is serious business for him. First, he slowly and meticulously snips off the end of the cigar and rolls it between thumb and index finger while lovingly examining his handiwork. The cigar seems to fascinate him. Lighting up, he draws the air in slowly with his eyes half closed, holds it for a few seconds, and then blows a stream of cigar smoke into the air. This is followed by another deep drag, again exhaling the smoke very slowly.

The entire ceremony from decanting the Napoléon to the Cohibas has taken the better part of ten minutes and commanded Trachtenberg's undivided attention.

Seeing him so intensely focused on these earthly pleasures is hard to square with any fear of impending violence and physical danger. That reassures me, and it reveals a whole new and softer side of this man. This wasn't the austere, poker-faced Adalbert von Trachtenberg of this afternoon. Up here in his library, I am seeing an unabashed epicure who likes top-of-the-line luxury and takes evident delight in feasting on its finest gifts.

He throws a fresh log on the fire and leans in to coax it alive. When he turns back to speak to me again, his fingers grip the sides of his chair, his thin lips revealing a set of perfectly white teeth, incongruously so for a man his age. His eyes have once again taken on the steely, forbidding quality I had seen before.

"I've been thinking about our mutual friend," he says. "Witty loved his profession, didn't he, Adam? I admired him for that. But to tell the truth, I pitied him too."

"For being a diplomat?" I laugh. "I can understand that. A gypsy life and low pay? All true. Or was it because you're one of those people who thinks diplomacy is a profession where they pay you to lie for a living?"

"It's not that," he says. "I know yours is an honorable profession, but these days, you're being asked to do the impossible. You're supposed to manage a world that is dying from within, and you're doomed to failure."

"You're right; our so-called rules-based world's a mess," I say. "Many countries have problems. For sure, the US. Europe as well. And I grant you that the institutions that are supposed to make the global system function need a lot of work. But it's not hopeless; give it time."

Trachtenberg won't let it go and shakes his head sorrowfully. "I'm not exaggerating," he says. "You need to see things the way they really are, Adam.

"The old order, the one based on democracy, liberalism, and open borders America set up after the war was held together by the Soviet threat, singular US military power, and lots of your dollars. People had jobs, living standards were rising, and voters, by and large, were content. The world was in equilibrium.

"But that world is gone. All that modern microchip technology destroyed it. They say change is a good thing because it's equated with progress. But that's not always true. Change can also be unhealthy and have the opposite effect."

"I see your point," I interject. "It's true that even where change leads to progress, it's usually not made without pain and inconvenience. There are always winners and losers. However, even if not all changes lead to progress, more often they do, so that's not an argument against change per se. Look at how much better off than past generations we are in our living standards, health, and well-being, and in the opportunity for greater happiness and a better life. In any case, technological change—whether it's the steam engine or the microchip—can't be held back. It happens when it happens."

"You misunderstand me," Adi says. "I know that we have to live in the world as it is and that modern technology has its benefits. I know we can't prohibit modernity. What I'm saying is that we need a different form of governance for the world of today and tomorrow. Because what's going on today isn't working and will destroy us."

"Explain that to me," I say. "What exactly will destroy us? New ways of governing—what do you suggest?"

He seems to welcome the question. "Look around you," he says. "It's right before your eyes. Parliaments are floundering and helpless. Politics are polarized and politicians are paralyzed. Your own country is a prime example. Cities deteriorate, public services are failing, infrastructure is crumbling, and crime is out of control. Meanwhile, jobs vanish across our borders, taxes keep rising, and incomes stagnate. For some people, they are falling.

"Western liberal democracies are consumed by political infighting that doesn't get anywhere.

"Polarization and paralysis are everywhere, including between us. Inaction and political mismanagement in one country spills across our borders, and our elected officials haven't the power to defend our people from the effects. Think of the dot-com crisis and the Lehman Brothers debacle in the US. Your congress, facing election every two years, is too divided to act decisively, and when it impacts us, our politicians are just as helpless. Competitive trade wars where each country tries to export its problems to the others make things only worse and help the Chinese play one democracy against the other.

"That's why ordinary people are rightfully scared, angry, and in a rebellious mood. They see uncontrolled numbers of illegals of alien ethnicities, races, religions, and cultures flood across their borders and correctly sense that when you no longer have a cohesive nation with common traditions, you have nothing."

"Democracy is always messy," I say.

"No," he says. "Democracy is obsolete."

His tone was chilly. I look at him, and suddenly I see the face of aristocrat enablers who'd thought the Nazi dictator a useful idiot, a means to an end.

There was a lot of passion in his lengthy speech, but the effect appears to have tired him. Trachtenberg stares wordlessly at me for several seconds while I try to process what I heard.

His half-smoked cigar has gone out, and he picks up one of the giant matches and focuses on relighting it, refills his glass, and does the same for me. When he looks at me again, a tight little smile curls around his lips.

"Have I persuaded you?" he asks.

I decide this isn't a question to tackle directly; he probably knows the answer anyway. "I don't need persuading about dysfunctional governments," I answer. "You've laid the problems out pretty well, though you certainly made good on your promise to paint in stark colors. These are big questions, but I don't see any good answers we can agree on. This newly wired global world of ours is pretty new. We'll need time to learn how to manage it. Sometimes—if answers are elusive—it pays to live with the questions for a while."

Trachtenberg shakes his head. "Why wait?" he asks. "Some realities are beyond dispute, and the pure and simple truth is that the failure of liberal democracy is one of them."

"I'm not so sure," I reply, still trying to be diplomatic. "One thing you learn in my business: the truth is rarely pure and never simple. Twenty-first-century modernity is full of contradictions and knotty challenges, but why blame democracy for that? It's just that it's complicated. I like what Churchill said about that: 'democracy is the worst form of government—except for all others.'"

Adi gestures dismissively. "I've heard that before," he says. "A long time ago, Homer, a wiser man, more aptly observed that 'a state cannot be governed when there are too many in authority.' That's as true today as when it appeared in *The Iliad*.

"As to equality—I don't agree either. All men are not created equal. The accident of birth matters. One man, one vote leads to the tyranny of the majority. Your own Mr. Hamilton called 'the people' a great beast. The average person spending most of his free time watching soccer or reading trash—if he reads at all—doesn't know a lot. It certainly doesn't guarantee personal freedom. The majority gave the most votes to Hitler. There was more freedom of thought and personal freedom in Wilhelmine Germany."

I have been listening to him closely. His voice is calm and his tone dispassionate, as if he is merely stating the most obvious and incontrovertible fact of life. He isn't debating or looking for an argument. His mind is made up, and I am startled. People don't generally come right out and tell you that universal suffrage is for the birds. I can see now that Trachtenberg is a close-minded zealot with unshakably undemocratic convictions, and he wants me to know it.

The question still is: Why? Does he realize that I know about his involvement in a conspiracy to put these ideas into practice? I am getting nervous again. It's getting late, and I decide it's time to let him get to the heart of the matter.

"I am impressed by the strength of your convictions," I tell him, "but you may have a distorted view of democracy. You describe a form of majority rule unchecked by laws. That's not the reality. In the US, for example, there are institutions that protect the rights of the minority. Our constitution guarantees the rule of law and limits what you call the tyranny of the majority. Germany's *Verfassung* contains analogous guarantees. Besides, there is also an important ethical and moral foundation to democratic governance.

"But leaving all that aside for the moment, analyzing a problem is one thing; coming up with a practical policy prescription for solving it is another. We know of the ones that have been tried and were disastrous failures, like the various forms of authoritarian dictatorships: communism, fascism, the Nazis' murderous racial nationalism. North Korean family despotism. Absolute monarchies too. I don't suppose you're advocating any of these. So, what's your idea?"

"A system in which power is returned to a smaller number of decisive leaders at the top."

"What kind of leaders?" I ask.

"Tradition-minded patriots chosen not by the masses, but selected from a natural aristocracy of men grounded in virtue and talent."

In full flight now, he grips my elbow and points to the ancestral horseman towering over our heads.

"Let me tell you about Gut Königsglück," he says. "My father was killed in the great tank battle at Kursk in '43, so when we had to abandon the Trachtenberg family home of six generations in '45, my eldest brother put me on his horse and we rode away, with the Bolsheviks on our tail. Left everything behind. It took us two weeks to get to the west.

"The Prussian king gave Adalbert Wilhelm five hundred hectares in the eighteenth century, and over the years, the estate grew to about four thousand, with three villages and close to a thousand souls. That's how we farmed the land. It included a brick factory and a brewery. In winter, we made straw mats and sold them in the area. There were many estates like ours all over that part of Prussia. Life was in balance. No liberal democracy, but no one questioned who was in charge, and the people were content. When there were problems, the *Gutsherr* presided over a meeting to find a solution, and when the government interfered, he went to Potsdam to negotiate with the king's ministers and officials, people just like him. I know we can't recreate that today, but it may be a model to learn from."

I try hard to keep a respectful tone, but it is difficult. "You're suggesting that eighteenth- and nineteenth-century absolute monarchies can be a model for today?"

"With important adaptations, why not?" He shrugs.

"For a million reasons. For one thing, because your picture of life in the time of your Prussian ancestors is a nostalgic fantasy. Nostalgia can be a seductive liar, Adi. Ordinary life wasn't in balance, as you put it. That's why there were bloody revolutions all through that period—people chafing under political and economic inequality that reduced them to cattle, demanding their individual rights. That's what the French and American revolutions were all about.

"Your startling position isn't widely shared, to put it mildly. How would you ever get agreement to scrap universal suffrage and go back to your kind of world?"

"Don't underestimate the mood for change today," Trachtenberg insists. "People are less attached to liberal democracy than you think. They want results, and if a different form of political leadership at the top protects their jobs and their culture, they'll back it. Strong leaders intelligently chosen can learn from the past and preserve what works."

"There'd be blood in the streets."

He shrugs. "In revolutions, there are always casualties, but there are ways to encourage such changes peacefully. I hate violence. In fact, I dread it. I'm a peaceful man, just a concerned old-fashioned conservative."

"No, you're not," I say, looking straight at him. "You're a reactionary extremist, Adi."

"Why?" he asks, sounding surprised.

"A conservative wants to defend the status quo and slow down change, but he works within the system. You want to overthrow the system and turn the clock back to a past colored by your wishes and romantic illusions. That's reactionary. You're also willing to use any means. That's extremist."

I don't think Adi von Trachtenberg likes the characterization very much. At any rate, he isn't smiling when he turns to look at me again, and his voice sounds cold. "It's late," he says.

I glance at my watch. "I know," I say. "It's after eleven; I really must go." But Adi waves me back.

"There's something I want to ask you," he says. "It won't take long."

He pauses to give me a mendacious smile. "We have talked frankly tonight, and that is a good thing. It avoids wrong ideas and misunderstandings," he begins.

"Wrong ideas?"

"You understand that this talk about political reform is entirely theoretical at this point. There are like-minded friends on both sides of the pond interested in the topic. We exchange thoughts and occasionally we get together to discuss them, that's all. Seminars, lectures, literature review, that sort of thing. Perhaps you've heard about it from Witty, who was a member of our group and a link to American friends.

"He'd had some files to share with us from his last trip to the US and planned to bring them to the dinner the night he was killed. So, here's what I would like to know: Was anything like that found in his apartment?"

"What kind of files?"

"I'm not sure. Could be position papers and program notes." He hesitates and shoots me a questioning look before adding, "Also, financial material and bank statements, perhaps. He was our treasurer. We collect membership dues, and he kept the records."

Trachtenberg was none too subtle as he probed. Obviously, this whole evening had been designed to soften me up.

"I can't answer your question," I tell him. "If they found anything like that, they wouldn't necessarily have told me."

"Weren't you personally involved in the search? You must know quite a bit."

"You're well informed," I say. "Unfortunately, nothing I saw fits your description. You'd have to ask the embassy and the *Polizei* directly."

This time he just stares at me coldly, then says, "That's too bad. I was really hoping you might be able to help us."

"Sorry to disappoint you. I can see that this must be very important material. For some people. Since you know about my part in the search, you may also have heard that someone tried to mug me that night. What do you think? A connection?"

Perhaps I had played him a surprise card of my own, but he doesn't blink. Not for a second. "Absolutely not," he says. "I hadn't heard about that, but it has to have been a coincidence."

"And then there was Witty's murder. Also a tragic coincidence?" I say it in an offhand way, but don't mind sounding a touch sarcastic.

It evidently isn't something Trachtenberg is anxious to pursue, but he does have a parting message of his own.

He continues his cold stare. "It's a dangerous world, Adam. I'm glad you weren't hurt. You're a very intelligent man, and you must take good care of yourself. There are a lot of bad people out on the street these days. Even in Berlin."

His tone is friendly, but his voice flat, and his eyes cold again.

And his message crystal clear.

My host insists on walking me to the gate. The street is dark, and I can't see Trachtenberg's face when Börries plants his massive frame in front of him.

"*Guten Abend, Herr Graf,*" he says in his gravelly voice, and doesn't budge until I am safely inside the car.

I'm pretty sure Adi got the message too.

Chapter 20

Washington, DC

Tuesday, November 14

7:50 a.m.

*D*eep into northwest Washington, the SUV turns into a cul-de-sac a block off McArthur Boulevard, then makes a right into the driveway of an unremarkable two-story colonial. The only distinguishing characteristic of No. 6 Potomac Lane is the intricate electronic surveillance and control system hidden behind a hedge. The driver slows briefly to allow an invisible tripwire to identify him and to deactivate the hidden fencing and alarm devices, then moves forward slowly before coming to a stop outside a screened porch at the back of the house.

For mid-November, it is an unseasonably mild morning, the temperature in the midfifties, bright sunshine, and only a light horizontal layer of stratus clouds across a cornflower-blue sky.

The heavily armored transport is ten minutes early, but the deputy director of operations (DDO), Richard S. Brewster III, chief of the CIA's directorate of clandestine operations, hurries from the house and clambers aboard. Though not in the best of moods after a restless night, and up since dawn ruminating about his German problem, he is eager to get to his morning meeting. Jack Furuno, his main security man, takes his usual place in the back seat next to him, and a second agent sits in front riding shotgun. The driver reverses the SUV, pulls back into the street, and heads south on McArthur Boulevard, across Chain Bridge to the Virginia side of the Potomac, then inches his way into the southbound traffic on Route 123.

The commute is bumper-to-bumper, but Brewster, lost in thought, hardly notices. They are on a direct course for the CIA's vast Langley campus, but this morning the driver passes it by. A few miles farther, at Tyson's Corner, suburban sprawl gives way to the bucolic Virginia countryside, traffic eases, and the SUV picks up speed.

Some fifteen miles southwest of Langley, they turn into a cheerless strip mall with the usual array of stores—supermarket, nail salon, Walgreens Pharmacy, Domino's Pizza, Burger King—and stops in front of a plain two-story office building at the far end, next to a car wash. A large black-and-gold sign over the entrance identifies the tenant as "Exeter-Humble, Inc." and its business as "Commercial Real Estate."

Brewster's security team walks ahead of him into the building, which belongs to the CIA's inventory of under-the-radar fronts and safe houses sprinkled throughout the Washington suburbs. A uniformed guard behind a glass partition stands to work the security mechanism that lets Brewster and his entourage pass. At the end of a secure second-floor hallway, Furuno punches numbers into a wall panel and activates the electronic lock with his ID tag. The door swings open, and the DDO walks into a windowless room with bare-bones furnishings in a style mixing Ikea chic with government drab. A conference table with chairs stands in the center, a console with drinks and glasses against a wall, and in one of the corners a small seating arrangement with a coffee table. For no apparent reason, framed photographs on the walls depict snowy alpine landscapes.

Brewster had chosen this venue sight-unseen because of its remoteness, and he now realizes his mistake. This is not the congenial environment suited to assuage the no-doubt bruised feelings of his visitor.

George Hartfield, alias Mortimer McLean, slouches on a sofa by the coffee table. When he looks up from his copy of *The Washington Post*, he isn't smiling.

"To what the fuck do I owe the pleasure?" he growls.

———

During four decades of service at Langley and in the field, Rick Brewster had gradually ascended the ladder to the top of the clandestine service. At the comparatively advanced age of sixty-three, he is somewhat of a rarity among the current professional leadership of the CIA, the barons who wielded the real power. Recruited in the year Jimmy Carter had moved into the White House and installed an ex-Navy admiral named Stansfield Turner, Brewster had outlasted not only Stan Turner, but the dozen or so hapless directors who followed him. Not to mention as many operational failures and debacles that had led most of the Agency's best and brightest to decamp for greener pastures.

Brewster was a third-generation Princetonian, and it was in that ivy-enriched environment that he'd been recruited toward the end of his senior year, seduced by the promise of a life of glamour and excitement in service to the country. The Agency paid scant attention in those days to politically correct notions of gender and race when trolling for the highest potential recruits. Unlike today, advertising for applicants was frowned upon, and "the most desirable targets" filtered up through an old boys' network, a process shrouded in mystery.

A faculty member with a line into the Agency kept a lookout for promising prospects among graduating seniors, then passed the word back to Langley. Following discreet preliminary vetting of background and suitability, of which the subject was rarely aware, the first contact was then initiated via some well-known, respected figure to impress the target. If he passed preliminary muster, the more intense, lengthy dance of hush-hush testing and interviews at various off-campus locations would ensue.

With a major in politics, a knack for foreign languages, varsity lacrosse, and a decent game of tennis, Brewster had been a natural to be fingered as a prize prospect. The senior partner of a white-shoe Washington law firm, a well-known Princetonian who also happened to be an alumnus of The Ivy, Brewster's eating club, was dispatched to the campus to take a closer look. Initially, he'd cornered Brewster at an Old Boys homecoming evening, and followed it up a week later with a three-hour lunch, *à deux*, in a quiet corner of the Metropolitan Club in New York City.

Against the promise of a life of risk and adventure, manning the ramparts against the nation's enemies in foreign lands, the tamer alternative of a career on Wall Street or in the law hadn't stood a chance with young Rick Brewster. The Ivy's alum, a veteran of top jobs in prior administrations with a national reputation for patriotic probity, had let it be known that service to country in the elite outfit in question was, in his opinion, a Princetonian's noble calling.

And wasn't their alma mater's motto: "In the Nation's Service"?

The sour mood of his man in Berlin didn't surprise the DDO. He had ordered him home for an immediate debriefing without prior warning, knowing full well that Hartfield would resent it. For one thing, he'd have a lot of explaining to do about his operational plan, which had gone nowhere, and Hartfield's well-developed ego didn't mesh with admissions of failure. For another, because of the short notice, he'd been forced to rush back on a commercial flight without first-class seating, which Hartfield, who hated transatlantic flying and was entitled to premium travel, undoubtedly considered a loathsome imposition.

The DDO and his Berlin emissary had been partners over many decades in any number of operations in world trouble spots, from Berlin to Baghdad and Vienna to Karachi. Over the years, their youthful exuberance for the work had given way to a jaded, cynical, yet still grudging loyalty to the outfit that bound them together. They trusted and respected each other, but it was a complicated relationship—at times cooperative, at times competitive. Brewster, actively wooed into the service from an elite university and with a private income to supplement his government paycheck, had joined up for the romance of adventure. Hartfield, of humbler background, had aggressively lobbied to get in because the CIA's culture of intrigue and deception suited his personality. He also appreciated a steady job with excellent benefits.

They were a study of opposites. With the easy charm and self-confidence of a man secure in his station and comfortable in his skin, the DDO preferred subtle deviousness and the avoidance of unnecessary rough stuff in the field. Hartfield, with a chip on his shoulder, cared little about such niceties and prided himself for having the toughness of an aggressive risk taker needed to get the job done.

In their standing within the Agency and advancement toward the choicer assignments, the difference in backgrounds had always been a significant but unspoken factor. Brewster correctly suspected that his making it to DDO, a career crown that had eluded

Hartfield, continued to haunt his friend.

In keeping with his "outsider" edge, Hartfield had shown up this morning needing a shave, wearing the same tan corduroys and blue workman's shirt he'd worn on the plane. Brewster wore the navy-blue suit, white shirt, French cuffs, and bright yellow tie of the ultimate insider.

Taking a chair opposite Hartfield, the DDO amiably rests his tasseled Ferragamos alongside Hartfield's Crocs and says, "Sorry to put you through all this, but I really had no choice." His voice is as soothing as a barrelful of scented liquid soap.

"The hell you did," Hartfield answers. "Where the fuck's the fire? I was in the middle of stuff. We could have done this over the phone."

The DDO shakes his head. "Not this time, unfortunately. There have been developments here. Not good ones, and we need to come up with something new, and fast."

"Bullshit. It's working, if you don't fuck it up by second-guessing me. I told you I was in the middle of things."

"It's too late for that, George."

"I need another week or ten days, max."

"We don't have a week. This can blow any day now."

"Goddammit, Rick. You're the one who sweet-talked me into coming out of retirement to handle this thing for you. You said I should do it my way. We had a deal, and you promised me full support. Unlimited funding from one of your little black cash drawers and no questions asked, remember? Then you pull me back without warning, or explanation, on that shitty United flight. In coach, for Chrissakes. I'm too old for this shit. You want me to go home and send someone else? Be my guest."

Brewster shakes his head and gives a little smile. "Of course not, George. No one can pull this off except you. I have full confidence in you."

"Fuck you," Hartfield says and looks away.

"Come on, partner," the DDO says. "I understand how you feel, and I don't blame you . . ."

"So?"

"You're not a quitter, George. You're better than that. And as you're about to find out, we're up against it."

Hartfield returns an ill-humored look and says nothing. The DDO is right, and he knows it. He's lost control over Jackson, the young American diplomat, and the plan to use him to crack the German conspirators is going nowhere. His grievance act is partly to keep his boss on the defensive, and partly wounded pride.

For about a half hour, they play the game: Hartfield venting, the DDO mollifying and flattering. Eventually, Hartfield runs out of steam and is ready to turn the page.

"So, what in hell is going on, Rick?" he asks. Then he listens quietly as the DDO fills him in.

Twenty minutes into the briefing, Brewster pushes his chair closer, leans toward Hartfield, and says, "So, let's be clear, George. The intel is this thing may be imminent, and if they find out the truth around here about how Emerson got himself killed, not to mention the truth about Trotter, it's going to be another Bay of Pigs moment. Right up there with letting Bin Laden escape at Bora Bora. And this White House hates us on a good day. Exposure would mean not just the end for you and me, but maybe the whole damn Agency shuttered."

Brewster pauses, giving Hartfield a long stare of genuine desperation. "We need ideas," he says. "I'll authorize anything. Whatever the risk, I don't care. Carte blanche."

Hartfield stares back.

"You mean that? Anything goes?"

"We've got no choice."

"Hmm," Hartfield says. "I can work with that."

Noon

"What I still don't understand," Hartfield says, "is why the pressure to pull the trigger now? This has been building for months. Why the rush?"

"POTUS," Brewster says.

"How d'you figure?"

"Reading between the lines, it's pretty simple," Brewster explains. "Poggi and the DNI are his lackeys, terrified they're going to be next administration hoo hah's to get the boot. But they're also feeling the FBI's pressure to move quickly. The Bureau thinks these bastards are dangerous and have to be eliminated. Plus, they think they've fixed on a Day X to pull the trigger and activate 'Thunderclap' soon. Trouble is, some of them are big money backers. POTUS may not even know about them yet, and if he finds out, he might well say 'lay off.' That's why the Bureau wants to move ASAP."

"And we're holding the missing piece," Hartfield says.

The DDO shrugs. "They want more US names and a fix on Thunderclap's international connection. Emerson was the guy they were counting on to lead us there, and we were supposed to deliver him. If they find out that we're the ones that got him killed, God help us."

Hartfield stands up and starts pacing the room. "Can't we stall a little longer?"

Brewster shakes his head. "They've booked the Situation Room for a full NSC deputies' review with all the bells and whistles. The Bureau will bring their guys Hinton and Castelyou back from Berlin for that, and they'd like nothing better than to screw us. They know Jackson hasn't worked out. They'll insist we produce Trotter and will want to know why we've had him under wraps. Castelyou hates him and will squeeze him, and Trotter will either take a powder, or he'll know the game is up and try to make a deal.

Castelyou has excellent relations with the German cops, and they will have fed him all they know. None of it good for us. Especially when they find out we've been working off the books.

"The only chance we have is to shut it down in Berlin before that meeting. If we can deliver them the names they want and the overseas connection so they can crush Thunderclap, we'll be in the clear. No one will care why and how Emerson was killed. That'll be collateral damage, and Trotter could be dealt with quietly. But that begs the question: How do we shut this down in Berlin?"

Hartfield gives a self-satisfied smile and says, "I think it's pretty obvious."

"What?"

"Trotter."

Brewster stares blankly. "Trotter, what?"

"Jackson didn't work as bait, so we plug in Trotter. If we're right about him, he's got the right entrée into that German gang. And in his case, participation won't be voluntary. Carte blanche, you said? I'll sit down for a long, intimate talk with him. I've got two fellows in mind who can hold up our end of the conversation. Trotter will have no choice but to learn their language. Shouldn't take long."

Brewster keeps staring. Then he smiles.

"Lunchtime," he says.

Chapter 21

Berlin

Tuesday, November 14

10:00 a.m.

Dwayne Hollander warily eyes the Stoli bottle atop the liquor cabinet. His head aches, and he's fighting intermittent waves of nausea.

"Bad idea," he mutters. He bites off a piece of buttered toast and washes it down with a swig of tomato juice. For a short moment he stares morosely at the half-empty glass in his hand, then sucks in his breath, makes a face, and reaches for the vodka. "One Bloody Mary to clear my head," he announces resolutely, to no one in particular. He is the only one in the room.

Eodosia, the Portuguese maid, has conveniently stocked the breakfast table with the fixings before leaving for her morning shopping. He spices the juice cum Stoli with a liberal slug of Worcestershire sauce, squeezes in a lime, drops in ice cubes, and stirs the mixture with his index finger, which he then subjects to an epicurean taste test. "That should do it," he announces.

That morning, he awakened late, an unhappy man with a giant hangover from the previous night's session with the unpleasant "Herr Z." There is also the petty annoyance of an email just received from Frances, his wife, back in Baltimore. She was extending her stay to enjoy being a grandmother. It irritated him, not so much because he wanted her close to him—that sort of thing had long since receded into the rearview mirror—but because he missed her managing his creature comforts and shielding him from Eodosia's little kitchen crises.

The situation with Herr Z, the boss of the Hassani organization—he'd never been able to pin down his actual name—was infinitely more worrisome. Z had insisted on the meeting, and Hollander had reserved a private room at the China Club behind the Adlon for their confab. His hope had been that the club's posh surroundings would put Z into a conciliatory mood. But though the dark-eyed, sallow-faced Albanian with abominable table manners had stuffed himself noisily and consumed prodigious quantities of schnapps with beer chasers, nothing had softened his crude threats. If anything, it had emboldened him to insist, in even more vulgar language, that he wanted the promised money that week, and that the cops sniffing around might need to be taken care of "more directly."

It worries Hollander that this will have to be the main topic of conversation with Adi von Trachtenberg that evening, with the strong likelihood of an unpleasant disagreement on what to do about it. What he craves more than anything is Adi's respect, not his tongue-lashing and reproval. As far as he is concerned, it all comes down on how to handle that snooty embassy cookie-pusher Jackson. This is the crux of their problem, and dealing with him effectively is definitely the key to resolving it.

Emboldened by the taste of his rapidly disappearing cocktail,

Hollander pours himself a couple of follow-up jiggers of vodka, tosses them back, and waits for the desired effect. Booze is his reliable remedy, and as it eases the previous night's hangover, it does the same for his sour mood. He pushes back from the breakfast table, maneuvers himself into the recliner by the fireplace, and further contemplates the problem. There is an answer to everything, he reassures himself. All it takes is some creative thinking.

His first visit to Berlin almost twenty years ago, invited by German tablemates from a five-star European cruise, had been a spur-of-the-moment decision, an afterthought.

The Wall had come down and Berlin was jumping, vibrant and bursting with energy—building cranes everywhere, top shopping, and great restaurants. What had hooked him, though, was the social scene they had fallen into during their stay. Some were real aristocrats, rich but with status beyond money, the kind of crowd far beyond his reach in the US.

To settle in Berlin was the best decision he'd ever made. He'd established a connection with the Rickenbom companies—a Texas-based, family-owned mini-conglomerate of drilling equipment businesses—and built himself a lucrative Berlin-based agency representing them in Europe. Then several other companies with complementary product lines had come along, and now he was rolling in it.

But beyond that, Hank Rickenbom had brought him into a circle of like-minded Texans and Oklahomans who were the kind of rich, tough, fiercely independent-minded entrepreneurs Hollander admired. If being with them included adopting their implacable opposition to anything they considered infringement on their freedom to pursue unenlightened self-interest, then so be it.

Eventually, the circle expanded to include people like the von Trachtenbergs and their upper-crust German friends—not as rich as his American partners, but with an old-money cachet he found irresistible. They had the same contempt for democratic culture and values, but coming not so much from an acquisitive instinct as from nostalgia for the authoritarian world of their ancestors.

How could it all have gone so wrong?

He leans into the recliner and lets his mind drift back to the beginning, when Hank Rickenbom had first invited him to join The Group. No question, the timing for a move was absolutely right. Events were evolving their way, not only in the US, but also in Europe. Authoritarians were in place in Poland and Hungary, with perceptible stirrings from the new ultra-right even in Germany. It was only when he'd brought in that rat, Witty Emerson, that things had hit the skids.

Then again, if not for "Strangefoot"—it was Hollander who had thought of that code name—they might never have known about the potential disaster they could have faced. They'd dodged that bullet, but now they absolutely had to take decisive action. The stakes were enormous, but so were the possibilities. Surely Adi would see that. How to put it to him and bring him around to accept what had to be done—that was the real question. The man is stubborn as hell, but ultimately, he is tough and nobody's fool.

Hollander pads off to relieve his bladder. When he returns, he feels better. Having pondered the issue, he can see the light at the end of the tunnel, and his mind turns to laying out the coming evening's line of attack.

By five that afternoon, the last of a weak November sun has vanished behind a dark and threatening cloud cover. As twilight turns to dusk, a damp, cold wind starts blowing from the east, and the blackening sky blitzes with flashes of light in the distance. An approaching thunderstorm hangs in the air.

Trachtenberg, already wearing a floppy rain hat and a padded greatcoat, meets him at the door and hands him a rolled-up umbrella, insisting that they talk in the garden. This isn't at all the setting Hollander is prepared for, especially with only a thin top-coat to protect him.

For the next twenty minutes, they tap their way along the wooded path around the villa in increasing darkness, Hollander talking earnestly in low tones, making his case to Trachtenberg, who listens but never says a word.

They are coming up to the kitchen door in back of the house, about to embark on their third circuit around, when Hollander decides to push the envelope for the reaction he's been waiting for. Stopping dead in his tracks, he turns toward Trachtenberg and says: "So the good news is that Strangefoot has taken soundings on the other side. He reports that the moment is right to seize the initiative and get it done. We don't have a choice anyway, and he counsels us to be quick and decisive. Also, he knows Jackson and thinks he'll fold like a paper napkin if handled the right way. It's what I think also, Adi. Is that your view as well?"

Trachtenberg starts to reply, but his words are drowned out by a sudden flash of lightning, followed almost immediately by deafening thunder. Before they can react, there is a quick repeat, and the heavens open up with a heavy downpour.

Trachtenberg quickly pushes the door open and beckons to his guest. "Inside," he commands. Hollander is only too happy to oblige.

In the library, Hollander settles uneasily into a chair by the fireplace. Turning toward Trachtenberg, he leans forward expectantly and waits for the German to pick up where they'd left off downstairs. The room is dimly lit by the upward reflecting light from a single standing torchière.

"You asked what I think," Trachtenberg says at last. "The answer is: I don't like it."

"Tell me why."

"I don't like violence."

"Neither do I," Hollander says. "And I don't think there will be. The circumstances Jackson will face are sure to scare him enough to tell us what we need to know."

"If he doesn't talk, these people will use force. You know they will. And even if he does talk, then what? Will they just let him walk home, or will they kill him too?"

"No, no, Adi," Hollander shakes his head. "We can insure against rough stuff, and we will. We've got leverage with these people, and Herr Z has been very clear: all he wants is money.

"And besides, what's our choice?" he adds, with just a hint of reproach. "You tried the gentle approach on Sunday, and it didn't work. Now there's no other alternative. I've checked it out from every angle with Strangefoot, and he fully agrees."

Hollander waits for a reaction, but there is none. He leans in even closer and continues to press his case. "Hear me out, *Lieber Freund*," he pleads. "Let's examine this coldly and without emotion. You'll see that what I'm proposing is really the only way.

"Here's the situation: our American friends are ready to strike. Hank Rickenbom is convinced this is the ideal time to take advantage of the turmoil the current administration has created. He'll stir the pot with demonstrations and street riots. Things will get so heated that the president will have no choice but to declare martial law, postpone elections—that sort of thing. The right people are already in place. In the military, in local offices. When the trouble starts in the US, they're counting on Urban in Hungary, Morawieki in Poland, the Slovaks, Turkey, and friends here in Germany to pick up the pace. It's why they trusted us with their money. They need the quick investment returns we promised. Revolutions are expensive.

"Which is why we absolutely need to get into Witty's bank

accounts. For Z's people, it's all about the money. They're greedy and they want the payoff that's in it for them. Now they are pressing me, and these guys aren't patient people. We also need whatever material and records Emerson kept, which could be highly incriminating in the wrong hands. So, once again, it all comes down to that bastard Jackson."

"And you're proposing to let Z do the dirty work," Trachtenberg observes dryly. "How can you trust these gangsters?"

"They've learned their lesson with Emerson," Hollander says reassuringly. "They're rough, but they aren't stupid."

"What exactly do they propose to do?"

"They know where Jackson lives. They'll pick him up at night—it's all set. They're confident it will work, so let's leave the details to them. They'll take him south by car and Jean-Luc will help with the banks. He knows all the tricks."

Trachtenberg sighs sadly. "It's dangerous. I don't want trouble. I'm not a violent man," he half whispers.

Hollander, sensing the opening, jumps in to press his advantage. "It'll be done elegantly, Adi. Trust me. There'll be pressure, but no violence. Enough pressure to get results, that's all we need. Let's be honest. This is a revolution, our revolution. And as Chairman Mao was so fond of saying, a revolution isn't a dinner party."

Chapter 22

Berlin

Wednesday, November 15

8:20 p.m.

*L*KA Keithstrasse is quiet as a morgue. The *Mordkommission's Mannschaft* went home hours ago, and in the rest of the building, only a few duty officers are dozing peacefully, hoping for a quiet night.

Bodo Kranmüller emerges from a stall in the deserted third-floor men's room and begins washing his hands. At the next sink, his deputy, Holzer, does the same while carefully studying his image in the mirror. The *Oberkommissar* dispatches a thin smile in his direction.

"Surprised, Karl?" he asks.

"What?"

"By that guy in the mirror?"

"Hardly surprised. I've lived with that ugly face for a long time."

"So have I."

"Thanks, Chief. I look like death, *ja?*"

"Looking for sympathy, Karl? If it helps, you can have all the sympathy you want," Kranmüller offers cheerfully, and, with one hand on the door handle, skillfully sends the used paper towel ball sailing into a waste bucket across the room. "Meanwhile, Karlchen, it's back to work for us."

In his office, Kranmüller produces a thermos, pours hot coffee into two paper cups, and slides one across the desk to his deputy. Holzer, yawning, regards it with distaste and keeps his arms folded across his belly to make a point of ignoring the offer. What he really wants is a Berliner Kindl, though he knows better than to say it out loud. The rule is, "no booze *im Dienst*," and the boss respected rules.

"This is the time when a case looks hopeless," Kranmüller mutters to no one in particular, not looking up. "Facts and theories don't easily fit together or give a full picture. Different-sized wooden planks piled up into a shapeless *Scheiterhaufen*."

Holzer nods. "*Scheiterhaufen*," he says. "I like that. But perhaps *Scheisshaufen*, a pile of shit, is more apt."

"*Na, ja*," Kranmüller responds. "That's where this case of ours sits right now. But, you know, I'm thinking: every so often, it happens."

"What does?" Holzer asks.

As if he'd been waiting for the question, the *Oberkommissar* says, "What happens is that without warning or explanation, a plank comes loose. Either it tumbles out accidentally or someone pulls it out. Doesn't matter, because—poof, the *Scheiterhaufen* collapses, implodes. And the planks get rearranged into a template that solves the problem."

"Has one of our planks come loose and I don't know it?"

"I wish," Kranmüller says, shaking his head. "Unfortunately, it's the same old slog, only now the senator is on my ass, and BND wants to move, and I'm told the *Kanzleramt* is getting impatient as well. And they're all waiting for us."

"Is that why we're sitting here, pissing the night away?"

"I'm here to find the right plank to pull. And you're here to help me look."

Kranmüller pulls two sheets of paper from his desk drawer, flattens them out, and rebalances his glasses across the bridge of his nose. "I'm going to run through the 'knows' and 'don't knows', Karl. If anything occurs to you, cut right in," he says, and Holzer nods wearily.

"First thing we know," Kranmüller begins, "the Hassanis killed Emerson. We can't prove it yet and we don't know who actually pulled the trigger, but I'd say we have enough to chalk that up as a pretty solid known fact. We also know why they did it—because their German clients found out Emerson had betrayed them to the Amis. And that there was money involved. It's all solid, because they actually told us. Couldn't be clearer from Adi's little powwow with Hollander. You heard the tape, right?"

Holzer, now fully awake, nods again.

"If you ask me, Bodo, we should pull these bastards in right now."

"Patience," Kranmüller replies. "Then there are the things we don't know. Number one, who's Herr Z? Number two, how did Emerson get turned into a double and why did the Amis never tell us? There's something fishy going on there. We need to understand the full picture."

"Number three, even more important," Holzer jumps in. "If it's Trachtenberg and company who hired the Hassanis to take care of Emerson, how'd they find out he was a rat? Want me to guess?"

"Go ahead."

"Looks to me that the Amis are up against a mole of their own, and if they've been penetrated, do they know it? Maybe they do, which is why they've been holding out on us. Which makes 'Strangefoot' the key 'don't know.' Who the hell is he?"

Kranmüller nods. "The question is, how do we handle this with the Amis? Do we tell them, or keep it as our ace in the hole?"

He pauses for a moment, then says, "Another big one is whatever it is beyond the money that this crowd is so desperate to get their hands on. We know from the transcript that they think Jackson has it. We just don't know what it is."

"Desperate enough to kill for it," Holzer comments. "That sanctimonious bastard, Trachtenberg, just gave Hollander the green light. Which puts Jackson in their crosshairs. And which means he better tell us what he's got, for his own protection."

"Jackson's coming here tomorrow," the *Oberkommissar* says. "He's supposed to tell us about his meeting with Trachtenberg. It's the right time to force the issue. I'm still thinking about how best to give him a dose of reality."

"Anything else?"

"Your favorite disciplinarian. Antonia Holzapfel, a.k.a. Antigona Duka. After you grilled her, she sent that message to Cousin Jermir at his garage on Turmstrasse, so we know she was involved. That's the trail to follow for nailing the Hassanis."

"The sooner the better. There are a few other loose ends."

Kranmüller continued. "Like, who else is in the Trachtenberg group besides Hollander and that Swiss banker? I'm told the BND is working on that. It will fall into place when we arrest them. Plus, we should find out more about Hollander and his business. Is it legitimate, or another can of worms? But these are 'don't knows' that can wait."

Kranmüller scratches his cheek while Holzer watches. When his patience runs out, he asks, "So, now what, Bodo?"

"What?"

"What's the next move?"

Kranmüller looks up, quietly. "Only two that I can think of, and I suggest we divide up the work." He shifts in his seat and says, "First, I figure out some way to get Jackson to tell us all he knows."

"Threaten to pull his protection, scare the hell out of him," Holzer says.

"I like your subtle approach."

"And what's my job?"

"Antonia Holzapfel, née Duka. Bring her in and make her talk. Tell her we know about Turmstrasse and Cousin Jermir. Then we grab him and try to get the rest of the story."

The *Oberkommissar* consults his watch. "Almost 22:00," he notes. "It will be a short night, Karl. Pick her up first thing. Get her out of bed and make her sweat. We need a confession."

Thursday, November 16

6:50 a.m.

The first signs of dawn are beginning to creep up on the eastern horizon. Gray buildings under gray skies on another drizzly November morning.

The green VW police van pulls out of the LKA garage and turns west. Not much traffic yet, but the driver accelerates and reaches for the siren. Holzer, next to him in the passenger seat, grabs his arm.

"No blue light, and slow down," he barks at the young cop behind the wheel. "I want to talk to the *Kollegen*."

"*Kolleginnen und Kollegen*," the brassy middle-aged detective corrects him from a row in back. Lorelei Zimmermann, a squat, full-breasted veteran detective with the build of a female wrestler, is the *Frauenvertrauensperson*, the female staff representative at Keithstrasse LKA and takes her job seriously.

"*Ja, ja, schon gut*, Lore," Holzer agrees, without turning around to look at her. "Women's rights, females and males, is what I meant to say, of course. A bit early for political correctness, I guess. I ask to be forgiven." Detective Stummer, next to her, laughs, and Angela Francke, the *Mannschaft's* young apprentice detective seated in the back row, makes a face but keeps still. Except for Holzer, who looks like he's slept in yesterday's clothes, everyone is in uniform and armed.

A mile and a half away from their destination, the driver turns left onto Kantstrasse, a boulevard parallel to the Kudamm, rolling at a more leisurely pace. Holzer wheels around to face the others.

"Here's what you need to know," he tells them. "The woman's name is Holzapfel, Antonia. She's suspected of involvement in the Ami murder. We know each other, I've interviewed her before, but no doubt she'll be surprised to see us. We're arresting her and taking her in for questioning. Shouldn't be a problem, but stay alert. Follow the protocols: correct, but stern and formal. I want her scared and worried.

"She lives alone, and we may be getting her out of bed, which is just fine. Lore and Angela, you stick to her like leeches. Don't let her out of your sight. Not even when she asks to use the you-know-what. Meanwhile, Stummer and I will look around the place.

"One final thing. Be forewarned: she's one of Berlin's top dominatrixes, so the place will probably look it. Don't let it distract you. All in a day's work. Any questions?"

"A new one for me," Stummer chuckles.

"I'm sorry, Karl, but dominatrix? I mean, are you saying she's a prostitute?" a visibly embarrassed Angela Francke wants to know.

"Not exactly," Holzer tells her. "You might say she's a business-woman whose specialty is a service dispensing discipline for men with tastes for that sort of thing. As far as I know, no sex in the usual sense, but I'm no expert."

"Crazy, you'll see," Lore says to Angela, matter-of-factly.

Wielandstrasse is quiet, enveloped in a slight mist. A uniformed policeman meets them outside 111a and salutes as the *Mannschaft* exits the VW.

"We've been here since midnight and it's been my shift since 05:00," he informs Holzer. We've been across the street keeping out of sight and watching the place. Everything's been quiet. A few people left for work this morning, that's all. You can walk right in, Herr *Oberinspektor*, he tells Holzer with obvious pride. "I stuck a wedge inside the front door."

"Thanks, man," Holzer tells him. "Smart thinking. Good work."

On the top floor, there's no doorbell outside the Holzapfel apartment, only an odd-looking doorknocker. Holzer silently signals Zimmermann forward, Francke moves in behind her, and the two male detectives take their positions against the wall on either side. The knocker is shaped like a mermaid, half woman and half fish. Zimmermann looks toward Holzer, points and shrugs her shoulders, then grabs the fishtail part of the naiad, and pulls on it to make herself known. The sound is loud enough to echo through the early morning quiet of the *Wohnhaus*, but inside the Holzapfel apartment, nothing stirs. A minute goes by before she works the fishtail again, longer and louder this time, but the result is the same. Two more times, then Holzer motions her aside and steps forward to press his ear against the door, listening for some sign of activity on the other side. Nothing.

He sucks in his breath, looks around and motions to Stummer, who's come prepared. The detective pulls a flat leather pouch from his anorak, extracts some tools, and goes to work. "Old-fashioned lock," he announces quietly, "shouldn't take long," and begins to attack the keyhole.

If there's an inside chain, is that a good or bad sign? Holzer silently wonders as he watches Stummer at work. Less than two minutes later, there's an audible click. Stummer pulls out the jimmy and pushes the door open. No chain.

Holzer is the first one through the door, right hand resting on his weapon. Behind him is Lore Zimmermann shouting, "*Polizei, Frau Holzapfel, kommen Sie raus!*" She repeats the invitation for Antonia to emerge, but nothing moves. She, too, has drawn her weapon, and all four officers are now through the entrance door. Francke, the last one in, has flipped on the light switch.

They cluster in a vestibule outfitted as a reception area. Holzer, trying to get his bearings, has raised his arm and is listening. The others have fanned out behind him to orient themselves. On the opposite wall are two doors, both closed, with a large mirror between them and two small, wooden, child-sized chairs nearby. To the left, a narrow corridor leads to the back of the apartment.

Off to one side, there's a coatrack with hooks affixed to the wall, from which dangle leather whips, a cat-o'-nine-tails, bamboo canes, chains, ropes, and handcuffs. The only items of clothing are several black latex wetsuits. Holzer points toward the hallway and three detectives, Zimmermann in the lead, hustle down it, opening doors and calling Antonia's name. A bedroom, bath, kitchen, living room—all empty.

Holzer signals them to stand back and approaches the first of the two doors, opens it, looks in, and then retreats. A treatment room, empty as well. He turns to the second door and feels a chill moving down his spine. Because by now, he knows. He knows before he's through the door because of the smell. He's smelled it many times before, but you never get used to it.

He sucks in his breath, turns the doorknob, and steps in, the others cautiously behind him. It's the second of Antonia Holzapfel's treatment rooms, and she dominates it now as she must have in life. She is naked, tethered to a large wooden cross sunk into the wall that faces the door. Her arms are spread out in a macabre gesture of welcome, her wrists cuffed tight to the horizontal crossbar, her legs spreadeagled, ankles chained to the floor, bare feet in a sea of coagulated blood. Dark red rivulets streak down her naked body to the pool surrounding her.

She stares at them with lifeless eyes. Her head lists to one side. As Holzer steps closer, he sees the deep, oblique, long incised injury on the front of her neck. On the left, the wound starts just below the ear near the upper third of her neck and deepens gradually to the mid side of the neck on the right.

"Secure the crime scene," Holzer says. "Put in the calls and touch nothing. You know the drill." Then he steps to a corner of the vestibule and pulls out his cell and briefly closes his eyes while he waits for Bodo to answer.

A moment later, he says, "There's news."

Chapter 23

Berlin

Thursday, November 16

4:35 p.m.

I'm back inside the LKA, in a familiar spot across from
Kranmüller's desk. At the last minute, owing to "an unanticipated development," he'd postponed my scheduled briefing to the
afternoon. His message said he'd explain later.

He greets me cordially, but this time he isn't smiling. "Nice to
see you again," he says. He pours me some barely drinkable coffee
into a small cup, which I politely pretend to enjoy.

I'm surprised how calm and reassuring it feels to sit across from
him again. The office is quiet, the desk orderly, the phones don't
ring. He's all business today, but the way he welcomed me back
gives me the feeling that he is a good one to have on your side.

"You've had a busy time since last Sunday," he says. "Tell me
about it."

"I suppose you know it pretty well," I say. "Your babysitters are good at keeping a discreet distance, but I see them around. Thanks for the protection, Bodo."

Kranmüller cranks me a wry grin. "I must say that red-headed giant of yours is impressive."

I laugh. "That's Börries, the bouncer at Die Bienen. You've seen him?"

"Only his photograph."

"Now I'm impressed."

"We keep informed, Adam. I'm glad you're looking out for yourself. But don't let your guard down."

"I wonder. After meeting Trachtenberg and his crowd, I'm not so sure all this protection isn't overkill."

"Really?"

I tell him about my afternoon at the Trachtenbergs', and my private chat with Adi.

"Hollander's a bully," I sum up, "crude and rough. But clearly Trachtenberg calls the shots. I couldn't believe he really thinks it's time to dial us back to the nineteenth century. The American conspirators may be more realistic, which makes them more dangerous, but if Adi's European crowd thinks like him, I have trouble taking them seriously."

Kranmüller nods patiently, then says, "Alas, that would be a mistake. Because the true circumstances you—and we—are up against are more dire than you realize. You are in real danger, and you'd better face it. Stepping back is no longer an option for you, I'm afraid. Once you hear what I'll tell you, you'll be able to judge for yourself. Starting with the 'unanticipated development' I mentioned."

I feel an adrenaline surge. His face leaves little doubt he is dead serious.

"Tomorrow you'll read about a murder on Wielandstrasse. A woman named Holzapfel, a dominatrix. Emerson was a longtime client and paid her a visit the day he was killed. Earlier, we questioned her about her relationship with the gang we think tried to kidnap you. She would have been a key witness . . . if they hadn't slit her throat. We found her this morning, and it wasn't pretty. These people don't fool around. And we have every reason to believe they have nothing benign in mind for you."

I swallow hard. My stomach tightens, and I try to deflect my anxiety. "Dominatrix? That's what Witty was into?"

Kranmüller nods. "If there was ever a security risk, he was it."

"Tell me more, but first, do you have some water? You're giving me a headache."

He watches me down half the bottle of Fachinger, then says, "Your DCM wasn't just a coconspirator. He was also a double agent. When the gang found out, they killed him."

"He was playing both sides, you mean?"

"He became a mole, presumably to save his skin. Someone on the American side got wise, then turned him back into informing on the conspiracy."

"That's incredible," I tell him. "I can't believe it. There was never even a hint about that in any of the meetings I attended. Our investigators knew? It doesn't make sense."

Kranmüller shrugs. "Don't ask me to explain your country's operations to you," he says. "To be honest, we've been astounded that no one thought it important enough to let us in on that little secret, either. Maybe that's why your side has been reluctant to cooperate. It's possible that only some of your people knew, but not others. But that's speculation. What counts is that we have proof."

"What proof? I'd like to see it."

"In a moment," Kranmüller says. "There are other developments you need to know about, and none are good. The first is that we have hard evidence the Trachtenberg group has penetrated your side with a mole of their own. They're getting inside information from a spy inside the embassy."

"I don't believe it."

"Codenamed 'Strangefoot.' That's all we know. We were hoping you might help us."

"An American? In our embassy?"

"We strongly suspect it."

"Could it be a German?"

"In theory, but very unlikely."

"*Herrgott*, Bodo," is all I manage to say and laugh a nervous cackle. "I'm not sure I'm absorbing all this. You better lay the last thing on me. Then I want to see your proof."

Kranmüller rises from his chair, walks around the desk, and leans against it, facing me.

"I'm afraid this next piece of intelligence concerns you directly," he says. "Hollander and Trachtenberg had a meeting to discuss your visit. They talked for a while. Then they made a decision."

"What decision?"

"That they have to move against you and can't wait any longer. That the material you have is absolutely vital, and that they're pre-pared to use any means to retrieve it. Trachtenberg gave Hollander the green light. So, you see, Adam, you can forget about overkill. As long as you have this stuff and keep it to yourself, the danger is very real."

"And how do you know all that?" I manage to ask.

"Come with me," Kranmüller says and points to the door.

Twenty minutes later, we're back in Kranmüller's office. My throat is dry, and my head throbs. I sit down and drain the rest of the Fachinger. Then Kranmüller hands me another bottle, and after emptying it into a glass, I busy myself wiping up a few drops of spillage. Mostly, I try to collect my thoughts.

In a secure room down the hall, Kranmüller had let me listen to a tape of the Trachtenberg-Hollander conversation, which substantiated everything he'd told me. Overhearing someone plan to give me the treatment, or worse, is an emotional experience, to say the least.

"So, how did you get the tape?"

"I can't tell you, because even I don't know that. The BND doesn't discuss its methods. They just pass along the output."

"Amazing."

"Everyone listens in on everybody these days. Windows can become mics. Weak phone signals can be picked up, and sophisticated computers are used to convert the data into ordinary speech. Then there are the drones and satellites."

Kranmüller pulls a chair close to mine. Watching him wordlessly come close like that, it's obvious that he's got something serious on his mind.

"I was permitted to share this tape with you because it concerns you directly," he explains. "But since our last talk, we've found out a lot more about this conspiracy, none of it good. We don't have all the details, but the plan is for some serious terrorist stuff that could mean real bloodshed. Plus, they've settled on the timing. Codeword: 'Payday.'"

"When?"

"We don't know for sure. Less than a week, we're guessing."

"Do our people know?"

"Washington tells us they do."

"What kind of terrorism?"

"We're still after the details. What do you know about the US Insurrection Act of 1807?"

"Why?"

"It's been mentioned."

"As far as I remember," I answer, "it's a law that goes back to Thomas Jefferson. Authorizes the president to deploy the military inside the US to suppress insurrection. It's been done very rarely, and only in a real crisis, because using the army or National Guard against citizens inside the country is considered a big taboo in the US."

"Would be in Germany too." Kranmüller nods. "So, with Payday imminent, and assuming this is a coordinated thing, Adam, the German government is very concerned."

He stops and gives me a hard stare. "The question for the German authorities is what to do next," he says. "As for you, Adam—you're a key in this; and the question is the same: What will you do next?"

I nod in acknowledgment. "Any suggestions?"

"Our people have decided that the time for surveillance is coming to an end. We don't know everything, but we've got enough. It's time to move in and act. Besides, we've already got two homicides, and we can't risk any more.

"Naturally, we've been in touch with your government at a high level and confirmed our desire to coordinate our moves between us. With your Berlin people stalling us, we hope it will work. But I can tell you that if it doesn't, we are prepared to act alone."

"So would I, if I were you."

Kranmüller gives me a weak smile. "You have to decide what role to play in all this—before events force your hand. For now, you've got a choice. You can go back to your people; give them the evidence you've got and let them tell you what they want you to do with it. Or—if you still don't trust them to keep you safe—you can tell us. And trust us. Continuing to fly solo isn't realistic. Not anymore. We can figure out your next step together and protect you. You have my word. Trust me."

"I do," I say. "All the same . . ."

And for a moment, I let that thought hang in the air.

We've been dancing around the problem for an hour and a half.

Outside, it's dark and wintry. I can hear raindrops and gusts of wind slapping the window. The pressure has been building steadily, and it's after six o'clock when I finally decide to tell him more.

"It's mainly numbers," I explain, filling Kranmüller in on the details of what I took from Witty's safe.

"What kind of numbers?"

"Mostly bank accounts, but I'm guessing," I say. "Others look like codes of some kind."

"Can I see them?"

"They're hidden. In a safe place."

"Where?"

"Doesn't matter. I can get them."

"That would be step one."

"It might take a day or two."

"We've no time to lose, Adam. One day is better than two," Kranmüller urges.

"I'll try."

"Getting into numbered accounts is tough. But those figures might tell us a lot of what we need to know, fill in the missing pieces, or lead us there."

"Let's hope."

"Who else has seen them?"

"No one," I reply, thinking it's technically true for Emmett and better to leave Anna out of it.

Kranmüller has remained calm and businesslike. On the outside, at least.

No doubt he's privately pleased and relieved, if not excited, but he doesn't show it. He doesn't ask whether I plan to tell my embassy now, an obvious question we both avoid. On my part, because I haven't decided, though the idea of stiffing the US team and confiding only in the Germans is already weighing on my mind. Is it disloyal? Or even legal? A priority problem to deal with when I get out of here, I decide.

There's some more back-and-forth between us. Kranmüller thanks me for what I've done and reminds me to take every precaution until we meet again, which I promise will be very soon. It prompts my last questions.

"Katharina Willmans, Bettina's assistant. Any information on her, good or bad?"

"We might have," he notes dryly. "Why do you want to know?"

"I knew her before her Trachtenberg job."

Heading back to his desk, Kranmüller half turns and answers over his shoulder.

"There's nothing more about Willmans I can tell you. But since you know her, I suggest you trust your instincts."

Chapter 24

Berlin

Thursday, November 16

Evening

It's miserable outside. The rain is coming down in sheets and pelting the sidewalk. Only a few brave souls slosh along the cold and wet Keithstrasse, bundled up in their rain gear, fighting the wind with their umbrellas.

Leaving Kranmüller, I feel unmoored. I want to get away from the LKA fast and find a quiet place to hide and think. Problem is, with my minimal wardrobe at the Osthotel, I'm definitely not dressed for this rain, and the chances of finding an empty cab are slim. Hoping for a miracle, I hunker down into my coat and jog the few blocks to the Kudamm, where I huddle for temporary shelter inside a narrow doorway. It's no more than a niche and barely keeps me out of the downpour, not counting the strong, intermittent gusts of wind still blowing plenty of wet stuff into my face.

Five minutes go by with no taxis and no miracles. I see a coffee bar across the street, and for want of a better idea, sprint over in my waterlogged oxfords. It's no Starbucks, but it seems safe enough—and dry. The two women behind the counter appear to take note that I'm soaking wet. The one who brings me my double espresso hands me a towel along with it.

"We thought you could use this," she explains.

Since the place is almost empty, I peel off my shoes and socks, towel off my feet, and try to warm up, relax, and get my bearings.

The session with Kranmüller has badly unnerved me. Being told that you're the target of killers and that opting out is no longer an option will do that to you. But that was only a part of it. This "Strangefoot"—a mole inside our tent—is shocking intel, and I realize it has a deep implication for my safety. And the likelihood of terrorism with an imminent Payday deadline puts me under a very different kind of pressure.

My head is swimming.

I need to get a grip and figure out what to do.

Letting the German *Oberkommissar* in on my haul from Witty's safe was a spur-of-the-moment response to the man on the other side of the desk. I like Kranmüller and I trust him, which is why I did it. But a nagging doubt has come back about putting my fate into the hands of all the other Germans he's bound to bring into this. If it serves their interest, how likely are they to see me as expendable? And what if our mole is a German and spills the beans to the other side?

I close my eyes and try to relax. These new pressures depress me. I'm tired of all the stress, not to mention living like a junkie at the Osthotel. I'm tired of the clothes I'm wearing, and I haven't read a book, listened to my music, or talked with friends in ten days. And I miss the touch of a woman. It's not just about sex, though. Ever since our night at Hanno's party, and then our reunion at the wine bar on Emserstrasse, I haven't been able to get Kati out of my mind.

And yet her involvement with the Trachtenbergs has me confused and concerned. What did Kranmüller mean by "trust your instincts"? A peculiar comment that sticks in my mind.

I'm still pondering the question when I pull out one of my throwaway phones and make the call.

She picks up on the second ring, and I hear concern in her voice. "Adam," she says, "I've been hoping to hear from you. I tried your phone, but you didn't answer. Is everything okay?"

"New number," I tell her. "But yes, I'm alright and want to see you. I've got more questions."

"I thought so," she says. "When?"

"Now."

"Fine," she answers.

"Your wine bar?"

"Not a good idea," she says quietly. "We'll talk up here."

"Where?"

"My place."

"Yes, but—"

"Don't worry," she interrupts and laughs. "He's in Vienna."

"A half hour, if I can find a taxi."

"It's raining," she observes.

"Hadn't noticed."

7:30 p.m.

It's still raining outside, but Emma, the waitress who gave me the towel, has worked her cell and a radio cab pulls up twenty minutes later. I tip her lavishly and settle into the back of the car for the short ride to Kati's place, my funky mood morphing into a state of elated confusion. I'm exhilarated, perplexed, and worried, all at the same time.

Why is she eager to see me? Or is she? She's invited me to her apartment, and her lover is out of town. I'm fantasizing about what I hope that means, but then I begin to doubt it, because she doesn't seem the type who'd go in for sideways trysts behind his back. And then there are all the warnings reverberating in my head. Nothing's changed. I can't afford risky adventures. I'm in hiding and have decisions to make, and she's an unknown factor. Can she help, or is she going to be my undoing? It's silent mental combat between desire and prudence—the heart and the head.

By the time the taxi reaches Emserstrasse, I have resolved to be cautious and keep temptation in check. But I'm not sure the resolution will stick. To be honest, I'm not even sure that I want it to.

The elevator is the old-fashioned kind from before the war. They keep them well maintained, but this one is agonizingly slow, rattling its way up to the third floor. I exit, and she's standing in her open door in a simple black dress, giving me a big smile.

We hug hello, cautiously, like cousins, and then she ushers me inside. We wind up sitting opposite each other by the living room window. She kicks off her heels and tucks her feet under her as she settles comfortably on a small sofa. I take an easy chair nearby. The overhead is off, and the single lamp standing near her provides the perfect, soft lighting.

"You look gorgeous, Kati."

"And you look tired. A hard day?"

"More like a hard two weeks. That murder and the fallout has all of us scrambling, and there hasn't been any let up. I'm grateful you're willing to answer more questions, especially after that strange day at the Trachtenbergs."

"I'll try," she says. "But you just got here, and there's plenty of time. I've got a better idea. You need to unwind and relax first. How does that sound?"

"Agreed."

She gets up, heads into the kitchen, and a few moments later reappears with a bottle of red wine and two glasses in one hand, a plate of appetizers in the other. Olives, mixed nuts, little cheesy things, and assorted canapés. I uncork the merlot, pour it into the glasses, and sit down next to her on the sofa.

"*zum Wohl.*"

We clink glasses, look into each other's eyes, and laugh in relief to have gotten beyond our awkward beginning.

"This feels amazing," I tell her.

For a while, neither of us talks as we concentrate on the wine. We're sitting close without touching, but I feel the vibe and am wondering if she feels it too. When it's not too obvious, I try to scan the room unobtrusively for signs of Guillermo. He's on my mind and it's holding me back. It's his place, too, after all.

"I've got to ask this, Kati—"

"I know," she interrupts and laughs. "You're so obvious. Stop looking around. He's not here because he doesn't live here any-more. That's what you want to know, right? We're still friends, and I'm still fond of him, but it's been over between us for months. I've tried to signal that, but you were too dense to figure it out. He's living in Vienna these days, where he's found a new model he likes to paint—and sleep with. Just like Schiele. He still pays half the rent for staying here when he's in Berlin, which is convenient for both of us. But he rarely comes."

"Well, then I believe I'll have some more wine," I say, but she ignores the request.

"Come here," she tells me, and I move closer. Her eyes are fixed on mine as she reaches for one of my hands, slowly lifts it to her face, and works her lips and tongue to cover it with soft kisses and caresses. She's made the first move, but then I withdraw my hand and take her into my arms.

The evening passes quickly. We talk, we flirt, and we laugh. There's music and occasionally we dance. She opens another merlot, and when we get hungry, she warms up a minestrone, and we nibble on prosciutto and cheese. It's getting late, past eleven, and Neil Diamond, her favorite, sings: "*You are the sun, I am the moon . . .*"

We're swaying in place, holding each other tight, and she ever so quietly sings the lyrics as she caresses the back of my head. I'm inhaling her fragrance and the pleasurable excitement of the earlier evening has been building into what is now a lustful longing. Sometime later, when my hand begins to travel lower down her back, she disengages and puts a finger to my lips.

"Patience," she whispers and disappears.

She stayed away a full fifteen minutes, testing my patience when I'm least prepared for it. When she finally reappears, she's in a floor-length robe, white silk, with a delicate floral design and loosely held together with a string belt. Her hair has been combed out, and she lets one side of it fall over her shoulder to the front. Standing in front of me, she searches my face for a reaction with a sly, expectant half smile lighting her eyes.

"How do you like it?"

"It's beautiful, Kati. You and this robe."

"Would you like to take it off for me?" she asks in a soft voice.

I'm desperate to take her into my arms, but I resist and take a half step back. Throughout the evening, she's made the first moves. Now it's my turn.

"No, you do it, please," I say.

She looks up and smiles at me. Then, taking her own sweet time, she pulls on the bow of her belt and lets the robe slip off her shoulders. We stumble toward the bedroom, fumbling off my clothes on the way in. The room is dark, and the light from the outside plays on the curves of her body in the rising urgency of our lovemaking to its inevitable conclusion.

For a while we lie close, limbs entwined. The second time, it is slower, more confident, and much better.

Afterward, we fall asleep in each other's arms, bathed in the warmth of our newfound intimacy.

It's morning. I'm alone in her bed with Kati's scent to remind me of our night, and I lie still with my eyes closed, remembering. I'd rather not think about anything else, but reality has its way of intruding. Yesterday it was all swept from my mind, but now the questions and worries about what's ahead come flooding back. I have Hollander to worry about, and Adi, and their considerably less refined associates who are out to kill me. But I also don't know whether to trust Kranmüller and the Germans, or my own people and the CIA. And then there's Kati.

She reappears so quietly that I don't know she's there until her hand is on my face, and I feel her lips lightly brushing over mine.

"Good morning," she whispers. "Breakfast's ready. I hope you like eggs."

I squint my eyes open.

"I do like eggs, but I'd settle for coffee."

"Not today," she says and shakes her head. "A special night deserves a special breakfast."

"To revive us from our weakened state?" I ask, and we both laugh.

She ignores my joke and says, "Nine thirty, in case you're on a schedule," and then heads out the door.

10:15 a.m.

We're on our second cup of coffee. We haven't talked much, but we've enjoyed this first post-coital breakfast together. It's getting late, and I'll have to leave soon, so I get on with it and ask the obvious.

"What's going to happen with us, Kati?"

She wags her head and answers in English. "You never know. We'll go with the flow."

"I just hope it flows in the right direction," I say.

We're silent for the next few moments, sipping the coffee. Then I say, "I don't understand about you and the Trachtenbergs. Why'd you take the job? They're not your kind of people. Actually, they're dangerous."

"I know."

"You do?"

I look at her, waiting for more, but she's silent, giving me just the hint of a smile.

So, I keep going. "Their invitation to tea was a pretext because Adi wants something from me. It's related to the murder, which puts me in a delicate position."

She nods. "I warned you, remember?"

"The restroom? How can I forget? But I don't know how much I should tell you."

She raises her eyebrows. "What was Bodo's advice?"

I'm confused.

"Which Bodo?"

"How many Bodos do you know, Adam?"

"Only one. Bodo Kranmüller, a homicide cop."

"And what was his advice?"

"You know him?"

Kati smiles, seemingly having a good time at my expense. Then something's dawning on me and my knees go rubbery. I feel myself starting to sweat.

"You haven't answered my question, *Liebling*," she insists. "What was Bodo Kranmüller's advice?"

"To trust my instincts."

"Good advice."

"I don't know what to say."

"Then don't say anything. Just listen. I'll clear it up for you. We have mutual friends, and they gave me permission to tell you that we are on the same team."

We've moved into the living room.

She'd planned to stay with the Trachtenbergs only for a few months, she tells me, a year at most, but then she'd been recruited by the German government to help with their surveillance. It's tricky and not without risk, but she got used to it, and she's glad to be doing it. Bettina's not part of it, she explains, though she knows what's going on. Adi's the one who's calling the shots, Hollander is pure evil, and de la Marre's in it up to his neck. Not to mention that he's been hitting on her for months. And yes, she assures me, they want what I have, and they're desperate enough to kill for it.

I reach for her hand. "Why do you do it, Kati? It's crazy."

She stares at me with a quizzical look on her face. I can tell she's searching for the right words. "Because I'm a German," she says at last. "Is that good enough?"

"I'm not sure."

"Okay," she says. "Someday I'd have to lay it all out for you, anyway, and it's a story you've heard in a million variations. Not that complicated, actually. My grandfather wore the black uniform of the SS, the one with the skull and bones. I never knew him, but I've seen the photographs. God knows what he did in the East, but he shot himself rather than face the consequences.

"German history is very personal for my generation, Adam. I was a kid at the *Wende*, when the wall came down. Reunification worked, and now we're one country again, and a decent one, part of Europe and a Western democracy. I feel a special responsibility not to see that destroyed. That's why I'm doing it."

I would love to take her into my arms again, but I don't.

"My grandparents were German Jews," I tell her. "One grandfather of mine died in the East as well. The Nazis murdered him. His name was Jakobsohn. That's partly why I'm in it as well. Maybe we're not that different."

"It's fate," she says, and I laugh.

"No, seriously," she says. "First there was that party at Hanno's I almost didn't go to. Hopeless, each of us with our baggage. Then I take the job with Bettina, almost by chance. Then you show up, and now we're involved in the same thing, on the same side, for the same reasons. With Bodo Kranmüller as my contact, same as you."

"Last night . . . Was that fate?" I ask. "Please tell me it wasn't part of your job."

Immediately I regret it, but the possibility has weighed on me.

"Forgive me," I say quickly.

Kati doesn't seem to mind. She simply looks at me and murmurs, "As Bodo would say—trust your instincts."

Chapter 25

Berlin

Friday, November 17

*A*t two in the afternoon, I call Tommy, who sends Börries to pick me up. I have some tough decisions to make, so I have him take me to the Havana Lounge.

After a few hours and a few Tia Marias, I've come up with a plan, which starts with a clandestine call to Emmett.

The adrenaline is pumping, and I'm no longer paralyzed by indecision and doubt—not that I can't see a million pitfalls still looming. But for the first time in days, I feel a pleasurable sense of excitement. I have to move fast, but I know I can do this. It's the victory of hope over fear.

I need more ammo for the Ruger and a new set of clothes, so I start planning a stealth visit back to my apartment. The last thing I want is for McLean or the rest of the embassy team to pick up my trail. No, the *last* thing I want is for Hollander and his thugs to pick up my trail.

I call Tommy again, who agrees to be my personal shopper,

at least for controversial items such as ammunition. Two hours later, he's back with a canvas bag full of merchandise stowed in the BMW's trunk. He promises to have the rest for me by tomorrow.

Getting in and out of my apartment unseen involves reconnaissance, so Tommy takes off again with Börries to survey the neighborhood. They're back by 7:30, and Tommy assures me they've walked and watched the area carefully and found it clean.

We leave the bar and head to Wittelsbacherstrasse. It's a clear night, but it's pretty dark outside, with no rain for a change. But my street still looks deserted. As is usual for this time of the evening, both sides are crammed with diagonally parked cars, and we check them carefully for hidden occupants. Nothing. Just empty cars of neighbors home from work and lucky to have snared a spot.

On the third drive-through, Börries and I pile out of the car and hurry inside. Unless someone's rigged up invisible surveillance, we're in the clear.

It feels odd to be back in my own place, a reminder of a routine existence that ended abruptly in Heringsdorf two weeks ago. Twice we hear suspicious noises inside the building, and each time Börries freezes and my hand travels to the Ruger inside my jacket. Each time it's a false alarm.

Twelve minutes later, we're done. I've packed my new dark-gray herringbone suit, a blue blazer, flannel trousers, and an extra pair of jeans, along with three of my good shirts, ties, and a few accessories. I've also picked up another pair of decent shoes, since my oxfords have yet to recover from the rain, and perhaps never will. A few more odds and ends, and, finally—very important—cigars from my humidor. It's all been crammed into an elegant Louis Vuitton carry-on that Fiona left behind. A gift from her mother; it's not my taste, but it's fine for what I have in mind. Börries walks ahead of me, checks the street, and stows the luggage in the trunk.

8:30 p.m.

Tommy deposits me at Kati's door, and her arthritic elevator noisily climbs toward the third floor at a snail's pace, but I don't mind. I'm being spared a night at the Osthotel, and Kati is waiting for me. Since making up my mind about a plan of action, and taking the first steps to implement it, my spirits have actually blossomed into something approaching buoyant eagerness to take it to the bad guys.

Kati greets me with a prosecco and eyes my suitcase.

"Planning to stay awhile?"

"Is that an invitation?"

I give her a kiss, which sets the tone for the rest of the evening.

Saturday, November 18

I wait until breakfast to tell her my plans. I've thought it through, I explain, and I've decided to stick to my original idea of dealing with the contents of Witty's safe alone. Nobody but my closest friends to back me up.

Kati looks horrified.

"Don't do it," she tells me. "That's a terrible idea. You'll be overmatched and out-gunned. Why, in God's name, wouldn't you want Kranmüller, the German government, and, for that matter, your American colleagues protecting you? Think again, Adam," she pleads.

"There's a mole on the American side. Could even be a German. Not even Bodo knows who it is. I'm not going to risk being double-crossed by an insider. Besides, I'm the one with the contents from the safe. That's my ace in the hole, my insurance. Tommy and Börries have my back. Emmett at the embassy is a pipeline to US assistance when needed. And I'm counting on you to play the same role with Bodo and the Germans—if you're willing."

Kati nods, listening intently. I think she can see that my arguments aren't totally without merit.

I hand her one of the prepaid cell phones Tommy picked up for me. "I'll be out of town for a few days. This has ninety minutes on it and a Hanover area code. Our calls will be untraceable if we keep them brief. I'll reach out to you."

I take her shoulders and say, "It's going to work out fine, *Liebling*. You can tell Bodo that it's my best chance to seize the initiative and get it done."

She stirs what's left of her coffee and stares into the cup for a while. When she looks up, she reaches across the table and squeezes my hand.

"My hero," she says. "You're either very brave or very stupid."

"Well, I always did okay in school, if that tells you anything."

She gives a wry smile. "I don't want this to have been a brief and tragic affair."

"Your words in God's ear."

Kati glances at her watch. "I'm late," she says. "I have to be at the Trachtenbergs' by ten."

I follow her to the door and help her into her coat. I try to be calm, but my heart's in my mouth as I'm wondering if I'll ever see her again.

We embrace. "You be very careful," I tell her.

"You too," she says.

Then she's gone.

I walk back into the apartment and sit down on the couch. Kati's presence is everywhere, and it upsets me that she's heading back to the villa alone. I'm haunted by her words. A brief and tragic affair.

But Tommy's waiting downstairs, I have things to do, and I'm on a tight schedule.

Our first stop is a nearby Deutsche Bank ATM, where I withdraw another three thousand euros from my now much depleted bank account. Börries hovers nearby. With what cash I have left, and two prepaid debit cards I asked Tommy to buy me, I'll be able to finance my plans.

With banking out of the way, Börries hands me two magazines with seven rounds each, adamantly refusing to tell me where he got them. Though I still have trouble imagining that I'll ever actually use the Ruger, the additional firepower feels reassuring. I bury the clips deep inside my luggage.

I've talked with Emmett twice. I have two more sensitive phone calls to make, and I need some privacy. Outside it's cold, and the sky looks dark and threatening, so I ask Tommy to drop me off at a small park not far from Kati's place. It has a playground complete with slides, swings, and a sandbox, and I'm counting on there being no parent or grandma crazy enough to take their tots out to play in this kind of weather. I tell Börries to stay with Tommy, who has parked the BMW on the street, then I bundle up and huddle on a bench in a secluded corner on the edge of the park, partly shielded by a waist-high hedge. Then I reach for one of my prepaid cell phones.

It's been two weeks since Wolfgang delivered my envelope to Anna, and she hasn't had a word from me since, much less an explanation. But she acts unsurprised when she hears my voice. Anna Rotbein is a cool customer, always keeping her thoughts and emotions to herself.

"*Wie geht's?*" I start off. "How's the weather in Heringsdorf?"

"It's November," she observes, not unreasonably.

"Have you missed me?"

"Why?"

"Just asking. Fact is, I missed you."

"So come back," she suggests.

"I plan to. Soon, I hope. But I can't just yet."

"Hmm."

"How are you, though?"

"*Wie immer*," she says. "I'm good."

"Glad to hear it," I tell her. And though she hasn't asked, I add, "I'm fine too. Everything's okay here."

"That's nice, Adam."

"Say, Anna," I ask. "About Wolfgang's thing. You still have it, right?"

"Why not?" she says. "No one's been around looking for it, if that's what you're asking."

"That's good to know. Thanks for keeping it safe, but now I need it back. So, I've got a big favor to ask and I hope you won't mind."

That wakes her up. "I hope you're not suggesting that I bring it personally to Berlin," she says with more emotion than is her usual style. "Because that would be a problem."

"You can relax." I laugh. "I wouldn't dream of asking you to leave Villa Ostwind. I've got a better idea."

"So have I. Send Wolfgang," she suggests.

"No, that won't work," I say. "But here's what I'm proposing. Put it into another envelope, seal it tightly and wrap it in more paper. Then call DHL, the transport people, to come and pick it up this afternoon. They'll put it into an outside envelope of their own. I want it sent to the DHL office in Geneva. Get a receipt."

"Switzerland?"

"Yeah, Geneva, Switzerland."

"Got it."

"And, Anna—one more thing. Put that receipt in a separate envelope and send it registered, addressed to me at Poste Restante, Bureau de Poste, Carouge, Switzerland. I'll spell it. It's a suburb of Geneva. Please try to get it all done today. Can you?"

"No problem."

"You're a princess," I tell her.

"*Quatsch*," she says dryly. "Nonsense."

"Thanks a million, Anna. *Tschüss*."

"*Tschüss*, Adam. And bon voyage," she answers.

Anna is no fool.

The cold wind is getting to me, but I've got one more call to make—to Emmett again, and on his cell, to minimize the risk of it being traced.

"Good news?" I ask when he answers.

"You don't want to know."

"Three p.m.?"

"Yeah, where?"

"I'm thinking Liz's favorite," I suggest. "They've got that private room."

For a moment, Emmett seems stumped. Then he realizes that I'm talking about Luigi's, their favorite Dahlem Taverna. The private room is accessible from the back, through the garden, which should allow me to slip in and out unseen.

"Oh, I get it," he says quickly. "Good idea. Three p.m."

"Ciao," I say, already back at the car and anxious to get out of the cold.

I glance at my watch and note that it's time for my lunch date. The next item on my checklist.

Chapter 26

Berlin

Saturday, November 18

12:15 p.m.

*M*y lunch with Jupp von Norden is set for one o'clock in Potsdam, and it takes at most a half hour to get there. Because Jupp is vain and full of himself, I'm hoping to feed his fragile ego by being the first to arrive and obliged to wait for him, rather than the other way around. I need him in a good mood.

Potsdam, once the residence of Prussian kings where Frederick the Great built himself his over-the-top Sans Souci Palace (and Truman and Stalin carved up Hitler's Reich after the war), is legally a separate city and the capital of Land Brandenburg. Viewed through a less romantic lens, it's also just another part of Berlin's sprawling suburbia.

I settled on Potsdam's Piccolo Pane for this lunch because it will appeal to my guest's pretentiousness. It's reputed to be the best—and most expensive—restaurant in an area where a certain type of

Berlin's business elite built themselves expensive lakeside villas. It's a place where they love to be seen, but mostly for dinner and on weekends. So, I'm also counting on it being mostly empty in the middle of the day when they're more likely to be in their offices.

I don't especially like Jupp von Norden—never have—and haven't seen him in a long time. Over the years, I've avoided his attempts to keep in touch, so he must have been surprised when I called to suggest lunch and is probably wondering what it's about. The answer is simple: he's the only one I can think of who might be able to give me some useful information about the ins and outs of Swiss banking and numbered bank accounts. Or, at least, lead me to someone who can.

When Fiona and I first arrived in Berlin, we bivouacked for a few weeks in an upscale *Pension* the embassy uses as temporary quarters for senior staff in transit. Jupp, who was moving to Berlin to open a branch for a Frankfurt boutique investment advisory firm, was our neighbor in an adjoining suite.

As soon as he discovered where I worked, he attached himself, trying to pump me for inside intel on US economic policy. He's a man well north of fifty, on the short side, but vain, always impeccably dressed, with a full head of silver hair and a face that suggests time spent under a tanning lamp. I found his wary, restless eyes and ingratiating manner annoying from the start, but Fiona liked his flirty attentions and thought he was cute. She called him Juppi and, being innocent of the German language, pronounced it the American way as "Yuppie" which, given his Germanic mannerisms and age, he decidedly is not.

When he wasn't regaling us with stories about his amatory adventures—invariably involving rich clients' wives or women half his age—he would boast about his prowess as a money manager for rich people, helping them avoid paying taxes. His bag of tricks included shell companies overseas, bearer shares, tax havens in places like Cyprus, Panama, and some Caribbean islands, as well as hard-to-penetrate nominee fronts for trusts in obscure places the world over. Also, numbered Swiss bank accounts, of course. "Only suckers pay taxes," he was fond of saying.

It wasn't the kind of conversation I found especially amusing at the time. Now I'm thinking—hoping—that he's the right man to point me in a fruitful direction for what lies ahead.

Norden shows up fifteen minutes late.

He hasn't changed much in the last three years. Same well-coiffed hair and sun-lamp tan, same classy Italian suit. Except that I detect a few deeper lines around the mouth and baggier eyes, which I first notice when he removes the wrap-around Ray-Bans he's been wearing against Berlin's nonexistent November sun.

My gamble for an empty dining room paid off. Only two tables are occupied, both by women lunch partners, and there's actually a small salon-like corner off to one side where we can eat practically unseen.

"You look great, Jupp," I tell him after we've exchanged greetings and settled down at the table. "How did you get here? Still driving your Porsche?"

"Oh no, VW has ruined that brand," he says, obviously pleased that I asked. "The car to drive these days is a Ferrari, the Portofino Gran Turismo. That's some machine. I'll let you drive it if you like. I've also bought myself a Tesla, the S-class. That's my fun car—a computer on wheels."

"Congratulations," is all I can think to say.

We order aperitifs. Jupp wants a Kir Royale and I ask for a prosecco. For the main course, he chooses a seafood salad with truffles, which sounds good enough for me to join him.

His stories haven't changed much either. I hear a lot about his current girlfriend: young but smart as a whip, the figure of a goddess, and a tigress in bed. All described in meticulous detail. Business is great, except he worries that US tax cuts for high earners might give the German Finance Minister similar ideas.

"Why is that bad?" I ask, momentarily lost. Wouldn't that allow his clients to have even more money to invest? Oh, no, he explains. The biggest fees come from advising them how to shelter income from taxes, and if the government takes less, it reduces the incentive. Which leads him into a detailed description of several arcane tax avoidance schemes he's invented for rich Germans, much of which I have trouble following.

When we've finished our salads and the coffee is on its way, we move from the table to overstuffed chairs. He's reclining comfortably, sipping his coffee, and feeding himself after-dinner mints. For comfort, he's unbuttoned his jacket, revealing an unmistakable bulge around his middle.

I decide now is the time to get my money's worth for this expensive lunch.

"Fascinating stuff," I tell him. "You're a very clever man."

"Oh, please," he says, and gestures modestly. "I'm a professional at my trade. Just like you. That's all."

"Then perhaps you can advise me," I say, and launch into a carefully concocted story meant to appeal to his conniving mind. "This is confidential, but an American friend of mine is going through a nasty divorce and needs a discreet way to park some money over here. Is a numbered Swiss bank account still the way to go?"

"Sorry," he says. "Definitely not. The Swiss caved to US and EU pressure some time ago. Swiss banking secrecy is no longer absolute. Nowadays, they tell your IRS anything they demand to know. He'll have to find other ways."

"It's not the IRS," I explain, "it's his wife . . . and her private eye. He has a lady friend here, if you know what I mean. Quite expensive. So, he's looking for a private way to hide cash and related evidence.

If his wife finds out, he'll be ripped open in the settlement."

"Oh, that. That still works."

"So, the wife couldn't go to his bank and get information?"

"Hell, no. They wouldn't even confirm the account exists. Swiss bankers know all about that kind of discretion. It's a long tradition."

"No tricks or ways around it?"

"None."

We carry on like this for a while, and Jupp's visibly enjoying it. He lounges in his chair, an ankle crossed over his knee, showing off colorful socks and fancy, tasseled loafers. He answers my questions with a permanent half smile on his face, and I'm sure he thinks it's all a charade and my "friend" is none other than me, but that's okay. Still, I get a lot of basic intel about opening a numbered account, typical security protocols, that there are twelve or thirty digits involved, depending on how you look at it, and so forth. But nothing about ways to crash into them. In fact, Jupp says it's impossible.

Remembering the various numbers on Witty's list, I then grill him about safe deposit boxes, and the rules à la Swiss. All banks have them, he explains, and very popular for clients with problems like my friend. Security is no less strict, but there are also non-bank companies offering the same service where there's at least less red tape, which is news to me. Still, if Witty's stashed contraband in one, I'll have the same problem. Security is meant to be foolproof: duplicate keys, elaborate ID requirements, and more. Since there wasn't a key in Witty's safe, the prospects don't look any brighter.

When it's time to wrap it up, I spring my final question.

"You've been most helpful, Jupp," I tell him. "My friend will be very grateful. The poor guy doesn't know anyone in Switzerland. Can you recommend a contact—some clever, well-connected professional like you—who knows everything and everyone in Swiss banking he could turn to for confidential advice? For a fee, of course."

Jupp stops, but only for a moment.

"Sure," he says, "I've got a lot of friends there. You have to, in my business."

"Who would be at the top of your list?"

"I'd say Tony's the best," he answers. "Antoine Ahmed Slinani. Ex-private banker, now a private consultant in Geneva. Highly discreet, a real problem solver, and very imaginative."

"An Arab?"

"Moroccan, with lots of Arab clients who need privacy and reliable advice. He knows his way around."

"Sounds great. My friend needs someone he can really trust."

"Absolutely. Tony's the man. A real straight arrow. Even a bit too much so, if you know what I mean. In this business, a bit of harmless deviousness isn't a bad thing." Jupp chuckles.

"But he's honest and gets results?"

"No one is better connected in Geneva than Tony."

"Would you email him to say my friend may be in touch?" I ask, and the question elicits a sly look.

"Sure," he says eagerly and smiles. "What's your friend's name?"

He's thinking now I'll have to come clean that it's me, but I'm ready for him.

"His name is Mark Miller from New York City," I say. "He'll call Tony when he arrives in Geneva. They'll like each other. He's a pretty smart fellow too, and no slouch with the ladies. Maybe Tony's got some phone numbers for him."

In the parking lot, Jupp edges himself behind the wheel of a fire-engine-red Tesla, gives a jaunty wave as he rolls past me, and accelerates at warp speed onto the Berlin highway.

The lunch took longer than planned. It's close to three thirty by the time Tommy collects me and drives to my next stop, Luigi's. I get out and hurry through the wintry desolation of the Taverna's garden to the back entrance.

Emmett's face lights up when I come through the door. He bolts from his table and crushes me in a prolonged bear hug.

"Goddamn, Adam," he says when we sit down opposite each other, "you're a sight for sore eyes. How the hell are you holding up?"

"I feel good," I tell him. "Considering there's a big target on my back. Scared shitless, occasionally, I don't mind telling you. But fear, I've discovered, is a fine spur to creativity. I know what I want to do, and now I'm eager to execute and get it done. I'm going to make it work, Em. With your help."

Emmett gives me a long look. His face has morphed into a mask I have trouble reading. Except for his traveling eyebrows—a sure sign of inner tension.

He's nursing a beer and shoves one across the table. Except for cryptic phone calls, this is the first time in ten days we are together, and it feels good.

"Fill me in, for Chrissakes," he says.

"Sure, but I've got a question first. Did it work?"

Emmett doesn't answer right away and shoots me another long, silent look that mixes concern with pride. "Yeah, Adam. I got what you asked for. Jesus—in twenty-four hours—it was touch and go," he says, and his face is more grimace than grin. "This is the craziest thing I've ever done. Whatever you're planning better pan out, or we'll both be on the job market. Or working on our backhand at some nice federal prison."

"It'll work. And we'll both be heroes."

"You're sure about all this?" he asks. He scratches his jaw pensively with the prepaid phone I've given him. "Some of it sounds like a real long shot."

"Best I could think of." I shrug.

"Well, good luck. You'll need plenty of that," he says and hands me an envelope from an "Official Use Only" government folder he's extracted from his briefcase. "At least now I know why you wanted these," he says.

"You said it's a long shot. So, I have to get all my ducks in a row. And these two babies are two of my most important little ducklings." I take a quick look, then let the envelope disappear in my jacket pocket. "The genuine article," I say, thinking about the unsolved problems still ahead of me. "How did you do it?"

"Wasn't easy," he says. "I had to pull rank on the passport guy in the consular section. Swore him to secrecy on his life, and actually made him take an oath and said it was all top secret and there wasn't time to go through regular channels for the Witty investigation's critical stage. I guess he was proud to be in on it. They issue quick substitute passports for tourists who lose them. A few dozen each year. So, luckily, we had all the stuff for it. Getting those photos in there almost didn't work, though."

"Thanks, brother."

With that business out of the way, I start at the beginning and tell Emmett about Tommy and Börries, my private bodyguards; about Hollander and my visit to the Trachtenbergs'; and all about the Kranmüller relationship. I also describe what the Germans know through their human and electronic pipeline into the conspirators and about Kranmüller's mention of the Insurrection Act.

Occasionally, Emmett interrupts with a question, but mostly he keeps quiet. It's when I give him the intel about the traitor, code name "Strangefoot," which is a big reason I'm going after the numbers alone, that he comes alive. We go back and forth for a while, but eventually agree that if it's one of ours, Trotter, our CIA station chief, has to be a prime suspect. It all points that way. It also would explain why McLean, who may know something, has kept him out of the loop. Emmett tells me that he's looking, but no one can find him. Incredible if true, and with all the makings of one more giant CIA disaster, we both agree.

Then I tell him about my plan and the traveling, but only in general terms. The details I prefer to keep to myself. Then we work out our communication strategy.

Emmett says, "You don't know it yet, but in light of the latest developments, you're really up against it, Adam."

The FBI, working inside sources, has learned a lot more about the conspirators, he explains. According to the Bureau's latest intel, they're planning to engineer coordinated attacks on cops and government installations, as well as conservative outfits like the Federalist Society, the Pomona Institute out in California, and others, plus on several prominent right-wing activists and politicians. Their idea is to provoke enough violence and rioting to generate public support for strong counteraction, like a presidential declaration of martial law or invoking the Insurrection Act.

What they have in mind is a classic false-flag operation, using neo-Nazi street gangs like the Proud Boys and Two-Percenters to get the ball rolling. Crazy as hell, but very scary, and with a real chance of serious bloodshed.

"When's all this supposed to start?" I ask.

"That's the thing," Emmett explains. "We don't know the precise date, but the code is Payday, and the betting is it's imminent. Three or four days at most."

"And over here?"

"Same idea," Emmett says with a nod. "There have been regular contacts, and the US guys are counting on copycat stuff here not long thereafter."

After listening to Emmett, I don't know what to say. "Jesus Christ," is all I manage. "Why doesn't the Bureau move in now?"

"A lot of what they know is based on intel they can't use. Wouldn't be admissible in court. That's why what you're after is the critical missing piece. Now do you see what you're up against?"

"Tell me about it."

I raise myself up and flash him a winning smile. "Okay, wish me luck, Emmett. I'm on it."

I'm putting up a good front. But it's not exactly how I feel.

Emmett gives me a hug, then calls out, "Watch yourself, brother," as I head for the door. "You'll be the guy who changes history."

"You, too, Excellency," I say and wave back at him.

5:55 p.m.

"All set?" I ask when I'm back in the BMW. "Where are our guardian angels?"

"Right where they're supposed to be," Tommy says, and points out the unmarked black VW Jetta parked at the corner behind us.

The time has come to shake loose from my *Kripo* protectors, and we've worked out a simple ruse to fool them. Still, the cops are good at what they do, and it makes me nervous.

"*Oberkommissar* Kranmüller won't like it, but it's now or never," I say.

"Don't worry," Börries chimes in from the front seat, "it's all set up. Can't miss."

Tommy is driving at a normal speed toward the Kudamm, a twenty-minute ride, the cops a block behind us, keeping their distance. It's 6:17 when we pull up in front of the Dressler, one of Berlin's better-known restaurants. Börries escorts me in while the cops are busy backing into a narrow parking spot on the Kudamm's center strip. They have us in their sight and I'm going in for dinner. All perfectly normal.

Except that we've picked the Dressler for a reason. It sits next to the Kudamm Passage, a crowded block-long shopping mall running to the Lietzenburger, a parallel street to Kudamm. There's a front entrance and a smaller side door straight into the arcade.

Börries and I saunter in through the front, but as soon as we're out of sight, we speed up and hurry out the side into the arcade and jog through the crowd to Lietzenburgerstrasse. That takes about a minute and a half. Börries, who has been huffing and puffing along just behind me, jiggles some keys and points toward a VW Passat parked at the curb. "Courtesy of Hertz," he says proudly. I hop in and we're off.

"How's our timing?" I ask Börries, while scanning the street through the rear window, but there's no sign of the cops.

"We'll make it with time to spare," he reassures me.

A minute later, I feel my phone vibrating and hear Tommy's voice.

"Bon voyage," he says. "In case you're wondering, your babysitters are across the street, relaxing until you finish your dinner. Clear sailing for you."

"One hundred eighty kilometers to Leipzig," Börries announces. "Autobahn all the way."

Chapter 27

Berlin

Friday, November 17

8:30 p.m.

When the email comes through on the encrypted system, Berlin's CIA station chief, Austin Trotter, is lying face-down and naked on Johanna's king-size bed while she, equally unclad, is massaging his neck and shoulders. Occasionally, she lets her hands travel lower and alternates the kneading up top with softer touches below.

He raises himself to read the message, then lets Johanna resume her ministrations. McLean wants to meet him urgently, not at the embassy, but at 22b Schumannstrasse, top floor, at eleven p.m. that night.

Trotter isn't surprised. He knows he's been under suspicion from the moment McLean showed up in Berlin, and for weeks he's been preparing himself for the inevitable confrontation. Now they are coming for him.

Nor is the venue of the summons totally unexpected. Trotter is as good at cultivating his sources inside the service as he is at intel-gathering in the field. His contacts at Frankfurt center had tipped him off about McLean's off-line safe house in Berlin. He's also kept his eyes and ears open, carefully observed the key players, and maintained his private contacts with counterparts in German intelligence: the BND and Staatssicherheit. So, the details of McLean's black Berlin mission weren't nearly as impenetrable a secret to him as the DDO back in Langley may have thought.

The radio is tuned to the Armed Forces network, and Conway Twitty is singing "Slow Hand." The volume is low, Johanna's touch is comforting, and he tries to empty his mind again and sink back into the feeling. Yet the magic is gone, his brain inevitably focused on what awaits him and how to play it.

The venue is meant to frighten him.

"Isolate the subject from familiar surroundings and put him off balance in a strange and forbidding place." Interrogation 101, the stuff they taught rookies. Did they seriously think the games he'd mastered years ago would work on him now?

Taking risks is what fieldwork in the Agency's clandestine service is all about, and this situation isn't any different, Trotter tells himself. Except that this time it is personal. He is in a tight spot, but he has been here before and has prepared himself for it by studying the forces arrayed against him, looking for weaknesses and thinking about how best to exploit them.

That's what tonight will be about.

Johanna crawls in beside him, and for a while, they lie side by side, enjoying the closeness of their bodies. Then they make love.

Twice divorced, Trotter long ago concluded that marriage didn't mesh with his undercover life, and Johanna, the forty-seven-year-old single mother and widow of an East German policeman, makes no such demands. He hasn't told her what he did for a living, and though she has probably guessed, she never asks. He protects her, supplements her widow's pension, and comes and goes as he pleases. Cara, her ten-year-old daughter with Down's syndrome, adores her "*Onkel Au*," and Johanna is happy that the feeling between the two of them appears to be mutual. Each time Trotter shows up, he brings a present—a doll, a picture book, a soft pillow, or new trinket—and devotes hours entertaining and reading to her. For Johanna, that is enough.

A little after ten, Trotter rises, stretches, and disappears into the bathroom. After a long shower, he stands before the mirror and gloomily examines his face.

The circles under his eyes seem deeper and darker than he remembers them, and he notes with distaste that his sparse hair is clearly losing its battle with the widening bald spot atop his head. His skin is blotchy, and he needs a shave. He considers that, but decides against it and reaches for a towel to finish drying off. As always, keeping it wrapped around his bulging midsection is a challenge.

In the living room, a half dozen talking heads on television are locked in an argument about some obscure aspect of Angela Merkel's energy policy. The radio is off and Johanna, in a flowing kimono, is listening through the open kitchen door. Austin would have preferred more Conway Twitty.

He begins to dress slowly. Blue jeans, roll-neck sweater over a white T-shirt, and tennis shoes. He checks his Glock, and is returning it to his shoulder holster when Johanna comes in with a platter of cold cuts and rye bread.

"Hungry?" she asks.

"Not really," he says. "But I'll have a drink. Get me the whiskey, would you?"

He pours himself a third of a water glass and downs it in several long swallows.

Johanna watches him silently.

"Not sure when I'll be back," he says. "Kiss Cara for me."

Johanna nods.

"Money?" he asks.

"I have enough."

Trotter moves toward her, and they embrace. Then he puts on a leather jacket, a raincoat over that, and says, "*Tschüss.*"

10:45 p.m.

The squat, broad-shouldered man who opens the door looks more bodyguard brawler than CIA agent.

"Gimme your coat and jacket," he says, followed by, "and your gun."

Trotter does as he is told and watches the Glock disappear behind the fellow's back.

"Hands behind your head and spread your legs," the man orders, and takes his time frisking Trotter thoroughly and none too gently. Front, back, and between the legs. Twice.

Handiwork completed, his host opens the living room door and points toward it. "Inside," he orders.

George Hartfield, a.k.a. Mortimer McLean, is sprawled comfortably on a couch, his feet resting on a coffee table, a pair of horn-rimmed glasses perched halfway down the bridge of his nose. Trotter's arrival seems to interest him far less than whatever he is scrolling through on his cell phone. A pencil-thin man with a hawkish face is in a chair to Hartfield's left. The beefy greeter takes the chair on the right and points Trotter to one opposite the trio.

Nobody says a word. Austin, recognizing it as more interrogation SOP nonsense, uses it to size up Hartfield's two enforcers. The big guy he judges to be in his midforties, and a closer look reveals his hooded eyes to be unpleasantly bloodshot. He has folded his meat-cleaver hands over an impressive belly. His fingernails have been chewed down to the base.

The other one is shorter and younger, with a full head of dirty-blond hair and rimless glasses. The most distinctive thing about him is his cowboy boots with metal tips. His ice-blue eyes dart nervously between Trotter and Hartfield. Austin concludes that he is probably the more dangerous of the two.

Unlike his associates, who are wearing jeans and wool shirts, Hartfield is truly playing it by the book, sporting a suit, white shirt, and red tie. Good cop/bad cop? Black hat/white hat? Roughnecks versus gentleman? That seems to be the idea.

The silence, which lasts a full three minutes, is also par for the course. Knowing the routine, Trotter tries to relax and simply wait for the show to begin.

At about the four-minute mark, McLean-Hartfield slips the cell phone into his jacket pocket, looks up at Trotter, and smiles.

"Welcome, Austin," he says pleasantly. "I'm glad you could come."

He waits a moment for Trotter to say something, but appears unfazed when no answer is forthcoming.

"You've met our two visitors, I take it."

"Not formally. But I assume manners aren't their strong suit."

More smiles from McLean.

"That's Asa on my left, and Rocco here's on my right. They've come to help with the investigation."

"Cut the crap, George, will you?" Trotter says. "What the fuck is this all about? Why the muscle? And while you're at it, perhaps you'll tell me why I've been frozen out of Thunderclap. You owe me an explanation."

McLean focuses on some invisible object on the sleeve of his suit jacket, flicks it away, scratches his nose, and then returns Trotter's stare.

"You're right, Austin," he nods approvingly. "But why am I not surprised? We've been through a lot of shit together, you and me. We understand each other. So, let's both cut the crap and get right to my question: Why'd you do it?"

"Do what?"

"Sell out. Go over to the dark side. Was it money? Boredom? Wounded ego? Surely not because of some deep conviction." McLean sounds genuinely curious, his tone conversational, non-threatening.

"You may not know this," he continues, "but the shrinks at the Farm have studied traitors like you, and they tell me you're their perfect prototype. The ultimate midlife crisis. You're at that stage of life, right?"

Trotter manages to conceal his inner tension, but he can feel his pulse banging.

"So that's it," he says. "You seriously think I betrayed Emerson? I guess because I'm the one who handled him? You're full of shit and you'd better look elsewhere. Where's the evidence? You're in the wrong pew, George."

"You sure?" McLean asks darkly and sounds disappointed. Next to him, Rocco grips the arms of his chair and leans forward. His cadaverous playmate gives a mirthless giggle. Trotter senses they are waiting to pounce.

"Damn right, I'm sure. You haven't got a fucking shred of evidence, because there *is* none. So, screw you. Why don't you flutter me, if you're so sure?"

"No need, really. Not with all the videos, tapes, witnesses," McLean says.

"Bullshit!"

"You're in it deep, Trotter, at risk of spending the rest of your fucking life behind bars. Lucky for you, we can still use your help. Come clean, tell us all you know, and I'll go to bat for you. I promise you that."

Trotter shakes his head as if trying to throw off a harness. "How often do I have to say it? It wasn't me, damn it. I've got nothing to tell you, because I don't know anything, get it?"

"Here's your problem," McLean says. "You betrayed a key government witness in a conspiracy that's a serious threat to national security, which makes you responsible for his murder. For all we know, you may have even gotten your hands dirty. We know you sold out Emerson, because you were the only one who knew he'd been flipped. The whole thing was being held tighter than a virgin's twat."

"More bullshit, George. Any one of a half dozen people from Langley could have passed the word. Emerson himself could have talked. All I know is that it wasn't me."

McLean shakes his head. "The tapes, the videos, the witnesses... They all say it was you. And what I'm trying to tell you is you have one more chance to save your ass. Help us catch these criminals. I'd much rather this stay friendly between the two of us, and we move ahead on that basis. For your sake and ours.

"So, one last time: I want your confession, with details—the works. Or else."

"Or else what? Fuck you, George."

"Austin," McLean sighs. "You're not being smart. You're wasting valuable time and you're beginning to piss me off. I've been trying to help you. Do yourself a favor and listen. For the last time: start talking."

"And once more: I told you," Trotter says.

McLean shakes his head, slowly stands up, and starts toward the door.

"I've got to take a leak," he announces, and turns to his two companions. "Take care of him for me, will you fellows? Make sure he doesn't do anything stupid while I'm gone."

The door has barely closed when the guy whom McLean called Asa has his gun out and points it straight at Trotter's face. "Get up, fucker," he orders. The gun is long-barreled, and the silencer makes it look massive.

It flashes through Trotter's mind that he's made the wrong bet. He's done as he was told.

From behind him, Rocco barks, "Arms over your head!" When Trotter complies, he follows up with "Higher!"

For a few moments, nothing more is said. Trotter stands with his arms high in the air, with Cowboy Boots making little circling motions with the barrel of his gun trained on a spot roughly between Trotter's eyes. He seems to be enjoying himself. Trotter decidedly is not, his mind working overtime trying to think of some way out of this.

He isn't too worried about being shot, except perhaps accidentally by this weirdo in cowboy boots. After all, McLean doesn't want him dead. He needs him. Clearly, these two goons have been imported to soften him up and make him compliant, which probably means that they are about to beat the crap out of him.

His best chance, Trotter concludes, is to stall for time until McLean returns. Once he is back, the strategy he's had in mind all along still makes sense. It's just that his timing is off. McLean pulled the trigger faster than he'd thought. How long did he intend to stay away, dammit?

It was Cowboy Boots who breaks the silence. "Why don't I just shoot the SOB, Rocky?" he asks his partner. "The guy's a traitor. Get it over with. Save the taxpayers a lot of money."

Trotter tries to join the conversation. "So, that's what you are, a killer?"

"Among other things," Asa replies.

"Well—" Trotter continues, until Rocco cuts him off.

"Quiet," he growls.

"What do you say, Rocky?" his partner says. "Let's do it."

"Not yet, bro. Not yet."

Trotter tries again. "So, here's a question for both of you—"

"Shut the fuck up and take off your pants," Rocco orders.

"What do you mean?" Trotter asks, knowing full well what it means.

"Your pants. Off with them. Now."

"I've got my arms in the air."

"Do it, smartass. Now."

Trying to kill as much time as possible, Trotter slowly sheds his tennis shoes and steps out of his jeans.

"Look at the sorry-ass bastard," Asa giggles. "Now your boxer shorts."

"Fuck you," Trotter spits at him.

That is the last thing he remembers saying before Rocco delivers a vicious blow to the side of his head that feels like he's being hit with a steel bar. The force of the blow buckles his legs; he sinks to the floor and promptly passes out.

He comes to when someone dumps water on his head. His face feels a size bigger than normal and hurts like hell.

"Get up," Rocco orders.

He doesn't move.

"Get your ass up, fucker," his partner chimes in, reinforcing the command with a hard kick of his boot.

Austin curls into a ball. The pain is very real, but he makes the most of it by shrieking and screaming as loud and for as long as he can. Then he pretends to pass out again.

When McLean comes back into the room, he says, "To be honest, I hate violence. It's messy and uncivilized."

He is trying hard to make it sound conciliatory and sincere, but Trotter isn't buying it. He musters a half smile, fully expecting to pass blood the next time he has to pee.

It is well after one in the morning, and for Trotter, the last two hours have been a jumbled haze of various forms of pain. His yelling had brought McLean back on the scene, and then Selena Kotzki—who went by the alias of Phoebe, a support staffer from Frankfurt he'd known for years—had busied herself cleaning him up and dressing his wounds. A nasty, dark bruise cuts diagonally across his face, his lip is split, and his nose is a swollen lump. As far as he can tell, nothing is broken. At least there's that, but he has a giant headache and his ribcage aches where Asa's boot crashed into it. Especially when he breathes.

He'd been allowed to put on his clothes and now everyone is back in their seats and ready for the next act.

"Look, Austin," McLean starts in again, "wouldn't it be best if you fessed up, so that you and I can proceed to something more constructive?"

Trotter breathes in and out, slowly and painfully, nodding as though he is seriously considering the proposal, and then says, "No."

"I mentioned proof. Such as multiple photos of the two of you with Hollander."

"So what? He's a source."

"And Trachtenberg?"

"Ditto."

They go back and forth like this for a while until McLean makes a noise in his throat, which Austin interprets as a sign of renewed frustration and the right moment for him to try to take control.

"Okay, George," he says dramatically. "You win. Let's assume I'm the guy who fingered Emerson. I'm not confessing anything, but let's stipulate it as a possibility. With that, I'm ready to talk. These two jackasses here have convinced me.

"So, here's my proposal. Send them to the kitchen to amuse

Phoebe. I'll tell you things if you and I can talk alone."

Rocco and his sidekick look none too pleased. McLean is clearly surprised. He hadn't seen that coming.

"You're shitting me," he says suspiciously. "It'll do you no good."

"Try me, then. What have you got to lose?"

McLean stares at him hard, trying to read his mind, and looks over at his two enforcers as if he wants their approval. Then he makes up his mind.

"I guess you're right. No harm in hearing you out. But this better be real, for your sake."

As soon as they are alone, McLean asks, "You want some water?"

Trotter shakes his head and makes a face. "Water's for fish. I need a drink."

"You earned it," McLean laughs. He gets up and produces a bottle of Johnny Walker Black Label, and half fills two glasses.

"Up yours, George," Trotter says, takes a few big gulps, and feels a whole lot better.

McLean does the same. "Start talking."

"Let's say I did it," Trotter answers. "For the money, the glory, ego—whatever. What does that get you? I'm betting my confession isn't your highest priority anyway, except as a means to an end. The way I see it, your number-one objective has to be to bust the conspiracy from this end. Number two, solve the murder. All designed to get a jump on the Bureau and the Germans so as to avoid the DDO coming out of this with his head up his ass, and another giant Agency fuckup. That's why they sent you over here, am I right?"

"Don't be a smartass. Get to the point."

"I can deliver the goods. That's what I'm telling you."

"How?"

"I'll get you Hollander."

"Explain that," McLean says.

"Let's be honest. You tried using young Jackson as bait to get on the inside and collect the evidence, but he fucked you over, right?"

"What makes you think that?"

"Come on, George. I'm the Berlin station chief. You tried to freeze me out, but I've got my sources. I worked the field, targeted Hollander, and got lucky. I've got the evidence that Hollander is in it up to his neck, the 'it' including Emerson's murder. I'll bring him in, we'll confront him with the evidence, and make him talk to save his neck. That'll be enough to bust the conspiracy wide open. And you'll get the credit."

"And you have evidence?"

"Documents, emails, and a tape. Hollander in his own voice. I got him cold."

McLean is highly focused now and listening intently, but remains dubious.

The two keep sparring. McLean questions and prods, and Trotter has answers for all his questions, some tantalizingly precise, and others maddeningly vague.

McLean isn't about to take anything Trotter tells him at face value, but he can't let it drop.

"You're not convincing me," McLean says at last. "Let's go take a look. Show me this evidence you've got."

Trotter doesn't bat an eye. The evidence is in a safe place, he explains, and there is no way to get it until the next day. Besides, he is half dead—and not through any fault of his own, he reminds McLean pointedly. Tomorrow afternoon, at the CIA station Tank, he'll have everything available. They'll review it together, then go and grab Hollander.

McLean's defensive antenna goes on full alert.

"Bullshit," he says. "I'm not going to let you out of my sight. If we have to wait until tomorrow, you can sleep here."

That causes another long argument. It is three in the morning, Trotter argues, he is sore and a mess. He needs to go home, sleep in his own bed, put himself back together again, and get some clean clothes. If McLean thinks he'll run out on him, he can send Rocco to tag along.

Reluctantly, McLean agrees. They'll meet at two o'clock the next day in the Tank. Meanwhile, Rocco will babysit.

Trotter heads for his car, the big enforcer leading the way to the street. "No funny business," he growls. "You try anything, and I'll have your nuts in a jar."

Chapter 28

Berlin

Saturday, November 18

2:00 p.m.

*I*t had been an up-and-down week with mostly sleepless nights, and Dwayne Hollander was feeling queasy.

Investigators and cops were getting uncomfortably close. Herr Z was clamoring for his money, and Hank Rickenbom's group in the US was pressing for a return on their investment. The loss of the cash in Emerson's safe had been painful enough. Losing the much larger Swiss deposits would be a disaster.

Payday was imminent. They absolutely had to get to Jackson and open him up, fast, but how to do it still wasn't settled. Getting Adi von Trachtenberg on board had been a big step, but Z's people, who do the heavy lifting, have been slow to respond. At least now they were ready to talk it over at eight o'clock that night.

The Portuguese maid Eodosia takes Saturdays days off, and Frances, Hollander's wife, isn't due back from Baltimore for another several days. Hollander had slept in late and was enjoying a treasured ritual—a quiet lunch in a corner of the Adlon dining room. The hotel does a particularly fine steak tartare, complete with raw egg, onions, capers, anchovies, a little parsley, and a splash of Worcestershire and lemon juice. He finishes it off, then orders *Baumkuchen* for dessert. The waitress has just arrived with it, a scoop of vanilla ice cream on the side, when Hollander feels the ping of a text message on his cell phone.

FYI Ruben to Hollander. Centrifuge heater and five hydrometer test jars shipping priority today Tulsa.

"Ruben" is Strangefoot's cover name, and any unscheduled communication from him in prearranged code spells an emergency of sorts. On the surface, the text reads like routine business, but the real message is something quite different. "Priority" and "five" mean Strangefoot is calling for an urgent meeting at five p.m. that day. "Centrifuge" is a secluded spot in the Tiergarten, the 500-acre parkland near the Victory Column.

Hollander runs his eyes over the message twice more. Strangefoot liked to keep face-to-face meetings to a minimum, and he doesn't panic easily. Something critical and unexpected must have happened. Suddenly, Hollander feels nauseous and a strong urge to relieve his bladder.

When he gets back to the table and his *Baumkuchen*, the ice cream has melted, and the appetite is gone.

He calls for the check and hurries home.

4:50 p.m.

Twilight has deepened into darkness on a starless, cold, and windy evening.

Avoiding the taxi stand at the corner, Hollander hails a passing cab a prudent distance from his house, and leaves it two blocks short of the Strasse des 17 Juni, the broad boulevard that cuts through the middle of the Tiergarten.

Traffic is heavy, a steady line of headlights stabbing past him through the gloom. No pedestrians are out, only an occasional cyclist. Emerging from the cab, he shivers in the chill, draws his overcoat around him, and starts walking toward the Siegessäule monument that marks the entrance to the boulevard, with Tiergarten's inky expanse stretching out on both sides.

He pulls a thick wool scarf around his neck high enough to hide the lower part of his face. A wide-brimmed fedora worn low on his head shields his eyes. Not the world's cleverest disguise, and it wouldn't have worked if not for the desolation of the night. Tiergarten walkways are messy and muddy in winter, and his unwieldy, oversized galoshes make walking awkward and unpleasant. A mummified, overweight man in a grotesquely large hat, stumbling awkwardly into the deserted Tiergarten, is not something that would have gone unnoticed.

Just short of the Siegessäule, a narrow path to his right leads into the park. Hollander casts his eyes carefully in both directions, sees no one, and hurriedly disappears into the darkness. The path leads deeper into the woods, and he taps his way forward cautiously for about fifty yards, fearful of tripping on the uneven surface. His destination is a small fountain, shut down for the winter, bound by an eight-foot-high stone wall. When it comes into view, he breathes a sigh of relief and slips behind the barrier.

"Over here," a voice calls out, and Hollander sees Strangefoot's shadowy figure astride a fallen beech tree. The fat man shakes himself and stamps his feet, walks over, then lowers himself laboriously onto the log.

"It's a terrible night," he complains. "I'm not made for this."

"You wanted in, nobody forced you," Strangefoot says. "Maybe you bit off more than you can chew. Revolutions aren't a tea party. Mao Zedong, right? Incidentally, what's with the galoshes? You look ridiculous."

"Never mind. I have my reasons."

Conspirators can make strange bedfellows.

Hollander is a not-very-fit and mean-looking man whose instinct for solving problems is to charge ahead against whatever impediments get in his way. Act first, ask questions later is his preferred modus operandi. Strangefoot, a younger man, prefers finesse to force. The stiletto rather than the sledgehammer.

They had joined the conspiracy for very different reasons. Hollander's motives were social ambition, vanity, and unashamed greed. With success would come status and prestige among a powerful crowd, and probably lots of money. What motivated him, above all, was to be part of Hank Rickenbom's group. Politics and ideology didn't really interest him, but if paying lip service to their way of thinking was the ticket into their club, then so be it.

By contrast, Strangefoot was a true believer. Ambition, personal power, and money were motivation for him as well, but first and foremost it was the creation of a new world order that had drawn him in. The secrecy, intrigue, and double-dealing of a political conspiracy he actually found exciting. Not so for Hollander, for whom none of these things were pleasant. Like many bullies, he is at heart a coward, and any suggestion of danger makes him prone to panic when things go off the rails.

"We need a change of plans," Strangefoot begins.

"Why? What did you hear?"

"Our boy Jackson's not in Berlin. He flew the coop. Vanished. No one at the embassy knows where he is, and the cops don't either."

Hollander was silent for a moment, then stands up and says, "I've got to piss."

"Not in your pants, I hope."

Hollander frantically looks around, disappears, and then sits back down in defeat.

"What are we going to do? We're out of time. Any news on Payday?"

"Soon. That's all I know."

"If Jackson has what I think he has, we're done for. This is a disaster."

"Cool down. Don't have a tizzy. I found the SOB. He's in Geneva."

"My God, great! How'd you find him?"

"I keep my ears open. Show up in the right place at the right time. People let things drop. That's how I found out about Emerson ratting on us, remember?

"The problem is, I pull the fat out of the fire and then, every time, you still manage to fuck it up. I warned you about trusting Emerson, but you insisted. You didn't even secure access to the numbers of our accounts. Then you ran crying to a bunch of gangsters who kill first and think afterward. That's what brought everyone down on us. Now you're whining again. It's all your fucking fault."

"It's not that simple," Hollander protests. "I didn't expect them to kill Witty.

"But let's not point fingers," Hollander continues. "Monday morning quarterbacking won't get us anywhere. We have to stick together. You need to help us think about what to do. If Jackson can follow the money trail and figure out what's behind our MFG setup, it'll lead straight back to Hank and the entire US operation, just when they're getting ready to act. We can't let that happen.

"And there's another thing. I'm seeing Z tonight and we owe him 250,000. Plus, we promised him a cut on the money he's supposed to invest for us."

"So—what do you want me to do about it?" Strangefoot asks.

"I discussed it with Adi," Hollander explains. "He agrees that Z needs to help us with Jackson. His people know how to get him to cooperate. Just scare him—no really rough stuff, I promise. But who goes to Geneva to grab Jackson? Maybe I should talk to Z? Any ideas?"

"Jesus, not those guys again. Are you nuts?"

"We have no choice."

Strangefoot shakes his head. "Even if we find him, Jackson more than likely has protection. He's not stupid. And you don't want the Swiss cops down on our head."

"What's the alternative?" Hollander asks.

"I don't know. We'll have to think. There has to be some other way to pressure Jackson. Give me twenty-four hours. Maybe I can find out exactly where the bastard is and who's with him. That may give us some ideas. I'll keep you posted."

"We're out of time! I have to tell Z something tonight!"

"Goddammit," Strangefoot explodes. "How do I get it through your thick skull? Brute force doesn't work. Haven't you learned anything? I've got to try to get more intel on Jackson so we can find him and put the squeeze on him some other way. Twenty-four hours is what I said. Don't tell Z anything. String him along. He's your guy. You figure out how to do it. Anyway, if we can't locate Jackson in Switzerland and communicate with him, we have nothing. Just keep cool."

"When will I hear from you?"

"Relax, Dwayne. Tomorrow."

"Okay, I'll brief Adi," Hollander says quietly.

"You do that."

"Who leaves here first?"

"You do. Just don't trip over those stupid boots."

7:50 p.m.

For reasons Hollander does not understand, Z has chosen Berlin's main rail terminal for their rendezvous. He would have preferred a more private spot, but Z insisted on this most public of all places and gave him no choice in the matter.

The Hauptbahnhof, a huge, modernistic glass hulk, sits across from the chancellor's office on one side, with Bundestag offices on the other. On Sunday nights, it was packed tight with weekend travelers on their way home. Hollander arrives early and manages to snatch a table for two at a *Kneipe* inside the station. He nurses a pilsner while nervously monitoring the crowd stacked three deep at the bar.

Both Trachtenberg and Strangefoot had argued against making any kind of deal with the Hassanis, and now Hollander wishes to hell he'd listened to them. "If you invite the devil to dance with you, he'll dictate the tune," Strangefoot had cautioned.

At first, it had seemed like a straightforward business relationship. It also looked to be a golden opportunity to get their hands on some big money to finance their operations. The US and German sides had managed to raise quite respectable initial funds on their own, though not nearly enough for all that was needed, and he'd been quite pleased with his idea to invest some of it with Z's organization for a promised triple return in a matter of months. That the profits were more than likely coming from the gang's usual rackets in drugs, human trafficking, loan sharking, and the like wasn't their business. Even Strangefoot agreed that revolutionaries couldn't afford to be squeamish. Everything had gone swimmingly at first. The initial trial runs had worked perfectly and paid off nicely. The MFG structure—his idea—had functioned faultlessly.

The big mistake had been bringing in Emerson to handle the money transfers, though there had been no way to predict that he'd turn out to be a rat, or that Z's people would respond by killing him. Now there simply was no choice but to stick with them to clean up the mess.

Hollander is still pondering how to use them to get what they need from Jackson without inviting another murder when a stranger emerges from the nearby crowd and sits down next to him. No more than twenty, he is wearing a black leather jacket and a reversed baseball cap emblazoned with an image of the Brandenburg Gate. When he puts his hands on the table, it is obvious that soap and water aren't part of his routine.

"Your beer?" the kid announces more than asks, reaches for Hollander's half-empty stein, and swills from it contentedly. Then he says, "*Komm mit*," and Hollander follows him into the chaos of the station.

The Hauptbahnhof takes up a whole city block and is a giant maze connected by long moving staircases shuttling travelers in all directions. Getting lost in this tangle is easy, but his guide knows his way around. Hollander follows closely behind, nervously checking his back.

For a while they seem to be going in circles, twice passing the same set of public toilets, the sight of which had awakened another strong urge in Hollander to again to relieve his bladder. It is on the third go-around that the guy stops and points toward the *Männer* side of the toilets. "In there," is all he says and walks away.

The entrance is blocked by a cart stacked with buckets, mops, and assorted cleaning supplies. A sign proclaims the facility as out of service, and a fellow in an orange jumpsuit helpfully directs would-be users to try the lower level. Hollander, having anticipated imminent relief, is momentarily perturbed and perplexed, but then breathes more easily when the orange suit waves him forward. He circles the roadblock and walks in, hit by a foul smell of damp and dirty air.

He goes straight for the nearest urinal, relieves himself, zips his pants, then looks around. The doors are closed on all the stalls but one. Hollander goes over to take a closer look.

"Not exactly the China Club," Z mutters. The chief of Berlin's Hassani gang, stylishly dressed as always, is seated on the commode. "A lot more private, though," he adds.

For a brief moment, the revolting thought passes through Hollander's mind that he is witness to the man actually using the toilet, until he realizes that Z's pants are up and the seat cover down.

He tries to mask his discomfort with an obsequious greeting. "Great to see you, my friend. And my compliments on the ingenious location. Complete privacy, right?"

The boss of the Hassanis isn't a big man, but the cut of his suit makes the most of his broad shoulders and muscular build. He looks at Hollander as if the American has just shit on his precious crocodile loafers. Then he gives a brief nod, as if to say "cut the crap and get on with it."

Hollander inhales slowly, trying his best to control his anxiety, and launches into the well-rehearsed story.

"As you know, my dear Z," he begins, "there have been a number of unforeseen developments, and I'm sure you'll agree that immediate, decisive countermeasures are needed. We have carefully analyzed our options and found a solution for which your collaboration is essential, and which we believe has an excellent chance of success. There's also a lot of money in it for you."

Hollander pauses dramatically to await a reaction. Z eyes him suspiciously.

"Get to the point, Herr Hollander," he replies, "and cut out the bullshit. I know the cops are sniffing around and that something's got to happen fast. And, believe me, one way or another, it will. We're not going to the *Knast* for you people. So, what's this about money and the bundle you owe us? Why are we here, and what are you proposing?"

Hollander raises a hand. "I'm coming to that," he says. "What I'm telling you is, if we work together over the next two or three days, there's a sure fire way to get the authorities off our backs and our hands on a lot of money. We'll beat them to anything incriminating, and they won't be able to touch any of us."

And with that, Hollander begins to supply the details. He talks for ten minutes as Z listens quietly. When he is done, the American asks, "What do you think?"

Z is silent for an uncomfortably long time. Then he stands up and said, "It's 250 you owe, plus 250 more, not counting investment commissions. That's the deal."

Hollander nods vigorously. "That's the deal. One hundred percent."

"You'll set it up, and we're free to handle it our way?"

"Absolutely."

"Then we're in," Z announces and sticks out a beefy hand. "My guys will be in Geneva by tomorrow. You'll find him, and we'll do the rest. He'll cooperate. I guarantee it."

"Excellent," Hollander says. "But no bloodshed."

"Sure. No bloodshed. Well, maybe a bloody nose, you never know. He might be a wiseass."

"You swear?"

"On my dear mother's grave, may she rest in peace," Hassani reassures him. The fact that his mother, age eighty-six, is still enjoying robust health, leaves him considerable flexibility.

He produces a hip flask from his pocket and takes a long pull from it before handing it to Hollander, who eagerly does the same.

"You can leave the shithouse first," Hassani said.

Chapter 29

Berlin, Leipzig

Saturday, November 18

I assume they teach CIA rookies how to disappear into thin air, though with today's detection technology, I wouldn't be surprised if it's a challenge even for professionals.

For an amateur like me, hoping to stay hidden for long was a pipedream. Even if I managed to give everyone the slip, Kranmüller and whoever else was on my tail were bound to find me sooner or later. The best I can hope for is to get a few days' jump on my pursuers. I need time alone in Geneva without having to worry about a posse of cops and killers crowding in on me.

Although it's a short, one-hour flight from Berlin to Geneva, I'd quickly ruled that out. Air travel leaves too much of a paper trail. Passenger lists can be giveaways, even with a fake name to match one of the fake passports Emmett had handed me. And there was the added problem of how to get the Ruger through security. Driving there I'd rejected as well—too many cops cruising the Autobahn.

That left trains. Especially with the circuitous itinerary I've chosen, which I hope even the professionals might have trouble figuring out. It won't get me to Geneva until late tomorrow, which, given the time pressure I am under, is unfortunate, but unavoidable. On the other hand, I don't consider a longish layover in Paris a hardship.

The train out of Leipzig had been Tommy's idea. Nobody drives 125 miles to pick up a train from there, which is precisely what I was counting on as we took off for J.S. Bach's old bailiwick. Börries had kept to a leisurely pace on the Autobahn, and still got me to the Leipzig station well before the 22:12 night train out of Prague arrived, on which I'd booked a sleeper berth to Mannheim, with a connection on to Paris. Giving the cops the slip outside Dressler's restaurant had given him a big sense of accomplishment and put him into a buoyant and talkative mood for the entire length of the trip.

When we pulled into the *Bahnhof*, he gave me a thumbs-up and a cheerful goodbye wave. "Be smart, and be lucky," he called out after me.

No one has shown up to claim the second berth in my compartment, and the miniature bottle of scotch the sleeping car attendant brought me as we pulled out of Leipzig is putting me in a relaxed frame of mind. Nothing to worry about for a while.

So far, so good.

Paris

Sunday, November 19

9:45 a.m.

My plan for Paris is to leave my bag at the Gare de Lyon station, then pick up an evening TGV from there. The high-speed train makes the trip to the Geneva area in a fast three hours. I'd had a good night on the sleeper from Leipzig, though the moment the attendant knocks me awake in the morning, my worries about pursuers crowd in on me again. But, when I step out of the Gare de l'Est for the short cab ride down the Boulevard Magenta and past the Place de la Bastille, I soon feel a whole lot better.

Paris will do that to you. I am in my favorite city, and despite everything, I am going to enjoy it.

The Gare de Lyon is one of the busiest of Paris's half dozen train stations. It took a good ten minutes of combat with equally determined travelers to capture an empty locker, followed by further minutes of futile struggle to squeeze my bag into it before dragging it to the *consignes bagages*. The grumpy Parisian bureaucrat in charge reminds me why I tried the lockers in the first place.

"We close at ten," is the only thing madame says during the entire transaction.

A quick café and croissant at the station bistro, and then I start my stroll. For late November, it isn't a bad day. Dry, windless, and fairly mild, with just a touch of chill in the air, the sun moving in and out from under a gray cloud cover. It had rained during the night, and the cobblestones glisten.

My plan is a pleasant interlude meandering along the Seine, and once again to inhale the special vibes of my favorite city. The bouquinistes are just opening their stalls for the weekend crowd of strollers. At the Pont St. Louis, I cross to the Left Bank and stop to watch jugglers on roller skates working the spectators for handouts. At Place Maubert, I buy a *pain au chocolat* from a hole-in-the-wall bakery. Then it is back to the Right Bank along the rue de Rivoli, past the Place de la Concorde to the Champs Élysée.

With the unseasonably mild weather, people are out in force. Throngs of tourists, families pushing strollers, pensioners on benches enjoying the November sun, and lovers' arms intertwined or in tight clenches.

It was all I'd hoped for, except that my frame of mind is not what I had expected. The couples I pass put me in a melancholy mood again. They remind me of Kati. I miss her desperately. Thinking about her exposed to great risk inside the Trachtenberg compound scares and depresses me. How would she manage the dangers there?

I have finally met a woman I've fallen in love with and care for. The bond between us is like nothing I have ever felt before. I want to be with her and I want her safe. Yet, the real possibility of disaster—that I might never see her again—keeps going through my mind.

A nearly unbearable thought.

By midafternoon, I need a rest, so I take a table at the Café Cluny, corner of St. Michel and St. Germain Boulevards in the heart of the Latin Quarter. Unfortunately, I've picked up the overseas edition of *The New York Times* at a kiosk.

Over a hundred experienced Foreign Service Officers have quit, I'm reading. The number of new applicants has dropped by half. In Virginia, police have been confronting right-wing street gangs, some of them armed, spouting slogans of hate and carrying neo-Nazi banners. Has it already started?

I turn the *Times* aside, lean back, and close my eyes for a moment before reaching for the rest of my café au lait.

How on earth I got myself into this situation runs through my mind. And what chance do I really have to succeed and come out of it in one piece? What kind of world will I be living in? Then I think about Kati again and worry for her safety. What if the mole, Strangefoot, has found out about her and tipped off the conspirators?

The Cluny has filled up. All around me, the early evening crowd is relaxing, laughing, flirting, and having a good time. Lost in my gloomy thoughts, I hardly notice.

The revelers around me are enjoying themselves and it occurs to me that perhaps that's how it was in the 1930s. Everywhere democracies were under attack from within, but not enough people cared to notice or were willing to stand up and do something about it.

So, will this be the '30s all over again?

Throughout the West, right-wing extremists are once again conspiring against democratic freedom and the rule of law. All the signs are there for history to repeat itself. Unless—this time—there are those ready to do what's needed to defeat the conspirators before it is too late. And, yes, even to risk their lives for it.

Perhaps that's what this is all about, it suddenly occurs to me. I'm in a situation not of my making. I may not be ideally suited for this role of conspiracy fighter, but now that I'm in it, I can't be a bystander any longer. Running away is no longer an option.

Maybe Kati is on to something—it's fate. I've been given a chance to strike a blow for the only kind of world I want to live in, and so has she. Sure, it's dangerous. There's plenty of risk for both of us, and we may fail. But to hell with fear and doubt. Kati has made her choice and—goddammit—so have I.

In a strange way, these thoughts lift my spirits. Until two weeks ago, life had been ordinary, predictable, and routine. The problems that worried me—career, my marriage—suddenly seem trivial. What I'm in now is much more important. And worth living for.

Most of the day I've been feeling low, but no longer. Suddenly I'm confident, optimistic, and inwardly I'm smiling. Perhaps this is my chance to do something meaningful to honor the names on that family plaque in Weissensee Cemetery.

The TGV to St. Gervais, a resort town in the Haute Savoie, is loaded with weekend travelers, and we pull out of the Gare de Lyon at 20:14 on the dot. Around me, people are talking and laughing, and across the aisle a baby is squawking. But I'm settled into a single seat by the window with my eyes closed, trying for a moment of Zen.

At Bellegarde, I'll switch to a local train, then another, and reach Thonon-les-Bains, thirty minutes from Geneva, on the lakeshore in France, just before midnight. It's not the spa season, and I am now Mark Miller, with a room reserved in a little hotel that's open year-round. I've got one of Emmett's fake passports to prove it. In the morning, there's a train to the border at Annemasse, where I plan to join the crowds of daily commuters crossing into Geneva on foot, in case my pursuers, friend or foe, check the local hotels and principal border stations.

Geneva

Monday, November 20

The Hotel Richemond, in the heart of the business district near the Quai du Mont-Blanc, is the favorite meeting place of Geneva's heavy hitters.

On the telephone, Jupp's Moroccan friend has suggested it for our meeting, but it's the last place I want to be seen. So, I countered with a small bistro he'd never heard of, out of the mainstream on the south side of the lake. Actually, I'd never heard of it either. It's behind the Place Bourg-de-Four in the Old City I happened to pass this morning.

I'd suggested eleven thirty to get acquainted, and then a meal. I'm under a bit of time pressure, I'd explained. He said I'd recognize him by his tan *pardessus* with fur collar.

I get there early, settle into a corner table in back and order a glass of Fendant. The morning has gone well—infiltrating Geneva under the radar worked as planned. Mingled into the throng of transborder commuters, the French and Swiss border police at the small Annemasse frontier post gave my documents only a perfunctory look before waving me through. Mark Miller apparently wasn't on any official shitlist yet, which was reassuring. In Geneva, I stuck to public transport or walked, first to the post office in Carouge, and then to DHL near the Gare Cornavin. Now Anna's envelope with Witty's secret numbers is resting securely in my inside jacket pocket, and the fully loaded Ruger sits in the other.

So far so good, but I remind myself that these are merely the preliminaries and no more than prerequisite first steps toward my real mission in Geneva: to figure out Witty's numbers, and then to find a way to use them. But after days—no, weeks—of thinking about it, I am still distressingly shy of a realistic plan of action.

My best hope is that this Moroccan guy can come up with some useful intel for fruitful avenues to pursue. That's the hope, but realistically, it's a modest one. If he's anything like Jupp, I can't really trust him or even tell him what this is all about, so it might easily turn out to be a dry hole. Alternatively, I could snoop around the local banks, come up with some tall tales, and try to bluff my way inside, which, according to Jupp, probably wouldn't work either. Swiss banks are supposed to be as tightly sealed off from unauthorized eyes as a CIA bag of dirty tricks.

That's about it. But something else better turn up, something unexpected. Some lucky break, I'm hoping.

It just has to.

Inside those numbers in my pocket is the evidence to convict the conspirators, and I remind myself that there's a reason why I am alone in Geneva. The investigators have been penetrated by some unknown insider, and I can't entrust my fate to them. So, I am willing to take my chances, but I am determined to throw in the towel if the government guys catch up with me first. If it's the conspirators who catch me, I won't have that option.

Josephine's has fewer than a dozen tables, and, except for three blue-aproned workmen on their midday beer break, I am the only one here.

Then I see a middle-aged man in a fancy overcoat, more yellow than tan, walk in.

"Monsieur Slinani?" I ask and reach out to shake his hand. "A pleasure to meet you."

"The pleasure is mine, Mr. Miller," he says and gives me a nice smile. "And please call me Tony."

"And I'm Mark."

"Indeed," he agrees and hands me his visiting card.

Antoine Ahmed Slinani, Conseiller d'affaires finances, it reads. The reverse side is in Arabic.

"I'm intrigued," he says and looks around curiously. "How did you find this—er, interesting restaurant? Is the food special, perhaps? I don't come to this side of the lake very often."

"It's a first for me also," I confess. "And I'm afraid the food may be quite ordinary. I chose this place not for its cuisine, but for quite another reason."

Leaning across the table, I lower my voice to a conspiratorial undertone, one step up from a murmur. "The Richemond in the heart of town is too public," I explain. "I may be under observation and need to be careful. There's a lot at stake for me. Including money. I have to stay out of the limelight."

Slinani doesn't seem surprised. "*Bien sûr*, I understand," he reassures me. "You see, most of my clients are from the Middle East, Saudi princes, Kuwaiti oil sheikhs, the Omani Emir's family, that sort of thing. When they come to Geneva and want my advice, they usually have two equally delicate problems to discuss: money and women. And not always in that order.

"So, discretion is a given. You can depend on it, Mark. How can I be of service?"

"Thanks, Tony," I say. "I mustn't be impolite. May I suggest that we order our lunch first? Such as it is . . . and then talk business?"

We decide on *omble chevalier*, the best fish from Lake Geneva which even a bad chef can't spoil. Slinani insists on selecting the wine and makes a show of taking his time about it.

"A Dézalay, Medinette Grand Cru," he announces triumphantly. "I'm amazed to find it here. It's one of Canton Vaud's best Fendants," he explains. "Their vineyards go all the way back to twelfth-century Cistercian monks. You'll like it."

His little ceremony meant to impress me has given me time to observe him more closely. He's a man in his early fifties, with a handsome Mediterranean face and deep brown eyes that suggest a confident intelligence. A full head of casually combed black hair gives him a slightly tousled look. His hands, I notice, are soft, with only a single signet ring on his left pinkie.

His easygoing manner and relaxed smile is not at all what I had expected, with nothing of Jupp von Norden's aura of brash deviousness. That surprises me. Whether I can trust him is still an open question. Though the fact is, I like him.

The *omble chevalier*, with a *macédoine de légumes* and *frites* on the side, hadn't been bad at all, and the Fendant has lived up to Slinani's prediction. During the meal he did most of the talking and I just listened. The first bottle disappeared quickly, and the second further loosened his tongue for a steady stream of inside Geneva gossip, including a discussion about the private banks.

The comfortably round, rosy-cheeked *cuisinière* who'd served us our meal, presumably Madame Josephine herself, has brought us espressos, but I decline her offer of a *digestif complementaire*.

The time has come to steer the conversation into more sensitive territory.

"You know, Tony," I say, "Geneva seems so solid and law-abiding a city. And the private banking houses here have a stellar reputation: Lombard Odier, Pictet, Cresset and the others. Which is why

I'm here, as Jupp may have explained. Can they be trusted for protecting my identity from prying eyes, and for keeping my money safe?"

Slinani nods vigorously.

"Of course, your money would be safe, and you can count on the banks' complete discretion. That's how Swiss bankers got rich and stay that way. Public or private, Swiss banking has its time-honored tradition of absolute safety and confidentiality.

"They are also solid money managers and provide any number of useful services to their clients; all legal, of course. When it comes to their clients' motives, it's no questions asked. That's a time-honored tradition of Swiss banking as well. To question that wasn't my point. Only to say that the banking fraternity has no illusions about their rich clients' priorities.

"Hmm." I take a deep breath and say, "I'd like you to help me with a very delicate matter, Tony. It's tricky, and I'm going to tell you things I haven't shared with anyone else. Not even my lawyers. There's a substantial amount of money at stake, so I'm prepared to compensate you well. I expect your expert advice will be worth it. We can settle that later, but first—can I trust you completely?"

"Completely. And don't worry about my fee. That's never a problem."

"Good. And you were right. There are women involved. As you said: *Toujours les femmes.*"

"*Evidemment*, Mark, ha ha! Why am I not surprised? Tell me more."

Slinani laughs and I join in.

"So, this is the situation," I say, and then I spin my tale for him. A contentious divorce with lawyers fighting over who gets what of assets in comfortable nine figures.

"I'm the one who was smart with my investments," I say, "so why let her have half of it, right? Problem is, she suspects I've hidden some of it away, which, between us, happens to be true. Her investigators—former US Secret Service agents—are on my tail in Geneva right now. That's why I'm in hiding. I need to make my private cache disappear into an anonymous account. And that's why I need your help."

Slinani lets his shoulders ride up and down nonchalantly. "No problem," he says.

"Great," I say. "That's a big relief."

But now I get to the tricky part of my fairytale, and I'm not sure he'll buy it. "Audrey—that's my wife—has a lover, lined up to be her next husband. I have a nasty suspicion he's helped her to rob me for years. Money she claims to have given to charity and her family, but kept for herself. Big money. And I have evidence—don't ask how I got it—a bunch of numbers that look suspiciously like Swiss bank accounts. If this is true, it totally changes my bargaining position, right? So, could you take a look and tell me about those numbers? And this might be too much to ask, but maybe you could use your excellent contacts to get a look inside for a few vital details?"

I hand him the numbers and he studies them silently for a minute or two.

Then he says, "From the look of this, your dear wife has been very busy, which means that she may be richer than you imagine. Why else would she have two separate accounts—or perhaps they're her boyfriend's—at Banque Martin, and a third at Lombard Odier? Plus, a lockbox at Sécurité Safes Léman, a private safe-keeping service?"

"You know these places?"

"Of course. All top houses, solid, dependable, and airtight. The Lombard people are my friends. Banque Martin's senior partner, Jean-Luc de la Marre, is a leading citizen with a stalwart reputation. And Sécurité Safes Léman? Excellent organization, very secure."

"So . . . getting in to find out more?"

"Impossible."

"But with your contacts—"

"Doesn't matter, can't be done."

I continue to press, but to no avail.

After much back and forth, I fall back on, "Maybe you can think about it. Maybe something will occur to you. I'm running out of time, and I'm willing to pay you well for your creativity."

Slinani looks at me, evidently considering my proposition. Then he smiles at me again and puts his hand on mine. "I really would like to help you, Mark," he says and sounds like he means it. "I'm not sure I can, but let me think about it. Do some checking around.

"So, here's my suggestion—meet me tonight at my club. It's a very special place, very discreet and quite secure. You'll like it. We'll have a quiet drink and talk some more."

Rue Rothschild 59b, right behind the Palais Wilson. 23:00.

And with that, we shake hands, and he heads out the door.

Chapter 30

Berlin

Sunday, November 19

1:40 p.m.

*L*iz Cunningham has been on the veranda all morning with her *Times* crossword and more coffee than is good for her, but Emmett is not himself. Distracted, distant, and uncommunicative, he's obviously under a lot of stress. He even canceled his tennis game and locked himself in his study.

She is concerned, because his unflappability has always been something she could count on. He's never kept her out of the loop on even the highly classified stuff he's not supposed to share with anybody. But this time, he's shut her out. So just how bad must it be?

She's placed their traditional Sunday fare on the little side table out on the terrace—Greek salad, cheese, freshly baked rye bread from the corner baker, and a pitcher of Bloody Marys. Rather than climbing the stairs, she calls him on her cell phone, wondering whether he'll pick up.

He does.

"It's almost two," she says. "Lunchtime. You want any?"

"God . . . sorry. No wonder I'm starving."

He comes bounding down the stairs, a bit too eagerly, and Liz takes one look and laughs.

"Have you looked in the mirror?"

He's unshaven, hair a mess, wearing a Holy Cross sweatshirt that looks like he's retrieved it from the lost-and-found bin at the Y. Rounding out his outfit is a pair of striped pajama pants that have seen better days, sockless moccasins, and a guilty expression that's a cross between contrite and coy. He grins at her, plants a quick kiss on top of her head, and takes a seat. He has two cell phones with him that she doesn't recognize, which he keeps within easy reach.

During lunch, he avoids her eyes and works hard at making small talk. It's after the salad and the cheese, while he's munching the grapes she's brought from the kitchen, that he opens up.

"It's about Adam," he confides. "He's overdue calling in, and I'm nervous as hell. More like scared shitless, if you want to know the truth.

"He's on his own, hiding out of town, while everyone's looking for him—the Bureau and the Agency people, the German cops, and some street gang killers, and I'm the only one who knows where he is. Now I'm thinking I may have done the wrong thing . . . covering for him."

Liz pours coffee. "Start from the beginning. I'm not sure I understand what this is all about."

So, he lays out the basics for her, and twenty minutes later, he is summing up. "Adam may have the evidence to put the conspirators away, but with a traitor inside our tent, he's in mortal danger. He's without protection, and he could get himself killed if the gang finds out where he is. Tomorrow there's an urgent 'all hands' meeting at the embassy. FBI, CIA, and embassy staff. The German cops also want to talk to him, so it's come-to-Jesus time for me. I could break my promise to Adam and send people to protect him and back him up. But if the mole finds out where he is, it might put him in even greater danger.

"So, what do I do, Liz?"

They're both quiet for a moment. Then Liz says, "I've got nothing you haven't already thought of, Emmett. Only the obvious. Keep your cool. Listen to Adam if he calls. Then trust your gut. That's all you can do. And quit blaming yourself. You'll do what you think is best. That's all anyone can ask. And I do love you for caring so much for your friend."

——•——

Liz had insisted on their usual date night at the Taverna, and he acquiesced, pretending to be cheerful and attentive, but he wasn't doing a very good job at it. Even Luigi's signature dish—eggplant parmigiana—with a top-of-the-line Barolo, hadn't done the trick.

It isn't until Monday, around two p.m., that his phone comes alive. Adam sounds tense and gives a bare-bones report of developments that seem both hopeful and scary. He is safe, thus far. He's found out what Witty's secret numbers mean and is chasing leads for possibly more critical intel later in the day. Pushing it, going fast. That was the good news. But the people he is dealing with are "a bit scary," as he puts it. And since last night, he thinks someone might be on his tail, though he can't be sure.

And that's it.

"More later," he says. "I might need help soon."

Then he signs off.

Berlin

Monday, November 20

2:15 p.m.

After the investigator team meeting, Public Affairs' Erica Baum-holzer is lying in wait outside the Embassy Tank, and when Em-mett comes through the door, she pounces. He knows that the way she sees it, most principals are uber-secretive and don't appreciate the importance of having the media on your side. But she does. It's her job to keep reporters happy and dole out newsy tidbits, so if she has to be a nuisance to get the job done, then so be it.

"Anything new?" she asks. "My media briefing is in an hour. What can I say?"

Emmett keeps moving and waves her off. Public relations is the last thing on his mind.

"No news, Erica," he says, and tries to push past her, but she stands her ground.

"This is really important," she pleads. "We have a flood of rumors and we have to get in front of them. I need to say something to keep control of the narrative."

"We're working on it," he says. "No further comment at this time. That's it."

Erica protests, and it takes a few more minutes of back and forth until she relents and beats a sorrowful retreat.

Upstairs, Jack Castelyou leans against the hallway Coke machine, waiting for him.

Emmett waves him inside, and Castelyou sits across from Emmett in one of his government-issue, brown leather armchairs, a small coffee table between them.

He leans in, pushes his rimless glasses back over the bridge of his nose and, unable to hide his discomfort, swallows self-consciously.

"I don't know about you," he explains, "but I'm worried. It's crunch time, and we're nowhere on the key questions."

"Which are, in your estimation?"

"Adam, the guy with the keys to the kingdom, has disappeared, and no one knows where he is or what he's doing. Meanwhile, McLean won't let us level with the Germans. The Agency is in charge here; he's their top guy. And until he says it's okay, I can't make use of my contacts. And on top of everything else, there's Trotter's vanishing act. McLean just isn't being straight with us. You gotta give me some help."

Emmett nods and affects a pained smile. He's got most of the answers, but has to pretend otherwise. Discretion is fundamental to his job description, but he doesn't like to flat-out lie. Besides, after three years at the embassy, Jack's earned Emmett's respect. Then again, he's an FBI agent, so there's never any question about where his primary loyalty is.

Still, Castelyou is a straight shooter who tries to be on the embassy team as well. When he's got a conflict, he levels with Emmett, who's worked with other attachés and knows that transparency is not all that common. Castelyou is also exceptionally smart, and when he talks, his legal training shows through. Short, concise, and to the point. And everyone at the embassy likes him. Except, of course, for Trotter.

Taking his time and measuring his words, Emmett nods and says, "I'm with you. I don't understand McLean's game either. There's something very fishy about him and Trotter's disappearance."

He pauses to let that sink in, then adds, "But whatever they're up to is a sideshow. Adam's the main event. He's definitely on our team, and he told us he'd go off on his own when we met at my place, remember? Right or wrong, he thinks it's the way to get results. So, we have to be patient."

Castelyou shifts uncomfortably in his seat, exuding anything but patience. "I don't agree. We can't afford to wait. This gang is dangerous, and it's crazy to leave him on his own. I say we insist McLean bring in the Germans and mount a full-court press to find him. Right now."

"Where the hell would we look?"

"Yeah, well, unless you have a better idea, I'll put my money on the land of the numbered accounts. Zürich or Geneva. Where else? Let's send out teams to look for him. Get the locals involved as well."

Emmett stares at Castelyou as he considers how to respond. He's really torn, and coming clean and getting some help would be a big relief. Then suddenly he hears himself say, "I know where he is, Jack. He's made progress. He's getting close and there's a good chance he'll pull this off for us."

Castelyou looks up, wide-eyed. "What are you telling me?"

Emmett sighs. "I've been sworn to secrecy, but if I can count on you to tell no one—and I mean no one—I'll explain."

Castelyou blinks and nods. "Christ almighty, of course, Emmett."

Emmett begins to lay out the key facts: that Adam is indeed in Geneva, avoiding hotels, and trying to stay invisible. That he has the numbers and is making progress figuring out what they mean. That he has been in contact with Kranmüller and the *Polizei*, and what the Germans have uncovered.

"He'll call me again today," Emmett explains. "Then we'll know more. But we have to be ready to join him, maybe even tonight. So, please help me, Jack: cops and robbers is your bailiwick. How do we prepare?"

Castelyou digests what he's heard for a moment. Then says, "I still don't understand why Adam went off on his own when he could have had us as backup."

Which is when Emmett explains about Strangefoot.

The blood seems to drain from Castelyou's face.

"My God. Who is it? Trotter?"

"A logical choice," Emmett agrees. "It would explain a lot."

"How in hell did the Germans find out about this?"

"It's their country, Jack. They've got satellites, drones—all the same toys we do. And possibly an inside source."

"A Strangefoot of their own?"

"It has been suggested."

Suddenly, Castelyou is on his feet.

"I'm late. Hinton's waiting for me. Back by five or six," he promises. He puts on his blazer and heads for the door. "If Adam calls, be damn sure you find out exactly where he is."

Chapter 31

Berlin

Monday, November 20

Zamir Hassani, a.k.a. "Herr Z," views himself as the chief executive of a healthy family business. It took him years of scheming to ascend to the top job of "Krye"—the boss of the Berlin Hassani gangs—and over the years he has built a highly profitable enterprise mostly involving drugs, loan sharking, and human trafficking. Plus, investments in a few legitimate businesses. These days, the organization nets a nice seven-figure profit, at least half of which goes into his own pocket.

It is the nature of the business that the law will always be on their tail, but he has a hand-picked staff to protect their franchise and to keep the *Polizei* and rival gangs at bay. Even so, the current crisis isn't the first time the cops have come dangerously close, or done some serious damage. The half dozen brothers doing time in Moabit are painful reminders of that, though supporting their families for years is a burden Z willingly accepts as a matter of clan loyalty, a necessary and proper part of his overhead cost structure.

As to his joining them in prison, he considers that a miniscule risk. In his quarter century in Germany, he has never seen the inside of a *Knast*, not counting a brief stint of pretrial detention leading, for lack of sufficient evidence, to neither trial nor conviction. Friends around the Berlin crime scene, as well as business contacts with lines into the police and the courts, have always run interference for him. His lawyers' skills exploiting the slow and ponderous German judicial processes have done the rest. So, Zamir sees no reason to feel especially concerned about his personal situation at the moment.

He grew up in a small farming village in the remote Dukagjin highlands of northern Albania. With only seven years of schooling, he soon came to the attention of the *bajrak*, the clan's overseas network elders, not for his book learning, but for being a tough alpha animal, shrewder, fearless, and more aggressive than most of the local youngsters his age.

In March of 1991, on a drunken Saturday night in Shkoder, the area's only larger town, a man named Besnik Murati was overheard referring to a Hassani mother as "the devil's cunt." Under the strict code of honor, so intolerable an insult of Hassani womanhood cried out for prompt retribution. Even more so since the Muratis were connected to a rival gang.

It was Zamir, though still a teenager, who had moved in and taken care of the matter. Days later, what was left of Murati was found in a hollow near Lake Skadar, his face bashed in beyond recognition, his tongue in his left hand, his penis in the other. The police investigated, but not for long or with great conviction. The ensuing blood feud lasted a full two years.

Zamir had earned his spurs, but had to be spirited out of the area. Before leaving, he took the sacred oath which sealed his submission to the Hassani internal code of honor and discipline. He then joined a group of Albanian men who that year crossed the

Adriatic in small boats into southern Italy.

Shortly thereafter, cousins arranged his onward journey north to Germany.

The deal with Hollander—that fatuous American and his German clique—had looked financially enticing, but it didn't play out as promised. The big capital infusions and fees he had been promised never materialized, and Hollander's allegedly foolproof system for laundering illegal cash had evaporated as well. In Zamir's opinion, the decision to appoint the traitorous government stooge Emerson as their courier and put all their chips on him was nothing less than gross incompetence.

Following his Hauptbahnhof rendezvous with Hollander, he'd assessed the situation and settled on a plan that not only would neutralize the risks, but actually allow him to profit handsomely.

The first step would be to preemptively capture Adam Jackson in Geneva and isolate him in a place unknown to Hollander and his crew. Gaining exclusive control of Jackson, then extracting all the information and materials about money and incriminating evidence from Jackson and keeping it in their possession, should put the family in the strongest possible bargaining position and assure them the largest share of the financial spoils. This would solve his problem with the cops, while opening up interesting new opportunities for future tributes under the threat of a little friendly blackmail of Hollander and his partners. Whether Adam Jackson survives this power play once he's squeezed dry is a matter of no great importance. A routine question of collateral damage to be resolved later.

12:50 a.m.

The small, indifferently furnished room over Jermir Duka's Turm-strasse garage is rarely used for meetings these days, but tonight the five men summoned there fill it to overflowing. Zamir himself is in attendance, which is unusual.

The oversized Kulla brothers—Fatback and Gezin—had shoehorned themselves into the small orange couch. With their amply tattooed, muscly bulk, they are easily the largest presence in the room. The one they call Marco, a well-dressed man in his forties with a drooping mustache and doleful eyes, is on a high-backed wooden chair across the room next to Zamir. Ahmed, "the Bosnick," sits next to him, and James, an athletic-looking, bald Albanian with lifeless blue eyes, leans against a wall.

Zamir splashes more whiskey into his glass, frisks himself for a cigarette, lights up, and maneuvers himself back into his leather armchair.

"You're going to do this. Am I fucking right, Marco?" Zamir asks, addressing the man in the tall chair, the leader of the group.

"*Keine Sorge, Chef*," Marco nods.

"*Mut po*, shit yes," Gezin chimes in from the sofa in Albanian.

Fatback agrees. "*Jan gati*, ready!" he announces. Both brothers, each with a can of beer in his hand, are in an excellent mood.

"As soon as we get there tomorrow," Marco continues.

"It's today . . ." James cuts in with a look at his watch.

"Right, today. Soon as we arrive, we'll get the house ready. Nicely secluded."

Zamir nods approvingly. "Where exactly?" he asks.

"Out toward the French border, off the Route de Florissant, on the south side of the lake."

"Okay," Zamir says. "Tomorrow afternoon, we should know exactly where our pigeon is staying. Then you take it from there.

No fuckups. I want it done smoothly. With no trigger-happy shit," he adds, directly addressing the gaunt young thug with the non-Albanian name.

"Swiss cops can be worse than Germans," the Bosniak observes sourly.

"Okay, then," Zamir says. This is serious. The cops are after us and this is how we stick it to them. If we fail, we're fucked. Remember that. And there's lots of money at stake, for all of us. So, no women, no nightclubs, and no boozing until it's done. Anyone does wrong, he pays a heavy price. I promise you that. Your job is to get Jackson ready for me. I'll handle him when I get there. When it's finished, we'll celebrate."

Then he turns to Marco, embraces him and kisses him on both cheeks. A blessing he bestows on each of the others before heading for his BMW in Jermir's garage.

Washington, DC

Monday, November 20

6:30 a.m.

Rick Brewster usually can smell an operational disaster well before the field reports it. Forty years in the Agency's clandestine service and years in the field will do that for you, and on this one, there is definitely that certain something in the air.

By Sunday night, what had begun as a faint whiff of a setback on Saturday morning has grown into the telltale stink of major trouble. So, when the red phone by his bed rouses him from a half sleep at six on Monday morning—noon in Berlin—he is not surprised.

"Berlin's requesting a video conference, sir. They say it's urgent. What shall I tell them?" the duty officer inquires.

"On the secure circuit. Fifteen minutes," the DDO orders, and heads for the bathroom.

Friday night, McLean had been all too eager to report his initial success, with the prospect of total victory within twenty-four hours. With only moderate persuasion, he said (sparing the DDO the details) Trotter had de facto agreed to deliver Dwayne Hollander, along with truckloads of incriminating evidence. Pending that, McLean had kept him under guard. He promised that by Saturday, Brewster would have all the missing pieces. The Agency would come out on top, and the small bumps along the way, like the defection of the Berlin chief of station and getting a principal witness killed, would soon blur into the Agency's long history of similar fuckups.

But as of Monday morning, the shit has officially hit the fan.

One brief glance on the video screen, and Brewster knows. George Hartfield, a.k.a. Mortimer McLean, looks like he hasn't slept in days.

"You won't like this, Rick," he says.

"Can't wait."

"Trotter got away from us. SOB's disappeared into thin air."

"You said you had him locked up."

"Yeah, well, he tricked Rocco with a drugged beer. Muscles instead of brains. Sorry, boss, but we're fucked."

The DDO was not amused, but he would save the shouting and the recriminations for later.

"You're sure Trotter is Strangefoot? And everybody knows it?"

"Most likely, though no one is willing to say it to my face."

"The Bureau guys? Hinton, Castelyou?"

"Not a word. But gloating, no doubt."

The DDO is determined to keep his cool, but this couldn't be worse. National Security Council principals meet tomorrow to finalize a joint move on Thunderclap later in the week, both stateside and in Germany, coordinating with the chancellor's office. But without the intel Hartfield had promised to supply, they have nothing that will stick.

"What about Jackson?" he asks.

"Disappeared too. No one knows for sure what he's doing, but he's doing it on his own."

"What a fucking shitshow," Brewster mutters.

"Hate to say it, boss, but unless there's a miracle, it may be over. We can try to grab Hollander, bluff him, and hope he'll flip. A long shot, though. If he has any doubt about what we have on him, he's got no reason to fold. But that's what I'm trying to set up."

Brewster sucks in the air through his teeth, then exhales. "Get it done," he says. "Now."

Berlin

1:00 p.m.

Precisely at one o'clock each day, the Trachtenbergs share lunch in their dining room. It's been a set routine of spousal togetherness over many years, though it's never been an especially sociable one. Adalbert von Trachtenberg isn't someone to share his feelings or say that much about anything, and Bettina has learned to live with that. Except that over the last several days, he's been even more moody and uncommunicative than usual. He leaves the lunch table hurriedly and rarely emerges from his library before dinnertime.

Bettina can tell that her husband is deeply upset, but she has no idea why, and she knows better than to ask or to intrude on whatever he's doing up there. So, when a leather-jacketed motorcycle courier shows up at the front door with a mysterious yellow envelope addressed to him and marked URGENT in bold block letters, she immediately realizes that she has a problem.

Send it up at once and interrupt him, risking his wrath, or wait until the six o'clock cocktail hour?

Considering the unusual object and manner of its delivery, she has decided not to withhold it even for a moment. She has, however, taken the precaution of sending her assistant to deliver it. Better to let her suffer her husband's displeasure. However, according to Kati, he tolerated the interruption surprisingly well, and, after a glance at the envelope, dismissed her with a not unfriendly, though hurried, "*Danke, mein Liebe!*" before retreating back into his inner sanctum.

An even greater surprise awaits Bettina and Kati a few minutes later. Without a hint of an explanation, Adi suddenly appears downstairs and reaches for his raincoat and umbrella. Then he bolts out the front door, where a taxi has just rolled into the circular driveway.

———

4:35 p.m.

Adi's cab makes it from Zehlendorf to the Adlon with remarkable speed. He doubles the fare and hurries inside.

During the entire twenty-three-minute ride, he's been staring at the envelope's contents. Three words and a number: "Ruben. Priority. Adlon 623" and an electronic room key. "Ruben" is Strangefoot's code name. The key, he assumes, is for room 623.

He's never before laid eyes on this mystery man. Hollander has always been the intermediary, an arrangement that Adi insisted on. Now the spy's direct summons has greatly unsettled him. An unwelcome break of precedent, because cloak-and-dagger meetings aren't at all his style. This time he's been given no choice.

At the Adlon, he takes the elevator to the sixth floor. The plush, carpeted hallway looks deserted. The room he is looking for is around the corner to the right. Adi looks around cautiously and then starts toward it. When a young couple emerges from another elevator, his heart seems to burst into his throat. He slows down and pretends to look in his raincoat pocket, then breathes a sigh of relief when they disappear into their room a few doors to the left.

Room 623 is near the end of the hallway. As Adi comes near it, plastic key in hand, he is startled to hear the blurred sound of talking inside the room. Not what he expected. He presses his ear against the door, hoping to identify the speaker, but doesn't get anywhere. The door is solid—it's the Adlon, after all—and the voice remains too muffled to make out.

He's momentarily undecided on how to proceed, then sucks in his breath, gently knocks, and waits. No reply, so he tries it again, harder this time, but the result is the same. No answer. Still uncertain on what to do, he cautiously swipes the key through the slot, but a red light comes on and the door remains locked. More and more anxious to get out of the hallway, he swipes more resolutely, the light turns green, and Adi, greatly relieved, walks in. He carefully shuts the door behind him, advances into the room, and looks around. In shock.

The room is empty.

By the standards of Berlin's leading hotel, it's simply furnished, and on the small side. A king-size bed, TV atop a sideboard, a faux-antique desk, and stuffed chairs near a small table with a Lalique lamp. The floor-to-ceiling drapes match the room's blue-and-gold décor. On the TV screen, an aproned, comfortably padded *Hausfrau* in her kitchen is letting her audience in on the secrets of her special gravy for *Königsberger Klopse* meatballs, which explains the voice he heard from the hallway.

What am I supposed to do now? he wonders.

Opposite the bed, an open door leads to the bathroom. Thoroughly puzzled by now, Adi turns down the TV and goes in to take a look. Empty.

What's happening here? Adi is thinking hard, willing himself to stay calm while trying to make sense of the situation. He's nervously listening for sounds outside the room but hears nothing. His unease is turning into alarm and panic. Is this a trap? What if he simply leaves? He's got to find a place to sit down and quietly consider his next move. In the corner, there's a small, white stool, and it's when he walks over to it that he hears the cell phone and catches sight of it on top of the sink.

"Thank you for coming, *Exzellenz*."

A foreign voice speaking American-accented German.

"Please make sure that the TV sound is on and speak directly into the phone. Don't say more than you have to. Walls have ears, and we have to be exceedingly careful. When we've finished, please take your burner phone apart, then destroy and dispose of the separate pieces in different, if possible, untraceable places. Do you understand?"

"Yes."

"Then I suggest you sit down and listen. Our mutual friend is also with us."

Adi, feeling distinctly squeamish, sits on the bed and presses the phone close to his ear, whispers a muted "*Jawohl*."

"Good," the voice continues, "we have to keep this brief. There have been several troublesome developments, which call for immediate, strong countermeasures. I'll get to that in a moment, but first, there is no need to panic. Our cause is righteous, and it will prevail."

Again, Adi whispers, "*Jawohl.*"

"Here's the state of play. First of all, it's now definite that the thief is in Geneva. He is alone, but more than likely he will have assistance from Berlin very soon. Worse, he may be getting close to evidence that could be used against us. That would be disastrous, so we must stop him now and be smart about how we do it.

"Unfortunately, it appears we're being monitored much more closely than we realized. The authorities are using every tool at their disposal, including—or so it seems—a spy within our tent. There is only one obvious suspect, but for the moment I'll let you come to your own conclusions.

"These new developments greatly limit our room to maneuver, which is why this meeting required so many special arrangements and precautions. However, as I'll explain in a moment, it also opens up an interesting opportunity for us to turn the tables on our opponents.

"The challenge we face is clear. We must quickly gain control of the thief in Geneva, either before he finds incriminating material or, failing that, before he can turn it over to the authorities. And at the same time, we must urgently agree on the best way to protect ourselves from the traitor in our midst. What I'm proposing requires each one of us to be fully on board and play his part. Let me lay it out for you. No doubt you'll have questions. But let's do this quickly."

The weather had been changeable all day. Rain, in the morning, heavy at times, has given way to weak sunshine through a partial cloud cover by midday. At twenty minutes to six in the evening, when Trachtenberg steps out of the Adlon, a nasty *Ostwind* is blowing and it has turned much colder.

His raincoat isn't much protection against the elements, but Adi hardly notices, ignores the taxi stand outside the entrance, and starts walking through the Brandenburg Gate, past the Holocaust Memorial's field of stones, toward the Potsdamer Platz traffic hub. A twenty-minute walk. Traffic around him is heavy with evening commuters, bicyclists hunkered down against the wind, and, very occasionally, other pedestrians. On a cloudy night like this, not many are out.

The entire conversation in room 623 lasted fifteen minutes at most. But now he wants to be alone, desperate to clear his head and to think. So, he keeps walking, past Philharmonic Hall, along the canal, and all the way to the KaDeWe department store in City West.

Finding no solace, he hails a cab and reaches home just in time for the cocktail hour, another of his rarely missed domestic rituals. Bettina and Kati are working later than usual, and the assistant has been invited to stay for dinner.

His precipitous departure that afternoon or where he went isn't mentioned. In fact, the mystery only deepens because Adi is now in a much better mood than he's been all week. Whatever had depressed him must have somehow resolved itself that afternoon.

Chapter 32

Geneva

Monday, November 20

*S*linani was a pleasant surprise, but can I trust him?
   He accepted the tale about my marital troubles and seems genuine about wanting to help. The allusion to "something positive" sounds promising and has me wired. Could it be that he was that lucky break I had been hoping for?

4:00 p.m.

I should stay out of circulation the rest of the day.
   But I don't.
   It's a fine afternoon, and, with the Haute Savoie on one side, the Jura mountains on the other, and the sun sparkling on the lake, I can't bear the thought of staying holed up inside.
   Stepping out of Josephine's Café, I cautiously check up and down the rue des Chaudronniers. Nothing out of the ordinary. No men sitting in parked cars or reading newspapers. No one inspect-

ing shop windows.

So, I turn up the collar of my Burberry and start walking.

I planned not to cross the Rhone into the center of town until just before my evening date. Old Geneva, with its maze of narrow cobblestone streets, somehow seems safer. Once in a while, I stop to study my reflection in windows for possible tails. Then I continue to stroll, keeping alert and occasionally doubling back through side streets and alleys.

Down by the lake at the Jardin Anglais, I mingle with hordes of tourists to admire the *jet d'eau* with its water column shooting skyward. Then I pass the time on a bench at the Horloge Fleurie, a clock made of flowers, enjoying the afternoon sun.

Toward evening, I head to the Café du Commerce, a famous old tavern on the Place Bourg de Four frequented mostly by locals. I picked it for a decent dinner, to kill time, and because at that hour it's usually jammed, making it as good a place as any for hiding in plain sight.

I get an out-of-the-way corner table in the back and order an *entrecôte grillé* with *sauce Bérnaise* and *rösti*.

Then I head for the men's room.

When I get back, the waiter has just arrived with the food and is pouring me a glass of the Dole du Valais from a liter carafe.

In a stall of the men's room, I transferred the Ruger from my jacket pocket to a small leather holster I spotted in a shop window on the rue du Rhone. Now the gun is resting comfortably attached to the belt in the small of my back.

I take a sip of the wine and allow myself a small smile.

I am armed like a professional and ready to go. Actually looking forward to my next encounter with Tony. The thought crosses my mind that maybe I am getting the hang of this "secret agent" thing. So far, I've stayed one step ahead of the bad guys, feeling confident about handling whatever lay ahead.

Perhaps a little too confident.

I have just finished the last of the *entrecôte*, when I look up and notice the man at a table diagonally across from mine. Our eyes meet for a few seconds; then he becomes interested in his newspaper again.

Something about him doesn't seem right. It may be his look when our eyes met, or the lush mustache and how it droops over the sides of his mouth. Maybe it is the ponytail, or the way he is dressed.

I keep him in my peripheral vision, but only once does he briefly look my way again.

Eventually, he calls for the check, puts down some bills, and walks out. Maybe it was nothing, and I was still edgier than I realized.

10:40 p.m.

I leave the café and am walking to the cab stand down the street when I see the mustache man again, talking to a guy about twice his size, at least a foot taller, and square-shouldered. They are both staring at me and it doesn't look too friendly. This time, the one that I saw before doesn't seem to care that I notice.

The obvious conclusion that the bad guys—Witty's killers and my pursuers—have picked up my trail so quickly hits me hard. This creates all kinds of unpleasant possibilities.

My stomach churns, something heavy rises into my throat and stays there, but for the moment there is nothing to do but to continue toward the taxis. Out the window of my cab, I watch them standing there with no indication that they are planning to follow me.

Except that the mustache man is talking into a telephone.

I am feeling pretty tense when I get to the rue de Rothschild, a short street a block off the lakefront in the high-prized Zone Internationale.

It's just after eleven o'clock when the taxi deposits me in front of 59b, an impressive three-story residence with a cupola on top. The kind a rich Geneva banker might have built himself a century ago, with lots of pillars, pediments, and decorative arches.

There's nothing to indicate that it's a private club. Only an antique lantern above the entrance highlights the house number. There's not even a doorbell, only a small doorknocker to signal my arrival.

The guy who opens the door is stuffed into a wide-lapel tux with a red carnation in the buttonhole and has the build of a middle-weight boxer with the face to match.

"Who may I announce?" he asks, blocking the entrance, and making it sound like he's not sure I belong there.

I flash him an indulgent smile and give him my name. The Mark Miller one.

He must be expecting me, because he steps aside, gives a little bow and says, "Of course, Monsieur Miller."

I hand him my coat and catch a brief glimpse of a circular staircase and sizeable room with bookshelves and antique furniture in the back of the foyer. Then he ushers me to a waiting elevator on the left, an elegant one, with walnut paneling and a mirror, but, oddly, no buttons.

It silently rolls shut; we start up and my stomach comes awake again.

On the second floor, I'm met by another carnation-bedecked tuxedo covering a massive torso, and behind him a stunning young Asian woman in an embroidered red side-split cheongsam, who steps forward with a warm smile and offers her hand.

"I am Mei," she says. "Your hostess. It's an honor to have you in our house, Mr. Miller."

"The honor is entirely mine," I say gallantly and return the smile.

"This way, please," she says.

"Where might we be going?"

"To Tony. He's expecting you," she says, and takes me by the hand.

"Tony?"

"Yes, Tony Slinani, your friend."

"Tell me about this place."

She stops, turns toward me.

"It's a gentleman's club. Very private." Then she adds softly, "You'll see."

Still holding my hand, she leads me through a small, sparsely furnished room. No one else is around, but I hear music coming our way as we mount steps into a good-sized dining room, dimly lit. When my eyes become accustomed, I see widely dispersed tables and people lounging around them on overstuffed chairs and couches. Middle-aged men, some in their Middle Eastern garb, and women in evening gowns who look more like daughters than wives.

Off to one side, an all-female orchestra—two violins, clarinet, piano, and drums—are doing a slow number, and several couples are swaying to the beat on a small center dance floor.

Mei steers me across the room to a table set into a niche where we find Tony, by himself, sprawled on a couch and smoking a cigar. He wears a dark-blue suit, white dress shirt, and yellow bow tie with matching pocket square.

"Mark," he says, with a big smile. "Welcome to Geneva's best-kept secret. How do you like it?"

"Tony," I say. "Quite a place."

He's wearing black velvet slippers.

We shake hands. I sit down next to him, and he props his feet up against the edge of a small table, puffing contentedly on a cigar. Then he reaches into the ice bucket on a silver stand next to him, extracts a bottle of Dom Pérignon, and pours me a glass.

He seems to be in an excellent mood.

"You've eaten?"

"I have."

"Cigar?"

"Sure."

I light up and lean back, trying to match his relaxed demeanor, which isn't exactly how I feel.

He toasts me with his champagne flute, and I follow suit. "*Bienvenue—et salut,*" he says. "Great to have you here."

"*Salut.*"

We sip, put our glasses down, and go back to our cigars.

He seems content just to enjoy the moment, but I'm anxious to press ahead. Also, I'm still not sure what to make of the surroundings.

"This is some place, Tony," I say. "Tell me about it."

"Just a private club and charming hostesses," he says modestly. "For entertaining our clients."

"I can see that."

"The Middle Easterners especially like it. Can you tell why?"

"Sure I can," I say, giving him a knowing grin and press it along a bit further. "The hostesses—that isn't the full story, is it?"

Tony doesn't seem surprised at my question and laughs. "You mean, are they working girls? Sorry, but definitely not. This is a club, not a *maison close*. If you want that, it can be arranged elsewhere. Our hostesses are here to be charming companions and to create the right environment to make our clients feel comfortable. That's all."

"Hmm. Looking around, they obviously are."

I am not entirely convinced by the answer, but it's getting late, and I decide it's time to get down to business.

"Thanks for inviting me here, Tony," I say. "But I'm wondering if you've thought of some way to help me. I'm really under time pressure."

He reaches over and pats my hand affectionately. "Perhaps, perhaps," he says. "I know it's important to you, but it's delicate and we can't talk about it here. We need privacy."

He picks up his glass and empties it down his throat, reaches for the half-empty bottle, and gets to his feet.

"Come on," he says.

He's moving toward a door discreetly hidden behind a heavy black curtain, which leads to a narrow passageway with doors running off it. From behind the first door, I hear music and women laughing.

We pass two more doorways before Tony stops at the third, opens it, and waves me in. The room is windowless and not very large. Two deep leather club chairs with matching footstools are against the wall on one side, and next to them, small tables with green-shaded table lamps, large bronze sculptures, and oversized cut-crystal ashtrays. A wine-colored Bokhara rug covers the floor. But what catches my attention is the sizeable rococo daybed against the opposite wall. No armrests, but lots of pillows.

We've arranged ourselves in the club chairs. Tony has emptied the rest of the Dom Pérignon into glasses and unburdened himself of his jacket. But owing to the gun in my belt, I keep mine on.

"About your problem," he starts in. "You've explained that it's a personal matter, and it'll be an honor to help you. No further questions. I'll leave it at that, because we need to trust each other—both ways."

He stops, searches my face, and I feel a surge of adrenalin. Is he trying to tell me he knows my story is bullshit?

"I trust you completely, Tony. Can you help?"

He nods and smiles slyly. "I've thought of something," he tells me. "It's tricky, but it can work. Let me explain.

"From what you showed me, we are talking about three numbered bank accounts. Those are the ones with lettered codes and thirteen digits. Two for the Banque Martin and one for Lombard Odier. Private banks and airtight. You could offer ten million and still not crack those accounts. No way. Can't be done."

"You've explained that. So, what's your idea?"

"There's a fourth number, remember? A letter code SSL, which stands for Sécurité Safes Léman. That's a private security company."

Meaning, Emerson rented himself a vault there.

"For access, an owner needs his key and SSL has a duplicate. Two keys to open the vault. And they let you into the vaults only with airtight ID to match the one on file. Business hours are nine to five weekdays. For emergencies, you have to make special arrangements. Someone's on duty until midnight."

"How does that help us?"

Tony pushes himself closer and lowers his voice. "I happen to know someone at SSL. Turns out he needs money. Lots of it. And he owes me. So, we can do business.

"Our way in is that SSL has a key safekeeping service for foreign clients who don't want to carry theirs with them. And guess what? Our good luck—my friend is on night duty this week."

"How would it work?"

"Simple: if you produce ID, Henri won't look too closely, will hand over the key SSL is holding, and poof—you're in. But it will cost you."

I'm feeling blood rushing to my face. I can't believe what I'm hearing. This might actually work.

"I have a passport. Will that do?"

"Absolutely."

We talk and scheme for another twenty minutes, working out a detailed plan for the next day. After haggling a while, we also agree about the money.

Henri Wahl, the crooked night gatekeeper at SSL, wants 300,000, and Tony has modestly suggested half of that for himself. A cut rate fee, he says, because he genuinely wants to help me.

It's a lot of money, but I eventually agree, though not before making a show of some pain and reluctance.

I don't have the money anyway.

Tony pours each of us a stiff three fingers of scotch.

To seal the deal, he says.

We click glasses.

"We need to eat something," he says and orders us food.

I glance at my watch. Past one thirty in the morning. I'm dog-tired, but my mind is churning. The big sofa bed looks inviting; I'm thinking of the man with the mustache and anyone else who could be waiting outside, and a vision of spending the night here flashes.

He's just refilled our glasses when there's a soft knock on the door and he immediately answers it with a cheery, "*Entrez, entrez.*"

The first one through is Mei. Another young woman, a blonde, is right behind her, both with sandwich platters in their hands and smiles on their faces.

Tony waves them in.

"That's Masha. She's from the Ukraine," he introduces the blonde and wraps an arm around her waist, which earns him a reproach-ful titter.

"*Mais, non,*" she corrects him. "*Je suis Belarusienne.*" The difference matters to her.

She's a full-figured young woman, early twenties, with a pretty, high-cheek-boned Slavic face and banana-yellow hair in a single braid down her back. A striking contrast to the lithe Mei, Tony has his eyes fixed on her and is beaming.

The women shed their stiletto heels, mount the sofa bed, and beckon us to join them and the sandwiches. Tony climbs aboard first, and, reluctantly, I follow.

Slinani has arranged himself close to Masha. Mei has taken my hand in hers but is keeping a small distance between us. This is totally weird, and even if it weren't for Kati, too weird for me to enjoy.

I guess this is Tony's idea of good hospitality, but I'm way too tired and wound-up to be in the mood for hanky-panky in this strange place with two young girls I don't know.

For the moment, there's only idle chatter and little else. Masha is doing most of the talking, asking about America, where I'm from, what I do, and what's brought me to Geneva. I spin her a pretty fairytale, to all of which Tony listens wordlessly, allowing himself only an occasional half smile. This goes on for quite a while until I decide to bring this odd scene to an end.

"Thanks for everything, Tony," I tell him, sitting up.

Then I turn to Mei, take her hand in both of mine, gaze at her fondly and say, "And thanks, Mei, for being such a gracious hostess. But I've had a very long day and—*malheureusement*—I'm beyond tired. I need to get some sleep. Will you forgive me?"

I am wondering how Tony will respond, but it's not at all what I expected. Even before Mei reacts, he's on his feet, pulling Masha up with him. He's in a hurry, moving quickly and eagerly.

"*C'est bon*," he says. "We're leaving. Please spend the night here. Mei will help you settle down, won't you *chérie*? There's breakfast in the morning, and please stay as long as you like."

A minute later he is out the door without looking back, Masha still climbing into her stilettos, stumbling behind him.

2:00 a.m.

Mei and I are on the sofa bed, alone.

When she glances at me, her eyes signal embarrassment. Then she smiles.

I smile back at her, but I can't help wondering what's really going on here.

She moves away, drapes a blanket over me, and I force another yawn.

"They left very quickly," I say. "Was that their plan?"

She laughs. "Perhaps."

"Why?"

A slight hesitation. Then, quietly, "Because they are lovers."

"Do all hostesses here have lovers?"

She laughs again, but this time it seems strained.

"Everyone asks that. But, no, that's not part of our job," she says emphatically. Then, a bit more tentative, "Most don't." Finally, wistfully, "Who knows?"

"Hmm."

"No more questions," she whispers. "I'll stay a few minutes until you're asleep. In the morning, ring the bell for breakfast."

I close my eyes as she quietly moves from the bed. From the distance comes the faint sound of music, but the room is quiet when suddenly I hear a woman screaming, followed by doors banging and people running down the hallway outside our room. A moment later, the sound of gunfire reverberates from a distance, followed by more yelling and commotion.

Boom, boom, boom!

A woman screams, and people are bellowing in voices I don't understand.

More gunfire, coming closer.

Then the lights go out.

I'm off the divan, using my cell phone light to find the door, listening to the confusion outside.

Mei looks at me. "*Mon dieu*," she says.

For a small moment, my mind slows. Then it speeds up again and goes into overdrive, trying to make sense of what I'm hearing.

Could this be a police raid or an ordinary holdup of some kind? The thought passes through my mind, but I quickly dismiss it. Too much of a coincidence. The much greater likelihood, I decide, is that this has to do with the people who've been tailing me.

That oddly calms me. I'm focusing intensely now, rehearsing possible scenarios and my best options.

I quickly conclude that to stay in the room is a bad idea. We'd be sitting ducks. Better to move into the open and look for a route to escape.

I look at Mei and put a finger to my lips, extract the Ruger from the holster in the small of my back, and transfer it to my front belt for easy access. Mei's eyes widen, but she says nothing.

"Come on," I say.

We lock hands. I pull the door open, and we move out. She has abandoned her heels and hurries behind me in bare feet.

Down the hallway, barely lit by dim emergency lighting, we head back into the main dining area where a confused crowd pushes noisily toward the exits. Mei knows a way, and has moved in front of me and tries to maneuver us toward an exit off to one side. We make some progress, but then our route is blocked by a club bouncer in a ripped tuxedo, struggling to subdue a bruiser in a leather jacket. It's the guy from outside the Café du Commerce. He's carrying a knife, and the bouncer, whose face is a bloody mess, has tackled him, and they're fighting as if their lives depend on it, which they might.

When the leather guy sees me, he grunts and lunges, but the guard doesn't let go.

I shout to Mei to push past them when I see the fellow with the mustache emerge from the crowd. He's got a gun and he's looking straight at me and closing in fast. Several other thugs are behind him.

In the far distance, I hear police sirens.

I stare back at him. Suddenly I'm very aware of the Ruger in my belt, reach for it, but then think better of it.

A gunfight in this crowded hall makes no sense. Besides, I've never shot at anyone in my life. And his gun looks a lot bigger than mine.

Retreat is the only option.

"Back," I shout to Mei, and pull her around.

A short minute later, we're back behind the locked door of our original room. I'm on one side of the door and point Mei to the other.

She nods, understands.

We wait.

For the moment it's quiet, but the thug wasn't far behind. I'm breathing hard, but I'm surprisingly calm. I have to think through what's next.

This has to be Hollander's gang tailing me to Geneva. Killing me won't get them anywhere, so they want me alive, which means I don't have to worry about this guy shooting me. Unless he's stupid. Or reckless. Or impulsive.

The only other options I can think of aren't that great, either. One: play for time until the cops rescue us. Two: fight him off when he breaks in. Which he will. Easily. The lock won't hold for long, and this isn't much of a door anyway.

There's a dim light in the hallway and he'll be stepping into a dark room. That may give me a small advantage.

I work the light on my cell phone, look around behind me, and my eyes fix on the bronzes on the side tables by the club chairs. There's a tall metal standing lamp next to them. I move the small wooden tables in front of the door, grab one of the bronzes, and pull up the lamp.

Mei has been watching me.

I nod at her.

She nods back.

A minute later, there are several loud blows against the door; it wobbles but holds firm.

Once, twice, a third time.

"Hey, Jackson!" he hollers. "I know you're in there. Let me in. We gotta talk. That's all—talk."

Mei looks at me and I shake my head.

"Come on, dammit. Let's just talk." Now he's almost pleading. He's talking German with an unusual accent I can't place. A few seconds pass, then I hear two gunshots and the door splinters. He's shot out the lock. Another heavy blow and what's left of the door flies open.

He's standing in the frame of the doorway, the gun still in his hand. He hesitates and squints, fighting to adjust his eyes to the dark. Then he moves forward, stumbling against the two tables. The moment I've been waiting for.

I step out from the side and swing the bronze statue hard. The first blow lands on his upper arm, but the gun stays in his hand. The second is a bullseye to the right side of his head.

He grunts, his knees buckle, he staggers but doesn't go down. There's blood streaming down the side of the face and dripping into his mustache. So, I pick up the lamp behind me and hit him once more. As hard as I can.

This time he goes down all the way, groans, and tries to talk. Then he passes out.

2:45 a.m.

Mei pulls her Fiat Spider into the underground garage of an apartment house behind the Gare Cornavin, just off the place des Grottes.

There is no elevator, and we climb the stairs to her apartment. It's on the third floor.

She double locks the door and hooks the chain. Then we turn toward each other.

"Thank you," I say. "You were incredible."

We both laugh crazily when she looks and points at her bare feet.

The exhilaration of relief.

It's the first time we've spoken since our escape from the club, through the pantry and a back alley into a chilly, windless night. Her car was parked on the street a block away. All the noise, confusion, and action had been at the front of the club and no one had been around to stop us.

It's a modest apartment, plainly furnished. One bedroom, tiny kitchen, and a small living area with a couple of pieces of Oriental art featuring golden flowers and a black wood panel depicting the face of a young Vietnamese woman. A Chinese calligraphy lithograph hangs near the entry.

She shows me around. "I won't be long," she says, pours me a glass of wine, and disappears into the bathroom. When she reemerges a few minutes later, groomed and showered, she is in a flowered kimono and her long jet-black hair hangs loosely down her back.

"Your turn to use the bathroom, while I fix your bed," she says, and heads for the other room.

When I come back, I see that the living room couch has been made up for the night.

I'm in my underwear, a towel wrapped tightly around my midsection.

"You look funny," she laughs and steers me toward the open bedroom door.

We stop and embrace.

"How can I ever thank you enough?" I ask.

"Just go to sleep," she says. "No more questions."

And exits the room.

Chapter 33

Geneva

Tuesday, November 21

9:00 a.m.

*A*lone in a strange bed, I come awake in a chasm of silence, except for the distant ticking of a clock.

The air is heavy and my head aches.

I lie still for some minutes with my eyes closed, fighting to come fully awake. Then my brain starts working overtime to make sense of last night. I think about the club's invasion by my pursuers and the mustache guy pointing his gun at me. I remember how I hit him and see him on the ground. Bleeding. Out cold.

Did I kill him?

A lot of feelings come and go, including a brief surge of elation over beating the bad guys at their own game. But now I have to face up to the reality of my situation.

Tony and I have a date at the airport this afternoon for a final run-through of the scenario at SSL. I'll be going there alone, because Wahl wants it that way, and Tony agrees he's too well-known around the place.

So, I'll be flying solo again. I let that pass through my mind, and the doubts flood in. I'll have to evade my pursuers, with plenty of ways for this thing to go wrong. But if it works, it'll all be over in a few hours.

Mei has made breakfast. Scrambled eggs and bacon. She pours the coffee, and we sit opposite each other, focused on the food. Nothing's been said about last night, but the way I catch her looking at me once in a while, I can only wonder what she's thinking. I'm nevertheless grateful for the silence, because my mind is mostly on SSL and my pursuers. I need a place to hide until this afternoon and a strategy for evading the gang when I leave here.

She pours me another cup of coffee and sends me a warm smile. "You can stay here as long as you like," she says.

She's read my mind. *An amazing woman*, I'm thinking.

More silence, then she asks, "When they came to the club, it was for you, wasn't it?" making it sound more like a statement than a question.

"Yes," I agree.

Then she asks quietly, "Who are you, Mark Miller?"

"I'm one of the good guys," I say. "I work for the American government. But don't ask me more, Mei. It's safer that way."

She nods. We're silent again; then she asks, "Are you married? Do you have children?"

"Neither."

"A girlfriend?"

"Yes."

"Do you love her?"

"Very much."

"Good. What's her name?"

"Kati."

"Good," she says again.

And hands me the *Tribune de Genève.*

It's just after two thirty in the afternoon when Mei shoehorns her little Fiat into a narrow parking spot across from the bus terminal at the Gare Cornavin.

She keeps the motor running and we sit and wait.

The weather has been unpredictable. After a mild day with plenty of sunshine, today it's gray and chilly and a cold wind is blowing down from the Jura. The queues of travelers waiting to board buses are bundled into their winter gear and look decidedly uncomfortable.

When the number 5 airport bus pulls in, we embrace, and I kiss her cheeks.

"Last night you saved my life," I tell her. "I'll never forget that."

She nods, with only a fleeting half smile.

"*Bonne chance*, Mark Miller."

"*Á bientôt*, Mei."

It's a promise I'm not sure I can keep.

3:00 p.m.

Cointrin airport is just four miles northwest of the city, a short fifteen-minute trip. The bus is a long and sleek late-model accordion type, filled to capacity with travelers and lots of luggage. I am standing wedged in the aisle next to two elderly women—American tourists—clutching their roll-ons, obsessing about how to get their heavy luggage off the bus at our destination. The closer we get to Cointrin, the more urgent their angst. To reassure them—and do myself a favor—I gallantly offer them my services. Pretending to be just another luggage-toting tourist could be excellent camouflage.

After I roll their two big trunks to check-in, they bid me a grateful adieu and, again unencumbered, I head for the airport bistro.

It's at the north end of the departures hall and I can't miss it, Tony has assured me.

When I get there, Tony is wedged into a small table amidst throngs of travelers crowding around him. He jumps up and greets me with a big hug.

Masha and he must have left the club just a minute or two before the raid, he says, but he's heard all about it and is mighty relieved that I got away safely. The cops are interrogating the thugs they arrested on the premises, and the rumor is that the whole thing was a kidnapping attempt focused on an Arab heavy relaxing in one of the private rooms. Quite near us, in fact.

"Interesting," I say and leave it at that. I see no purpose in enlightening Tony about the real target of that raid, though I do fill him in how Mei helped us get out of the club through one the of the back doors.

We move our heads together and briefly review the plan. I tell him that I'm good to go and he's full of optimism that everything is set with Wahl at SSL. Afterward we'll meet and celebrate. "No problem," he says. I'll collect my stuff, and he'll get his payoff.

Then he's suddenly in a great rush. A client urgently needs him in Geneva, he says. So, with that, he excuses himself, grabs his precious canary-yellow overcoat, and is gone.

I am on my own again.

I look around, scan the crowd snaking past my table, and glance at my watch. Not yet four o'clock. Three hours to kill, which is a very long time when someone may be trying to kill you. In search of a safe spot to wait, I make my way through the terminal to Lufthansa check-in. No one's in the first-class queue, so I walk up to the counter, flash the agent my diplomatic passport—the genuine one—and ask for an urgent word with the station supervisor. For what I have in mind, I'm counting on the innate respect many Germans still have for titles and authority.

A gray-haired woman shows up a couple of minutes later and greets me with a face suggesting officiousness and a touch of subservience. She's just what I'd hoped for.

Handing her my passport, I introduce myself as the ambassador's confidential assistant at the US Embassy in Berlin, and in urgent need of a discreet place for some very important telephone conversations. I drop a hint that it involves vital US-German relations and suggest that Lufthansa's first-class VIP lounge is just the right place. Since there are always a few private rooms in that kind of lounge, I would be most grateful if she would see to it that one of them is made available for my exclusive use. And would she please personally accompany me through the Swiss police checkpoint?

Frau Töpfer—that's her name—listens respectfully, briefly glances at my passport, then raises herself up straight before executing ever so slight a forward bow. Had she been a man, I wouldn't have been surprised to hear the clicking of heels.

She fully understands the situation, and Lufthansa is honored to assist. She calls me "Excellency," and will gladly lead the way past the Swiss police.

A few minutes later, I am comfortably installed in a room inside the lounge. The attendant has come up with a frosted bottle of Holsten lager, sets it down near a bowl of pretzels, and offers dinner at my pleasure. Frau Töpfer hands me her card, thanks me for the opportunity to be of service, and quietly leaves me to the conduct of US-German diplomatic affairs.

The door is locked, and I'm settled into a comfortable chair.

My jacket's off and my feet are up. For the moment, I feel safe and optimistic, especially when I remind myself that the end is in sight.

I put a call in to Emmett, and in a few hours, I'll have plenty of help.

First, though, I'll have to walk into SSL, and everything will be riding on how that works out. Because—for better or worse—there's no turning back now.

I take my time rehearsing the scenario over and over again, considering all the risks and what-ifs, looking for weak spots and pitfalls. I'll still be extremely vulnerable and very much on my own. If I fail to get into Witty's safe, or don't find what I'm looking for, this whole exercise will have been for nothing. And it still might get me killed.

Chapter 34

Berlin

Tuesday, November 21

5:15 p.m.

*I*nside his compound, Adalbert von Trachtenberg, Dwayne Hollander, and a third man in a heavy winter jacket, his face obscured behind dark glasses and the visor of a black nautical cap, are silently making their way toward the street. Their path through the large, parklike garden lies in tenebrous darkness, but Trachtenberg leads the way. At the gate he works the security lock, and they pass into the street, turn left, and disappear into the night.

The hooded figure crouched low behind the thick shrubbery on both sides of the walkway who's been watching them has snapped the last of a dozen takes from his microcamera as they pass by him. After the gate snaps shut, he waits motionless for several more minutes, well hidden behind a tall clump of purple bushes. Having concluded that the coast is clear, he stands up and stretches, pockets his night-vision glasses and special camera inside his hooded parka, and allows himself a satisfied, tense smile. Another minute later, he cautiously exits the gate and hurries off in the opposite direction.

———

The car parked around the corner a block away is an older VW Jetta, metallic gray with tinted windows and Hamburg plates. The three men climb aboard and the one with the nautical cap gets behind the wheel and carefully eases the sedan from the curb. He is driving cautiously and doesn't accelerate until they reach the nearby AVUS speedway, which leads out of Berlin and connects to the Autobahn southwest past Potsdam. It's the route he follows for the next half hour while his two passengers, left to their own thoughts, sit in silence.

He has insisted on absolutely no talking, and neither Trachtenberg nor Hollander have been in a mood to argue.

Twenty minutes out of Berlin, he pulls the VW off the Autobahn to a deserted, wooded rest stop, kills the engine, and cuts the headlights.

"We'll talk here," he says, breaking the silence, "but keep it down." His voice is soft but his manner leaves no doubt who's giving the orders. First out of the car, Hollander loses no time to hurry into the bushes. Tense situations—and this is one of them—have that kind of effect on him.

When he reemerges—his bladder appeased—he looks around. He sees two picnic tables still wet from the rain, a small detritus-laden fire pit, and little else. From the Autobahn comes the steady *swoosh* and *vroom* of passing traffic and headlights shafting through the night.

His two companions have settled themselves on top of one of the tables, and Hollander, stumbling to join them in the dark on unsteady legs, suppresses a shiver, then tries to transfer his nerves to the loose coins he's fingering in his pocket.

Less than two hours ago, following news from Geneva that the plan's last pieces had fallen into place and that the incriminating stuff would soon be secure, he'd been on a triumphant high.

But that was then, before the urgent summons to Adi's villa and finding Strangefoot there. That had seriously rattled him, because Trachtenberg and the American spy had never before met face-to-face. They had both insisted on that, and now Strangefoot evidently has outed himself, or is about to. A sure sign of some sudden turn of events that spells trouble, reinforced by their grim, sphinxlike faces and the baffling silence Strangefoot has imposed.

Hollander wants to know what this is all about. He's got excellent news from Geneva, he blusters, but is rudely cut off. Strangefoot says he knows all about the deal with Z's gang and that local crook, but Hollander is being ineffably naïve and stupid to believe their stories that any of that is working. The Moroccan is as twisted as a corkscrew. Is he aware that Z's people had their noses bloodied last night? Strong-arm tactics are working no better in Geneva than anywhere else. Hasn't he always warned him about that?

Hollander is in shock.

"Christ, how do you know all that?" he asks, a question Strangefoot dismisses with a tired wave of his arm.

"Because the other side told me. I know what they know, so shut up and listen," he commands. "We're desperately short of time. Stop wasting it."

Hollander lapses into sulking silence after he looks toward Trachtenberg, whose face signals zero support.

"Here's the latest, and it's all bad news. I'll keep it short. We have no time to lose."

Strangefoot continues in a tone that is flat and dispassionate.

"Adam Jackson has been sharper—or perhaps just luckier—

than I'd expected. He's been hiding in Geneva and, courtesy of you, Dwayne, is about to gain access to Emerson's secret safe deposit box within the next hour or two. Who knows what he'll find. Money would be the least of it. The US group's and Herr von Trachtenberg's organization, minutes of meetings, correspondence files, membership lists, etc. is a real possibility. A total disaster.

"He can no longer be stopped because bodyguards, and perhaps even Berlin *Polizei*, are arriving to protect him as we speak."

Strangefoot has their full attention now, stops and takes a short breath, then continues. "In the US, the group's leadership is well aware of this imminent threat to everything they've worked for," he explains. "They've authorized me to do whatever is necessary to avert catastrophe, which is what I plan to do." Hollander can't believe what he's hearing. He's always been Rickenbom's designated liaison to Berlin and his most trusted advisor. Now he senses his world collapsing.

"How do you know the group's position?" he sputters. "I'm the one who's privy to their thinking!"

Next to him, Trachtenberg stiffens.

Strangefoot takes a breath, then lets it out slowly. "I've been a member of the group's ExComm for a long time. No reason for you to know that, Dwayne," he adds dryly.

———

Throughout the evening, Trachtenberg has listened wordlessly with a face that has been hard to read. He is a tightly controlled, disciplined man with an ingrained habit of keeping thoughts and emotions to himself, which is not to say that he's without them. At the moment, he is struggling inwardly to assess what he's hearing.

"*Staatssicherheit* and Kranmüller's *Polizei* know just about everything about us," Strangefoot says. "They've been recording everything going on inside your property, Adi. That's why we're out here together."

Trachtenberg's look remains fixed. He senses there's more coming and waits.

Hollander proclaims his doubts. Haven't they always been extra careful?

"Not careful enough," Strangefoot responds sadly. "They use technology no layman understands. The latest highly sensitive surveillance devices, virtually undetectable, remotely activated microphones all over the place, laser beams that reconstruct the slightest audio signals through windows and walls. Even drones.

"Unfortunately, they've also had help from the inside. Direct human help, Herr von Trachtenberg. I have just learned—and that's a certainty—your wife's assistant Katharina Willmans works for *Staatssicherheit*. Furthermore, she and Jackson are lovers."

"*Unmöglich*, impossible!" Trachtenberg almost shouts it.

"A disaster," moans Hollander.

"Not really," Strangefoot responds. "Actually, it's a gift she's handed to us. Our last best chance. Let me explain."

Chapter 35

Geneva

Tuesday, November 21

*A*irports aren't my favorite for spending an afternoon, espe-cially if I'm not going anywhere. Even if it's in a Lufthansa first-class lounge, which is better than most.

Considering my situation, Frau Töpfer was a godsend. The effi-cient Lufthansa station manager personally stood guard at the lounge the rest of the afternoon, seeing to it that I remained dis-creetly shielded inside one of the private rooms to conduct what she assumed was important diplomatic business.

A most productive and successful arrangement, I assured her.

Which wasn't a lie.

Thanks to Töpfer, I was left undisturbed for my final contin-gency planning, and ended the afternoon with a nice salad and sandwiches she thoughtfully sent in. It has left me in an upbeat mood for a quick call to Kati before leaving. I want to hear her voice, and a minute on the burner phone doesn't seem too risky. Just long enough to make sure she's okay and to tell her that I miss her and can't wait to see her again. Which—good news—will be very soon. A day or two at most.

It takes a while before she picks up, and when she does, she speaks hurriedly, her voice low and sounding on edge.

"I'm glad you called," she whispers. "I can't talk. Watch your back, Adam. Don't trust anyone where you are. They're after you."

Then, before I can react, she cuts it off and is gone, leaving me staring at the phone and fighting panic, both for her sake and for mine.

Is she in danger?

What has she picked up about Geneva that I don't know?

Hoping Emmett might know something, I make a quick call to him, but his tone is completely different and reassuring. No new developments or new news. Everyone is good to go. They'll be there and not to worry.

Emmett says that his chartered plane will avoid Geneva and fly into a local airport near Annecy, France, about thirty miles away. They will arrive before seven, which is cutting it close, but the best they can do. Timing is crucial because I absolutely need him nearby when leaving SSL.

Tommy is hitching a ride, and Börries has recruited a few of his best no-neck nightclub bouncers. That was it.

The train is leaving the station. I am on it, and there's no turning back.

I check my watch. Six thirty p.m.

Time to go.

I promise my guardian angel at the airport that her stellar contribution to the health of the US-German relationship would not go unnoticed within Lufthansa, well above her paygrade. Then we air kiss goodbye, left cheek, right, and left again. Töpfer was pleased.

The rue de la Confédération is full of life during the day, but after seven in the evening there isn't much going on there. Stores and offices have closed, and commuter traffic has thinned. On a cold November evening, not many pedestrians are around.

Most of the small Geneva private banks like to impress with inconspicuous locations that project discreet wealth. SSL—Safes Securité Léman—is the opposite. It sits in the middle of a central crossroads by the Place de la Fusterie, and the busy Pont des Bergues across the Rhone, an ugly gray cement block that has more the look of cheap offices or a warehouse than a bank. Which actually makes sense—SSL is in fact more storage facility than bank—a warehouse for the convenience of rich people. Behind a locked fifteen-foot-high wrought-iron fence, it is set back about ten yards from the street with room for a half dozen parking places.

An embossed gold-colored nameplate lists the business hours: "*Heures 9-17. Lundi–Vendredi.*" With a bell next to it proclaiming "*sonnez-içi, s.v.p.*"

Showtime.

I suck in my breath and ring. As I wait for someone to answer, I grip the Louis Vuitton duffel bag in one hand. The other, I keep on the gun in my pocket.

Eventually, a voice comes through the intercom, wanting to know my business. I announce myself as Monsieur Emerson, a client with an appointment with Monsieur Wahl, and immediately the gate swings open.

Slinani has followed through. They are expecting me.

The bulky young guard at the door wears a charcoal-gray uniform with brass buttons and a matching Keystone Cop cap, but doesn't have much to say. He asks for ID, gives my phony Witty passport a cursory look, and then waves an arm toward an open elevator door.

"*Troisième,*" is all I hear. Third floor.

The door rolls shut, and the elevator starts moving, with me concentrating on trying to swallow the lump in my throat.

I am actually inside. The question that concerns me now is what comes next, and most of all, how do I get back out?

When the elevator door opens, I am greeted by a cadaverous-looking man of about sixty, wearing a blue suit, white shirt, and red bow tie. "Mr. Emerson. So glad to see you again," he says. "Good trip, I hope?"

Henri Wahl extends his hand, and when I shake it, his skin feels cold.

"Thanks for this after-hours accommodation," I say.

"As always."

He has thin lips, hollow cheeks, and what is left of his gray hair has been arranged diagonally across his scalp. With watery blue eyes behind wire-rimmed glasses, he has the look of a petty bookkeeper worried about an audit. Accordingly, he keeps me in the hallway with nervous chatter, and I play along with the pretense that we've met before. Considering that we are alone, I can't quite figure why he is making such an effort. Then I spot the surveillance camera mounted in a corner of the ceiling: Wahl is talking for the record.

Eventually he ushers me into a well-furnished client reception room—sofa, conference table, bookshelves, lots of framed certificates and diplomas—and installs himself behind a large double desk. He hands me a bottle of water and motions for me to sit in one of the chairs facing him. On the ceiling beyond his head, I spot another surveillance camera.

I unscrew the cap to the water and take a drink while he keeps chattering about the weather and the rigors of travel, and I have to assume that he is stalling, but I can't figure out why. I continue to play along, but I am on a schedule—Emmett and his team are due outside before eight.

He knows and I know why I am here and what is supposed to

happen. And he knows that I know.

So, I blow out my breath and cut him off midsentence to tell him I am late for an appointment and need to get into the vault.

He stiffens, falls silent, and stares at me for a moment.

The guy is more nervous than I am.

"I understand," he nods. "There are formalities."

He opens a folder on the desk, pulls out a form, and hands it to me.

"Please write down your secret access code here. And I need your passport. To record your ID."

"Of course," I say.

I write down the number from Witty's Berlin safe, hand the paper back to him, and give him the passport.

"Formalities are vital for security," I say with my best smile.

I am actually enjoying this.

That earns me another blank stare. "I'll have to record these," he says. "Excuse me a moment," and disappears.

He is gone for a good five minutes, which leaves me wondering about possible reasons, none of them reassuring. When I hear him talking to someone out in the hallway, it doesn't exactly add to my peace of mind. If need be, handling Wahl alone would be one thing. Two against one might be a different story.

I move quietly toward the door to see what I can hear, but I've only made it halfway there when Wahl suddenly reappears with the taciturn uniformed guard from downstairs looming up behind him.

"Santiago will accompany us to the vaults," he says.

"My key is in safekeeping," I remind him, which he seems to have expected.

He pulls another printed form from the folder he is carrying. I enter the key code on it, sign my name, and he hands me a double-sealed envelope. While he watches, I break the seals, fish out the key, and stick it in my pocket.

Then the three of us head toward the elevator. Wahl leads the way. I hoist the duffel bag over my shoulder and follow, and Santiago falls in behind us. In the elevator, I notice for the first time that he is carrying a gun, and that a good-sized billy club dangles from his belt. He is a strong-looking guy who evidently spends a lot of time at the gym. He still isn't talking much, but keeps close to me all the way.

I feel boxed in.

The safe deposit boxes are in the basement. Witty's vault number 18 is in a special section for the larger ones and, even so, looks surprisingly big. About twice the size of an airport locker.

Wahl sticks his key into the top lock, and I insert mine in the one below it. He turns his key around twice, and I do the same with mine. There is a buzzing sound, and the door swings open, revealing a large metal container that completely fills up the inside.

It looks heavy.

Santiago steps forward.

"He'll lift it out for you," Wahl announces.

"No, thanks," I demur and block his way. "I prefer to do it myself. In privacy."

Santiago doesn't budge, looks toward Wahl, who hesitates and then nods his assent. Santiago steps aside.

A tense moment has passed.

Wahl points toward a bank of enclosed cubicles and invites me to choose one.

"Ring the bell when you're ready," he says.

The cubicle reminds me of my study carrel in college, except that this one is a lot larger. The only pieces of furniture are a deep, built-in, wall-to-wall ledge that serves as a table, a chair in front of it, and a desk lamp. The color scheme is avocado green.

I wrestle the container onto the ledge and lock the door. Then

I take my time to search for hidden spy holes, cameras, microphones, and such. I check under the ledge, run my fingers across every part of the chair, inspect the door and the walls and unscrew the light bulbs, but don't find a thing. If they have spiked the place, it's been done by experts.

The adrenaline is pumping and I can feel my heart pounding when I turn to the box itself. This thing is actually going down exactly as Slinani said it would. So far, at least.

The first thing I see when I pull the lid open is a cardboard carton the size of a shoebox, and behind it: money. Lots of it. Stacks of dollars in bundles of fifties and hundreds. A far bigger stash than the euros in Witty's home safe.

I half expected it and am surprised mainly by the amount of cash involved. This isn't conspiracy on a shoestring. This is big—in the millions. Witty has been their courier between the US and Berlin, which was what that phony MFG employment letter signed by Hollander in his home safe is all about. What I am seeing probably is a supply he brought in from the US for Hollander's money-laundering operation, with the help of de la Marre. Destined somehow for Hollander's Panama/Cyprus/Bahamas MFG setup. It all makes sense.

The IRS will have their fun with this.

It's when I turn my attention to the shoebox that I get a bigger surprise.

I am searching for evidence of a conspiracy, but right now I am looking at a carton-full of dirty pictures, a private trove of special-taste erotica, which includes at least a dozen photos of a very naked Witty. Standing straight, eyes cast downward, with hands on his crotch. Another of my erstwhile boss on his knees, arms tied behind his back. And one with a racket-ball-sized gag in his mouth getting the whip. A large photograph—in color—licking an Amazonic dominatrix's boot.

The others were more of the same. Men, young and old, singly and in duets with a selection of disciplinarians in various poses.

Our deputy chief of mission definitely got around.

I am short on time, so I put the porn aside and turn my attention to piles of manila folders, bundles of correspondence, files of memoranda, and financial statements crammed into the rear of the container. Some are stacked neatly and tied together with ribbons or rubber bands. A couple of piles are loose.

I pick up two folders at random and rifle through them, put them down, and do the same with some of the loose papers, but then it is clear: I am looking at Dwayne Hollander's office files.

Apparently Witty hadn't merely been his courier, he'd been his archivist and file clerk as well.

Big mistake.

By God, it is all here.

Action plans, timetables, minutes of meetings and names galore. Enough evidence for sure to put the noose around the conspirators' necks on both sides of the Atlantic.

No wonder they were desperate to get their hands on this stuff before we did.

The files and erotica go back into the container. I close the lid and focus on the last tricky hurdle ahead of me and the strategy for handling it that Emmett and I discussed in great detail.

I'd never planned to carry the evidence out with me. That would have put it up for grabs by anyone. My duffel bag was simply a prop, stuffed with newspapers and old paperbacks to approximate the weight of the archives in question. These documents will stay safely inside the vault, the conspirators will be pulled in, and the damning evidence retrieved by the cops with the key I provide.

At least that was the plan.

8:03 p.m.

I've seen enough.

The box is back in the vault.

It is time to get out of here.

I have my left hand firmly around the strap of the duffel bag slung over my shoulder. Wahl, who's been waiting outside the cubicle, keeps his eyes on it with the furtive intensity of a glutton who doesn't want his greed for another helping to be too obvious.

"Did you find all you were after?" he asks.

"Indeed, I did. Thanks to your excellent arrangements."

We are both speaking in code, which is a bit odd under the circumstances, but I am trying to keep it light.

We ride the elevator up to the ground level. I ask to use the toilet, which is at the other end of the hallway from the exit. He lets me go in alone, and after I've locked myself into one of the stalls, I quickly work the small, flat key to the vault into a camouflaged spot in the seam of my overcoat I've carefully prepared for this purpose.

When I come out, Wahl is leaning against the wall at my end, and I see Santiago on his feet at the other end, near the door.

This doesn't look good, but I give a confident smile and say, "I'll be going now, so, *au revoir.*"

Wahl and I shake hands, and I start walking.

"I'll accompany you," I hear him say.

"Not really necessary," I answer and keep walking until I felt the pressure just below my shoulder blades.

I wheel around.

Wahl has taken a half step back and has a Glock in his right hand, pointed straight at my midsection.

"What's this?"

"Keep walking."

"Is this a holdup?"

"Keep walking, I said."

So, Kati had been spot-on. For all his endearing goofiness, Slinani is a crook, just like all the rest, a testament to the pervasive power of greed. Frankly, I am surprised. I hadn't seen that coming. But I can't see him as a cold-blooded killer, and I don't think Wahl has it in him either. Assuming that the cavalry has arrived and is waiting outside, I should be okay. But now that I am staring down the barrel of a gun, I recognize the large element of hope in that assumption.

Neither Wahl nor Santiago seems like a hardened criminal—employment in this venue would have been unlikely if they were. But this is not an unalloyed positive given the case of nerves Wahl is beginning to show. How is he going to react when he finds himself facing Emmett and his bouncers? A panicked rookie firing at random could be deadly enough, and all it takes is one bullet.

I still have my gun, and Wahl, who is prodding me forward, hasn't even frisked me. So, I relax and continue walking. Slowly.

Santiago pushes the door open and gestures for me to step outside. I comply, followed by Wahl, and when I glance back over my shoulder, I see that the security guard now has his truncheon in his hand. I walk toward the gate, expecting that these guys are about to get the surprise of their lives.

The night is exceedingly dark. There is no street lighting, and the only surprise is no surprise. An eerie quiet, and no sign of my protectors. I am getting that sinking feeling that something has gone very wrong.

Then, out of the gloom, I see a black Mercedes, which gives me a jolt of hopeful adrenaline. Until Santiago jabs me toward it with his stick. This is no rescue posse in an expensive rental. Who it is, exactly, I can't tell, but the thought flashes through my mind that it might be Tony and some goons. Within the next thirty seconds, I either have to do something heroic, or I am going to be in the back seat, very likely with a bag over my head.

I take a deep breath, sidestep to the left, and swing the duffel bag at Wahl's gun. The blow to his arm is enough to knock him off balance, which gives me just long enough to reach for the Ruger.

He raises his gun arm toward me again, and somehow, I manage to react exactly as Tommy instructed. Feet wide, arms extended, aim for center mass, two rounds. The first hits him in the gut; the second, given the recoil, hits him midchest.

He crumples to the ground, and I stare in disbelief. I actually killed a man. That moment of lost concentration is all it takes for Santiago to pull out his gun and press it into the back of my skull. He simultaneously slams his truncheon into my wrist, and the Ruger falls to the ground.

"*Voiture,*" he commands and, as I clutch my arm to my chest, prods me toward the car again. The pain is excruciating, but when he tries to wrest the bag from me, I manage to fight back. Admittedly, my effort against this guy would have been pathetic if I had two hands. Fortunately, he uses his club and his boot rather than his gun as I hold on to the duffel, and he drags me toward the limo.

With my face in the dirt and blood in my eyes, I can hardly tell what was going on, but suddenly I hear the limo speed away. I look up and see a hand the size of a catcher's mitt wrap itself across Santiago's face, and two thick fingers gouge into his eyes.

My memory of what happens after that is unclear. Santiago drops to the ground, and a muscleman with a friendly face has taken his place above me. Then Börries reached down to lift me off the ground. Which is when I pass out.

When I come to, Emmett and Tommy are by my side, smiling.

"Sorry about being late," Emmett says. "Lousy flying weather."

Chapter 36

Geneva

Tuesday, November 21

9:45 p.m.

*I*t's evening, and Emmett and I are finally alone at the Hotel d'Angleterre on the lakefront, where he's booked us into a suite. The marines he brought along—Gunnery Sergeant Matt Poggi, or "Gunny," the head of the embassy security detail, and Corporal Skip Hopper—are outside in civvies, keeping watch.

The rescue plane actually delivered quite a team. Alcaro and Hinton from the FBI and the *Kripo's* Holzer, who came as liaison with the local cops, are at a meeting with the Swiss, filling them in on the mess outside SSL. Tommy, Börries, two of his bouncer pals, and several other athletic-looking types I've never met before, have gone off for well-earned refreshments and dinner.

I have been fielding questions about the contents of Witty's safe and everything leading up to today for more than an hour, and my throat is as dry as an arroyo in July. Even after a big bottle of Perrier.

Emmett sent someone to retrieve my carry-on luggage from the little auberge in Thonon where I checked in as Mark Miller Saturday night. I haven't been back there since, and now Miller has faded back into the fictional world from whence he came.

I am dog-tired, but still coming off a high and too wound up to care. After a long shower, letting the hot water pound me for a good fifteen minutes, I've put on fresh clothes.

Emmett has moved his big frame to a lounge chair and parked his stockinged feet on the one next to it. He's acting cool and in control, as he always does, yet I can tell he's as worked up as I am. His mop of red hair is a mess, and his handlebar mustache has been in motion for much of the last hour.

He's ordered in some food, but I'm still too keyed up to eat. The excitement of the last hours seems to have had the opposite effect on him.

"Raclette—along with their knives—is one of the better Swiss inventions," he observes appreciatively, takes a slug from his Feldschlösschen bottle, and helps himself to one more boiled potato, prosciutto, and another generous portion of melted cheese.

With his mouth still full, he says, "Don't let it get to your head, but you did one helluva job, and just in time. The FBI has narrowed it down. Payday is Friday or Saturday. They have to strike, and this evidence will seal the deal."

"I'd say; we cut it close."

"Just in time."

"I was lucky."

"False modesty," he says with a smile, and turns his attention back to the cheese. I'm nibbling the gherkins and pickled onions that are part of the fixings.

Eventually, I say, "But I still don't get it. Slinani was onto me from the get-go? And who were the guys in the Mercedes?"

"An excellent question," he says. "I suppose we really won't know the answer until they're all behind bars. Which I hope will be soon."

"Any guesses?"

"Friends of your Mr. Trachtenberg and Hollander, I'd say."

"And the Hassanis?"

He nods. "Sure, but given the confluence of conspirators and criminal goons, I think your Moroccan pal may have been playing his own game. Maybe he knew he'd be overreaching if he tried to make off with the money in that vault. Far better to cut a deal and pocket a handsome finder's fee. Avoid having to be glancing over his shoulder for the rest of a very short life."

"But the lines of communication. A hell of a lot of coordination going on. Was it Strangefoot?" I ask.

"Just guessing, once again, but yes. A man with tentacles reaching far and wide."

"You still thinking Trotter?"

He nods, wiping some cheese from his chin. "The fact that he's disappeared does not build confidence in his integrity. Neither does McLean's silence on the matter."

"But Trotter's been gone for days. How could he have known what was going on in the embassy? The plans you and I had worked out? You didn't tell anybody, did you?"

"Of course not."

"No one?"

"Only the Bureau guys, and strictly on need-to-know."

"So, where is Castelyou? Why isn't he here?"

"We were moving fast, and he didn't answer his phone. You want another beer?"

Emmett reaches for the room service phone, but I stop him.

"What I need is sleep. I'm dead. I need to crash."

"Sure you do. Let's tuck you in."

He pads over to me in his stockinged feet, takes me by the arm, and moves me toward the bedroom.

"Meanwhile," he says, "one more mountain to climb—convincing SSL and the Swiss to give us access to the vault. Ideally, tomorrow. Wahl had the second key in his pocket, you know. Takes two to tango. You've got yours safe and handy, right?"

"Yep."

"Where is it?"

"None of your business."

"You stuck it up your ass?"

He looks at me and we both laugh.

"I'm dedicated," I say. "But not that much. Let's just say it's in an undisclosed location."

"Going underground has gotten to you. The man with many secrets."

"Strictly need to know," I say.

I'm heading toward the bed when I feel the phone vibrating in my pocket.

I stop and pull it out. "This is the last of my prepaid burners. Nobody knows the number but Kati. Emergencies only."

I swallow hard and put the phone to my ear.

She speaks softly, but her voice is quivering.

"Adam," she says, "I need you."

"What's the matter?"

"They want you to come."

"Who?"

"I don't know."

"Where are you?"

The next voice I hear isn't hers. It's a man's, muffled and distorted, but clear enough to understand. He's speaking accented German.

"Listen very carefully, Jackson," he says. "You'll do exactly as I tell you if you want to see your woman again. Alive. Got it?"

"Who the hell are you?"

"Listen carefully," he repeats. "You deliver fucking full duffel bag to Berlin tomorrow. By three p.m. No excuses. No funny business. You bring it, she walks. You walk. You give it to your friends, she's dead. Get it? And not nice. We start with fucking pretty face. Get it?"

"I get that you're a thief and probably a killer. How do I know you'll do as you say?"

"You don't. But all we want is the stuff. No more excitement. No more stiffs."

"I want to talk to Kati again."

That earns me a laugh.

"Forget it. Just come."

"Where?"

"Berlin. Alone. By three o'clock tomorrow. We'll contact you. Get it?"

"I'll be there."

But then I add, "And listen to me, you bastard. You harm one hair on her head—I'll track you down and kill you. Slow and painful. Get it?"

But he's gone already.

11:25 p.m.

After the phone call, Emmett and I almost come to blows over how to respond. The only thing we could agree on was not turning over the evidence.

"I'm leaving for Berlin," I tell him. "I've got until three to turn up."

"That's crazy," he says. "This is an emergency and way beyond you. It's time to call in the *Polizei*. This is what they do."

"I'm not taking that risk with Kati. We have no idea where they're holding her, and there's no way the cops are going to find her by tomorrow afternoon."

"You go," Emmett says, "and all you accomplish is to give them a second hostage."

"I'm the one holding the trump card. I've got the key. They let her go, I stay and lead them to what they want. Or at least that's what I'll say I'll do."

"Then what?"

"Then I'll need some help. We'll figure something out."

"No, we need help now, which is me telling you I'm not going to let you do this. I understand your feelings, but this is official business, with far wider interests here than your own. I'm still your senior officer, and I'm ordering you to stay put."

I can see this isn't going anywhere, so I tell him, "Okay, okay. I'm too tired to think. Let me get some sleep. We'll see what it looks like in the morning."

Alone in the bedroom, sleep is out of the question. More arguments with Emmett would have been a waste of time. What he doesn't understand is that logic may have been on his side, but right then, I didn't care. Even if Payday is tomorrow, I wouldn't care. Kati needs me and her safety comes first.

I am determined to go to Berlin, with Emmett's approval or not.

Keeping my ear close to the living room door, I wait, assuming Em would leave to meet with the others. Twenty minutes later, when he does, I simply take off, borrowing a busboy's white cap and jacket to sneak past the marines.

There's a 7:45 a.m. Swiss Air flight from Zürich, and I intend to be on it.

Wednesday, November 22

1:00 a.m.

I've barely made the 11:20 train to Zürich, the last one of the night.

I have no luggage, only the clothes on my back, plus the over-coat with the key in it over my arm, passports, cell phones, wallet, and some cash. Alcaro is turning the Ruger I used on Wahl over to the Swiss.

It's a three-and-a-half-hour trip from Geneva, and apparently not too many people are thrilled to arrive in Zürich at three o'clock in the morning. I'm not either, but I'm counting on Emmett and the others taking a while to figure out the route I'm traveling.

Only a handful of night owls are dozing in my car when the train pulls out, and most get off at Montreux and Neuchâtel. Hurtling along the shore of Lake Biel, I have the entire carriage to myself, except for a young couple fast asleep at the opposite end.

I squint out the window and watch the night roll by, still wide awake. Splotches of moonlit sky flash in and out through the broken cloud cover and light up windswept waves rippling across the lake.

Calmed by exhaustion, I begin to think more clearly, and some obvious realities come to mind. Primary among them is the fact that I can no longer afford to operate alone. In Berlin, I'll have at most five or six hours to figure out how to both force Emmett's hand and line up his full cooperation. I wrestle with the problem when my eyes close and I stop thinking.

Berlin

9:10 a.m.

My plane is five minutes early as it comes in low over the Charlottenburger Schloss, the sprawling palace of Prussian kings. Nowadays it's used mainly for state dinners, and the last time I was there, Angela Merkel was throwing a big one for Barack Obama.

It's a bright morning. I'm in a window seat taking in familiar landmarks and strangely excited to be back in Berlin. It helps that I was able to sleep for a few hours in a cheap hotel near the Zürich airport.

Once on the ground and off the plane, I'm soon in the back seat of a taxi, but my forward progress has come to a dead stop. I'm thinking about Kati, looking out the right-side window at the jam of cars, buses, and taxis clogging the exit. My blood pressure rises as I contemplate the wasted minutes when the cab's door opens and I hear a familiar voice say, "Mind if I bum a ride?"

It's Austin Trotter, our elusive CIA station chief, and everyone's prime Strangefoot suspect.

I stare at him, speechless.

"What's the matter? Aren't you glad to see me?" he asks, but doesn't await an answer.

"Change of plans," he tells the driver. "Take us to Rosenthaler, corner Sophienstrasse."

The last time I laid eyes on him was that fleeting moment in Adi's garden, when he scurried by me through the bushes. He seems to be wearing the same "cat burglar" outfit of jeans, black parka, and tennis shoes.

I have no idea what's going on, but if he is indeed Strangefoot, it means the three o'clock phone call was only a ploy, and I've just been kidnapped.

"What's the deal, Austin? Where are we going?"

"Hakesche Höfe," he says.

"For what?"

"A nice little chat. Can't talk here, now, can we?"

"Forget it. I think you'd best go back to the embassy and square things with your playmate, McLean. Meanwhile, let's stop this cab and get out of my face. I'm busy."

"Not a good idea, Adam," he says firmly, and wags his head.

"Or what? You going to shoot me? I assume you're armed, but you know, so am I. Is this going to come down to a quick-draw contest?" I bluff.

"I'm just a messenger, taking you to someone you need to talk to. A friend of yours—and mine."

"I don't think we have many friends in common."

"You'd be surprised," he says.

The Hakesche Höfe are interconnected *Mietshäuser* courtyards, now with art galleries, antique shops and restaurants, and always crowded.

The cab drops us about ten yards from the Höfe's entrance, but when Trotter gets out, he heads in the opposite direction. For a short, fat man, he's surprisingly light on his feet, an athletic side of him I hadn't noticed before.

"I thought we were going to the Höfe?"

"That was for the driver."

A block away, he makes a right onto Münzstrasse past a U-Bahn stop, and turns into the archway of a slightly dilapidated tenement. We cross the inner courtyard to the *Gartenhaus* in back.

"Third floor," he says and starts climbing, taking two stairs at a time and not looking back, me hustling up behind him.

I realize he's no stranger here.

The middle-aged woman standing in the open doorway of one of the two third-floor apartments greets us with a smile. She's wearing a blue apron over a blouse and skirt. A pleasant face, red cheeks, and no makeup.

"Johanna," Austin says, and pecks her on the cheek. "This is a business friend of mine."

"*Freut mich*," she nods.

"Likewise," I say.

In the hallway I detect a not unpleasant kitchen aroma. Johanna is walking ahead of us and points to a door on the right.

"In the *Wohnzimmer*," she says, and continues straight ahead.

Oberkommissar Bodo Kranmüller is sprawled on the floor, cradling a doll with blond pigtails.

A small girl next to him is hugging a larger doll in *Lederhosen*.

"Cara and I are playing house," Kranmüller says, grinning cheerfully. He hands the girl and both dolls to Trotter, who scoops her up in his arms. When the girl's head comes to rest on his shoulder, I notice the distinctive features of Down's syndrome.

"I'm her *Onkel Au*," Trotter says, then tells her affectionately: "Let's go see Mama," and carries her out of the room.

For a moment, it's just Kranmüller and me in this small room furnished in Communist German chic, circa 1987. Nonetheless, a large rubber tree plant in one corner, wall-hangings, and photographs give the place a feel of cozy comfort.

I look at him and ask, "What's going on?"

Bodo simply smiles, hiding behind his professional poker face: a friendly sphinx, impossible to read. It's only been a few days since I ran out on him and tricked his people into cooling their heels on the Kudamm. So, I'm thinking I better start with an apology.

"A nice surprise to see you," I say. "Especially after I ran out on you. Sorry about that."

"No apology needed, Adam. Frankly, I was more impressed than annoyed. And concerned for your safety, of course. But you handled yourself like a pro. My compliments."

"I was afraid of being betrayed from the inside," I explain, and avoid looking in Trotter's direction, just as he comes back into the room and starts pouring coffee.

"Another one of your safe homes?" I ask.

"More than you can ever know," he answers.

I look at my watch and feel my blood pressure rise again. I'm thinking of Kati and Payday.

"So. Now that we've caught up, how about somebody telling me what we're doing here? I'm on a pretty tight schedule."

Kranmüller sends Trotter a questioning look. Kranmüller nods and stands up. He takes off his suit jacket and drapes it over the back of his chair. A sizable automatic is strapped under his left arm.

He sits back down, turns to me, and says, "We know about the timetable. Holzer has reported in from Geneva. Obviously, we're as concerned as you are. Kati is one of our own. We sent her in there, and we intend to get her out. We simply have to work together this time. You can't do this alone. That's why we picked you up at the airport. That's why you're here."

"How'd you even know I'd be on that plane from Zürich?" I ask, turning to Trotter.

"I didn't," he says. "But the odds you'd be landing on an early morning flight were pretty high. A train or the Autobahn would have taken too long. So, I placed my bet and it paid off."

Until this morning, I had Austin Trotter pegged as a traitor, a mole, maybe a killer. Now I'm seeing him in a surprisingly different light and don't know what to make of it. I need to fill in some gaps.

I hesitate for a moment, then say, "The last time I saw you, you were lurking in Adalbert von Trachtenberg's bushes. What's the deal? Why have you been hiding?"

He gives me a long, silent look, digs a wrinkled red handkerchief out of his khakis, wipes it across his mouth, then flashes a smile.

"I decided to lay low for roughly the same reason you did. A lot of bullshit, backbiting, and blame gaming. You didn't want to be used as bait; I didn't want to be made the fall guy. I had no choice but to try to solve this little mystery on my own."

"Why you? Why were they going to make you the patsy?"

"Because I'd been Witty's Berlin handler. He talked too much and to the wrong people, which got him killed. This created a shitstorm for Operation Thunderclap, and for Langley. Another giant screwup to add to their sterling record of screwups. They panicked, figured they'd blame me, then hope McLean could figure out some way to save face."

"While playing their cards very close to the chest," Kranmüller interjects.

Trotter nods. "FBI and CIA doing their usual tribal war dance, maneuvering against each other and too embarrassed to let the Germans see it. But I had my contacts with BND and *Staatssicherheit* and no such inhibitions."

"It's been a good collaboration," Kranmüller agrees. "But now we've got three murders. And big pressure to make arrests."

"Three? Emerson, the dominatrix—who else?" I ask.

Kranmüller opens a folder and extracts a large black-and-white photo. "Know him?"

The body is on a gurney under a white sheet that only exposes a brutally battered face, virtually unrecognizable. Except for the dense mustache.

"He was tailing me," I say. "At the club in Geneva. I–I hit him with a statue, but this . . . What's his story?"

"Marco Kosta, age forty-nine. Albanian-born German national. Three arrests, one conviction for trafficking women, with four and a half years in the *Knast*. Pretty high up in the Berlin Hassani hierarchy, we think."

"So, why'd they beat him to death?"

Kranmüller's tone is dispassionate and matter-of-fact. "There's no 'do better next time' in an organization like this. Kosta was supposed to capture you and secure the contents of the vault. He failed. Wound up in a cow pasture just outside the city. Hands tied behind his back. Two broken eye sockets, fractured skull, smashed jaw. Nose busted in two places. Cigarette burns on his neck. In the end they shot him, but he was probably already dead."

"These are the people who have Kati? The ones who called and told me to show up by three?"

Kranmüller tries to sound reassuring but is only partly successful. "Letting a Hassani make the call was meant to scare the hell out of you. Fortunately, our intel is that for you and Kati, it's the conspirators running the show, not the gang. They want the contents of the vault, including the money, and they'll make a deal. Assuming they can keep the Hassanis under control."

I'm feeling slightly nauseated. "Not terribly reassuring, Bodo."

"It is what it is. What's next is up to you."

"With Kati in their hands, I've got no choice. But one thing I've got to know—who am I playing against? Who is Strangefoot?"

"I was waiting for that question," Austin chimes in. He hands me an envelope with a half dozen photographs. "Take a look," he invites me. "It took a while, but I finally nailed the bastard."

"Is that what you were doing in Trachtenbergs' bushes?"

"Among other things."

I look at the images slowly, one after the other. But I don't really need to.

I'd figured it out already.

12:15 p.m.

We've moved from coffee to beer and pretzels, as Bodo Kranmüller lays it out methodically.

"The key to everything is for us to know where they're taking you. That's tricky, because we can't be anywhere near the *Treff*. Strangefoot is smart. He'll spot any traditional surveillance.

"Also tricky is the fact that you'll be walking in without the goods. They won't like it, and that's the moment when it's up to you to keep the game alive. Make or break. You need a plausible story that gives them a reason to keep talking. Once we know where you are, we'll bring in our top team, but they'll need time to set up. We need surgical precision, not mayhem. That's the only way to keep you and Kati alive. It's also true—we want them alive."

I'm listening carefully, and I like what I'm hearing. It makes sense and once again I find myself energized, not scared.

"Fine," I say. "So, they'll take me and you won't be anywhere nearby. But you'll know exactly where to find us. You want to tell me how that's supposed to work?"

Kranmüller pulls out a small plastic box and opens it. Inside is a capsule about the size of a small vitamin pill.

"What's that, cyanide?"

"A nano-tech tracking device. Connected to a drone."

"And what am I going to do with that?"

"You're going to swallow it."

Chapter 37

Berlin

Wednesday, November 22

2:45 p.m.

A half hour later, I'm in my Westfälischestrasse apartment. To wait.

It's the first time I'm back in over a week, and it feels good to be home.

The burner phone they'll use for making contact is on the table in front of me, and to kill time I scroll through my regular one, the one I haven't dared use in days.

Charlotte, my secretary, has left two voicemails to alert me that Benninger, our AWOL ambassador, is back from Tulsa and wants to see me, so would I please call Betty Kowalski ASAP. Significant primarily because I do not recall his previously showing the slightest interest in what I do. One call from Jack Castelyou, our FBI guy, from two days ago. "Please call back," which I presume Emmett has taken care of. Two messages from McLean who has some news and wants to talk. Says it's urgent. Ha!

Let him wait.

Other than that, nothing of significance, except for a half dozen voicemails from a progressively angrier Fiona, making me realize that I haven't thought about her in days.

Her last message: "Have we stopped talking?"

Good question, I think, with only a twinge of guilt before turning back to more immediate concerns.

Another look at my watch: it's well past three o'clock and so far, nothing. *Come on, let's get this over with.*

I walk to the window and survey the street below. A wintry afternoon with daylight slowly beginning to fade.

Back at the kitchen table, I riffle through a pile of junk mail and bills, and busy myself consigning spam to the trash file on my cell.

Time is dragging and I'm beginning to worry.

Then at 4:15, my phone vibrates, and a familiar voice gives me instructions.

He wants me to go to the Sony Center on Potsdamer Platz, a complex of eight high rises with a giant atrium in the center. Shops, restaurants, hotels, and entertainment venues, with thousands of locals and tourists crowding in every night.

"Buy yourself this week's *Spiegel*, and keep it visible in your hand."

"No problem," I say.

"Go the Cine Star cinema, purchase a ticket—any ticket—and go to the waiting area on the right."

"Will do."

"Look for chairs against the wall next to the ice cream and candy concession stand, and sit down as close to it as you can. Put the *Spiegel* on the chair next to you."

"Then what?"

"You wait."

"For what?"

"Don't ask questions."

A half hour later, I am sitting by the candy counter in this movie palace, watching people stock up on popcorn and Eskimo bars. Waiting, and on high alert.

As instructed, I have this week's *Spiegel* on the chair to my immediate right. So far—for the last fifteen minutes—nothing. Though I have a feeling I'm being watched.

The foreign-looking young couple to my left by the door, perhaps? He tall and muscular in a leather jacket, she in a hip-hugging denim skirt with a heart tattooed on the calf of her right leg. Or what about the older woman with a black scarf who briefly locked eyes with me when buying her caramels? She's still standing around, and perhaps just pretending to wait for someone. The German guy a few chairs away studying the sports section of *Bild-Zeitung* is another possibility.

The woman with the headscarf and caramels disappears into the theater. The young couple is joined by friends, and they wander off. The *Bild-Zeitung* guy is still checking the soccer scores, and I'm debating whether I dare make a trip to the men's room to pass the time and show a little independence when the cell phone in my pocket vibrates again.

Same voice, informing me that next it's not the movies I'm to go to, but the Hauptbahnhof.

"Take the S-Bahn. Walk out the station's Europaplatz exit, stand at the curb ten meters from the car drop-off, and wait. No tricks. We're watching you all the time. Don't forget the *Spiegel*."

"How much longer for this merry-go-round?"

"No questions."

It's a twelve-minute S-Bahn ride from Potsdamer Platz to the Hauptbahnhof. Daylight's gone, but the Europaplatz exit is brightly lit and busy with early evening commuter traffic. Dense crowds hurrying in and out of the station, buses, taxis, and cars disgorging departing travelers and picking up arrivals. A long queue bundled up against the chill are in line at the curb, waiting for their rides.

I walk past them, clutching my *Spiegel*, and step to the curb a few meters ahead in a red no-parking, no-standing zone.

Almost immediately, I see a paneled truck, slate-gray with white lettering on it, inching forward in the pickup lane. "Crown Services," it reads on the side. I remember thinking, *what services?* when the truck suddenly veers to the left, swings around the cars ahead of it, and comes to a quick halt in front of me.

The side door rolls open, arms reach out from the truck and pull me inside. The door is shut, and I'm pushed to the floor. Someone pulls a black hood over my head.

"Lie down, fucker."

It's the same voice I've been hearing all afternoon.

"Is this necessary?" I ask, and the answer is a hard kick that lands just below the rib cage. It knocks the wind out of me and hurts like hell.

Fighting back isn't an option. I concentrate on breathing, close my eyes, and lie very still.

I'm flat on my stomach, immobilized and in the dark, with someone's foot resting on my neck. It hurts when I breathe.

We were heading west when we took off, I'm guessing along Alt-Moabit, which is a major artery that runs past the Moabit *Knast*, Berlin's high-security prison. I'm trying to follow the route in my head, but before long I've lost all sense of time and direction. I feel us turning left, then a right, and two lefts again, around something round, perhaps a U-turn, then longer stretches of rapid driving interrupted by more turns. Traffic noises near us come and go; the wailing of a police siren passes us and fades.

At least a half hour later there's a sudden jolt, the truck stops, and I find myself being non-too-gently dragged out of the vehicle. Two guys, one on each side, walk me down a long flight of steps into a dank place that assails my nose with the carious smells of kerosene, tobacco, sweat, and shit.

Pushing me onto a straight-backed chair, they immobilize me with Velcro wrist and ankle restraints, after which they pull the hood off my head.

I squint and blink, then realize that we're in a cellar storeroom of sorts, with cardboard boxes piled high, as well as oil cans and empty bottles. I see a rickety wooden table, a few chairs, and in one corner, an ancient refrigerator.

One of my two captors is a pockmarked crusher with sledge-hammer arms. The other one's a lot younger, rail thin, with a voice I recognize. He's the one who's doing the talking. His German is accented, but fluent.

He steps close to me and rams a work boot into my shin. "Where's the stuff from the safe?"

"Hey," I holler. "Stop that. Where's Katharina? You'll get it when you release her and me. That's the deal."

He answers with the back of his hand across my mouth.

"Where is it?" he repeats, hits me again and adds, helpfully, "if the cops have it, we'll kill you."

My lip is bleeding and my jaw feels dislocated.

"Listen!" I yell. "Cut my balls off. Poke my eyes out. Threaten anything you want, but it won't get you anywhere. The cops don't have the stuff. Not yet, at least. But if there's no signal soon that we have a deal, it'll be out of my hands. The cops will get it. Is that what you want? If you're too dumb to understand that, take me to someone who does."

The big guy moves forward and gives me a look that spells real trouble, but my tirade has stopped his partner, who tells him something I don't understand. There's some back and forth, and then the work-boots thug picks up the hood and pulls it back over my head.

"Fucker," he says, a four-letter word which, in its various configurations, seems to be the anchor of his English vocabulary.

The overhead lights are switched off, and I hear them climbing the stairs.

I'm back in the dark again.

To think clearly when you've been smacked around and left in a stinking cellar Velcroed to a chair with a hood over the head isn't easy.

My head feels like someone's rapping a door knocker against the inside of my skull. My side hurts, and so does my leg. Mostly, I'm afraid that my brilliant plan might be too subtle for these knuckle-draggers. I thought I'd be bargaining with conspirators, but so far, it's nothing but gangsters. Under the circumstances— the bleeding, the chair, the hood—I'm also not feeling complete confidence in the little bot Kranmüller had me swallow. What if it's a dud? What if their server's down? It's not like we can call IT and get it running again.

In this very dark moment, I realize that we've gone for a truly all-or-nothing approach, with the nothing being Kati and me with our throats slit, dumped in a field somewhere. I'm wracking my brain to come up with plan B, but I'm drawing blanks. I try to console myself that Kranmüller said it would take time for them to set up a foolproof rescue. Okay, I'll give them some time. Meanwhile, my tirade at least seems to have confused my captors enough to send them off for new instructions, maybe even someone higher up the food chain.

Then again, maybe they just went to get a body bag.

The sound of footsteps descending the stairs.

I can't see, but my hearing's sharp, and it registers the steps of a single person. I'm going to take that as a good sign. Still, my heart rate is jacked, and my pulse is pounding in my ears.

I hear the click of the light switch, and from beneath the hood, I can see a pair of running shoes.

Then there's a familiar voice.

"Jeez, Adam. These guys are idiots. I'm sorry. Let me cut you loose."

The hood comes off—and Jack Castelyou flashes me a crooked grin.

"Ah, the mystery of Strangefoot revealed."

"Surprised?"

"Not really. I'd figured out it was you. Figuring out *why* is another matter."

"Happy to explain, but let me liberate you first."

"Where's Katharina?"

"Your lovely spy girlfriend? Don't worry, she's okay."

"I want out of this shithole, and I want to see her."

"Sure you do," he nods, then rips off the second ankle restraint.

Dangling a black eye mask in front of me, he smiles apologetically, pulls it over my eyes, and leads me up the stairs, blind again, and on wobbly knees. I listen for telltale sounds, as if it might help Kranmüller locate us. I hear traffic, but nothing distinctive. We could be anywhere.

When the eye shades come off, I find myself in a windowless room that someone's using as an office. Chairs, a lamp, empty bookshelves, and two large ashtrays—one overflowing with butts—sitting on a battered wooden desk. The room smells of garlic, sweat, and a thousand cigarettes. Castelyou is a nonsmoker.

He sits down opposite me.

"Let's talk," he says.

He seems relaxed, wearing a tracksuit, as if he's just come back from the gym. We've been embassy colleagues for years, and I always thought of him as a typical by-the-book, white-shirt, drab-suit Bureau guy. I'm watching him closely, and I still can't wrap my head around this new version of him.

"I want to see Katharina."

"I promise you she's fine," he tells me. "Nervous, no doubt scared, but no one has mistreated her. You'll see her soon enough." He leans in toward me, and his congeniality seems to fade.

"Right now, we need to know where we stand with you, and we don't have time to waste. You and I know each other, so let's not screw around. You came here for Katharina, so we know what you want. I take it you're clear what we want. Specifically, Witty's stash of documents and money, and proof that your colleagues didn't get them."

"Good. We can do business, then. I laid it all out for your leg-breakers. Kati goes free, I lead you to your stash. Simple as that."

He shakes his head. "Not quite so simple, I'm afraid. We've made commitments, and regrettably, our partners are not of the highest moral character. They'd slit your throat as soon as look at you."

"That's what I can't understand, Jack. You're law enforcement. The straight arrow. The fucking FBI. I've seen what's in that safe, and if the government gets its hands on it, you and your friends are all going away for a very long time. Lucky for you, though, you called just in time. So, I made up an excuse and didn't give them anything. I'm the only person on the planet who can get it for you. It'll land me in a tub of shit, but frankly, working for the government's getting old, and I'm willing to take my chances. Bottom line: you bring Kati to me, we both walk out of here, and I hand you the keys to the kingdom."

"Exactly how?"

"One more thing," I continue, ignoring his question. "You keep your hoodlum friends off my back. I never see them again."

"I'll do my best," he says. "They're not my friends. I didn't bring them into this."

"Who did? Hollander?"

He doesn't answer, but it's obvious. He's too smart to admit anything, but I need to kill time. Assuming that Kranmüller's little gadget down in my digestive track is doing its job. If it's not, then I guess I'm just delaying the inevitable.

"They're the ones who killed Witty," I continue, making it more a statement of fact than a question.

"I had nothing to do with that," Castelyou says.

"Yeah, well—you lie down with dogs, Jack, you catch their fleas."

He gives me an unfriendly smile. "That's deep, Adam. I'm going to have to remember that one."

He walks out of the room and returns with a carafe of water, fills two glasses and shoves one over to me. He looks tired. He takes a long, slow drink, then surprises me by opening up.

"You want to know why I lay down with these 'dogs,' Adam? I'll tell you why. It's because I'm a goddamn American patriot."

He moves closer, staring at me with an intensity I do not recognize. I'm no longer looking at a rule-following FBI agent, but into the eyes of a madman.

"I've been with the Agency for fourteen years, and for most of that time, I kept my mouth shut and my head down, followed orders and did what I was told. But our country's no longer drifting, Adam, it's sinking. Everything we have was built on Christian morality and testosterone. Now the liberals and the Jews, the women, the gays, the transgenders—they're shitting on all of it. Tearing it down. And don't even talk to me about the blacks and the immigrants. The libs think they can run a global economy the way they run their health-food co-ops. We're up against the Taliban, China, the Russians . . . and the faggots and feminists are worried about pronouns and safe spaces? Are you fucking kidding me!

"But you know what? Not everyone is willing to cave. There are still plenty of swinging dicks, and we're ready to take it back. The guys with the private jets supply the money, and the cops and the military supply the muscle. We've got plenty of them on our side. Not to mention the millions of ordinary dudes who just happen to own AR-15s. That's called *power*. And we aim to exercise it."

He seems to have run out of rant. I watch as he takes another long swig of water.

"Interesting," I say. "But ever hear of a little thing called democracy? Thomas Jefferson. Ben Franklin. The US Constitution? Isn't that what you swore allegiance to? Isn't that what being a 'patriot' means?"

He gives a laugh. "You know who wrote the Constitution, Adam? Rich white men. Slave-owning white men. They rebelled against a crazy foreign king—over taxes, I might add—because they wanted liberty, not democracy. You think the Senate and Electoral College would be set up the way they are if your Founding Fathers had wanted democracy? 'Your *people* sir . . . a great beast.' Alexander fucking Hamilton."

"Maybe. Otherwise, not so sure about your version of constitutional history, Jack."

"You know the beautiful part, Adam? The Constitution is whatever the fuck the high court says it is."

Castelyou pours the rest of the water into his glass and downs it in a single gulp.

"Okay, enough fucking around. Number one: hand over the stuff. Now. Number two: convince me the authorities haven't seen it. Satisfy us on these two scores and both of you walk. I guarantee it. If not, all bets are off."

"You're threatening me?"

"Just stating facts. As previously mentioned, my partners 'in crime,' as you might put it, are not known for their patience."

"I appreciate the candor, Jack, so I'll return the favor." I steal a glance at my watch. Seven o'clock, and still no sounds of armored vehicles rumbling up to the door. I need to keep stalling.

"As I told Dumb and Dumber when I got here, I'm ready, willing, and able to give you everything you want. But I'm not stupid. It would take a real idiot to show up with the goods in tow, with no leverage, saying, 'Please, kind sirs, now let us walk away unscathed.' So, I left the stuff with a neutral party, 'in escrow,' so to speak. They don't know what they're sitting on, but they absolutely will not release it, even if I call them up and tell them to. The only way they'll give it up is for Kati Willmans to go there in person—alone.

"It's all set up, Jack. Like those nuclear retaliation triggers from the Cold War. Mutual deterrence through mutually assured destruction. Torture me till I sell out my grandmother, and it still gets you nothing, 'cause it's out of my hands.

"So, here's the deal: set her free. She goes there alone and gets you your stuff. I'll stay as your hostage."

Clearly this last bit is not what Castelyou had expected, but just as obviously, he doesn't like it.

"I don't seem to be getting through to you, Adam. What happens here is very similar to what you're describing: 'Out of my hands.' Your little fail-safe makes perfect sense—in a rational world. But while my associates are neither moral nor patient, they are even less rational. Push them too far, they'll kill us all just for spite and eat their losses."

I shake my head. "That sounds like you'd better get your most spit-and-polished FBI self in there and convince these bastards to go along. Cause otherwise, we're all fucked."

He gazes at me for a long minute.

"Sit tight," he says. Then he gets to his feet, goes out the door, and locks it behind him.

Castelyou comes back a few minutes later followed by a kid who's probably no more than seventeen, but big for his age. Castelyou stands to the side while junior frisks me and shoves me toward the door.

Outside, the kid pushes me along toward a cinderblock building across a courtyard. Apparently, we're in a complex of storage sheds and workshops, enclosed by a high red-brick wall. I'm heading toward a doorway that says AKA-Industrie, GmbH. An entity no doubt owned and operated by a certain Mr. Z.

The whole gang's inside this stinky, overheated office. Nobody's wearing a mask, which is not a good sign.

Hollander, in shirtsleeves, is sweating profusely and glaring as if about to explode. In a far corner, Trachtenberg sits stiffly on a chair, his hands folded in his lap. Castelyou crosses over to him and leans against the wall as Hollander takes the lead.

"You better come up with something better than this, Jackson, because we don't buy it," he barks. "Your life is on the line. And don't even think what they'll do to her."

He points to a sliding window that reveals an adjoining room where Kati is tied to a chair. The upper buttons of her blouse are missing. I count five gang members lounging around near her, including the one who brought me here, and two nasty-looking thugs I recognize from before.

My throat is dry, and I'm really having to work at it to appear nonchalant. But until that rescue party shows up, I'm shooting blanks, and false bravado's the only kind I've got.

"Good evening, Dwayne," I say pleasantly. "I'd like to say it's a surprise to see you, but actually it's not."

The teenage goon shoves me down into a chair. At least there're no straps this time.

It's way past when the *Polizei* et al are supposed to be here, and I'm wracking my brain for options. I now have that sick-to-my-stomach, lightheaded feeling that they really may not make it. Maybe their little tracking gizmo isn't what it was cracked up to be. Maybe their armored car got stuck in rush-hour traffic.

I look around, making eye contact with all the boys. Then I focus on Hollander.

"We had a deal, right? I get you what was in the safe, you let us go. I went along with your little bag-over-the-head routine, and here I am, ready to deliver my end of the bargain. So, what's the problem?"

Hollander leans down and gets in my face. "Where is it?" he blusters.

"I explained all that to Jack. It's so simple. Do I really have to go through it all again?"

"It's unacceptable—to them!" He nods toward the other room. "And to me."

I force a laugh. "What is with you? You expect me to walk in here with no leverage? And what . . . expect you to just *do the right thing*? I'm not an idiot."

"You're stalling, dammit. These people don't fool around, and you're going to get us all killed! So, stop playing games."

His face is beet red, with sweat pouring down from his hairline. He could be on the poster demonstrating the warning signs of impending stroke.

"Then let's go and talk to them," I suggest bravely.

I'm shuffled into the next room, where Kati and I make eye contact.

"Are you okay?" I ask her.

"*Es geht,*" she says, giving me a weak smile. She's so lovely, and I so want to hold her, but somehow it all comes down to being able to bullshit my way through the next twenty minutes.

The thug who picked me up in the panel truck steps between us. From behind me, Hollander says, "Go ahead—tell James all about your proposal."

This is the first time I've been able to get a look at this guy beyond the heavy work boots I so fondly remember. Bald, about my age, he's rail thin with olive skin and creepy, comatose eyes. The two bruisers with tattooed arms the size of thighs sprawl on a bench behind Kati. Two other thugs hover behind me, along with Castelyou and Trachtenberg. Hollander is to the side, leaning against a heavy metal shelf littered with what looks like auto parts.

James gives me a "fuck you" look, and even though I'm scared enough to wet my pants, I give him my best "fuck you" stare right back.

"Very simple, James," I tell him. "Turn her loose, you get everything you want. In business, they call it a win-win."

James doesn't seem impressed. His eyes don't move.

"*Nimm ihn*," he says, and one of the guys behind me grabs my arms and pins them behind my back.

Very tight.

It hurts.

"Not smart, James. Kill us, you get nothing. How much money is that you're giving up? A million? Two, three? And I do seem to recall the last guy who fucked up an assignment got his head crushed. Where'd they find him? In a potato field?"

I can see from James's face that my last statement may have registered. I detect in his eyes what might be considered a glimmer of calculation aimed at self-preservation.

But it's Hollander who loses it. He turns around, grabs a pair of bolt cutters off the shelf, and comes toward Kati.

"New bargaining position, Adam. For every minute you keep up this bullshit, she loses a finger. When she's down to nubs, I start in on you."

Castelyou comes toward him saying, "Back off, Hollander. You don't cut it as a tough guy."

Enraged, Hollander swings at him with the bolt cutter. Castelyou kicks him in the groin, and Hollander doubles over. I wrest my arms free and reach for the tool.

James bellows orders in Albanian, then presses an automatic into my cheekbone.

"Stop that," he snarls.

Suddenly I'm crushed by two goons, my head pressed to the floor. Twisting my neck, I can see Hollander struggle to his feet, holding his crotch, glaring at Castelyou. Then he pulls out a gun and lunges toward Kati. Then his head explodes.

My first thought is that James has had enough of this bastard. But then I twist around further and see Adi von Trachtenberg lowering a large-caliber revolver.

Then everything goes white, and my head swells with the sound of an explosion. The room fills with smoke, and the goons fall to the side. Everyone's coughing, gasping for breath, and I hear someone yell "*Polizei!*" A dense cloud lingers from the flash-bang grenade. I can barely make out men in body armor pouring into the room.

"*Waffen runter. Hinlegen!*" the cops shout. Arms down; get down.

There're too many guns, too much confusion. I need to stay low, but I also need to get to Kati. I try to crawl toward her, but in all the smoke I can't really tell. I call her name and reach out. And that's it. Silence.

Chapter 38

*R*eports of the Moabit raid came too late for the next day's papers, but the networks featured it on their morning news shows.

A police spokesperson said that several suspected members of a street gang and others connected to a kidnapping and murder investigation had been arrested. At least two suspects resisting arrest were killed, and several others, including law enforcement officials, were hospitalized. The full names of suspects and victims were being withheld, which is standard practice under German law.

Ten days later, there still hasn't been any significant official follow-up. Only *Bild-Zeitung*, Germany's top tabloid, ran a story speculating that there might have been more to the raid at Friedrich Krause Ufer than the authorities had revealed. One of those involved was a US diplomat, suggesting a possible connection to the earlier murder of the US Embassy's deputy chief of mission. *Bild* also thought that the casualties pointed to a bloody affair, which raised additional questions.

The persistent absence of official information on the background and details of the events at AKA-Industrie was no accident. Law enforcement on both sides of the Atlantic agreed to remain closemouthed until a string of arrests in Germany and the US were complete. That the authorities had succeeded in holding things close for weeks—a bubble that could have burst quickly in notoriously "leaky" Washington—had been a minor miracle. When it did break, the story of Operation Thunderclap and its successful outcome and German connection was sensational news, spun by both governments as a stirring example of fruitful cooperation between the two key partners of the Atlantic alliance.

If enterprising investigative reporters one day dig deeper into the behind-the-scenes of Operation Thunderclap, the real story of what went right and wrong and who deserves credit or blame may come out into the open. Like the reasons for the disarray between the US and German sides, which cost time and impede progress, or interagency politics among the Americans and the ponderously slow German rescue operation of the hostages, which cost lives and barely snatched victory from the jaws of defeat—elements of the real story that official accounts hadn't mentioned.

Success has many suitors, and there were many in Germany and the United States who eagerly lined up to stake their claim for the credit of a successful operation. Admitting to a share of the blame for what had gone wrong had few takers.

Berlin

December 3

I only remember the dreams.

A few had been standard cauchemars, like running on legs that don't move or being pinned down in a hopeless fight with no way out. Mostly though, what sticks in my head are disjointed fragments of bizarrely ethereal dreaming: flying in an open airplane through a perfect azure sky or gently floating suspended in a parachute and enjoying a mind-blowing view. Also, oddly disjointed bits of a wildly erotic dream involving vague foreplay with a mysterious partner, where nothing really happens and her face remains obscured.

Later I was told that any dreaming during the days I had been kept narcotized is unlikely, the intent having been to keep me unconscious and to give my shaken brain a complete rest. So, all those scenes must have been conjured up in just the last hours when they were slowly bringing me back to life.

This was ten days after the rescue.

I have absolutely no memory of what happened in that crappy industrial park in Moabit, except that a serious concussion and gunshot wound landed me in this hospital, the Park Klinik in Dahlem.

According to the doctors, a grade-three concussion is serious and takes time to heal. They tell me that I have been making excellent progress toward a full recovery, although my body still refuses to believe it.

I'm hooked up to an impressive array of electronic monitors producing ominous pinging sounds, and two rubber tubes sprout from somewhere near my backside. All this keeps me uncomfortably immobilized, and it hurts when I try to move. My head is trussed in a bandage down to my ears, and the lower part of me is tightly pledgetted too.

Today is the first day they're allowing visitors. The room is full of flowers. Kati is sitting on the bed, holding my hand. Emmett is doing the talking, filling me in on what happened during the rescue and while my brain has been asleep. He's strategically positioned himself on a chair where I can see him without moving my head, which the doctors say is important.

He's in a buoyant mood and glad to have me back and on the mend.

"It's all over," he says with a big smile.

The tracking technology worked just fine. The cops simply took too long planning the raid and figuring out how they were going to break through AKA-Industrie's outer wall. When they finally stormed in, it was pretty crazy, with a short and violent fight and lots of confusion. Trachtenberg apparently couldn't stomach the criminality and shot Hollander dead, which saved Kati's life. Then he took his own.

"What about Castelyou?" I ask.

"Slipped out. Disappeared. Figures that a guy like him would have planned for contingencies. As you can attest, passports are not so hard to fake, if you know the right people. They'll find him, though. They also know the right people."

"The rest of the bad guys?"

"The big guy named Fatback Kulla was killed by the cops. He's the one who gave you the concussion. With a bolt cutter, evidently, but I guess you wouldn't remember. The rest are all behind bars. Even Zamir Hassani is in protective custody, locked up in *Untersuchungshaft*. The cops are pretty sure they can link him to the murders, which should put him away for good."

"What about Witty's treasure trove?"

"Safe and sound. Eight million euros in Swiss accounts, mostly US money waiting to be laundered via a Panama cutout Hollander had set up. But more than enough evidence in the SSL vault alone to convict all of them. Multiple indictments have been handed down in DC. Hank Rickenbom is top of the list, and already out on bail."

There's a pause in the conversation. I'm a little fuzzy from the painkillers, but even without them, I think I'd be feeling pretty good. It's a relief to be done with all the derring-do, to be here safe and sound with this amazing woman holding my hand.

I give her a smile. "I think Kati's going to get a medal," I say. "I've seen the papers. She's a national hero."

"You're not doing so bad yourself," Emmett says. "Even the ambassador wants to come and congratulate you in person. Typical political horseshit, though. He also gave a statement saying he knows Rickenbom and associates, and that they're all 'good people.'"

Kati and I share a look.

"You both deserve the recognition," Emmett says. "You were brave and smart when it really counted. But all in all, I'd have to say you were damn lucky too."

"Lucky? Look at me—you call this lucky?"

"Sure. You got clocked on the head at just the right moment. Otherwise, James, that gangster, might have shot you someplace a little more critical than the gluteus maximus."

"The what?"

"Gluteus maximus. He shot you in the ass. If you have to take a bullet, they tell me it's the best place."

"Thanks," I say. "Try it sometime."

Emmett continues to fill in details of how things wrapped up, but now my mind is drifting and it's a struggle to follow what he's saying.

I try throwing in an occasional question, but the answers hardly register and don't mean much. I feel flat. Disconnected. And frankly, not all that interested.

Kati's still got my hand in hers. We've hardly talked. I want to be alone with her, but when I think about all the things to say, I'm not sure I know where to begin.

It may be the drugs, or it may be exhaustion, but I'm feeling disoriented and down, maybe just a little depressed. I guess you could say I've been through a lot. I'm trying to process everything that's happened.

I turn my face to the wall and fall asleep.

Chapter 39

Heringsdorf

December 21

*T*he first day of winter, and there's a light dusting of snow on the ground outside the Villa Ostwind, Anna Rotbein's bed-and-breakfast.

I have been recuperating here for a week, and now feel almost normal again. The bandage on my head came off a while ago. I have a good-sized scar on my backside where I took James's bullet, and Kati assures me it improves the attractiveness of that part of my anatomy. I told her I'd take her word for it, but she insisted on holding a mirror at an angle where I could see for myself.

Anna has let me know that Kati's a definite improvement over Fiona, which is as far as she's willing to go, and I'm cheered by her way of saying that she approves.

I'm on sick leave until mid-January, with another month of home leave to follow. It's our last day before heading back to Berlin, and then Kati will come home with me. Except that I really don't have a Washington home anymore. Fiona is getting it in the divorce. I've told her to sell the house, and good luck.

So, it'll be Christmas in New Jersey with my folks, and their reception of my German girlfriend has me slightly on edge. For my parents' generation, there's still lots of ambivalence about all things German. I've briefed Kati about the problem, and she says she's ready for it, so we'll see.

12:30 p.m.

Anna is decked out in full regalia. Rings on every finger and a blue-and-black Eskimo pendant on a stainless-steel necklace dangling low from her neck. Because it's a special occasion—a surprise farewell party of sorts with visitors from Berlin.

The Cunninghams, Liz and Emmett, are the first to arrive, followed by Tommy in his Gran Turismo, and then *Oberkommissar* Kranmüller and deputy, Karl Holzer. Austin Trotter has been invited too.

A feast.

Anna and Kati have had their heads together for days planning it, with a menu of favorites conceived in my honor. This morning they've been up early, and Kati's been allowed to help get everything ready. The kitchen is Anna's sacred domain, so that's a big concession. *Kartoffelsuppe mit Einlage*, slices of wieners floating in Anna's special potato soup, followed by *Sauerbraten* and *Rotkohl* with parsleyed potatoes. For dessert, *Baumkuchen* and *Obst*, an assortment of fresh fruit which aren't easy to come by in wintry Heringsdorf.

Anna has poured the coffee, put a bottle of Jägermeister schnapps on the table, and is handing out cigars. Except for Kati and Liz, everyone lights up. Today they're willing to tolerate the poison, they say. But never again, please.

"Come on, Herr *Oberkommissar*," Tommy insists. "Tell us where you hid it."

The hiding place of the GPS device that kept tabs on me has been the subject of outlandish suggestions and much hilarity throughout the meal, but Kranmüller insists it's still classified information.

"Maybe it was stuck in Adam's gluteus maximus, which would explain why James plugged him there," Emmett suggests.

Every conceivable body part gets its turn, but the *Oberinspektor* has refused to let me tell.

"Okay," he finally grins. "Go ahead, tell them."

I look around with a suitable blush. Then I tell them, "You know that saying, 'This too shall pass'?"

This prompts howls of laughter, followed by more toasts.

Anna's Jägermeister is getting a workout. I'm receiving my share, but then Bodo Kranmüller proposes a special one for Trotter: "An American secret weapon in the success of Operation Thunderclap," he says gallantly.

Trotter's actually shown up in a suit and tie, which is the first time I remember seeing him dressed up. He's telling stories about his time underground tailing Strangefoot, which earns him a second toast.

"They fed Austin to the wolves," Emmett says, "and now the Agency is celebrating him as their hero. McLean claims the whole thing was his idea and wants to take credit."

Trotter merely smiles.

"No problem," he says. "Standard Langley operating procedure. And frankly, that it makes even more of Jack Castelyou's defection to hang around the Bureau's neck doesn't bother me a bit."

"But how did he get all that inside information?" I say.

"No mystery," Emmett observes ruefully. "I'm the idiot. I trusted the bastard and told him more than I should have."

That earns Emmett a toast of his own, with me raising my glass to him.

"I forgive you, brother. You redeemed yourself many times over. Couldn't have done it without you."

Holzer tells us how Slinani was pulled off an Air Maroc plane at Cointrin at the last moment. And Wahl actually survived. He's been moved from a hospital to a Geneva jail. But the really big story was the breach of security at SSL. The Swiss sweated bullets about this undermining their reputation for absolute privacy in their banking system.

At five o'clock the Cunninghams announce they have to get back to Berlin, and everyone's saying their goodbyes. Emmett explains that the ambassador has asked to see the draft of my "efficiency report" and wants to add his own praise to it.

"You're a legend now, Adam." Emmett smiles with a sigh. "You belong to the ages."

9:00 p.m.

In the morning we made slow and languid love. Tonight, we've turned in early and there's been more of the same. Kati's resting her head on my shoulder and we're enjoying the warm afterglow of a wonderful day.

"Do you want to be a Foreign Service wife, or is a more stationary existence closer to your heart?" I ask her quietly.

"Is that a proposal?" she wants to know.

"If you want to look at it that way," I tell her. "But haven't my designs on you been clear for some time?"

"I guess," she says and comes a bit closer.

"So, what's your answer?"

"If the diplomatic life is like the last two months, forget it," she says.

"Trust me, I've been at it a while, and it's usually boring as hell."

"Then okay. But let's just give it time."

"We've got all the time in the world," I say and kiss her on the lips.

Then I turn off the light.

Afterword

I have forgotten when a book about an imaginary ultra-right conspiracy first crossed my mind, but in view of current political trends, the idea appealed to me as intriguingly topical. Of course, nothing like it had ever happened and my protagonists are equally fictional. (Though I know a few Americans, Berliners, and people from my Foreign Service days not unlike them.) I liked the plot, but wondered occasionally whether readers might find it a bit over the top.

I needn't have worried. Not long after the manuscript was finished, Germany announced the breakup of an extreme rightist, so-called "Reichbürger" conspiracy startlingly similar to what I had imagined. It involved plans for the violent overthrow of the German government, far more extreme and potentially lethal than anything I had dreamed up for Payday. Led by a man named Prince Heinrich XIII of Reuss, with a noble pedigree similar to that of my own invented plot leader, this conspiracy was real and taken very seriously by the Germans. A case, one might say, of life imitating art and taking it a level further.

Payday Conspiracy ends on a positive note, but I might have been too optimistic. With assaults on democratic institutions in many countries, including actual violent coup attempts, how confident can we be that it will always end well?

A word about my choice of Berlin as the center of the action.

I was born near there and lived in that city for the first dozen years of my life. Half of that time it was Adolf Hitler's Berlin, of which remain as many bad memories as good ones. On the gray April evening in 1939 when we left, I assumed it would be forever.

That's not what happened. Whatever my jobs over the years, there were always situations involving visits to the city of my youth, and for almost two decades, I was thrust deeply into its cultural and political life to an extent I couldn't possibly have imagined. In 2015, Berlin officially anointed me an Honorary Citizen. Who would have thought?

I have lived in some storied world cities—Paris; San Francisco; Washington, DC; New York; and Geneva, Switzerland. For most of my adult life, my permanent home has been in Princeton, New Jersey, which even Albert Einstein (another ex-Berliner) thought was, and still is, a very special place. Yet, though I never lived there again, no place on earth is today as much in my head as Berlin. That's a big surprise even to me.

Berlin is once again a great world city with impressive museums, operas, orchestras, fine restaurants, and a vibrant art scene. Exciting things are always happening there, and young people who flock there will tell you that at night, Berlin rocks! But that isn't why it stands out in my mind. Other great cities have as much to offer. What is different about Berlin is its unique vibe, an indefinable special aura that has made it a magnet for creative people and avant-garde artists from across the world. No less also the native Berliners in this now very cosmopolitan and multicultural place. Throughout its often-tortured history, they have always maintained a special attitude toward what's happening in their city—cynical, irreverent, proud, to the point, and often very funny.

Berlin lifts my spirits, and whenever I return, I feel more hopeful. In a word, I've become reattached to Berlin's unique spirit, which is why it was probably inevitable that I would put the city at the center of Payday action.

Writing a book can quickly turn amusement into an abiding passion that holds one in its grip and won't let go. It is also lonely work, strictly between you, a yellow pad, and a pen (or, nowadays, a computer). I am therefore especially appreciative that there were always a few professionals, friends, and family I could count on when I most needed them.

I especially want to thank my editor, the incomparable Bill Patrick, for his wise counsel and for teaching me that less can be more.

My sincere thanks go to my agent, Gail Hochman, for her efforts on my behalf, and to Maggie Kneip for her advice on publication matters. I am particularly grateful to the very capable Betsy Thorpe who managed that process, to copy editor Katherine Bartis, and to interior designer Diana Wade. My admiration also goes to Duncan Blachford for the design of the cover.

I am indebted to Chief Inspector Ingo Kexel of the Berlin Police for his patient and generous guidance on local homicide investigative procedures.

My warm thanks go to those who read early drafts and offered helpful advice. First among them is Michael Naumann, publisher, journalist, and former German Culture Minister, whose encouragement and guidance meant a lot to me. I am also very grateful to Lauren Tarshis for sharing the secrets of a best-selling author and to David Dreyfuss for his many timely suggestions and help.

From beginning to end, I had two indispensable partners at my side.

As with all my previous books, my longtime assistant and friend, Marie Santos, dug up sources, did research, ably converted illegible notes into readable drafts, and took charge of managing the many details involved in turning out the finished product. I am deeply grateful for all she did.

My wife, Barbara, was my inspiration and kept me going. She encouraged me, contributed many good ideas and pointed out the bad ones. Without her, this book would not have been written.

About The Author

Former Secretary of the Treasury Mike (W. Michael) Blumenthal is the author of two prior books of non-fiction. He also served as a senior U.S. diplomat and CEO of two major U.S. corporations. A German-born ex-Berliner, he was more recently the founding director of the renowned Jewish Museum Berlin.

Printed in October 2024
by Rotomail Italia S.p.A., Vignate (MI) - Italy